W9-CGK-402

This is a work of fiction. Names, characters, places, and incidents are either the product of the author's imagination or are used fictitiously. Any resemblance to actual persons – living, dead or undead – events, and locales is entirely coincidental.

Library of Congress Control Number: 2014901523

ISBN 978-0-9914702-0-4
10 9 8 7 6 5 4 3 2

Covers by Terry Fogarty
Edited by Judith Swain

www.DayZeroBook.com

For lovers of walkers everywhere.
I hope I can make you proud.

DAY ZERO

Written by Charles Ingersoll

Edited by Judy Swain

Table of Contents

PROLOGUE

DAY ZERO

EPILOGUE

PROLOGUE

1

Whirly Bird

minus 63 days – 1915 hours

Dusk flirted with the darkness as we huddled in the back of the Black Hawk that raced thirty meters over the sands of southwest Pakistan. The crystalline sands burned a thin line of fiery red in the last moments of the setting sun.

"… vo teams are in position," crackled over the headphones.

"Ten minutes!" I barked to the squad.

Corporal Rosalita Alvarez continued to sleep, her helmet against the helo's bulkhead.

I didn't mind.

She had checked her gear several times in-flight and was a superb sniper spotter.

The other member of my team, Corporal Peters, patted down his vest, comforted by the .308 Winchester rounds there. Sergeant Daniels' team, including PFC Manuel and Private Jacksey, checked their gear.

"…air support…"

"Repeat!" I replied into the comm. A pause. "Roger that!"

"Mission correction!"

The Marines perked up.

"Our AC 130 gunship air support is returning to base due to a mechanical failure. The Black Hawks will have to provide cover until a second gunship is inbound. Ooh rah?"

"Ooh rah, Sergeant!"

I checked my Cobra and signaled three minutes to mission go.

"This gonna be another dry hole, Sarge?" Jacksey asked.

"Not based on intel."

I slapped the top of Alvarez's helmet.

She opened her eyes, already sharp and clear.

My headphones squawked again.

"Roger that," I said. "30 seconds! 2nd and 3rd are on the ground. Ooh rah?"

"Ooh rah, Sergeant!" They replied in unison.

"Outstanding."

One more command filtered to my ears.

"We're a go! Go! Go!" I yelled over the whine of the engine.

Jacksey and Manuel opened the side door, threw out thick black nylon and fast-roped out of the Black Hawk as it hovered twenty meters off the rocky ridgeline. Ten seconds later, the rest of us followed.

2

Nest

minus 63 days – 2145 hours

Nothing stirred at the sandbagged guard station at the south end of the village.

"2nd in position," came over the mic.

"Roger that," I replied, touching my own throat mic.

Alvarez set up her scope next to me. Peters moved ten meters into a high cover position behind us. Daniels' team set up eighty meters to our north. Two other Marine sniper teams were positioned on the opposite ridge.

"Heads up, John."

Alvarez knew I hated when she used my first name in the field and loved when she called me Sarge in the cot.

I repositioned my Barrett 998 sniper rifle, using the scope to follow the incoming convoy. The Iranian security force's armored column stopped one hundred meters from the guardhouse. Jeeps and the Russian manufactured Gaz 69s had their lights off, the Iranian drivers using US government supplied night vision goggles. US Marines from 5th and 11th squads moved to the gate on foot.

The Marines cleared the guardhouses and adjoining shacks. One of them raised and secured the gate. Organized chatter came through the comms.

"…no guards here… clear…"

"…guard shack clear…"

Encountering no resistance, the leader of 5th squad motioned for the vehicles to move in. The Jeeps started rolling through the open gate.

"…clear…"

"…moving southeast…"

Darting movement.

Blankets swept aside the open window frames.

Multiple muzzle flashes.

"...ambush!..."

"... check your six...agh!"

"...return fire!..."

"...return fire... all teams!..."

"...Prospero's down! Levy's down! Fall back! Son of a..."

"Find me a target, Alvarez!" I ordered.

"I'm trying! Shit!" Alvarez hissed as she pivoted her tactical scope. "Everyone's off the streets, Sergeant. No targets."

The transports reversed out the gates, taking the brunt of the gunfire. The ground forces retreated, their weapons flashing in the darkness. One vehicle attempted a three-point turn in a ditch, exploding a landmine under the chassis. The blast blew three retreating Marines off their feet.

"Peters? Any joy?" I commed.

"No joy, Sergeant. No joy."

Gunfire erupted all along the ridgeline.

"...we're taking fire..."

"... Manuel's been shot..."

The gunfire continued.

Loud detonations followed piercing whistles, rocket propelled grenades raining down on our positions. Three massive blasts bloomed in yellow and orange on the far ridge.

Dozens of ground-to-air missiles sputtered over us into the eastern night toward the hovering Black Hawks. I heard faint explosions, but couldn't confirm if the helos had been hit.

More RPGs arced down around us. One incinerated Jeffries and Peters. The insurgents' AK-47s popped all along the ridge top. The return fire from our MK-12s stopped. A few more pistol shots rang out but that ended as well.

"We have to bug out, John," Alvarez whispered. "They're going to find us."

The limestone boulders provided us with adequate cover but we would be found out soon enough if we laid low – sooner if I fired back.

"Team leaders report," I whispered.

Nothing came back, not even static.

The Marines' retreat below was visible in the glow of the burning Gaz. The remaining vehicles reversed back two hundred meters from the village. Marines limped or ran after them for a safe ride out of the fire zone. Insurgent gunfire continued from the windows.

"We gotta move, Sergeant!" Alvarez insisted.

I calculated the angle of the hillside and the weight of our gear.

"Corporal, we need to get down this hill, pronto," I said. "Ooh rah?"

She peered over the edge.

"Ooh rah, Corporal?"

"Ooh rah, Sergeant."

We collected our gear and scooted to the edge.

Alvarez moved into cover position behind me.

Knowing the descent would be loud and slippery I opted for speed over silence. Securing my sniper rifle tight across my back, I pulled my Glock 18 and dropped off the ledge.

Rocks and pebbles dislodged. Digging in with my boot heels did nothing to slow my descent but at least kept me upright.

Bullets embedded into the slope around me.

I fired at the flash points. Four of the seven insurgents fell to the dirt. Skidding to a stop at the bottom I killed the remaining rebels with one shot each to the head.

Rocks, dirt and stone shifted behind me. Alvarez slid to a stop against my leg. Blood bubbled from the edge of her temple, her breathing shallow. I pulled her onto my shoulders in a firemen's carry.

Moving out into the desert, we headed past the smoldering wreck of the Gaz.——

I shot two rebels in the side of the head as we passed them.

One hundred meters farther south than expected two of the remaining security vehicles sat peeled open and ablaze, dead soldiers around them. The last Gaz and a Jeep with a retro-fitted 7.62mm swivel gun mounted to its roll bar stood another forty meters away.

Five 11th Squad Marines defended them. They had stemmed the tide of the advancing rebels.

That was, until five rebel vehicles roared through the village's gate with their automatic rifles blazing...

3

Hump

minus 63 days – 2205 hours

…away from the village east of Zaranj with Rosalita laying in the back of the Jeep.

I stood behind the mounted swivel gun, firing away at the insurgents. Tracer rounds streaked through the night as they pierced through the vehicles. Dozens of shell casings and connectors fell to the floor.

The driver shouted into his radio between the blasts.

"… under fire!... need support… where's that air support?..."

One of my rounds shattered the windshield of a pursuing Ford F150, blood from the driver's head and chest exploding in the interior cab. The truck careened off the road, several more shots finding their way into the engine block and into two of the rebels who had been firing from the truck's bed.

An older model Chevy S10 raced along behind us, its own machine gun mounted on the center of its roll bar. The gun jammed as soon as the operator pulled the trigger. He slammed his palm against the feed while the truck bounced over the potholes at fifty miles an hour.

"…need support!... driving southeast at coordinates…airship inbound?... say again?..."

Three of my shots ripped through the top of the cab and the operator's chest. He fell back into the bed before sliding off the bumper onto the sandy road.

I directed my fire onto a Jeep Wrangler.

A RPG tore through the night, exhaust trailing behind the rocket engines. The ordinance whistled and arced toward our vehicle.

I dove over Rosalita just as it struck the windshield…

4

Semi-Conscious

minus 62 days – Night

… vaporizing the Black Hawk escorting us. The helo's fiery wreckage fell away, its rotors continuing to spin without the bulk of the fuselage. Our medic knelt between me and Rosalita, an IV running into each of our…

… armored HumVees racing from the helo pads. Blades of the Black Hawk slowed above me. A medical trailer to my right. An eagle with a sword in each talon emblazoned the trailer's black…

… rubber restraints around my wrists, forehead, waist, ankles. The pain in my legs and back screamed… Did I scream?…

…blood-stained sheets… masked men hovering… I hovered over a…

…heart monitor lead ran to beeping machine. Rosalita on next gurney. Men huddled over her. Orders barked to…

… a thin pale man with a black suit stood in the corner, smiling.

A heart monitor beeped, slowing.

Forms blurred into the olive drab background.

The gaunt man in the suit smiled wider. He stepped between the gurneys.

Beep. … Beep. … Beep.

He reached out.

Beep.

Lips pulled back, revealing razor sharp teeth.

Beep.

I screamed. Or did I?

Beep.

He leaned over me.

Beep.

"Marine, you and your spotter have served your country well."

Beep.

"This will hurt quite a bit."

Beep.

A long black needle in his fist.

Beep.

And plunged it into my neck…

DAY ZERO

1

Too Far To Run
Day Zero – 0935 hours

Sixty days after my last mission in the desert and three days after my general discharge from my career in the Corp, I started my walk home. No one had come to pick me up. I had not told anyone of the disgrace of what had happened.

My rucksack contained my entire life but seemed to weigh nothing. What it represented weighed me down. The only job I ever loved or was good at had disappeared in an instant. The Corp couldn't use an operator who no longer had the power of speech. And sitting behind a desk would have been an agonizing death sentence.

The two-lane blacktop warmed the soles of my boots. In another month the black top would start to belch out rubbery tar bubbles, but for now the asphalt absorbed the heat just fine.

I crested the top of a rolling hill, hearing the unmistakable downshifting of gears and the increased torque of a diesel engine. A gasoline tanker truck rumbled up behind me, its shimmering chrome giving way to a deep metallic cobalt blue.

Air brakes hissed the lumbering Detroit steel to a stop, the driver tapping his air horn twice. The cab shuddered as the passenger window eased down.

"Hey there, Marine! You need a ride?"

Shrugging off my duffle, I lifted myself to the window.

With a hand on one of the gear shifters and the other leaning on the window, an unshaven man in a flannel shirt and an oily Mac Truck ball cap stared back at me with a grin.

"You looked like a prairie dog, popping your head through the window like that." He laughed good-naturedly. "You need a lift?"

I looked around the cab.

"Well, Marine, I'm going down Route 5. If you need to get off your boots awhile I can get you along a few klicks before I have to head north again."

He continued to smile, his face crinkling the corners of his eyes. A faded menacing blue-tinted bulldog with USMC dog tags was visible in the man's thick gray arm hair.

I tapped the top of the door panel then hopped down to open the door. I grabbed my duffle and climbed in.

"Name's Sebastian, by the way," he said, shooting out his right hand.

I took it and shook it.

"Don't talk much, huh?" he asked.

I shook my head and put my hand to my throat.

"Well, alright then. Ooh rah!" The driver shouted, slipping the truck back into gear.

2

Checkpoint

Day Zero – 1155 hours

"Seeing the world during my stint in the Corp definitely put the traveling itch in me. I couldn't scratch it! Might have done the same to you if you had had the chance to finish out your career. It's a shame what happened to you. Good thing I had that notepad around, John, 'cause I suck at Charades.

"I knew a woman who wanted to anchor me down in a relationship. We left on good terms, Marie and me." He threw me a wink. "Whenever I get back to Philly I look her up. I may get down that way on my next run. Exxon has me running the entire northeastern coastline. Not enough operators to go around these days, I guess."

I listened to the Marine veteran and stared out at the New England countryside.

Sebastian downshifted as we topped another hill.

"What's going on here?"

I looked through the sun glare on the dusty and bug splattered windshield. We started our descent to a longer flattened stretch of road. Three state police cruisers sat along the road's grassy shoulders, their roof bubbles turning and their engines idling. Flares and cones had been set up in both directions on the two-lane highway. Officers manned the checkpoint, outfitted with tactical vests and semi-automatic rifles.

Sebastian added the air brakes to bring the tanker to a stop.

Two vehicles idled in the line ahead of us, sitting between the cones.

The oncoming lane was empty.

The cars ahead of us inched forward.

Sebastian left the rig idling.

17

A trooper with a full thick mustache pointed to the driver of a Crown Vic to stop. A second trooper with a pleasant smile and beaming face, wearing a flat-brimmed Mountie style lid, approached the car.

Officer Friendly motioned for the driver to lower the window. For a moment the driver did not comply.

The trooper continued the gesture and moved his other hand to his revolver. Officer Magnum, P.I., who had directed the car to stop, pulled his sidearm with the barrel pointed at the asphalt.

"Geez! What the hell?" Sebastian whispered.

The driver finally rolled down the window and Officer Friendly peered through it. He spoke to the driver, nodding several times and looking around the interior. He motioned for the driver to calm down.

After several moments, the officer finally straightened up and waved the driver through the checkpoint.

The sedan sped off.

Officer Friendly exhaled sharply and adjusted his lid, waving a VW forward. The distance between the Beetle and us lengthened.

Sebastian sat with his right hand on the gear shifter, a toothpick swimming around his mouth. The bill of his cap had dropped a bit over his dull blue eyes.

"We'll just wait here 'til we have a clear path. No worries."

The Beetle stopped in front of Officer Magnum. Officer Friendly approached the driver's side and pantomimed the same as he had with the driver of the Crown Vic.

He leaned down to the window.

Just as quickly, Friendly straightened up.

Friendly nodded to Magnum.

Officer Magnum pointed the driver to the side of the road with his weapon held at the back of his thigh.

The driver and the rear seat passenger both threw their hands up in the air, the passenger moving slowly. The driver shook his head at something the passenger said but put his hands back on the steering wheel and eased the Beetle to the soft shoulder.

Two blond officers, who had been standing at the police cruisers, walked over to join Officer Magnum. Their fingers were pressed down hard on their rifles' trigger guards.

Officer Friendly waved to us and pointed to the ground in front of him.

Sebastian moved the rig forward. When the trooper stood even with the driver's door, Sebastian re-engaged the hissing air brakes.

The officer hopped up.

"Sorry for the delay, gentlemen."

Behind the tinted sunglasses, his eyes darted around the cabin.

"What can we help you with?"

"We have an Amber Alert for a young boy. Just checking all vehicles."

"No problem, officer."

"How you gentleman feeling?"

"All good," Sebastian responded.

The trooper looked at me.

I gave him a smile and a thumbs-up.

"He just got Stateside from the Gulf. Got a little pinch in the neck that keeps him from engaging in stimulating conversation." Sebastian grinned. "Best passenger ever!"

The trooper gave me a long appraising look over his sunglasses. After a few seconds, Officer Friendly looked back at Sebastian.

"Okay, gentleman. Drive safe."

He stepped to the pavement and waved us forward.

The occupants in the Beetle opened their doors as we passed. Sebastian double-clutched into a higher gear, exhaust billowing from the double stacks.

I watched the checkpoint recede in the huge vertical side mirror. The blond troopers rushed over to the Beetle as the passenger struggled out.

As we turned around a bend, Sebastian shifted again. The truck's exhaust pipe caps exploded and popped, similar to the sound of rifle fire.

3

Lessons

Day Zero – 1241 hours

The one-sided conversation from Sebastian had tapered off after the checkpoint. To fill the silence he turned on the radio to WCBS FM, a news station. A female radio announcer rattled off the news for the top of the hour.

"Uncharacteristic floods rage through small towns in southern Ohio and parts of Tennessee today. The governors of both states announced that the declaration of their states as disaster areas by their outraged citizens is premature.

"A Florida native allegedly chewed off the face of another man, forcing Miami-Dade police officers to shoot him dead. As of this report, there has been no determination as to whether the man was under the influence of drugs or alcohol.

"In sports, the Atlanta Braves sealed a mid-season deal to trade injured All-Star Javier Ramirez for two promising L.A. Dodgers AA-Ball minor leaguers, causing an uproar from other MLB front offices.

"Traffic and weather up next on the 1s."

Straight ahead, a gated chain link fence separated us from a narrow one-lane asphalt road. A pristine reflective sign mounted on the fence read 'Rainier Island Energy Project'.

Sebastian turned down the radio volume as Route 5 curved west to hug the shoreline. Bark and foliage flashed by. To our left a wide river cut the island from the mainland, a series of concrete dams stringing the span from shore to shore.

"Yeah, Rainier put together a great eco project." Sebastian gestured toward the water. "Provides about a third of the electrical power to the island. Not as advanced as the Bay of Fundy in Nova Scotia, but very cool stuff."

A cube-shaped concrete power substation stood nestled in well landscaped trees and bushes. The forest continued for about a half mile before it petered out into more scrubby brush. Soon the flat roofs of buildings appeared, a church tower rising beyond them.

Sebastian drove the rig around a large bay, heading toward a half-mile long arched concrete bridge joining the mainland to the westernmost tip of the island. Every third archway opened with its own spillway, emptying the water back into the Atlantic.

"This corner is always a little tricky."

Route 5 approached the bridge at a severe angle. Sebastian slowed and turned the rig's oversized steering wheel hand over hand to keep the truck's tires from rubbing against the edges of the narrow sidewalks.

We made our way across the bridge.

On the other side a wood carved sign marked our arrival.

The fresh white background of the sign gave way to muted painted reliefs of sea gulls and a crab boat surrounding a carved, stylized gold-leafed cursive 'Welcome to Rainier Island'. The bottom of the sign read 'Population 417' and 'Home of the Casper Lighthouse'.

Past the sign and down a slight incline the whitewashed single-gabled church sat on a bright green lawn, the bell tower I noticed earlier rising from one side. Behind the building the Atlantic Ocean crashed its waters against a narrow strip of rocky beach. Beside the red double doors was a large letter sign touting "Don't Forget God! This weekend - Spiritual Retreat - Boston!"

Sebastian guided the tanker truck along a street next to a rectangular manicured plaza. Intersecting curved stone walks broke up the lawn, leading to a white octagonal gazebo at its far eastern section. The structure was complete with a black roof of architectural asphalt shingles.

The shops and stores surrounding the plaza conformed to a salty white New England style, most with picturesque awnings and painted signs at the end of chains on wrought iron braces.

At the corner of the plaza Sebastian slowed the rig and pulled into an Exxon gas station. A small mart was built in the same island themed white and blue. Its roof pitched steeply with deep gray roof shingles and a brass weather vane with a swooping seagull flying around the four points of the compass. A covered concrete island sat in the middle of the sea of blacktop with two modern gas pumps.

Sebastian brought the truck to a stop.

"Here we are, Johnny. Welcome to Rainier Island."

We climbed down to the blacktop.

I walked around the front of the rig, feeling the heat from the engine. Sebastian stood at the fender, stretching out his back.

"Hey, my man, I have to transfer some of my precious cargo."

He thumbed over to the fuel tank access covers.

I moved toward him, but Sebastian held up both hands.

"Whoa there, Marine! I appreciate you wanting to help out a fellow leatherneck but this is a boring one-man job. Plus, I don't think my bosses would appreciate an outsider handling their equipment. I definitely don't want you handling my equipment!"

He laughed and pointed across the plaza.

"Check out the Oceanside Diner. Carol will hook you up. That Carol is a fine, fine lady," he said with a wink.

I smiled and headed off in the direction of food.

23

4

Oceanside

Day Zero – 1311 hours

The inside of the Oceanside Diner crackled with life, the din of a dozen conversations overlapping in small town chatter. Patrons filled most of the booths, fake oak paneling running floor to ceiling. Three ceiling fans provided a comforting swirl of air.

Making my way to the closest available vinyl cushioned chrome stool at the counter, I pulled out a menu wedged in a condiment holder. As I looked it over, I realized I was hungrier than I thought. The meatloaf with mashed potatoes and gravy sounded good. A diet Coke would top it off nicely.

My stomach growled in agreement.

I watched the closer of two televisions mounted above the counter. The news was on. A man in a raincoat with an umbrella in one hand and an ABC affiliate microphone in the other talked about an explosion. In the background, a fire raged through a warehouse behind a fenced-in perimeter.

"Hey, Carol!" a man shouted.

A stocky woman popped her head through the saloon doors from the kitchen.

"What, Ralph?"

"Can you turn the TV up?"

With a sigh, Carol came through from the clanking in the kitchen, grabbed a remote and pointed it at the television at the far end. She did the same to the television near me.

With the volume coming up, the reporter's lips gained substance.

"… the fire here at R&R has raged unabated for three days. The result of an underground gas main rupture, according to an R&R spokesman, the fire you see behind me has engulfed the warehouse and has countered any attempts by local firefighters to subdue it. As of today, R&R announced it would let the fire burn itself out, concerned that the continued battle between the blaze and local engine companies could result in unnecessary injury.

"Carl Stack, ABC 7, reporting from Farson, Wyoming."

The on-scene reporter disappeared, replaced by a young in-studio female anchor.

"Thank you, Carl," the anchorwoman responded. "In related news, as the winds push the smoke east from Farson toward Cheyenne, Casper and Medicine Bow, R&R has asked Wyoming's governor to bring out the state's National Guard to assist in possible evacuations. R&R still claims the warehouse holds no hazardous materials that would affect public health. The company, known for its decades-long work as a defense contractor with the United States government, asserts it is only looking out for the safety of the public.

"In other news, a rash of attacks has been reported in the outskirts of Rapid City, South Dakota. Local authorities have reported several young men and women, experimenting with an LSD-laced batch of the drug Ecstasy, have shown aggressive behavior as a result of drug-induced hallucinations. When local authorities arrived on scene, the officers were forced to resort to Tazers and non-lethal measures to subdue the group. Several officers were injured and sent to local hospitals with contusions and bites, resulting in the dispatch of the Rapid City SWAT team to bring the tense situation to a close. All suspects are now in the Rapid City jail awaiting arraignment.

"Finally, on a more upbeat note, Biskist the German Shepherd returned home ..."

"What can I get you, hun?"

I looked down from the TV to Carol staring at me with one hand on the Formica counter and the other on her curvy hip. Her features were soft and youthful in spite of the gray streaks in her hair.

Picking up the menu, I pointed to the meatloaf.

"Interested in the meatloaf?"

I nodded.

"Having trouble with your voice? I'll bring you some hot tea and lemon."

Before I could figure out how to object, she strolled away and disappeared into the kitchen.

5

Something Wicked This Way Comes

Day Zero – 1344 hours

I sat in a café area on the sidewalk in front of the diner.

"How was the food?" Sebastian called out as he crossed the street.

I gave him a thumbs-up.

"Good." He laughed as he walked toward the door. "Wait here a bit. I want to get some hot food and chat Carol up a bit. I have to get back up north but I want to make sure you have the next leg of your travel set. Let me see what I can do."

I waved him away so he could continue his obvious courtship.

At the next wrought iron table, a silver haired heavyset man in a summer suit absently stirred his cup of coffee. Next to his coffee sat a leather briefcase. On its latched edge the name Felix Laraby was etched in script on a riveted gold-colored placard.

Mr. Laraby put the newspaper on top of the briefcase and stood, the legs of the chair screeching on the concrete.

"What the hell?" he asked as he stared across the plaza.

I followed his gaze.

A girl wearing a gauzy white sundress walked across the grass, the white two-story limestone and marble Town Hall rising up from a columned portico behind her. She walked with a slight limp. Her dress was torn and muddy, her face and forearms dirty, her hair wet and stringy.

A dog barked in the distance.

The girl stopped and cocked her head.

Mr. Laraby walked toward her.

Maybe he knew her.

With each step, the girl appeared more wrong. At thirty meters, I realized the girl's summer dress was actually a filmy nightgown.

At twenty meters, the dirt on her skin and clothes looked more like drying blood. A single red tear ran from the corner of each eye, dust sticking to it. More blood coated around her mouth, droplets splattered between her slight breasts.

Once Mr. Laraby closed to within five meters, she blinked out of her stupor and raised her arms to him. Her sleeves pulled back to reveal multiple parallel cuts along the forearms, with two deep slashes running up from the wrists to the middle of the forearms.

Mr. Laraby swung off his suit jacket and wrapped it around her shoulders.

The girl emitted a sound that was half moan, half hiss.

Her lips peeled back, revealing bloodstained teeth and blackened gums. Her jaw opened as if she could no longer stifle a ferocious yawn.

She lunged toward his throat.

What the hell?

I got up to assist.

Luckily, he had sidestepped to get the jacket tighter around her.

She struggled against him with her arms pinned, still trying to get at his neck. Mr. Laraby spun behind her, wrapping his arms low around the jacket and her chest. When she could not get anywhere close to his neck, she bent forward to snap at his arms.

I could smell blood and dirt, mixed with urine and feces.

Mr. Laraby picked her up and took a couple steps toward me.

Her whole body thrashed.

He lost his grip and dropped her.

As soon as her feet hit the pavement she spun around, shrugged off the jacket and lashed out at him.

Mr. Laraby tripped backwards, his ass hitting hard on the pavement.

She settled on his chest with uncanny speed, forcing him onto his back. Grabbing handfuls of his graying hair, she plunged her mouth toward his left shoulder.

A pistol shot.

The bullet ripped through the girl's shoulder.

She twisted off Mr. Laraby and rolled into a coiled crouch.

A uniformed man ran up, a smoking Beretta M9 in his right hand. He kicked a steel-toed black work boot across her jaw. It cracked and hung askew, still producing a horrible humming sound.

She readied to pounce on the officer.

That thought was fleeting as a second pistol shot blew brain matter and skull fragments out the back of her head.

6

But He Did Not Shoot The Deputy

Day Zero – 1359 hours

Two Oceanside diner patrons had screamed after the second shot rang out.

Most of the customers continued to press against the plate glass window.

The deputy with the nameplate Garrett stood with shaking hands. His Beretta still pointed at the girl. He was medium height and stocky, with a slight belly.

"Christ, Jared," Mr. Laraby muttered.

"I had to, Felix," Jared Garrett whispered.

Mr. Laraby rolled onto his knees.

I offered him a hand up.

His hands trembled as much as the deputy's. The adrenaline was bleeding off and turning into shock for both of them.

"Yeah. I know," Mr. Laraby said to the deputy, slapping the dirt off his crumpled pants. To me he said, "Thanks, son."

I put my hand over the slide of the deputy's weapon and flipped the safety off with my thumb - automatically bringing the hammer back with a soft click.

"I had to," Garrett said, defending his action.

I put my other hand on his shoulder, giving it a light squeeze.

"Sheriff told me to do it. No exceptions!"

Sebastian appeared through the crowd and steered Deputy Garrett to a chair. Garrett slumped down with a hollow, tinny thud. Mr. Laraby sat next to him.

The girl was now covered head to waist with the suit jacket.

"She was crazy strong," Felix admitted. "I didn't expect that."

Sebastian took the radio from Garrett's belt and pushed it into the deputy's numb hands.

"Call Frank, Jared," Sebastian told the deputy sternly. "He needs to get a handle on this."

7

Getting Into Gear

Day Zero – 1407 hours

The girl lay covered in the street.

Deputy Garrett sat with his radio in hand.

The diner patrons ventured out to gawk.

When a hand from the crowd slapped Garrett on the shoulder, the deputy yelled out. He spun out of the chair and backed into the street, nearly tripping over the body. He stopped short when his radio squawked.

"Garrett, are you there? Over?" A faint steady hiss replaced the bodiless voice. "Garrett, come in. Over?"

The deputy slowly raised the radio.

"I'm here, Sheriff. Over."

"I need a sit-rep!" the voice crackled with authority.

"One down," Garrett replied more loudly.

"Down for good? Any more?"

"One down permanently." He paused and looked around the plaza. "No other threats. Repeat. No other threats. Over."

"Secure the Stretch. Barricade the bridge with cars, trucks, whatever you need to. Need it tight enough to keep a person from slipping through. Lock it up! Keep everyone off the streets. Over and out."

Before the radio cut out two pistol shots echoed through the radio.

Deputy Garrett pointed at me.

"What's your name?"

"That's John Walken, Deputy Garrett," Sebastian said. "He don't talk but I vouch for him."

"Mr. Walken and Sebastian, put a cordon around the girl!" He looked at the crowd. "Don't let anyone near her!"

Garrett ran over to his cruiser, popped the trunk with his remote, grabbed a roll of yellow police tape and tossed it back at me. He turned to the crowd and pointed to three men.

"Kyle, Diggs, Simon. Come with me."

The men whose names he called out hopped into Garrett's cruiser.

I stood there with the yellow tape in hand, watching them drive off.

The crowd stared at me.

Mr. Laraby came up to Sebastian and me.

"Let's get this situation cordoned off, gentlemen," he said, a café chair in each hand.

8

Glimmers of Preparations

Day Zero – 1420 hours

The yellow police tape flicked in the breeze, wrapped around the backs of the café chairs surrounding the body. Mr. Laraby's suit jacket still covered her.

Deputy Garrett led a convoy of vehicles past the Town Hall to the bridge. With a little maneuvering, the men parked four cars side-by-side on the bridge. A young man parking the last sedan next to the guardrail had to shimmy out the driver side window.

The largest of Garrett's men stood and gazed over the Atlantic, scratching under his flannelled armpit.

Once done Deputy Garrett loaded the men into his cruiser and drove them back to the diner. He and the flannelled blonde exited, both opening the back doors for the others.

The deputy shook the lanky young man's hand. His toothy grin widened after the deputy patted him on the shoulder.

"That's Simon Russell," Sebastian informed me. "He works at Erma's Groceries."

Garrett walked around the back of the cruiser and extended a hand to the other rear seat passenger.

"Kyle Foster. A good kid, high school senior." Sebastian continued his introductions. "He works at the diner. Not the brightest bulb in the box but a good kid."

Last for congratulations was the large flannelled man. He clasped Deputy Garrett's hand with both of his, pumping twice and smiling the entire time. Garrett took a step back, unbalanced.

"Harlan Dickerson. Lifelong islander. He has a farm mid-island. Most people call him Diggs because of a former roadwork occupation."

Deputy Garrett veered off toward the gawkers.

34

"Everyone needs to go home! No one is going to work on the Main today. If you encounter anyone like this," Garrett said, pointing to the covered body, "do not approach them! They are highly infectious! Sheriff Wayne is working with the state police on the Main trying to figure things out. When he gets back, we'll get you more info."

"What about the girl?" a woman asked.

"Yeah! What about the girl?" from someone else in the crowd.

"What's going on, Garrett?" a third voice chimed in.

Garrett climbed onto one of the remaining café chairs.

"I will only say this one more time. Go home! Anyone here in three minutes that I did not ask to stay or does not have a business to run will be arrested! Move!"

The crowd mumbled, but slowly dispersed.

Some glanced at me with a wary eye.

I stood fast.

My home was too far away.

9

First of Many

Day Zero – 1436 hours

Sebastian, Mr. Laraby and I stared at the dead girl in the street under the jacket.

Deputy Garrett pulled his cruiser next to the body, popping the trunk as he exited. He grabbed a duffle bag, unzipped it and extracted two black body bags. Reaching back into the duffle, he pulled out a box of blue latex gloves and plucked two for himself.

Garrett donned the gloves and tweezed a corner of Mr. Laraby's jacket collar with a thumb and forefinger, the latex drooping beyond the tips of his fingers. He slid the jacket off the girl and draped it inside one of the bags. The girl stared up at the sky, a fly scurrying across one of her amber and gold eyeballs.

The blood under her body had dulled to a dusty flat stain.

"Mr. Walken, grab a pair of gloves," Garrett ordered.

I grabbed two and wiggled my fingers into them.

"Grab the feet, please."

He bent his girth over the girl, a bead of sweat sliding off his nose and onto the girl's cheek. Garrett grabbed her under the armpits and I lifted her by her ankles. Her flesh felt much too cold, especially in the heat of the day.

"Okay, Mr. Walken," Garrett said. "One, two, three."

We placed her in the body bag. I zipped the bag halfway over the girl, Garrett reaching over for the tab to finish the job.

We lifted the bag, Garrett sweating more profusely and his skin turning an unhealthy red. We sidestepped and placed it into the second bag.

Garrett snapped off his gloves and tossed them in an evidence pouch from his pocket. He held the pouch out to me for my gloves.

He dropped the evidence pouch in with the girl and zippered up the second bag.

"Help me get the bag into the back seat."

I grabbed the body bag handle and crawled through the cruiser's rear bench, sliding the bag through behind me.

"You in the military, right?"

"Him and me both, Deputy," Sebastian added.

Garrett walked past Sebastian and reached into the trunk.

I came around to the bumper in time to have a pump-action shotgun pushed into my hands.

Sebastian got one too.

We both instinctively checked the breaches before slinging the weapons.

"Sebastian, you haven't seen action in some time," Garrett commented.

"That may be true, deputy," Sebastian responded with pride, "but shooting stuff is like riding a bicycle!"

10

In the Oceanside

Day Zero – 1503 hours

Deputy Garrett drove off to a parking lot between the Town Hall and a low-roofed brick building.

I turned back to Mr. Laraby.

He sat in the same café chair with his head in his cupped hands, elbows on his knees and shoulders slumped. Spittle clung from his chin and regurgitated coffee and pastry pooled at his feet. Some of it had splashed up onto his wingtip dress shoes, but he seemed not to notice.

I lifted him to his feet.

Careful to avoid the vomit puddle, I steered him into the Oceanside Diner. Sebastian held the door before coming inside.

The last remaining patron, an old man, sat at a window table and gazed at us as we steered Mr. Laraby toward the counter.

"Hey, Sam," Sebastian called out.

"Hey there yourself, Bastian," the old man responded. "How're you feeling, Felix? What the hell happened out there?"

Sam wore a light flannel shirt, cinched denim jeans and muddy work boots. With a shiny balding head, wrinkled weathered face, and sharp blue eyes, the man kept staring at us.

"You saw what we saw," Sebastian replied. "I wouldn't have believed it if I hadn't have seen it."

Carol came over with a tumbler of ice water.

"Drink slow, Felix," Carol said before disappearing into the kitchen.

He did take a slow sip, still half-choking.

A series of clattering and clanking came from the kitchen before Carol appeared again. She approached Felix, her hands behind her back.

"Carol, hon? Can I get some more joe?" Sam whistled through his dentures.

"Sam, can't you see I'm busy?" Carol replied, slightly disgusted.

"Don't worry. I'm not goin' anywhere."

"Yeah. Anything for free refills."

"Don't make me change a policy that's been in place since the diner opened."

Sam chuckled, until a coughing fit stopped him. Once the worse of it had passed, he sipped his coffee to drive back the rest. He cleared his throat and returned to looking out the window.

"Felix," Carol cooed.

Mr. Laraby looked up.

She pulled a shot glass and a bottle of whiskey from behind her back. Unscrewing the cap, she poured a full shot and slid it in front of him. She set the bottle on the counter.

"A little medicine to take the edge off, hon." She patted his hand and walked away.

Mr. Laraby eyed the glass and swirled it for a moment before gulping it down. He poured a refill, banged the bottle back on the counter, downed the second shot and banged that to the counter as well. He stared at the bottle for a moment before flicking away the shot glass. It scooted to the counter's edge.

"That lady, there," Sebastian said, "has put her blood, sweat and tears into this place after her husband died. I'm proud of her."

I gave him a wink.

"Shut up," he responded.

Felix looked a little better, the whiskey having calmed him.

"Carol? Can you watch over our friend here?" Sebastian asked. "Deputy Garrett asked us to join him at the station."

"Yeah. You go ahead. Sam and I will look after Felix."

I clasped Mr. Laraby on the shoulder. He surprised me by reaching up and squeezing my hand for a moment. Giving him a final pat, I went to the door and held it open.

Sebastian slipped through.

Sam took a deep drag of his cigarette and coughed, catching my attention.

"Have a fabulous day, young man."

11

The Sheriff Returns

Day Zero – 1522 hours

Garrett's cruiser sat idling at a ramped lower entrance at the Sheriff's station, its back doors open.

Sebastian and I peered at the back seat.

The body bag was gone.

A siren wailed.

Another cruiser screeched to a skidding stop behind Deputy Garrett's vehicle.

The car door flew open, its lights still flashing.

Muscular and tall, the lawman approached us. His beige shirt was coated in drying blood and his left sleeve was partially torn away at the shoulder. His black trousers were muddied and tattered. Blood and matter streaked through his blonde hair, his tan cheeks and neck.

The nameplate read Wayne.

The sheriff walked past, appraising me with his steel green stare.

"Hi Sebastian," he said, and then gave us an order. "Come with me."

We obediently followed him down the ramp.

Inside, the room opened up to a square-shaped receiving area. Janitorial supplies and palettes were parked around the perimeter. Sheriff Wayne went through another set of doors to a hallway. He stepped into the first room on the right.

"What do we have, Doctor Rawlings?" the sheriff asked, his voice booming in the small space.

Deputy Garrett and the doctor looked up with a start.

The Sheriff stopped at the near side of a steel morgue table.

41

The girl from the plaza lay naked on its cold surface, a towel covering her private areas.

Sebastian and I stood in the doorway.

The doctor held a scalpel over the bloody girl, his medical mask unable to hide his sharp features.

The deputy's surprise turned to shock. "Christ, Frank. Are you alright?"

"Later," Sheriff Wayne said. "Doc, was she dead?"

"Of course she's dead, Frank!" Garrett blurted out. "I shot her!"

"Doc?" Frank asked again.

Doctor Rawlings took off his glasses and pinched the bridge of his hawk-like nose.

"With no disrespect to the good deputy here," the doctor responded after a moment's consideration, "this girl was dead before she was shot. Both wrists were slit at the radial artery. She surely bled out and died some time during the night. Time of death, though, is inconclusive due to continued muscle function."

"What the fuck?" Garrett exclaimed.

"Just like the ones we put down over on the Main." Wayne turned to Garrett. "That's why I gave you the kill order. They're all over."

"What do we do, Chief?"

"You barricaded the Searing Bridge. I came over the Norte Dam Bridge through the utility gate. It's more isolated over there, but it will need to be barricaded too."

The sheriff rubbed his smooth face with a still bloody hand, depositing a smear on his check.

He pointed a thumb over his shoulder.

"Who's this guy?"

"Walken," Sebastian chimed in. "He's ex-military."

"Is that the case, soldier?" the Sheriff asked me.

Before I could respond, Garrett spoke up. "Sebastian says he can't talk. Claims it was from an accident in the Corps."

"Ok," Sheriff Frank Wayne said. He rested his hand on the butt of his service revolver and gave me a once over. "Let's get Glenda on the phone tree."

12

Phone Tree

Day Zero – 1540 hours

We went up a stairwell that emptied into a large office area.

A woman with raven hair and a fair complexion sat at one of the desks.

"Don't worry, Kathy," she said into the phone. "I'm sure Harland's goat will not continue to trample through your rose garden... Yes... Yes, I will make sure Frank speaks to him. Okay... Okay..."

The woman slowly spun in her chair. Her face drained to a chalky color. The finger stopped twirling the phone cord. Her mouth continued to move without making a sound.

After a few seconds she turned back to her desk.

"Kathy. I will talk to him. I will call you back."

She hung up the phone, pushed her shoulders back and spun back around.

"What the hell, Francis?" she shouted at the sheriff.

Garrett, Rawlings and Sebastian backed away.

"It's alright, Glenda."

"Are you kidding me? Look at you! Whose blood is that?" She pointed at his uniform.

"Glenda!"

"What?"

"We don't have time for this. I'm fine. It's not my blood. There's a situation we have to deal with now. Do you hear me?"

She gaped at him for a moment before rushing to give him a hug. When finished she stepped back and wiped a stray tear away.

"What do you need, Sheriff?"

"Call the Tree. We need everyone to stay indoors with doors locked."

"What's the reason?"

"Tell them we're sorting that out."

She went to her desk, opening a folder with a list of numbers.

"Jared, I need you to call the Gun Toters," Wayne ordered.

"All of them, Frank?"

"Yes. All of them except the Councilman."

"Shit! What do we tell Anderson?"

"Nothing. Keep him in the dark. I don't need his crap. This is police business, anyway. Glenda, that goes for you too!"

"Yes, Sheriff," Glenda acknowledged, dialing her first number.

Deputy Garrett sat heavily in his chair and started to dial from memory.

"Doc, I need you to take stock of your medical supplies. Get Basia to help." Sheriff Wayne pronounced the name Basha.

The doctor left without a word.

Sebastian eased into an open office chair.

I stood at ease.

The sheriff stepped close to me.

"Ex-military, huh? Hope you aren't one of those Army pussies."

I shook my head.

"Can you shoot?"

With that, I gave him a wide grin.

13

News

Day Zero – 1620 hours

Sheriff Wayne had cleaned up and changed uniforms, and was sitting in an enclosed office in the corner of the lobby.

Eighteen men and women stood in the stone walled lobby. Driftwood sculptures and beige office furniture with colorful throw pillows offset the crowd's mood.

Mr. Laraby and Sebastian walked through the crowd.

"Hey there, Johnny," Sebastian said with a grin. "Felix is almost as good as new."

Alcohol drifted from the swaying Mr. Laraby's breath.

The Sheriff emerged from his office and turned to the gathering. Glenda moved away and stood with Garrett.

"Alright. Let's get started!" Wayne boomed.

The crowd quieted.

"Thank you for coming on short notice. The Searing Bridge has been blocked off. Some of you were in plaza this morning when Felix came in contact with the girl that Deputy Garrett shot."

With his last remark, a murmur came over the crowd.

"Listen," Sheriff Wayne said in a raised, commanding voice. "I asked Deputy Garrett to have you bring your firearms. The girl was a carrier of a lethal infection. Had she come into longer contact with anyone her contagion could have spread.

"On the Main, several Massachusetts State Troopers and I encountered more than a dozen of these infected people. They attacked without warning or reason. One of the troopers, while fending off one of them, was bitten in the shoulder. In a panic, he accidently discharged his sidearm into his assailant's chest. To no effect!"

Sheriff Wayne took a long breath. Everyone stared at him. Glenda had a hand over her mouth, her eyes moist. Garrett looked pale again, his bravado and adrenaline from earlier seeping away.

"I shot that assailant in the temple just before he took another bite out of that officer," Sheriff Wayne continued, his voice even and eyes sharp. "The assailant did not get back up. We killed the rest with a bullet to the head. When the bitten trooper showed signs of the virus and attacked us we shot him, too."

"What were they, Sheriff? Vampires?" Kyle Foster asked. "In the daytime, no less!"

Nervous laughter echoed throughout the lobby.

"Kyle. The idea of vampires is absurd." Sheriff Wayne clenched his left hand. "Men and woman have died. Good men I have known for my entire career."

"Sorry, Sheriff," Kyle muttered, dropping his eyes and losing his grin.

"Whatever the cause, know this. The infected will kill you. They have no reasoning. If you encountered a rabid dog or 'coon, you don't try to catch it… you put it down. The same rule applies here. They're aggressive and strong. They will not hesitate. You can't hesitate."

The sheriff paused.

"I need volunteers to stand post at the bridges. The Norte Bridge still needs to be blocked off. I need calm, reasonable islanders for sentry duty until further notice. I will expect any sentry to be ready to eliminate any obviously infected persons that come across either bridge. Do I have any volunteers?"

"You can't just shoot people, Sheriff!" someone hollered.

"Yeah!" another cried out.

I looked through the crowd to see who had yelled out. Others did the same.

"Walter, Pete," Sheriff Wayne started, knowing exactly who had blurted out their opposition. "I see you brought your Winchesters. And I know you have always been first in line in times of community need. But if you cannot stand with me on this thing, you need to go home. No guilt, no pressure, no judgment. All I ask is that you lock your doors and protect your homes and families. That goes for anyone else here."

The Gun Toters murmured to each other.

The sheriff glanced back at his wife and the deputy.

"Okay," Wayne said.

The crowd continued to talk.

"People!" Wayne yelled, following it with a piercing whistle.

The crowd quieted.

"I need ten volunteers. If you think you can keep a clear head, meet me back here at 3pm. That is all I have to say. Anyone not volunteering goes home. Thank you."

Sheriff Wayne finished and went back into his office.

Felix, Sebastian and I stayed put.

The rest of the Gun Toters gravitated into groups to discuss their options. Glenda pointed a remote at two flat screens on the wall. They came to loud life as a weekend anchor for CNN stared back at us.

"...scattered reports from Nevada and surrounding areas have come in regarding panic and violence in major urban areas..."

Everyone quieted and fixated on the screens.

"... the Center for Disease Control has released a statement that these outbreaks are not part of any pandemic they are familiar with. The CDC cautions people to stay indoors and away from populated urban areas as a precaution."

The male anchor paused, his eyes darting left to right on the teleprompter.

"Pittsburgh's Mayor Thomas Gleeson, three hours ago, called for the state's National Guard to be called up to contain both the violence and the possible spread of contagion. We go now to Mario Vendez in downtown Pittsburgh for a complete report."

The weekend anchor faded away, replaced by a young reporter with slicked back black hair. Microphone in hand, he waited for an off-camera prompt. During the few seconds of awkward silence a platoon of National Guardsmen sprinted down the street toward a concrete barricaded intersection where a large group of civilians had gathered.

"As you can see behind me," Vendez started, "the National Guard has been called in at the request of Mayor Thomas Gleeson. A group of protesters has assembled on Grand Avenue and look as if to overrun the barricades."

The camera panned and closed in on the intersection.

"The violence within the group has led to many injuries. As you can see, several of the protesters are bloody or have visible wounds."

One of the Guardsmen tossed a smoke canister into the crowd. The camera focused on a man in the crowd near where the canister landed, the bystander's Polo shirt streaked with blood. The man looked dazed, but kept up with the stumbling crowd moving through the swirling acrid smoke.

A mass of people bumped against the concrete dividers, a few of them falling over the waist high barricades. They got to their feet and howled. The platoon of Guardsmen raised their weapons and ordered them to stop where they were.

"Some of the protesters have come over the barricade," Mario Vendez continued off-camera, "and seem to be ignoring the orders of the National Guardsmen."

One of the bloody protesters rushed over to the closest Guardsman and made a grab for his weapon. The Guardsman batted the protester's hand away with the rifle, still shouting for him to stay where he was. The protester lunged and bit the Guardsman on the thigh. He screamed and slammed the butt of his rifle into the protester's head. A fellow soldier pulled the protester off his comrade, the biter coming away with a chunk of thigh meat.

We stared at the hi-definition flatscreens.

"Oh my god," Vendez continued, "the protesters have attacked the Guardsmen. Truly out of their minds…"

More protesters surged over the concrete rail. They got to their shambling feet and converged on the closest soldiers. When rifle butts to the head did not quell them, they opened fire on the crowd.

"The soldiers have been overrun! They have opened fire on the civilians. I can't believe this…"

"Shit," Sebastian whispered.

Mr. Laraby sat down hard on the couch.

On the screen, the remaining Guardsmen retreated as the infected crowd advanced.

"… the soldiers are down! The guardsmen are down! The crowd is… oh my god… they're eating the soldiers… what the hell?... Louie, let's get the fuck out of here!"

The cameraman held the shot for a moment longer before the image spun toward the ground and to a pair of running feet on the asphalt. We heard their curses as they ran down the block. A screech of metal and a loud bang from off camera followed. The camera steadied and auto-focused on the interior of a reporter's news van.

The feed turned to static before cutting back to the weekend anchor. He sat behind the CNN newsdesk, his skin now an unhealthy waxy shiny color. He didn't say anything for more than a minute, the news crawl and the spinning station logo the only indication the news feed had not frozen. Finally, the anchor stirred enough to deliver his last line in a hushed, subdued tone.

"We now turn to Harris Shaw in our New York studios."

The camera shot cut away to another anchor behind another CNN newsdesk. Before Harris Shaw could utter a word the flat screens went dark.

The Gun Toters started muttering.

"Now you have a real picture of what we're facing." Sheriff Wayne stood tall with the remote in his hand. "Whoever is volunteering, let's get to work."

14

Gun Toters

Day Zero – 1713 hours

Almost all the Gun Toters stayed. Kyle and Carol from the Oceanside talked to each other. Mr. Diggs Harlan, from the barricading crew, leaned against the stone lobby wall. Sam from the diner stood next to a young man.

"That's Sam's grandson Patrick." Sebastian leaned in. "Great kid. Like his granddad was in his younger years. All Sam has now is bitterness and old age to fall back on."

A hulking man stood under the television with a Winchester 30/30 cradled in his arms. Next to him, a smaller mousy man with sparse beard and thin straight hair sat on a bench with two rifles slung across his back and a handgun holstered to each hip

"Over there is Derek Block. Works part time in the Town Hall. I am not sure what he does there." Sebastian continued. "The tiny Rambo is Pete Newman. He's the wisecracker during the Sheriff's speech. You may have noticed his name on the awning of the gun shop. He may not seem like much, but he sure knows his weapons. Can be a prick sometimes. If he carried all the time he might be a danger to himself."

Kyle wandered off.

Two women joined Carol on the sofa. They talked in whispers. One wore loose jeans and an oversized gray knit sweater, rimless glasses on her nose and her hair pulled back in a tight ponytail. The other woman had dark almond-shaped eyes, filling out her black denim jeans with wider hips. A tight Bob Marley T-shirt covered her developed and toned upper body.

"The one with the glasses is the librarian, Emily Proctor. I know, stereotypical. I'm surprised to see her here. She doesn't seem the type but she loves to target shoot. I have no idea who the other girl is. She isn't an islander."

Sheriff Wayne, Deputy Garrett and Glenda rejoined the group.

"Everyone have their guns?" the Sheriff asked.

A few Gun Toters held up their weapons.

"I have a licensed sidearm in my rig," Sebastian chimed in. "I think maybe Johnny here may have something in his duffle."

I had, in fact, two weapons. One was my personal Glock 18 and the other was a M-45 MEUSOC. Sebastian was not a stupid man.

"Pete, I will need you to supply ammunition and any additional hardware as needed," Wayne instructed.

"Long as I get compensated," the gun shop owner replied.

"Alright. Let's get ready."

15

The Guests Arrive

Day Zero – 1803 hours

A series of faint pops came from the west, maybe a couple miles.

"Sounds like the Main is still having trouble," the sheriff said.

I stared across the Searing Bridge's span.

Sheriff Wayne and Doctor Rawlings huddled, discussing the dead girl in the morgue. Carol and Pete talked about how well their businesses were doing. Apparently, firearms and coffee were big island business.

Two minutes later, the world according to Rainier Island changed forever.

A lone staggering figure came into view.

I peered through the .223 Remington bolt-action rifle's scope, sliding the bolt back and chambering a round. Everyone else turned his or her attention to the bridge.

Blood surrounded the infected man's mouth and washed down his T-shirt. Wearing gray sweat pants and asphalt blackened socks, he walked down the yellow center divider stripe.

"Shit," Pete whispered.

"Stay calm," the sheriff responded. "It's only one."

"But look at him," Carol added.

Wayne stepped over to me.

"Mr. Walken, can you take it out?"

I glanced away from the scope.

Wayne nodded slightly with a grim look.

When I returned to the scope, the figure was much closer. Lining up the crosshairs with the man's mouth, I adjusted up to the bridge of his nose for distance. I slowly exhaled and pulled the trigger.

The muzzle flashed with a crack.

A red dot appeared at the man's receding hairline, blood splashing off the top of his head.

He fell out of view.

I looked over the scope in time to see him slumped on the pavement. I pulled back the bolt on the rifle.

"Good job, Mr. Walken."

Sheriff Wayne climbed over the barricade.

I stayed kneeling on the car trunk, the rifle resting on its roof.

"Please assist me, Doc," the sheriff called back.

Rawlings approached the barricade. Pete helped him up. The doctor crawled over and slipped down to the other side. He caught up to Wayne, the sheriff holding his pistol against his thigh.

The rest of the group stayed where they were.

Wayne and Rawlings approached the body.

Wayne kicked it in the leg. He nodded to Rawlings who knelt down for a closer look. The sheriff stood to one side with his pistol aimed at the body.

A low mewing sound came from the dead man's throat.

Rawlings stumbled backward.

The sheriff put one bullet through its brain.

The mewing stopped.

Wayne pulled Rawlings up.

The doctor slapped the dust off his pants. He brushed past Wayne and approached the body again. Without kneeling, they both surveyed the body.

Something moved in the background.

I looked over the scope.

Twenty-five infected people advanced from the mainland, thirty meters from the Sheriff and the Doctor.

I chambered another round and fired.

A man in overalls, untied boots and a huge sticky gash on his arm fell to the ground.

The sheriff, hearing the pop of my rifle, looked in our direction then toward the lumbering mass of infected people coming his way.

He swept Rawlings behind him and fired three shots. A woman in a navy blue suit with her head tilted to one side, a thin businessman and a state trooper with his throat torn out crumpled to the pavement.

Wayne walked backward, Rawlings already running toward the barricade.

Mangled men and women pressed forward, stumbling over the bodies.

I squeezed the trigger.

An obese woman in a housecoat, with curlers in her thin hair, snapped her head to the sky before falling backward.

Pete fired several times into the crowd.

The infected swarm quickened their pace, guttural sounds rising from their throats.

Firing into the head of a teenage boy with shaggy black hair, my stomach turned.

The sheriff stepped backwards a few meters before stopping and firing.

Rawlings scrambled over the barricade. Sweat poured down his forehead and neck, his breath short and ragged. He brought a shaking cupped hand over his mouth, closed his eyes and threw up.

Carol rubbed his back.

I pulled the trigger twice.

Two men with Massachusetts Bell uniforms, one of them with a piece of collarbone sticking out, crashed into each other.

The magazine was empty.

I replaced it with a spare from my pocket.

Wayne lined up his shots.

Bodies dropped with each muzzle flash.

Thirty meters remained between him and the barricade.

The Sheriff released the magazine. He snatched it as it dropped, returning it to a spot on his belt. He grabbed a full magazine and slid it home.

I continued firing to cover the sheriff's slow and deliberate retreat. The others tried their best to take down the infected without putting the sheriff in the crossfire.

Sheriff Wayne closed the distance to the barricade to fifteen meters. He shot one wide-eyed pursuer wearing a wife beater T-shirt, a loose flapping red Hawaiian shirt and cargo shorts.

His second shot took out a businessman whose foot dragged at an obscene angle. The third shot killed a young man with a green apron still hanging around his neck. A pale young woman wearing a tank top and tight jeans - looking normal other than a gaping hole in her belly – sidestepped around the falling barista. Three more shots dropped her to the pavement, plus two young twin girls in billowy yellow linen dresses with blood dripping from parted lips.

With all the infected killed, Wayne leaned against the hood of the station wagon. He holstered his weapon and stared at the carnage we had left behind.

16

Remnants

Day Zero – 1836 hours

The Sheriff, Carol and I walked to the municipal building, leaving Pete at the bridge. Doctor Rawlings had opted to go home to change clothes some time before.

As we crossed the stone steps of the Town Hall Mr. Diggs Harlan, Sebastian and Glenda passed us on their way to the barricade.

"Sheriff," Glenda nodded.

"Wife," Wayne replied.

A wail of sirens pierced the air.

A police cruiser screeched around the corner from Mall Street to North Plaza Street. The car revved toward us and popped over the parking lot apron. The cruiser came to a smoking stop at the delivery bay.

Garrett and Kyle rushed out of the front seats. The deputy reached inside to the back, dragging Ms. Greenfield and someone else out.

"Christ, Garrett!" Sheriff Wayne boomed. "What's going on?"

"Shotgun blew up in Steve's hand!"

Ms. Greenfield and Garrett pulled Steve to his feet. The remains of his right arm came into view, the ragged bloody meat below his elbow peeked from under a makeshift bandage of a gray sweatshirt.

"Where's Rawlings?" Garrett yelled.

"He went home," Carol answered. "You must have just missed him on the road."

"Get him downstairs, Jared," Sheriff Wayne ordered. "Kyle! Get on the phone in my office and get Rawlings back here now!"

Kyle raced off to the lobby.

57

Deputy Garrett dipped under Steve's good arm while Ms. Greenfield pressed the sweatshirt into Steve's stump. They escorted the semi-conscious man down the ramp. We followed them to the same room where Doctor Rawlings had performed the girl's autopsy.

"Tourniquet above the elbow," the Sheriff ordered. "Walken, get some rubber tubing out from the top left drawer in the cabinet over there."

I rummaged through the drawer and pulled out a length of amber rubber tubing, grabbing a socket wrench from the countertop.

"Keep it tight!" Wayne yelled. "Jared, keep him from thrashing. Hold him!"

Steve howled as Ms. Greenfield pressed the sweatshirt harder into his elbow. The deputy wrapped an arm around the man's shoulders.

Pushing against Ms. Greenfield, I wrapped the tubing around Steve's bicep above the bloody sweatshirt. I wrapped the tubing twice around the arm, slipped in the socket wrench handle and twisted it and the tubing as tight as I could.

"Yeah. That's it, Marine."

The Sheriff came around and pushed his big hand into the sweatshirt that Ms. Greenfield was holding.

"Okay, Lucy. I got it."

Ms. Greenfield stepped away to the wall. She wiped her hands on her shirt. As the blood transferred, she stopped when she realized what she had done.

Carol put her arms around Ms. Greenfield's shoulders just as her legs gave way. They slid down the concrete wall to the tile floor.

"Who's at the Norte Bridge?"

"Felix, Emily and Patrick are at the service road," Deputy Garrett responded.

"How did *they* get in?"

"Could have only been through the utility gate," Garrett said.

"Christ," the Sheriff whispered, his face losing color.

He pulled the bloody sweatshirt away from Steve's elbow. The bleeding had slowed to a trickle from the ragged open wound.

"Jared," Wayne said to his deputy. "Get some gauze. We need to wrap this now. We can't wait for Rawlings."

"Roger that," Garrett replied, letting go of Steve.

I held the socket wrench tight.

The Sheriff pressed a clean patch of sweatshirt into the wound.

Garrett banged open several drawers. A minute later he dumped a bunch of sealed packages of pads onto the metal table between Steve's legs.

"Okay, Garrett," the Sheriff instructed, "take the pads and stack them up."

The deputy did as he was told.

"Okay. When I take the sweatshirt away, press the pads into the arm and wrap it. Ready?"

Garrett swallowed twice, sweat streaming down his face.

"Okay, Now!"

The sheriff tossed the sweatshirt away and Garrett pushed the stacked pads into the stump.

Steve's eyes opened and he screamed.

Gasps came from the corner.

The Sheriff held Steve tight. Steve's screams and thrashings ended as abruptly as they had started. His eyes fluttered and closed.

"Keep going, Jared!"

The deputy wrapped the stump quick as he could.

"Walken," the sheriff said, "turn the wrench parallel with his bicep."

I did as I was told.

The Deputy wrapped the gauze over the wrench.

Steve's breathing turned ragged, eyes closed and skin clammy.

"He's going into shock," Carol said.

"Lay him back. Get his feet up. Keep that arm elevated!"

Sheriff eased Steve's head to the tabletop.

"Keep that arm up, Walken."

Carol grabbed a bag of snow salt and hefted it onto the table with a dull crunch, positioning it under Steve's legs.

"What do we have, Sherriff?" Rawlings inquired from the doorway, Basia standing behind him.

"Tourniquet twisted down with a wrench handle. Sterile pads on the wound with gauze dressed around it."

"Thanks, Sheriff," Doctor Rawlings replied. "Basia, see what else we need. And get a saline drip running."

Basia took inventory in the drawers before going to a small fridge. She hung the bag of saline on a hook mounted in the low ceiling, fed a needle into Steve's good arm, taped the line and opened the IV drip.

"You got this, Doc?" Sheriff Wayne asked.

Doctor Rawlings looked over Steve, timing his pulse then checking his pupils with a penlight.

"He's in serious condition, but we'll get him stabilized."

"Good," the sheriff said. "We have to get back to the bridge."

17

Clean Up

+1 Day – 0818 hours

Two had died.

Steve was recovering at Doctor Rawlings' home office.

The Norte Bridge had been defended.

We stood at the Searing Bridge barricade.

"We can't leave the bodies out there," Sheriff Wayne said.

"Where are we going to put them, Frank?" Garrett asked. "I don't think people want them rotting on the island."

"We could burn them," Mr. Diggs Harlan offered.

"I don't want to waste fuel," Wayne shook his head, "or draw more attention."

"We have an entire gas tanker truck sitting on the tarmac over there, Frank," the deputy added.

"And I want to keep it that way, Deputy."

Felix and Pete stood off to the edge of the road, each smoking a cigarette with shaking hands. Sebastian stood next to me, listening to the Sheriff's conversation.

Across the plaza, Emily Proctor walked up the steps to the library door, her slight weight leaning on the handrail. She dug out a set of keys from her purse and dropped them. After retrieving them, she waited a moment before plunging and twisting the key into the door's deadbolt. Opening the door and walking through, she flipped the sign on the door from 'closed' to 'open' before shutting the door.

"We need a system for the disposal of the bodies," Sheriff Wayne said. "Let's get the flatbed through the barricade. Maybe we can stash the truck on the Main. Diggs, any ideas?"

"Sure, Sheriff. There a couple spots I can think of."

"Okay. We move the cars, get the truck on the bridge, dispose of the bodies, stash the truck and get everyone back to the island. Clear?"

Deputy Garrett pulled out a keyring. He shimmied along the bridge's rail then struggled to lift himself into open window to the driver's seat. He started the Buick sedan and parked it off the bridge. He got out and jogged over to the next car.

"Great barrier until you need to get through it," Sebastian mused. "Sorry I picked you up?"

I shrugged, figuring the island wasn't the worst place to ride out an undead invasion.

"When we get through it," Sebastian added, "we'll figure out how to get you home."

Felix and Pete walked over, cigarettes dangling from their mouths and smoke drifting up behind them.

"How you faring today, Felix?"

"Alright, Sebastian. I appreciate you asking."

"Smoking again?"

"Yeah. Bummed a couple off Pete."

"Yeah. I'm keeping count, Felix," Pete added.

"I know. I'll be sure to get you a fresh pack."

"None of those pussy girly cigarettes, either!"

"So... don't get you what you usually buy?" Sebastian interjected. "Understood."

We smiled.

Pete stammered then started cackling, his grin showing gaps where teeth used to be. A light bout of coughing soon took the edge off the amusement.

"I like you, Sebastian. You fit right in. Too bad you're not an islander."

"I count my blessings every day I was born on the Main," Sebastian replied.

"Your loss, my man."

Diggs started his Ford flatbed truck, black exhaust billowing from the twin vertical exhaust pipes. He puttered the truck through the opened barricade and left it idling.

"Okay, Gentlemen... and Pete," Sheriff Wayne started. He looked out across the bridge's span then back at us. "We should be okay. Felix, you, Sebastian and Pete will be hauling the bodies onto the back of the truck. Diggs, stay close to the truck in case we need to move it. Mr. Walken and I will walk ahead. Garrett, stay at this end in case we need support."

The Sheriff looked at each of us in turn, his gaze reinforcing the severity of the situation.

"Courtesy of Carol and the Oceanside diner, gentlemen," Sheriff Wayne said, providing a plastic milk crate full of yellow rubber dish gloves from the truck's flatbed.

"Lovely lady, that Carol." Sebastian beamed as he took a pair.

Felix and Pete grabbed gloves for themselves.

Sheriff Wayne handed a pair to Diggs, who tossed them up on the dash.

"Join me, Mr. Walken," Sheriff Wayne instructed.

"I see you found your weapon."

My Glock 18 sat in its shoulder holster. Not U.S. military issue, I had bought the weapon after trading with an Austrian Special Ops team member during my second tour overseas. The Austrian military forces loved their Glocks. Many United States military and law enforcement agencies had started to adopt the series as their primary weapons, but some still clung onto their Berettas.

We walked ahead of the truck, leaving Diggs in the driver's seat and Felix and Pete grabbing the first corpse.

"Mr. Walken," the Sheriff said, regaining my full attention, "Sebastian says you are a good man to have in a fight. Based on how you handled yourself so far I would agree. The others aren't prepared for this. I know I wasn't."

We stopped at the crest of the empty bridge. Sheriff Wayne drew his service weapon and held it at his side. I kept my Glock holstered.

Behind us, the others, with their bright dish gloves took turns swinging the bodies onto the flatbed. Diggs stood on the cab step with his rifle resting on the roof of the truck. Deputy Garrett stood on the other side of the span with his sidearm in his hand.

"Dark days, Mr. Walken."

He stared off to the west, his jaw clenched and his eyes narrowed. He sighed and raised his pistol. The knuckles of his fingers bled white.

I looked down range.

A single limping woman had appeared from behind the curving tree line of Route 5, still a couple hundred meters away.

I pressed down the top of his gun barrel until he relented.

The rumbling of Diggs' truck grew louder. He stopped next to us. The others held onto the mounted floodlights on the cab's roof, sweat clinging to their clothes.

"All set, Chief!" Diggs said with his head out the window.

"Diggs," Sheriff Wayne said, "you know where to dump the bodies?"

"Yeah. That ravine three miles up on Route 5."

The Sheriff nodded. "We have another one coming."

"Yep. I see her. I'll take care of it."

Revving the engine, Diggs drove across the Stretch.

As the old Ford rolled onto Route 5, Diggs swerved over the yellow line. The high grille of the truck clipped the woman, splattering fluids onto the fender and sending her to the soft shoulder. Diggs swerved back to his lane, rolled onto Route 5 and disappeared around the bend.

As the rumbling diminished, we waited in silence at the high point of the bridge.

Too quickly we didn't hear the engine at all.

18

Patience is a Virtue

+1 Day – 1107 hours

"Shouldn't be taking this long," Sheriff Wayne said, glancing at his watch.

Two rifle shots rang out.

A flock of sparrows lit from a tree on the edge of the road.

Wayne tapped his pistol against his thigh.

A minute later we heard the Ford's diesel motor. It appeared from behind the tree line and accelerated toward the bridge, the doubled back tires kicking up dust and gravel. Sebastian rode shotgun, with Felix and Pete on the flatbed with their gloved hands gripping the truck's floodlight rack.

The truck raced toward us, brakes squeaking loudly as they stopped. The Sheriff moved to the passenger's side and climbed up on the step.

"We heard shots."

"Yeah, Chief. Sorry about that," Diggs said. "Sebastian had to shoot a loner. We didn't see any more of them but we thought we'd better hightail it back."

"Okay. Head over to the Norte Bridge and start the clean up there."

Felix and Pete frowned.

"I appreciate what you're doing, gentlemen."

"Thank you, Sheriff," they responded hollowly.

Diggs surged the truck forward.

The Sheriff took one more look at the mainland before starting back.

I followed, glancing back periodically.

"Guess we should have hitched a ride," the Sheriff mused.

We humped back to the barricade.

The spillways opened. Water rushed through the spinning turbines, generating electricity for the island.

"Okay, Jared. You can move the cars back."

"Sure, Sheriff," he said, walking over to the closest car.

Sheriff Wayne gazed at the plaza, a smile drawing wider.

"I think I have a better spot for us to keep an eye on the bridge without being so exposed," he pointed.

I looked to where he had pointed, and smiled too.

19

More Clean Up

+1 Day – 1626 hours

We arrived at Norte Bridge much later than Diggs and his crew. Derek's 4x4 sat across the entrance to the dam's service road, a pile of bodies under the rear bumper and chassis.

Ms. Greenfield pulled up in an old red Ford Pinto station wagon, a white pinstripe running along its side panels.

"The infected started to crowd through between the police car and the truck as soon as we set up." Ms. Greenfield said as she walked over to me. "They came up around the bend of the dam. I guess the utility gate was left open on the mainland side."

Diggs backed his truck up, maneuvering it next to Derek's 4x4. The clean up crew went to work hauling the bodies, still wearing their yellow gloves.

"Once the bodies started plugging up the gap, they started crawling underneath." Ms. Greenfield stared at the bodies under the 4x4. "Derek, Patrick, and Emily were up in the bed. The things kept grabbing at their rifle barrels so their shots weren't very clean."

Garrett climbed onto Derek's truck bed and pointed his shotgun downrange.

With Diggs' truck lined up and idling, Felix and Pete started loading the bodies onto the flatbed. When finished with the dead by the 4x4 they walked farther out onto the service road.

"The rest of us were positioned here behind the truck and cruiser." Ms. Greenfield continued. "The deputy and Felix shot everything coming through the gaps. The rest of us tried to handle the strays."

She wiped a salty tear back with the cuff of her shirt.

"Steve got pulled under. Greg went after him and got bit." She paused and looked at the ground. "I tried to get a clear shot. Greg punched the FRAC in the face as we dragged Steve out. Once he was out, I pretty much blew the FRAC's head wide open."

Sheriff Wayne came over to us.

"Ms. Greenfield, what are you calling these things?"

"When Felix was shooting at the infected that were trying to get through between the cruiser and the truck, he kept muttering that they were 'fucking re-animated corpses'. Not sure if the phrase applies, but I liked the acronym."

"Just as good a name as any other," the Sheriff replied before returning to his cruiser.

"Anyway. Steve wrapped Greg's arm with T-Shirt strips before getting back to shooting." Ms. Greenfield continued as we took up position at the truck's front bumper.

"Garrett!"

"Yeah, Sheriff."

"I'm going back to the Searing Bridge. I'm taking Sebastian. Keep an eye out."

"Sure thing, Sheriff."

They got into the cruiser and backed off the access road.

"Pete. Felix. Take care of the bodies behind us first," Deputy Garrett said, eyeing the service road. "We'll move Derek's truck to get Diggs onto the bridge after."

Pete and Felix stood with their arms on top of their head before walking to the stack of bodies. Diggs stepped in and hauled bodies to the back of the truck by himself.

"I couldn't see Emily, but I heard screaming. Greg was propped up against the transformer station. Switched out the Remington with Steve's rifle and told him to reload. When I was out again I went to get the shotgun back, but one of the FRACs was grabbing at Steve's boot. He screamed and fired the shotgun. Nothing happened. He pumped it and pulled the trigger. That was when it blew up in his hands."

I stared across the bridge's deserted concrete.

The air was still and quiet.

"Felix took off his sweatshirt and held it to what was left of Steve's arm. That was when the gunfire and the FRACs stopped coming. Thank god. Derek hopped off the truck. Patrick stayed up on watch. I know I heard Emily sobbing then.

"Derek went to check on Greg. Said that he was dead." Ms. Greenfield stopped for a moment to clear away one more tear. "How could he be dead already?"

"All of a sudden, Greg opened his eyes and bit out Derek's neck. He was dead in seconds. Thank god Derek's weight pinned Greg down or he may have gotten to the rest of us. Garrett came over to shoot Greg but his Beretta was empty. Mine was empty, too. But I don't know if I could have shot him.

"Patrick ended up taking care of it. Said he didn't want Greg to have a chance to come back." Ms. Greenfield air-quoted the words 'come back'. "Patrick told Garrett we needed to lock up the utility fence before any more FRACs got onto the island."

At that moment, Diggs got back in the Ford's cab and cranked the engine.

Deputy Garrett dropped off the back of Derek's truck bed, hurried around to the driver's door and climbed in behind the wheel. He reached for the ignition and groaned.

"Shit!" Garrett banged on the steering wheel.

Leaving the shotgun on the dash, he slid across to the passenger's side, got out and walked over to Diggs.

"Where's Derek? I need the keys."

"He's right behind the cab, along with Greg," Diggs replied, thumbing over his shoulder.

Deputy Garrett stared at the bodies on the flatbed. He cursed under his breath.

"I'll get 'em for ya, Garrett."

Diggs hoisted himself up to the bed. He stepped around the bodies until he got the back of the cab. Patting down Derek's pockets, Diggs fished out the keys. He tossed them to Garrett who juggled them for a moment.

"Thanks, Diggs."

"Get that truck moved, Garrett, so we can finish up here."

"Yeah. I'm going."

Ms. Greenfield and I moved to the back of the truck as Garrett climbed into the cab, slid across the bench and settled behind the steering wheel. He picked the key with the Ford emblem and started the truck with a roar.

"Garrett!"

Diggs ran past us to the passenger door, his pistol pointed at Garrett.

"Get the fuck down!" Diggs yelled, grabbing Garrett by the collar and jerking him down to the bench. Diggs extended the pistol through the open driver's side door and fired three rapid shots.

"Shit!" Garrett yelled as one of the spent brass casings burned him.

Diggs slid back out, Garrett straightening up. Two FRACs slumped against the driver's door.

"Sorry, Garrett."

"Christ, Diggs!"

With his hand cupped over his right ear, Garrett kicked at the head of the closest corpse. And kept kicking.

Once the walkers cleared the frame, he slammed the door shut. The deputy grabbed the steering wheel until his knuckles turned white.

"Take a breath, Jared," Diggs assured him. "It's okay. Let's just get this goddamn truck moved and the bodies out of here, Deputy. Okay?"

"Yeah. Okay."

Garrett turned the key over, the starter screeching.

"Good looking out, John Boy," Diggs said as he walked past.

"Sarcastic, much?" Ms. Greenfield whispered.

Garrett backed the truck away from the rail. Almost touching Diggs' truck, he stopped, threw the transmission into Drive and surged forward, kicking up loose gravel. He ran over the two bodies with a bump, stopping once the truck was clear of the road.

Diggs backed the flatbed onto the bridge.

Felix signaled Diggs to stop.

They started picking up the remaining bodies that had not made it past the original barricade.

Garrett sat in Derek's truck, staring through the dusty windshield at the edge of the bridge. Ms. Greenfield and I kept our eyes down range.

A few minutes later Diggs pulled up to Garrett's window and honked the horn.

"We'll dump the bodies in the ravine up the 5 and be back as soon as we can. Are you good here?"

Garrett took in the words, but didn't say anything.

Diggs opened his mouth to repeat himself.

"Do what you have to do. We're good," Garrett responded. "Mr. Walken, Ms. Greenfield and I are going to walk the fence line."

20

Chains

+1 Day – 1740 hours

We walked along the curving roadway over the spillways, the concrete structure arching out into the Atlantic before bowing back to connect to the wooded mainland.

The deputy wiped sweat from his forehead and adjusted his black ball cap over his eyes. "I wish Linc was back."

I shrugged.

"Sorry, John. He's the other deputy. Lincoln Reynolds and his wife Trisha went on a boat excursion Friday."

"I'm sure they'll be back soon, Deputy Garrett," Ms. Greenfield said.

I pointed to the bridge.

"Yeah," Garrett said, leading the way. "Let's take a look."

We walked another forty meters on a gravel road until we approached a razor-wired chain-link fence. An obese man in flannel, with a chunk of flesh torn from his meaty shoulder, reached through the gate opening. The FRAC strained to grab us, unable to squeeze farther between the gates and the taut chain.

Fucking reanimated corpse. Yeah. I liked the acronym too.

"I guess they were still able to get in until this fat one plugged up the gap."

The Deputy sighed and pulled his gun.

He touched the muzzle to the FRAC's forehead and pulled the trigger. The gun did not make much sound but the back of the walker's head blew out a large bloody hole.

The fat man slumped with his armpit over the chain, dangling on its full body weight.

I kicked the fat man in the face, sending him flying back off the chain and into the gravel.

"Let's tighten this up," Garrett said.

Ms. Greenfield and I pushed the gates together, the chain giving up plenty of slack. Garrett took off the padlock before tightening the chain and locking it again.

"Thanks," Garrett said, walking away along the fence line. "Let's see what else we can find."

21

Blind Mice

+1 Day – 1954 hours

There had not been any other spots on the fence line where the FRACs could get through.

We crossed back to the island as the sun sank behind the trees of the mainland.

"Where are you, Jared!" The Sheriff's voice came through the radio.

"At Norte Bridge."

"Get to the Tunnel! We have more infected on the island!"

"Copy that. Out!"

We raced to the deputy's cruiser.

Garrett slid past the driver's side door before grabbing the handle. I rode shotgun while Ms. Greenfield climbed into the back.

The deputy started the cruiser and slammed on the accelerator, gravel spitting out from under the tires. Pebbles bounced off the underside of the car until the tires shrieked onto the asphalt road.

We quickly hit fifty miles an hour as we headed along the curving road leading to the tree canopied stretch of road nicknamed the Tunnel.

Something large crashed into the front grille with a wet thud, then disappeared underneath the cruiser. Garrett yelled and slammed on the brakes with both feet.

The body dragged against the undercarriage as we skidded to a stop.

Deputy Garrett leaned into the door.

"Stay inside, Garrett!" Ms. Greenfield shouted.

I grabbed the deputy's collar.

"What are you doing, Walken? We have to check the body!"

I turned on the dashboard searchlight and turned the inside handle to shine the light into the black of the road's soft shoulder.

Five infected people wandered through the beam ten meters from the car. Their eyes glowed gold and red in the light.

Powering down the window I pushed my Glock through the opening and fired.

The head of one of the dead snapped back with a spray of matter.

"Shit, man!"

The driver's door slammed shut.

"Garrett! Get back here!" Ms. Greenfield slapped against the Plexiglas divider.

Garrett's weapon flashed.

I got out and shouldered the rifle. Locking the tactical light into the rail under the Glock, I turned on the Xeon LED and moved to follow Garrett.

"Hey! Hey!" Ms. Greenfield shouted. "Don't leave me in here."

I backed up and opened the rear passenger door.

Thirty meters away Garrett fired at a woman lunging at him.

A slumping, lurching bloody man crossed my beam of light.

I double-tapped him in the head.

More infected shambled toward us from the Tunnel.

The Deputy and I continued to fire, the pops of our weapons echoing.

I double-tapped a quick, younger woman with a dislocated left arm.

A shot rang out behind me as a longhaired boy skidded into my legs.

"You're welcome, Marine." Ms. Greenfield flanked me.

We pushed forward, putting down targets with headshots.

Garrett picked off a few FRACs in a haphazard fashion.

Ms. Greenfield shot the closest targets that were too fast for the deputy. I took the longer shots as FRACs came into view.

Gunfire echoed from deeper inside the Tunnel.

We rounded a slight bend.

The taillights of a flatbed truck lit up the trees.

Diggs shot at the infected from the cab's open window.

Felix and Pete stood on the flatbed firing down into the crowd.

Pete pointed the rifle's barrel just inches from the most ambitious of the group, hollowing out what used to be its brainpan. He ejected the spent cartridge and loaded another round.

Felix pumped his shotgun, firing a round directly through the teeth of a man in a hospital gown with his ass hanging out. As the patient fell, a hollow-eyed topless woman pressed upward with a foothold on the wheel rim. Felix pumped another round and shot her in the throat, her head dangling by shreds of muscles.

A banging noise turned Felix around. A buzzard-looking man clamored over the side and fell onto the bed. Pete put a boot on the infected man's back, levered his rifle and reduced his head to pulp.

"Get small!" Felix yelled.

Pete dropped to the bed as Felix fired over him.

A stocky man in a bloody butcher's apron and a pair of basketball shorts changed direction with a backward snap from the bullet's impact. The meat carver hit the tailgate, slipped in a puddle of gore and flipped off the back of the truck. He made a thud on the pavement.

Pete couldn't suppress a giddy laugh.

He got to his feet and turned to Felix. "Thanks, man!"

We approached the truck, firing at some of the strays.

I whistled loudly to signal our approach. The trio on the truck looked in our direction. So did the remaining undead.

"Stay sharp!" Garrett called out.

I took down four FRACs.

Seven remained.

Garrett shot two in the head, emptying his weapon.

I dropped three more in slow smooth succession before the Glock's magazine emptied, leaving one round in the pipe. I reloaded.

Garrett reloaded.

An old man lashed at him, his glasses hanging from one ear lobe. The deputy fired at the last moment, succeeding in making the man's glasses fly off.

I fired into a teenaged boy's temple, a trickle of blood and gray matter spattering on his varsity jacket.

"Is that it?" Garrett called out.

I glanced around the empty road.

Ms. Greenfield had positioned herself behind me in a crouched position guarding our rear flank.

"Nothing here, deputy!" she called out.

"Clear up here, Garrett," Pete responded, out of breath.

I whistled twice.

Blue and red light painted the trees and high beams glared against the truck. Wayne jumped out of his cruiser, a pump shotgun in hand. He rushed over to the truck and banged on the driver's door.

"You okay, Diggs?"

"I will be." Diggs stepped down to the road. "Felix and Pete are the men of the hour, Chief. Garrett, and Mr. and Mrs. Gung Ho came up in the nick of time to take all the credit!"

Diggs let out a hearty snort.

"You all did good," Sheriff Wayne said.

Deputy Garrett doubled over with his hands on his thighs.

Sheriff Wayne placed a hand on the back of his deputy's neck and gently pulled him close. Although spoken in whispers, I could still hear them.

"You did fine, Jared. None of us could have foreseen every scenario."

"You would've, Frank."

"No, Jared," Sheriff Wayne responded with a sigh. "I didn't."

22

It Only Takes One

+2 Days – 2007 hours

Hot water ran into the basin, steaming up the mirror.

After cupping a last splash of water over my face and through my brown hair, I turned off the water with a squeak of the faucet. The steam receded to the mirror's edges, letting me get a better look at my face.

I needed a shave and some rack time.

Dark circles had formed under my eyes.

I looked closer.

The bruising on my throat had all but disappeared. Only a slight yellow tinge and a red dot marked where the needle had impaled me and destroyed my career.

I grabbed the rifle and went back into the sheriff's department lobby.

Sheriff Wayne sat in his office shouting at someone.

"Listen, Foster! We need to keep people indoors. Until we can ascertain that every threat to the island is not on the island, I want the residents inside…"

Wayne paused, looking at the ceiling with the phone cradled to his ear.

"Fine, Foster. Bring it up at the next meeting. Until then, I'll continue to make the calls in this matter. I am going to hang up now. Goodbye."

The Sheriff put the phone on the cradle and leaned back in his chair. He grabbed a racquetball from the corner of his inbox and squeezed it a few times before tossing it in the air.

"Do you need ammo?" asked a voice from behind me.

Glenda held out two 9mm boxes.

"Bullets?"

She held a box of Winchester Silver Tip Hollow Points in one hand and Cor-bon HP in the other. I held out my hand for the HPs.

"Figured that would be your choice. Want to reload inside?"

I gestured for her to lead the way.

She smiled and headed into the back office.

Pete sat at a desk cleaning his rifle.

I sat down at a desk with the nameplate of Reynolds.

Placing the ammunition on the blotter I drew my weapon and disassembled it.

"Hey, Deputy!" Pete called out.

Garrett came in through the basement stairwell, put his shotgun on his desk and sat down hard.

"Garrett, when is Lincoln back?"

"Don't know, Pete. He's supposed to be back tomorrow."

"Definitely need him back."

"Yeah. Don't remind me."

My weapon sat on the desk in its four major components – barrel, spring, slide, and body. The magazines sat next to them. I loved my Glock. You could drop it in a river, snow bank, or dune and it would still fire. Reassembly took less than a minute as I placed the barrel into the slide, set the double recoil spring behind it, and slid the slide back into place on the composite body.

I started to reload the magazines with the HPs.

Sebastian came in and made a beeline between the desks until he plopped down on the hard office chair next to me.

"Heck of a day and night, huh, John?"

I raised an eyebrow at Sebastian, making him laugh.

"Something different than what you're used to in the sands, I bet."

I continued reloading.

"Sorry I missed the action, friend. The sheriff wanted someone to stay at The Stretch. By the time he got the call from Diggs about the – what does Ms. Greenfield call them? FRACs? – on the road, he really had no one else to count on.

"The Sheriff has Diggs, Carol and Kyle from the diner, and a guy named Jackson keeping watch on the bridges. I think he said that Jackson was good with a rifle and was going to be up in the church tower tonight."

Made sense.

"I think Lucy is sleeping on a cot in the back of the diner."

Closing the ammo carton, I holstered the magazines and the Glock.

"You have good hands there, John," Sebastian commented.

"Amen to that, brother," Pete added. "If my hands weren't as gnarled as they are, I'd smoke you in a strip down."

"No one wants to see you in your long johns, Pete," Sebastian argued.

Pete chuckled, returning to his guns.

Garrett sat with his elbows on his desk blotter and his head in his hands.

Glenda walked over to him, put a bottle of water on his desk and put her arms around him. He leaned into her as she whispered something.

Garrett squeezed her arm.

Glenda gave him one final pat before coming over to us.

Sebastian craned his neck around.

Pete swiveled his chair to get a good look at her backside.

"Pete has a place to stay," Glenda said, "plus is getting a free pass for staring at my ass."

Pete smiled with surprise but did not look away.

"As for you two," Glenda continued, "Frank and I would like the pleasure of your company at our place. We will find you better accommodations tomorrow for the duration."

"We can sleep in the truck cab, Mrs. Wayne."

"Don't you dare," Glenda said. "You're staying with us. Case closed."

"Sounds fine, Mrs. Wayne," Sebastian said.

"How about you, Mr. Walken?" Glenda asked, leaning against the desk.

I gave her a thumbs-up.

"Good!" Glenda said. "Because we're hitting the road in one minute."

Glenda headed back to her desk.

"Pete! Go home and be safe. And, Jared, remember what I said."

"Yes ma'am," Garrett replied.

"Good, because you are the officer in charge until morning." Glenda confirmed. She turned to Sebastian and me. "Saddle up, grunts!"

Sebastian gave me a shit-eating grin. "Ooh-rah, Johnny."

He stood with some pep and fell in line behind Glenda just as she put her hand on the lobby doorknob. I rolled the chair to the desk and headed after them.

Glenda stood at the entrance with a pump-action shotgun. Sheriff Wayne had replaced his racquetball with his own Remington pump-action. She unlocked the door and swung it open, the Sheriff stepping through with the shotgun at chest level. Sebastian followed with his Beretta M9, flanking opposite the sheriff. I stepped out with my Glock and tapped Sebastian on the shoulder. He moved left and I moved right, Glenda coming out last and locking the door.

"Okay," Glenda said.

We moved across the empty lot in formation to the Sheriff's cruiser and climbed in. The Sheriff started it up and we pulled out of the lot.

Glenda spoke in hushed tones, though still audible to me through the separator.

"Did you get through to the boys?"

"I did last night for a minute. Nothing since then."

"Do you think they're okay?"

"My dad knows what to do. He taught me, so I'm sure they're holed up fine. His house is remote enough outside Boston."

"I hope so."

Sebastian nudged me in the ribs.

"Not sure what they're saying but the Wayne's have two boys vacationing for the month with the Sheriff's dad. They're both worried sick, but you would never be able to tell from looking at them. All business, those two."

We sped through the Tunnel.

The bodies had already been picked up and carted away.

We passed the access road to the Norte Bridge and closed in on the west edge of a residential tract. Parallel streets lined with Cape Cod style houses bore the names of United States presidents.

"They call this area," Sebastian said, pointing to the houses, "the Presidency."

The full moon shimmered across the Atlantic's waves, a sea of stars spread across the sky. The cruiser descended a hill and hooked lazily to the right as the road cut through dunes to the shoreline.

We stopped in a gravel driveway in front of a small Cape Cod beach cottage.

Two lampposts and hidden landscape lighting gave the property a warm inviting feel. Weathered cedar shakes were covered by black architectural shingles on the roof's steep pitch. A red six-panel door with a crescent window stood at the center of the house.

The Sheriff and Glenda exited the cruiser and let us out.

We closed our doors with soft clicks, the crashing of ocean waves loud behind the house.

I flanked out to the edge of the stone driveway, Sebastian doing the same on his side. My sightline along the edge of the house revealed a grassy dune and the Atlantic beyond.

I whistled to Sebastian.

He gave me an okay.

DAY ZERO

Glenda trotted to the door with keys in hand. She opened the screen door and put the key in the dead bolt. She went into the house and shut the heavy wood door.

Sheriff Wayne disappeared across a side deck, his boots thumping on the wood.

Sebastian and I regrouped in front of the cruiser.

"All of this heightened alert shit is going to give me a heart attack, Johnny. Damn! That's why I drive a truck now."

My eyes darted from one clump of shadows to another. I tapped Sebastian and pointed to the side of the house where the sheriff had disappeared.

"Got it, Sergeant."

Sebastian's footsteps went from a crunch to heavy thunks as he moved to the deck. He disappeared around the corner of the house.

I took one last look at the driveway and retreated to the front door, reaching for the door handle.

A gunshot boomed from inside.

I stormed into the house with my Glock raised and tactical light on.

A FRAC lay half on the hardwood floor. One hand was missing. Where the back of his head used to be lay open a hole with blood seeping from the exit wound.

In the archway to the kitchen, another man bent over a prone body. I shone the light on the moving form, ready to fire.

Glenda lay on the floor in a pool of blood, her weapon beside her. A large jagged gash in her shoulder blossomed blood onto her blouse.

"It's going to be okay, baby," Sheriff Wayne whispered, kneeling at her side with a dishtowel pressed to her bite wound. "Going to be okay."

Sebastian came through the rear patio door. He looked at Glenda and the sheriff and turned pale. Slumping against the doorframe he lowered his weapon and stared out into the night.

I flashed my weapon down the hallway.

Three of the four doors were closed.

The last door was halfway open.

I advanced and tapped it with my foot, letting it squeak fully open. I backed into the door and shined the light around.

Empty.

Closing the door I stepped back into the hallway.

A shot rang out.

"No!" Sebastian screamed.

A pause.

Then another shot.

I hurried back to the kitchen.

Frank slumped over his wife's body.

His gun, still in hand, hit the linoleum.

Sebastian stood at the back sliding door, unable to move.

"He shot her," Sebastian whispered.

I stepped over the bodies, took Sebastian by the arm and steered him to the rear deck. He steadied himself on the railing.

Then he bent over to dry heave.

I went back inside.

The air was still, the house heavy with the smell of gunpowder and ocean salt. Three bodies crowded the space between the kitchen and living room. On the wall next to the refrigerator, a phone hung with the receiver and cord on the floor. Above the phone was mounted an answering machine with the message light blinking.

I picked up the receiver.

From miles away, a chipper crackling electronic voice told anyone who would listen that *all circuits are busy... please try your call again later.*

23

Overdue

+8 Days – 0948 hours

I sat in the Oceanside Diner sipping a cup of black coffee.

Sebastian sat next to me eating his runny eggs on a piece of toast.

"How you holding up, Carol?" Sebastian asked.

"Alright, I guess. I can't believe they're gone almost a week now. I knew Glenda all her life."

"Sorry."

"Thanks for taking care of the burial. You too, John."

"It was the least we could do, Carol."

I looked at remnants of dirt under my fingernails as the doorbell chimed.

"Hey, Lucy. What can I get you?" Carol asked with a tired voice.

"Morning, Carol. Are you holding up?" She touched Carol's hand.

"I'll survive. Just need a little time."

"We're here for you."

"Thank you, hon. What did you need?"

"I was actually looking for Deputy Garrett. Has he come in today?"

"Not yet," Carol answered. "Can we help you with something?"

Erma Hilger leaned over from her place at the counter. Her thick wavy hair fell to her shoulders, shockingly white. She had also attended the burial. "Mentioned that he was heading to the lighthouse."

"Did he say how long he'd be, Erma?" Carol asked.

"Didn't mention it. Probably until lunch, I'd say. Didn't seem like it was going to be a quick trip." Erma finished. "Sorry."

"Thanks, anyway." Lucy replied.

"Erma, I hate to impose," Carol asked, "but do you have any more lettuce from your greenhouse?"

"Carol, send someone over to the store later and I'll have them ready."

"Thank you," Carol said. "I'm running low."

"I don't think you will be getting any more deliveries, Carol," Sam shouted from his seat by the window. "Don't think barricades and rampant infections on the Main are good for food deliveries at the moment. Even Sebastian and his truck are stuck here."

"He has a point, Carol," Sebastian said. "The last I heard from dispatch was to stay put until things evened out. That was when the phones were still working. I haven't heard anything since. Not much on the CB either."

The two televisions were on mute, only showing white snow. The last broadcast was four days ago and the last emergency broadcast signal yesterday.

Carol absorbed what Sebastian and Sam said, biting her lower lip. Then she offered a thin smile. "At least we have Erma and her greenhouse supplied general store right here on the island."

"I was thinking the same thing!" Sam replied.

"I'll have those heads of lettuce ready when you are, Carol." Erma said, heading toward the door.

"Remember when we dated, Erma?" Sam asked.

Erma stopped with one hand on the handle, a floppy sunhat in the other. "No, we didn't."

"We had that wonderful midnight picnic at the lighthouse," Sam added. "Watched the submarine races."

"No, we didn't."

"Then how do I know about that birthmark at the small of your back?" Sam ventured.

Erma looked at Sam with a bemused thin smile.

"I believe the correct term is senility," Erma responded with a wink. With that Erma pulled the door open, put her earbuds in and her hat on.

"That girl is still in love with me," Sam chuckled.

"Carol," Ralph said. "Can you please shut those goddamn televisions off?"

"Keep 'em on!" Walter said. "I want to see if something comes back on!"

"Ain't anything coming back on, Walter. You're an idiot if you think so."

"Screw you, Ralph!"

Both men stood from their chairs and approached each other.

"Hey!" Carol shouted.

She leaned under the counter, brought up her shotgun and banged it on the countertop.

"You want to go at it," she warned, "you take it outside. The TVs stay on until I say so."

Ralph and Walter looked at Carol, her finger on the trigger. Both raised their hands in surrender and quietly went back to their respective tables.

"Sorry, Lucy," Carol apologized. "What did you need Deputy Garrett for?"

"I noticed the 'Closed' sign was hanging in the front library door window. Ms. Proctor has turned the sign every day at 9am since I've been here."

Carol leaned her elbows on the cracked Formica surface.

"Mr. Walken, I know you are enjoying that wonderful black coffee, but would you and Sebastian mind taking a look at the library while I try to hunt down Deputy Garrett?"

"It would be our pleasure, ma'am." Sebastian beamed.

Sebastian slathered the rest of the egg yolks onto his toast, wolfed it down and licked his fingers. I held out a napkin, but he used his sleeve.

"Thank you for the grub, Carol. Let's go, Sarge."

Gulping down the coffee, I followed Sebastian out of the diner. Before the door closed, someone else tapped it open again.

"Wait up." Ms. Greenfield trotted up between us. She wore black denim jeans and a tucked in olive T-Shirt, outfitted with her Sig Sauer handgun in a belt holster.

"I'm sure we can handle this op on our own, little lady."

"That may be true, Sebastian, but I think I will tag along anyway."

"Suit yourself, Ms. Greenfield. Probably nothing."

A few moments later we stood at the stoop of the white clapboard library. A red sign announcing 'Closed. Please come back again!' did indeed stare back at us.

I cupped my hands to the windowpane.

The interior was dark.

Sebastian knocked on the doorframe, the glass rattling.

Nobody stirred inside.

"How you want to handle this?" Sebastian asked.

I looked at the doors. We could try to slip the latch. Or find an open window.

"Excuse me, gentlemen."

Ms. Greenfield brushed past me and turned the doorknob. The door banged open and she walked inside.

"I like her. She's fun." Sebastian laughed.

I had to agree as we went inside after her.

"Hello?" Ms. Greenfield called out.

Books stacked up on the circular return/checkout desk at the back center wall of the main hall. Three aisles of bookshelves lined up on either side of the desk, with round tables and chairs between the main desk and us. Nautical themed paintings adorned the walls under the skylights; with netting, small model ships, and other seafaring knick-knacks mounted around the space.

Lucy stepped out from a room behind the desk.

"Nothing in the back. Looks like she was sleeping here, though."

"Nothing here," Sebastian called out from the other side of the room.

At the end of the aisle on the back wall, a heavy oak door stood ajar.

I swung it open.

It revealed the landing of an enclosed stairwell.

A three-legged stool lay on its side in the landing.

The smell of Murphy's Oil Soap filled my nostrils.

Risers ascended into blackness.

I switched on the Glock's tactical light, casting the beam up the stairs. Stacks of books piled up on random steps.

Toward the top of the stairway, the circle of light landed on a pair of argyle-socked toes. The feet did not touch the risers, hovering a couple feet above the closest stair.

"I found a note from Emily!" Ms. Greenfield shouted.

One of the feet twitched.

I raised the light higher.

"I think it's a suicide note!"

At the end of a noose cast over the base of a heavy wrought iron light fixture, Emily Proctor swung. Her lips were purple, her wide eyes bloodshot, and her skin a yellowed and gray tint.

When the light lit up her face, Emily's mouth opened, her lips peeling back to reveal blackened gums and chomping teeth. They bit straight through her swollen tongue, spewing blackened blood down her chin.

She growled.

Keeping the light locked in on Ms. Proctor, I pressed my finger to the trigger.

"What did you find, John?" Ms. Greenfield blocked out the light from the doorway.

She screamed at the sight at the end of my beam of light.

Emily's growls turned more insistent.

The discharge of my Glock drowned out both.

24

Closed Session

+10 Days – 1021 hours

Sebastian and I sat on the steps of Town Hall, the morning sun warming our faces and brilliantly bleaching the marble and limestone. Across the plaza, in the church tower, Jackson's rifle barrel stuck out of the shaded western archway.

A bit of grave dirt lined the edge of my fingernails again.

Most people had remained in their homes after finding out about Ms. Procter's undead suicide, opting not to come to her burial. A few of us had attended, just as we had for the Sheriff and Mrs. Wayne, and the other islanders.

There was still life in town

Some people walked around the plaza. Three more sat outside the Oceanside. A couple ate inside by the window in Sam's usual spot.

"Hope Garrett and Sam don't have any problems" Sebastian wondered out loud, rubbing his left arm and wiggling the fingers.

Sam was inside the Town Hall's main chambers in a closed session.

"These nights of sentry duty are taking their toll on this ole body, that's for sure. Maybe I'll ask Garrett for a day off."

Sebastian continued to talk, but my attention snapped back to the diner as a reflection of light bounced off the door. Ms. Greenfield came out, skirted around the café tables and walked down the sidewalk.

Striding with a casual determination she passed the library, slowing only briefly to touch the stoop handrail before continuing on.

The double doors of the Town Hall behind us banged open.

Sam came out, squinting his weathered eyes against the sun. Behind him a large man in a gray suit and cobalt blue tie walked out, buttoning the flaps of the suit across his expansive belly.

Sebastian got to his feet and nodded to the dapper obese man.

"That's the one and only Councilman Anderson Foster. Third generation islander."

Mr. Foster stopped at the edge of the porch and interlaced his fingers on top of his belly. A lanky younger man with oily shoulder length hair and acne scarred skin hurried up to Mr. Foster with a pair of Ray-Ban sunglasses in his hand. He held out the sunglasses for several seconds before the large man accepted them.

Once the thin young man's hand was empty, it went up to his mouth to gnaw on his fingernails while his other hand rubbed his chest.

The pair walked to the sidewalk, Mr. Foster in the lead.

"Son of a bitch, he is," Sam said, a toothy grin emerging from behind his chapped lips. "It's true, young man. That man has always been looking for the brass ring."

"I see he still has his lap dog," Sebastian said.

"Yeah. Monroe wouldn't know what to do without having Anderson to serve."

"So, how did Deputy Garrett do?"

"Not deputy, no more. Ain't gonna be able to live with him now that he's sheriff," Sam cackled.

The new sheriff of Rainier Island came out. He was trying to pin the five-star sheriff badge to his uniform.

"There's the new sheriff now," Sebastian called out.

Garrett looked up and stopped.

"What's the matter, Sheriff?" Sebastian asked, emphasizing Garrett's new title. "I figured you would be glad that the councilman instated you as head constable."

"Now I know why Frank was always so miserable after meetings with Foster. You could have warned me, Sam," Garrett groaned.

"It's like marriage, son. Nobody tells you the downsides until afterwards. That way you both have something to bitch about." Sam laughed as he gingerly descended the steps.

Garrett followed the old man.

"Come on, Sarge," Sebastian said, slapping me on the back. "Let's try to keep up."

We walked to the sidewalk and waited on Sam's slower pace, before heading toward the sheriff's office.

"Sam," Garrett continued. "Get the Gun Toters on the phone. We need to talk about long-term defense. John and Sebastian, I need you there, too."

"Sure thing, Sheriff."

We crossed the parking lot.

Ms. Greenfield leaned against the bricks of the sheriff's station, her white blouse hanging open to reveal a scoop neck tank top. Both were tucked into the waistband of a snug pair of straight-legged blue jeans, complete with studded black belt and a pair of low-heeled boots.

"Be sure to count me in, too, Sheriff," she added.

25

Help Wanted

+10 Days – 1219 hours

With the loss of the sheriff and his wife, and with Lincoln Reynolds still missing at sea, Garrett needed to refill the department's roster.

I waited under the eaves, the midday sun fighting the overhang in an attempt to beat its rays down on me.

Sheriff Garrett came out with Sebastian.

"Hey, Johnny," Sebastian called out, "you ready for a recruitment drive?"

I hiked up the strap of my rifle.

The new sheriff walked down the sidewalk to the diner. He didn't slow down until he pulled the handle and entered.

I grabbed the door before it swung shut.

Garrett went to Sam at his usual window seat. Patrick sat across from him.

Sebastian and I stood back at the counter as Sheriff Garrett pulled a chair over to their table.

"Sam, I need to talk to Patrick."

"The boy is right here."

"Thanks, Gramps." Patrick spoke up. "What do you need, Sheriff? I think I can guess."

The sheriff leaned on the tabletop.

"I need you as a deputy, Pat. You more than proved yourself at the Norte Bridge"

Patrick tapped the ceramic mug with his college class ring, glancing at his grandfather who stared back with a grim weathered thin-lipped smile.

"I appreciate the offer, Sheriff. You know I have your back if you really need it, but I can't. As capable as Gramps says he is, I want to be close to home."

Garrett looked from Patrick to Sam.

"Listen, Sheriff, Patty's as stubborn as I am. Don't look to me to change his mind."

"Okay," Garrett said. "I understand."

He stood and started walking away.

"Remember you made the offer, Patrick"

"I would expect you to."

The Sheriff walked over to Carol.

"I know why you're here, too."

"Can you call him out?"

"Sure, hon."

Carol poked her head through the silent butler and whistled. Pots banged before Kyle pushed through the door, his apron ties dangling.

"Hey, Deputy! What's going on?"

"I need a deputy."

Kyle grabbed Garrett's hand, pumping it furiously.

"Yes! Yes, sir!"

Kyle looked at Carol and his face fell.

"Don't worry, Kyle. We'll limp along." Carol waved him off.

"Thanks, Boss." Kyle lit up again. "When can I start, Garrett?"

"Meet me at the station in an hour and we'll get you filled in."

"Cool."

"Let's go see if Pete is as receptive," Garrett said as he walked past us, becoming a silhouette as the door closed behind him.

"You heard the man." Sebastian smiled. "Let's go to Pete's."

We caught up with Garrett as he crossed the street to Pete's Guns, Ammo, Bait, and Tackle shop. Garrett tapped on the doorframe, waited for a buzzing sound and opened the security door.

Pete sat behind a glass-cased counter, the air heavy and dusty.

"You coming to take more guns and ammo?"

Garrett leaned over the case and looked at the pistols. The cabinet was filled with a variety of handguns, including Glocks, Berettas, Sig Sauers, Smith and Wessons, and Springfields.

"Sorry, Pete," Garrett said, still looking in the case. "You know we need you and your guns. It's the only way we can defend the island."

Pete closed his outdated gun magazine and leaned back on his stool.

"And you brought a couple of your heavies to persuade me?"

We stood at the end of a metal shelf stocked with fishing supplies, Sebastian concentrating on a tackle box label.

"You know that isn't so, Pete."

"Maybe not, but what are you going to do when my supplies run out. It's not like a new shipment is coming anytime soon."

"I understand your point. But I would like to make you a deputy, if you're agreeable."

"I'll be there, Jared. Only part time, though. I don't think these old bones could take forty hour work weeks anymore." Pete looked over at us. "Captain America over there can work non-stop but I'm sure Sebastian knows what I'm talking about."

Sebastian peeled his eyes up from the tackle box. "What?"

"Anyway," Pete continued, "I'll do what I can."

"That's all that I ask, Pete."

Garrett extended his hand.

Pete leaned forward and shook it.

"Still owe me for the guns and ammo you already have."

"Yeah. I know."

"Until I get paid, there's no way I'm showing you the real good stuff." Pete smiled wide and withdrew his hand. "I guess you better get back to business."

"Yeah. I guess I better."

Garrett pressed the paddle on the security door.

"See you later, Pete," Sebastian said with a wave.

He responded with a gnarly-fingered flip of the bird.

We left Pete to his magazine.

A slight breeze hit my skin, the sweat cooling instantly. The saltiness overpowered my senses. I exhaled sharply through my nose.

"Yeah. This fresh ocean air is a little much sometimes."

The sheriff stood at Diggs' truck parked in front of the Beloved Books and Antiques. Garrett pointed in the direction of the sheriff's station. Diggs raised his hands in surrender, shaking his head.

Garrett walked toward us, slicking back his hair under his ball cap.

"I guess we're barely two out of four," Sebastian surmised.

Diggs' truck rumbled to life and pulled out from the curb. He honked the horn.

"He's a bust," Garrett said. "Says he has too much to do on the farm. Said he'll be around for any heavy lifting if we need him."

Garret adjusted his cap again.

"With Jackson, Lucy, and a few others, we should be okay for sentries... for a little while, anyway. Wish we had more help."

A squawk on the sheriff's radio cut into his assessment.

"Sheriff," Ms. Greenfield announced, "we have a development."

"What is it, Lucy? Over."

"I think your ship has just come in. Over."

26

Port of Call
+10 Days – 1241 hours

Several sailboats and cruisers bobbed, anchored in slips on both sides of the main pier. At the end of the T-shaped dock, a forty-foot cruiser knocked lightly against the rubber bumpers mounted to the pier's pilings.

A tanned tall muscular man carried a Rubbermaid container from the boat's lower deck to the gray weathered pier.

Sheriff Garrett jogged over to the larger man and waited for him to set down the container before throwing his arms around him.

"That's Lincoln Reynolds, all right," Sebastian said as the pair broke their embrace. "Now that the bromance is over, let's go see what's up."

Our boots resonated on the planks.

"Where's Trisha?" Garrett asked, wiping his finger through one of the pink splatters streaked along the sides of the cruiser's fiberglass hull.

A woman with long wavy red hair and a loose fitting white sundress over a blue one-piece bathing suit stepped out from under the captain's awning. She pushed her sunglasses up onto her forehead, drawing her hair back and revealing dark circles under her eyes.

"It's been a hard week. Jared," she said.

"Yeah, Tricia. For us, too."

She looked at the island with a quick scan before coming around the rear bench to slide her hands around her husband's neck. He locked fingers with hers, both of them wearing simple gold wedding bands.

"We expected you back sooner, Linc," Garrett said. "I was kind of losing hope."

"We were, too," Lincoln murmured. "It's chaos out there, man."

Lincoln squeezed Tricia's hand, leaning his cheek into her arm. She kissed the back of his blonde crew cut hair.

"We weren't even sure what we would find once we got back here. Thought it might be overrun like the Main."

Lincoln glanced up at Garrett's new ball cap.

"Frank's dead, isn't he?" he asked.

"Yeah," Garrett muttered. "We lost him and Glenda, both."

Tricia buried her face in Lincoln's shoulder.

"Honorably?" Lincoln swallowed.

Garrett looked out over the breakwater for a moment before answering.

"None of us would probably be here if it wasn't for him."

"Good. Wear the mantle well, Jared."

"I'm trying. Every day."

The conversation stopped, the slap of the waves against the boat's hull suddenly too loud. Sebastian broke the silence with a question of his own.

"How bad is it out there?"

"Hey, trucker! I wouldn't have thought you'd be here. Who's your friend?"

"This is my pal, John. He doesn't talk much. Got himself a little problem in the voice box from his service in the sands. He's real good with a gun, though. Almost better than me."

I stepped forward and extended a hand. Lincoln unlatched a hand from his wife and pumped my hand in response.

I nodded to his wife. She smiled weakly.

"How about the Main, Linc?" Garrett insisted.

"The coast is overrun. We were sixty or seventy miles north of Boston when it first started. We had to anchor in Danberg Bay. Lots of gunfire that first night."

"And screams," Tricia mumbled.

"Yeah. We saw a few people on the beach that night. Thought they were injured. I was prepared to go ashore, but a bunch of teenagers shot them before I could even react. We didn't have our lights on at the time, so we just hunkered down.

"The next morning we pulled anchor and piloted north up the coast. We saw infected people all over the beaches and the interstate. State troopers were shooting anyone who looked off." Lincoln air-quoted the last word.

"The radio and CB alerts told anyone on the water to stay out of the major ports."

Lincoln looked off to the other side of the bay, Trisha rubbing his back.

"We saw plenty of small boats on the water. But a couple days in, we started seeing twenty- and thirty-footers overflowing with people. Looked like refugee barges.

"The water is a great place to keep away from the infected. The problem was that several of those boats were already infected. We passed a yacht teeming with them. Some of them went overboard trying to get at us."

Lincoln stopped again and rubbed his face.

"The entire boat was filled with them."

Another pause.

"But we heard a scream for help coming from below deck. The infected were clawing against the door. I had my service pistol, so we trolled closer to see what we could do.

"The infected in the water pressed against the sides of our cruiser. A couple of them climbed over the rail from the lower deck to get onboard. Fortunately, they couldn't get a grip and slid back into the water.

"I shot a couple of them, but they kept coming. Finally, I shot one in the head and it went down for good. I didn't have enough ammo to get below deck to help whoever it was. The people couldn't escape through the forward hatch because the infected were trying to claw through it too.

"We left them. I can still hear the man pleading for us to come back."

Trisha stopped rubbing Lincoln's back. She went to sit in the captain's chair. Lincoln snapped the lid back onto the container and patted it.

"For a while, we kept chugging north."

"Until we ran out of fuel," Tricia commented.

"Yeah, until we ran out of fuel," Lincoln agreed. "I had to break into a few diesel pumps along the way. Trisha stood watch while I siphoned fuel. Had to refill off a couple moored yachts, too."

With Lincoln's last words finished, no one said anything while we absorbed what he and his wife had experienced.

"Glad you're back, Linc," Garrett finally said. "We need you."

"Thanks, Jared. But one more man ain't going to do much against what's out there."

27

Brat

+10 Days – 1430 hours

After we helped Lincoln and Tricia carry their supplies to their Ford Explorer, Sheriff Garrett, Sebastian and I walked back to the plaza.

In front of Beloved Books and Antiques, Ms. Greenfield had finished her turn at dispatch and stood by the open hatch of her Pinto. She set a Hammermill box overflowing with paperback books on the curb in front of the store owner Gloria Steiner.

They talked for a few minutes. Ms. Greenfield occasionally pointed at the box or turned her hands over in the air. When Gloria bent over to pick up the box, Ms. Greenfield walked back to the Pinto's driver's side door. She reached into the back seat for another box. As she retrieved it, one of its corners caught on the doorframe.

We reached her just in time to see books bounce off the cobblestone.

"Having problems there, Ms. Greenfield?" Sebastian asked.

She looked up from the scattered mess, her hands on her full hips. "Well, truck driver, you think I may have a situation here?"

"Looks that way."

"Well, if that's the case, a gentleman would certainly come to my aid. I would think so, anyway."

"That certainly would seem to be the protocol," Sebastian agreed. He slapped me on the back. "Help the lady out, John."

I looked at the books, then at Ms. Greenfield. Her hands still hung on her hips and one of her eyebrows remained raised. A mesh scabbard with an Army Defender fixed blade combat knife looped through her belt.

Righting the box, I started collecting the stray paperback novels. Ms. Greenfield had traded her boots for an open-toed strapped wedge. Her toenails were painted a deep pink with the second toe on her left foot sporting a silver ring.

"What's with the books, Ms. Greenfield?" Sheriff Garrett asked.

"Well, I heard that the bookstore offered vouchers for most books that were brought in. I figured I would turn in my bookshelf for a few paperbacks that I haven't read. With everything going on, I forgot they were even in the back of the car. I still have one more box in the back."

"I'll get that for you, miss."

"Thanks, Sheriff."

As Garrett skirted around the books I was collecting, Ms. Greenfield's left foot started tapping.

"Come on, soldier. Gloria's waiting."

I reached for Stephen King's *The Dark Tower: The Gunslinger* and Tom Clancy's *The Bear and the Dragon* and placed them in the box. The last stray paperback was a well-worn copy of *Slaughterhouse Five* by Kurt Vonnegut. I grabbed the cardboard container and got to my feet.

"My hero," Ms. Greenfield mocked, pointing to the bookstore. "That a way."

I followed Sheriff Garrett into the store and placed the box on the counter. Ms. Greenfield and Sebastian came in behind us.

"A good day to you, Gloria," Sebastian said.

"Thanks, Sebastian. You have a good selection here, Lucy."

"I thought you'd like it," Ms. Greenfield said, bending over to adjust her sandal straps, her holstered .239 Sig Sauer showing at the back of her waistband.

"You got a license for that firearm, Ms. Greenfield?" Garrett inquired.

"Sure do! I'm an Army brat from way back. Dad's a big gun nut. Got me into all sorts of things in his spare time."

"Where's home?" Sebastian asked.

"Camp Edward in western Barnstable County."

"Let's hope we can get you there," Garrett remarked. "It's been quiet lately."

Just then the church bell started to ring.

28

Fangs

+10 Days – 1503 hours

Garrett ran out of the store as soon as we heard the second resonant bong. Ms. Greenfield pulled her Sig, beating Sebastian to the door.

We raced across the plaza to the church.

Kyle came out from the diner, beating both Garrett and Sebastian to the steps.

"What's going on, Donny?" Garrett asked.

Donny, a large olive skinned man with rimless glasses and a ball cap, stood at the base of the church steps.

"More problems than just FRACs!"

"What do you mean?"

"Come up and see!"

Donny retreated up the steps into the church's vestibule. Sebastian remained outside, out of breath.

Donny led us to a stairwell, then to a metal ladder in an alcove that led up to the belfry.

"Look," Donny pointed to a western facing archway.

"What the hell?" Garrett said to himself.

The rest of us crowded into the other archway that looked out to the bridge.

On the Stretch were dozens of FRACs. But they weren't alone. Around them, almost herding them like cattle, were a pack of canines. They barred their teeth and lunged at the undead, biting and shaking random legs or loose clothes.

Strangely, the walkers did not respond.

A dog with a red collar charged in and bit the leg of a FRAC, pulling on the walker like a tug-of-war chew rope. The walker lost its balance. The dog dragged it around until it lost interest.

Another dog lunged in and clamped down on the calf of a heavyset FRAC wearing just a pair of striped Joe Boxer shorts.

A larger wolf leapt up and clamped down on Joe Boxer's arm, shaking the FRAC in its jaws until the arm finally ripped off at the shoulder socket. Joe Boxer responded by spinning away and bumping off another walker.

"What the hell, Deputy?" Kyle asked.

"It's interesting." Garrett picked up Donny's rifle and looked through the scope.

"Why don't we let the dogs deal with them, Deputy?" Kyle asked.

"One, because we do not know how infectious the dogs are. Two, even if the dogs aren't infectious they could become infected. Three, what happens when they get tired of ripping up walkers? Last, I'm Sheriff now."

Kyle opened his mouth then shut it again.

Some of the dogs turned on each other. One German Shepherd and two mongrel dogs stalked the largest canine in the pack, an Eastern Coyote. The shepherd, with a bloody yellow bandana around its neck, stalked the coyote from along the left side rail while the two mongrels circled it from the right. The coyote would have been overpowered, but just as the shepherd crouched to leap one of the mongrels lunged at the shepherd and bit it in the throat until it bled and gurgled. The shepherd whined and fell to the pavement. The mongrel released its grip then lifted a leg and pissed on the dying animal. The coyote jumped on top of the second mongrel and bit its ear off. The mongrel howled in pain and crept away with its tail between its legs.

"What's the plan, Garrett?"

"Don, keep watch. If any dogs make a break for the barricade, put them down. John, you stay with him."

Garrett gave Donny back his rifle.

"Kyle, you come with me. We'll go check out the Norte Bridge."

I picked up a scoped M4 from a shelf behind the trapdoor and returned to the windows. As Garrett descended the ladder, I heard Sebastian panting below.

"What's going on, Sheriff?"

"I'll tell you on the way to the station," Garrett responded.

"More walking?" Sebastian complained.

Kyle and Ms. Greenfield followed the Sheriff down the hatch. Kyle closed the door and cut off their conversation.

On the bridge the dogs growled and fought among themselves. They darted at the walkers, swiping at their legs or gripping a wrist to drag them off their feet. Once prone, the rabid canines leapt up on their chests and ripped at their throats. The canines did little damage to the walkers aside from the occasional lost limb or missing chunk of rotted flesh, but the fact that the FRACs presented little resistance surprised me.

Below, Garrett, Ms. Greenfield and Kyle jogged across the plaza, Sebastian panting and lagging behind.

29

White As Snow

+10 Days – 1635 hours

For an hour the canines continued to attack and herd the
FRACs.

Ms. Greenfield, Kyle and Sheriff Garrett huddled together
along the front corner of Town Hall with rifles slung across their
backs and handguns in hand.

Sebastian was not among them.

Garrett pulled out his radio.

"Donny. Over."

"Yeah, Garrett. Over."

"You see us?"

Garrett waved. I gave Donny a thumbs-up.

"Yeah. We got you."

"Okay, Don. We're going to move up to the barricade."

"Copy that, Chief."

Garrett waved once more and started toward the bridge. The
rest followed at arms length. The ramp to the bridge inclined
several feet, allowing them to walk without crouching. Once at the
barricade, Garrett and his two "deputies" stopped and squatted
against the cars.

Donny received a message, almost a whisper.

"We can see them, Donny, but we have an obstructed view.
What are they doing?"

"Same as before, Chief."

I looked back through the scope. The dogs continued to growl,
whine and nip at each other. They defecated and urinated without
realizing it.

Kyle peeked over the barricade with his back pressed against a
bumper. Ms. Greenfield knelt next to him, leaning her rifle against

the car. Sheriff Garrett glanced through one of the windows before talking into his radio.

"Donny?"

"No change, Chief."

A breeze puffed through Garrett's hair as it pushed west.

One of the more aggressive mongrels stopped biting the haunch of a smaller retriever mix.

It sniffed the air.

The retriever took the opportunity to retreat.

Sniffing the air again, the mongrel growled once and began pacing in a circle around the herded FRACs.

I snapped my fingers three times before pointing down to the bridge, to my nose, and then made circling motions with a downward wag of my forefinger. Donny looked out at the bridge and fumbled with the radio before making contact with Garrett.

"Sheriff?"

"What is it, Donny?"

"The dogs may have your scents. They're more agitated."

"Okay, Donny. If they make a break... put 'em down."

"Copy that. Out"

The mongrel alternated between sniffing the air and circling. One by one, the others followed suit. The breeze had died down again, but something clung to the air just the same. The coyote stretched its neck and let loose a piercing and guttural howl.

The hairs at the base of my neck stood at attention.

My unease lasted only moments before the mongrel and the coyote started padding toward the barricade. The others whined, considered the FRACs they would be leaving behind, then stepped in line behind their pack leaders.

"Shit! They're coming," Donny called out.

My answer was a sharp crack and a muzzle flash, dropping the lead mongrel with a bullet to the top of its skull. The coyote scurried left, away from the pack's now-dead beta male. All of the canines stopped in their tracks. One lifted and cocked its head with its jaws still nipping another smaller fox's neck.

With a deep growl the coyote charged the barricade at a full run. Donovan hit the send button on the radio.

"They're coming, Garrett! They're coming!"

I fired.

The pavement sparked next to the coyote as it veered right.

I fired again.

The bullet found the mark, but it was not a kill shot. The bullet ripped open the back of its spine, sending it to the ground. Its back legs useless, the coyote crawled forward with its front paws. Its eyes shone red and its muzzle frothed.

The dog that had enjoyed the fox's neck dug into the coyote's scruff and dragged it over to the side of the bridge to finish the job. The coyote whimpered in pain as it bled out.

The rest of the pack charged at the barricade.

I shot three of them in quick succession.

Donovan fired several times, chewing up more pavement than fur, only killing one of them.

The remaining dogs reached the barricade.

I picked off two as they clawed their way up onto the front hoods.

Four more slid across the hoods and car roofs.

Ms. Greenfield dropped her rifle and swung her Sig up into the gaping mouth of a massive Rottweiler.

She fired down its throat.

A Doberman dropped to the trunk behind the slumping Rottweiler, stopping as the Rottie's blood and brain matter sprayed into its eyes. Kyle fired into the Doberman's belly, sending it into the windshield. Sheriff Garrett finished it off with a pistol shot to the head.

The injured fox leaped onto the top of the barricade and slowly stalked around the dead Doberman and Rottie. My next shot opened a hole in the trunk lid, but missed the animal. The red and brown animal cocked its head at the new ding, sniffed at it and moved forward.

The fox leaped at Kyle, sliding in the Rottie's blood but still managing to tumble into him. The animal forced him to the ground, Kyle raising his rifle in time to ward off the fox's drooling muzzle.

Garrett swung his rifle butt into the teeth of the last dog making its way across the car trunk lids. It yelped and slid down to the asphalt. Garrett drove the rifle butt into its head three more times for good measure.

A flash of white fur approached the barricade but I did not have a clean shot.

Ms. Greenfield aimed her Sig at the fox and Kyle. The fox snapped at Kyle, its frothing jaws biting into the rifle stock and slobbering on Kyle's face.

He yelled out.

A 6-3/4 inch steel blade plunged through the back of the fox's neck, the tip piercing two inches out the other side toward Kyle's face.

On the bridge, a few FRACs noticed the gunfire and were moving toward the barricade. I squeezed the trigger, the head of the closest walker exploding.

I fired again.

The second of the three curious walkers fell to the ground.

A third shot rang out with a fiery muzzle flash.

Another FRAC dropped.

The other walkers on the Stretch continued to mill at the center of the bridge.

At the barricade, Ms. Greenfield put a boot on the fox's neck. With the fox's dead weight and the pressure from Ms. Greenfield's foot, Kyle let out a heavy exhale. She pulled against the fox and withdrew the blade. Then she kicked the body off Kyle and put out her hand to help him up.

He screamed.

The mongrel that had dragged off the dying coyote on the bridge was shaking Kyle's pant leg and trying to pull him under the car.

Garrett and Ms. Greenfield circled behind Kyle, each pulling an arm. Kyle screamed louder as the dog shook harder. Garrett leaned down at a low crouch and fired at the animal.

From the bridge came that white blur of movement again.

I adjusted my position but still couldn't get a bead on it.

The white blur ducked behind the barricade.

A high-pitched whine came from under the cars.

Kyle flew backward into the road's shoulder, landing on top of Ms. Greenfield and the sheriff.

More whines and yelps.

Then nothing.

Garrett pointed his pistol under the cars.

Kyle doubled over with his hands pressing the bit denim of his leg, Ms. Greenfield trying to look at the damage through Kyle's protests.

A loud resounding woof came from the darkness under the car frames.

Ms. Greenfield and the sheriff grabbed Kyle by the collar and pulled him away from the cars, their guns both pointed at the barricade.

Another woof came from their left.

They swung their pistol around.

Raised up on its haunches like a prairie dog, with a muddy belly and its tail swishing back and forth, a Pekingese Poodle sat licking the mongrel's blood off her white chops.

She barked again.

Batting her paws in the air, the curly white dog cocked her head looking for a treat.

30

Precious Resources

+10 Days – 1748 hours

"Donny," the radio crackled, "We're taking Kyle to Rawlings, just in case."

"Copy that."

Garrett and Ms. Greenfield holstered their weapons and lifted Kyle to his feet. They hobbled him to the main street. The new four-legged arrival ran after them with its bushy tail wagging.

The bridge was empty of fur and fangs, only FRACs wandering the span.

I glanced over at Donny.

His left eye twitched.

"Donny," Garrett said though the radio.

"We're here. All's quiet."

"Stay focused."

"Copy that, Chief. What about that other dog?"

"She seems okay. Lucy and her seem to be getting along pretty well."

"Okay. Over and out."

Donny breathed a sigh of relief.

Looking at my Cobra, I realized that my normal shift would have just started.

A faint popping sound came from the north.

Then another.

Followed by a third.

Soon came a steady stream of gunfire.

"Donny!" the two-way radio squawked. "We have an overrun of FRACs at the bridge. I called Garrett for support. Keep your eyes open!"

The frantic voice of Lincoln Reynolds cut out.

During the message, the sound of gunfire came through loud and clear. Reynolds, fresh from his adventures at sea, had little opportunity to replace his sea legs with land legs before being pushed into the fray.

The FRACs on the Searing Bridge became agitated. A quick head count of forty-three walkers marched onto the bridge to join the dozen that had already set up camp on the Stretch.

I calculated our ammunition. 'One shot, one kill' would leave us with sixty rounds.

"John, this is your bag, man," Donny spoke up with a strained voice. "I ain't good enough at the long range stuff. And I can't even focus through the scope no more!"

I reached for Donny's rifle.

He quickly gave it up.

Leaning the second rifle against the wall, I took a moment to recalculate my inventory. I slid the ammo box over to Donovan and pointed to his rifle's magazine.

Donny pressed the Send button on the radio.

"Sheriff?"

He waited ten seconds, and repeated the process.

"What is it, Donny?" Garrett squawked back.

"What do you want us to do here? We have about..." I showed Donny an open hand, then a fist. "...50 infected here on the bridge."

"Take them down, Donny. They're pressing hard against the utility gate here!"

I gave Donovan a thumbs-up.

"Okay, Sheriff. Over and out!"

With the go ahead, I sighted a FRAC closest to the barricade and fired. A woman in a bloody hospital gown fell back.

Another shot and a nurse joined her patient on the ground.

A third shot dropped a brown-shirted deliveryman.

Settling the rifle, I pulled the trigger again.

The bullet careened off the pavement, missing a well dressed, but mud-strewn woman.

A second trigger pull sent a bullet that caught her wide on the top of her head.

Compensating, I fired again.

Donny reloaded the magazines as I fired.

"Shit! Shit! Shit!" Donny muttered, as he struggled to fill the magazine quick enough to be ready for the exchange.

A burly man with a Mack Truck ball cap fell as soon as I put a bullet through the bulldog logo.

My stomach turned as an image of Sebastian flashed through my mind.

A toothless frail old woman with her lower jaw missing received the next round. I was sure that her dentures had fallen out when she lost her mandible.

Another shot dropped a wispy gray haired man of the cloth, his vestiges missing.

I could still hear faint pops in the air from the north, the report from my weapon's discharge adding to it.

The smell of gunpowder filled my nostrils.

Smoky haze heated the air in the small space.

Sweat poured down my face, neck and back. I wiped the sweat from my eyes with my forearm before settling in.

Hot cartridges spun and fell to the floor, tinkling off the other spent brass.

I fired again and emptied the weapon. I released the magazine and handed it to Donny.

"This is the last one, John!"

I took the fully loaded magazine.

Fitting the butt to my sore shoulder and looking through the scope, I counted eleven targets. FRACs had continued to wander in from Route 5, attracted by the continuous gunfire.

A young woman wearing a red-stained salon smock around her neck and a curler grasping onto the last inches of a strand of hair came into view.

I exhaled and pulled the trigger.

Her milky eyes rolled back and her back arched as she fell to the pavement. Another walker flailed over her body. I put a bullet into the top of his balding head as he fell, ensuring that he submitted permanently to gravity.

Thirteen more shots killed twelve more FRACs.

The next pull of the trigger resulted in nothing. I looked at Donny.

Donny fumbled for the radio and pressed the Send button.

"Garrett!"

"What, Donny?"

"We're out of ammo!"

"How many FRACs?"

I looked out the window.

Four more had shown up since my last gunshot.

I held up my hand, wide open then closed it into a fist.

"How many, Donny?" The radio crackled.

"Over fifty!"

"Stay put. The herd is thinning here. I will send someone over when I can. Out!"

The last word was punctuated with the report of a pistol shot.

I looked at the stumbling remainder of the new FRAC contingent. They didn't navigate around their fallen comrades. Their legs dragged on the arms, torsos, and legs of the bodies underfoot.

Adrenaline had kept my body and mind focused.

With it now receding, soreness and fatigue seeped in.

I walked over to the cooler, pulled out a bottle of water and took a long swig. I took another swig then poured the remainder of it on my head and neck. Wiping my face with the bottom of my T-shirt, I looked out the archway again.

Bodies peppered the bridge, over a hundred in all. The remaining walkers had finally made their way to the barricade. They clawed at the cars, not lifting their knees high enough to crawl up on the car hoods. Several bodies were piled up at the base of the bumpers.

"Hell, John! They're going to get over the cars."

He was right.

I pulled open the trapdoor and slid down the ladder. Taking the stairs two at a time, I jumped to the first floor landing, ran through the vestibule and out the church doors to the front steps.

Circling around to the grounds keeper's tool shed, I looked for anything suitable to assist me. Gardening tools of all types lined the walls. I found what I was looking for and grabbed it off its hook.

Running back outside, I sprinted up to the barricade.

Two FRACs stood up onto the front hood of the first car.

I took two long strides and leaped onto the trunk.

The swinging arc of the spade shovel's flat blade sliced into the walker's head. I wrenched the handle upward to free the blade as the FRAC fell backward off the hood, the top of its face separating a little from the rest of its head.

A second walker stood up.

I swung the blade again, catching him full in the face with the edge of the shovel. The blade dug deep, almost buried to its ears. Gravity pulled the undead man back off the car. I pulled the handle, letting the FRAC's fluids lubricate the blade enough to slip it free as he fell off the car.

Fifty-three FRACs remained.

Taking a knee on the roof of the sedan, I dropped the shovel with a clank and drew my Glock.

Dozens of FRACs reached out at me.

I squeezed the trigger and shot two women in sundresses, plus another wearing overalls and garden gloves.

Fifty FRACs. Fifteen rounds.

I fired.

A stock boy in a blue apron from a Kroger's supermarket fell backward. Then came an old man with a pair of glasses hanging from his neck on a chain. Following the old man were two Massachusetts highway patrol officers, one with half his neck missing.

Forty-six FRACs.

Eleven rounds.

Clambering against the barricade were seven young men. Two of them wore MIT licensed shirts.

Thirty-nine FRACs.

Four rounds.

An overweight man in a business suit with a blood darkened sleeve pushed against the falling college students.

Thirty-eight FRACs.

Three rounds.

Two teenage girls reached around the fat FRAC. One had bright red lipstick over her metal wired teeth. The other wore a blue hoodie sweatshirt.

Thirty-six FRACs. One round left in the pipe.

I released the magazine and let it fall to the hood of the car with a metallic thud. Reaching to my holster, I pulled the second magazine and reloaded.

More FRACs pressed against the barricade, stomping their legs on top of the fallen undead piling up under their feet.

Seventeen more pulls of the trigger.

Seventeen dead.

Nineteen FRACs.

Eighteen rounds left.

I reloaded.

Eighteen shots.

Eighteen dead.

The slide locked open.

I closed the slide, holstered the weapon and grabbed the shovel.

The last FRAC had been joined by seven more who had come into view over the rise of the bridge.

Not waiting for them to mount an assault over the cars, I jumped to the other side of the barricade to face them head on.

The first swing caught the closest FRAC flat on the side of the ear. I pulled back the handle, turned the blade and swung it hard enough to decapitate the walker.

The second walker moved in close.

I hook kicked it, letting it take a companion corpse down with it. Diving forward with the shovel like a spear, I drove the blade into the first walker's neck. Pulling the blade up, I jumped on its fallen compatriot's chest and repeated the technique.

The five surviving FRACs closed in.

With tense muscles I swung the shovel again and again.

One of the last three FRACs grabbed at my shoulder.

I turned to face it, a brutish muscle head in gray sweatpants, muddy socks and nothing else. The other two pawed at me, one on each arm. I butted one of them with the shovel handle, shoving my shoulder into the other one. The first fell to the pavement. The second only pin wheeled.

The Brute bore down on me.

Backing up, I cornered myself against the bridge's rail.

I took a desperate swing with the flat of the shovelhead, only succeeding in turning its head away for a moment. The pin wheeler charged at me. I raised the shovel and speared it in the chest. Shoving it backward, I pulled out the shovelhead and thrust it into its face.

As I pulled the weapon out of the slumping walker, The Brute and its remaining small FRAC friend pressed me against the rail. I got the shovel up in time to fend off Sidekick FRAC as it surged at my face.

Sidekick staggered backward as the Brute pressed against the shovel. My muscles strained against its bigger mass. It craned its neck forward as it chomped the air in front of my face, saliva dribbling from its mouth.

The Brute's mouth inched closer to my jugular. Surprised at my strength, I kept it off me. Sidekick FRAC pressed against the Brute's back, adding to its weight. The Brute's stared at me with its unblinking milky red eyes as it continued to bite at the air.

The razor tip of an arrow erupted through its forehead. Its eyes rolled up as if to see what jutted from over its eyebrows.

Crashing to its knees, the Brute leaned to the right but did not fall to the pavement. Sidekick FRAC was connected to the Brute's back by a second impaling arrow through the head. They expired this way, propping each other up.

I kicked them over to the ground.

Four men stood several meters away.

Three of them stood in the middle of the bridge, dressed in hunter fatigues and carrying compound bows.

Standing away from the others, a gaunt man in a black suit gazed at me with a thin smile and dark eyes. He nodded to me, his skin waxy and yellowing.

The largest of the three hunters walked up to the Brute, braced a combat boot on the back of its head and pulled out the arrow. He then pulled out the second arrow lodged in the Sidekick.

He spoke up, a toothpick dangling from his mouth. "Hey, pal. Looked like you needed a little assistance."

With my shirt covered in matter and fluids not my own, a shovel dripping with blackened blood, and surrounded by the dead, his assessment was spot on.

Behind the three hunters, the man in the black suit had disappeared.

31

School's Out

+10 Days – 1811 hours

The three men, holding compound bows and quivers of razor tipped arrows strapped to their thighs, stood over me. The group's leader outstretched his hand.

"Let me help you up, sir."

I raised my blood sprayed hand. He grabbed my wrist and pulled me up. I clung to the shovel's handle with the other hand.

As the toothpick rolled around his mouth, he scratched his scraggily beard and adjusted the bill of his cap.

"Looks like you made quite an impact before you ran out of bullets." He swept his arm behind him in a grand theatrical gesture. "Especially in these plaguers' heads."

The other two men looked unkempt, unshaven and disheveled. Spots of dark blood splashed across their clothes. Their leader was much more presentable.

"What your name, friend?" Toothpick asked.

Donny slipped over the barricade.

"He doesn't talk much, mister."

"Yep. He looks like a man more of action."

Toothpick approached Donny, slung his bow and extended his hand.

"The name is Taylor. Professor Anthony Taylor."

He pointed back to his compatriots who remained where I had first spotted them.

"With me are Misters Sanchez and McDougal."

Each tipped a finger in salute.

"We heard the gunshots and were as interested as the plaguers. We did not know this island had a community, but we are glad you are here. When social services started shutting down, radio stations started blinking off the air, and anarchy started to rise up, we figured we better move out of Boston to the countryside."

"Well, Dr –," Donny started.

"Taylor. And it's professor. But I do not think that my pedigree is going to be of much use at this point. So Anthony is fine."

"Well, Professor Anthony Taylor. It is good to meet you," came a voice from behind the barricade. Garrett came up with a pump action shotgun.

"I am Sheriff Jared Garrett of Rainier Island. How many more in your party?"

"Just us three, Sheriff," Taylor said with a thin smile, the toothpick running from one side of his mouth to the other.

"Try again, Professor."

The Professor's smile waned. He panned up to the church tower. I followed his gaze and caught a reflection.

"You are right, Sheriff." Taylor responded in a serious tone. "I apologize. I have a contingent of two men, three women and six children in addition to myself, Sanchez and McDougal here. But I can assure you we come with the best intentions."

"You surely haven't gotten off on the right foot then, have you?"

"Quite right, Sheriff. Quite right."

The professor pondered the situation, the toothpick still dancing around his lips. I edged closer to the barricade and to Donny.

"What are you thinking, Professor?" Garrett asked.

"I want to make amends. We have run into some resistance and ill-mannered people along our way over the last week, and I am afraid that it has already left me a little cynical."

"What is your proposal?"

"My friends and I will clear the bodies off the bridge to a location of your choosing. I hope the act will show you the strength of our intent."

"Three conditions. One, no one in your party comes to the barricade until I say so. I will have snipers with full view in case you start feeling entitled."

The three men glanced up at the church tower.

"Agreed," Taylor answered.

"Second, do not ask me or my men for any amenities."

The Professor started to raise his hand with a point to be made, but thought better of it.

"Agreed."

Sanchez started to speak up, but Taylor cut him short with a wave of the hand.

"Agreed," he replied again, with more conviction.

"And lastly, if you finish and I still have a bad feeling about you or any of your people I will ban any or all of you from entry to the island."

"Agreed, Sheriff. You have a deal. I appreciate the opportunity."

Taylor turned and walked to Sanchez and McDougal. Sanchez shot Garrett a quick piercing look, but Taylor grabbed him by the arm and spun him away in the direction of the mainland.

Donny and I shimmied back to the other side of the barricade.

"Seriously, John?" Garrett looked at my shovel and shook his head. "What the hell?"

"We ran out of ammo, Sheriff."

"I know you did, Donny. But sacrifices like this," Garrett said, pointing to me, "is not the way to work."

He shook his head again and sighed. "Great job with the shovel. Really great. I am sure Pastor Dorsey would want his spade back where you found it. Clean it up first."

32

Promises

+10 Days – 1838 hours

Lincoln Reynolds was perched at the belfry window, letting me change out of my bloody clothes.

I tossed my soiled shirt into a small garbage pail in the corner. Streaks of pink seeped through the cotton of the clean T-shirt I pulled on from a shelf.

"Here they come," Reynolds tilted his head.

From the windows, the remains of the undead littering the pavement along the length of the bridge looked like a wartime killing field.

A small group of men, women and children walked onto the bridge. A pick-up truck puttered slowly behind them, spewing dark smoke. A woman stood on its bed, steadying herself with both hands on the roof.

A thin tall woman hooked a FRAC under the armpits while a young man grabbed its feet. They dragged it over to the truck. As the pair hoisted the rotting remains up onto the back of the truck bed, the woman in the bed - visibly pregnant - impaled it with a hay bale hook and pulled it toward the cab.

A young boy and girl grabbed a walker by the feet and tried to move it, unable to slide the body more than a meter.

"Heartbreaking," Reynolds commented.

Mr. McDougal shooed the kids away, grabbing the corpse by the belt and tossing it up onto the truck bed.

Two other young teenage boys grabbed a smaller FRAC by the arms and dragged it toward the truck. They broke into a run with the body, making a game out of it.

33

New News

+10 Days – 1958 hours

I looked out over the bridge, perched in the archway with my rifle.

Deputy Reynolds, relieved from overwatch duty, used his flashlight to direct the flatbed truck to a stop twenty meters from the barricade. Next came a beat up "woody" station wagon that the deputy motioned to park behind the truck. After the station wagon turned off its ignition, Reynolds walked toward the Main. At the crest of the roadway, he waved the flashlight. Beeping followed the rev of a diesel motor. A Winnebago backed up onto the bridge. It parked at the end of the vehicular column.

Reynolds returned to the barricade as Taylor's men reunited with their group. The kids and women, who had been sitting on the curb, walked over to the barricade. Mr. McDougall, Professor Taylor, Mr. Sanchez and two other men – twins – helped them across the cars. Sheriff Garrett helped each member of Professor Taylor's party down to the island side. Once all the women and children were safety back on the pavement, the men were allowed to join them.

Both the islanders and the new group walked down the road in the direction of the Oceanside Diner.

Two FRACs wandered onto the bridge.

One leaned against the Winnebago, patting it with its hand. The FRAC snapped its teeth at the air and head butted the aluminum siding of the vehicle before losing interest and staggering away.

Behind me, Jackson Parson climbed up the ladder.

"Sheriff wants you over at the Oceanside."

I stood and returned the M4 to the shelf.

Jackson set his own scoped rifle up at the window I had just vacated.

Whistling my goodbye, I dropped down the ladder and made my way out of the church and double-timed over to the diner.

Inside, the three visiting women were wiping grime off themselves and the kids with dishrags, a steaming pot of water sitting on one of the tables.

Garrett and Reynolds sat with Taylor's men.

I headed to the end of the counter next to Sebastian, sliding around to face the conversation.

"Welcome to the welcoming committee, Johnny," he said in a low voice.

"Now that we are all settled, I guess formal introductions are in order," Professor Taylor began.

"You have already met Mr. Rodrigo Sanchez and Mr. Noel McDougal."

Taylor pointed to the gentlemen at the far end.

"The rest of the men of my company consist of the Tewilliger Brothers, Michael and Mark. They hail from Long Island, joining up with us a couple days ago."

The Twins leaned on the table looking like they were ready to fall asleep.

"Sarah and Margie were desperate to get off Boston College campus. They were trying to hitch a ride on one of the outbound Greyhound buses, but organization was so chaotic most were left behind. Once we started northeast, we picked up Rod and his wife Petra. She's the one bringing a new life into the world."

"What's on the news?" Garrett asked.

"Before it went dark? Everything on the radio, the web, the broadcasts are contradictory. The religious zealots are claiming this is a form of the Rapture, spouting that at the End of Days the dead would walk the earth. The local television stations found blame where they could when no real information came across the AP – chemical leaks, radiation explosions, and government conspiracies. The radio said the same. The web showed multitudes of plaguer forums and shaky home vlogs. It was all very flummoxing."

"What did you see?" Reynolds asked.

"Well," Taylor responded, "once we all got together we compared notes. Noel evaded police blockades and saw National Guardsmen shooting people they felt were infected. Near the Boston College campus emergency service bulletins told residents to report to the local Light Guard Armory for processing. When we came close to the Armory from a secondary road that Sarah knew, the entire complex was engulfed in flames."

"Holy hell."

"Holy hell, indeed, Sheriff." the Professor paused. "You know in the movies when the major cities are evacuated, and the highways and interstates are gridlocked with cars?"

"Yeah."

"This epidemic, pandemic, whatever it is, spread so fast that most planned evacuations never occurred." The Professor air-quoted the word planned. "The news outlets encouraged people to stay home with their doors locked or go to a central metropolitan triage location. Once people wised up and tried to get away from populated areas, the plaguers greeted them at their door or local or state authorized roadblocks stopped them. The fact that most people thought the stories of these roaming flesh-eating ghouls were biblical level hoaxes doomed most from the start.

"Public spaces and care centers were the worst and the most quickly affected. People die everyday, Sheriff. On the first day – in hospitals, senior centers, convalescent homes, emergency rooms, in their homes – people died of natural or accidental causes. Imagine the doctors, nurses, support staff, visitors and patients suddenly confronted with the rising dead. Two plaguers become four, four become eight and so on, the mass of undead increasing exponentially. Care centers were overrun within a matter of hours, when the outbreak was most potent and turned the infected into plaguers most quickly. We have run across bite victims recently that have taken longer to come back, so I am making the assumption that the infection is burning itself out."

"You have an opinion on the source?" Garrett asked.

"Certainly. Once you open your mind to previously impossible notions, a valid postulation is fairly easy to discern. The only thing I am not certain of is from where the outbreak originally heralded. All of the major metropolitan centers across the middle of the country and east were affected at roughly the same time. Chicago, Detroit, Atlanta, Pittsburgh, New York, and Boston; all seemed to start broadcasting the event within a few hours of each other. The spread was so rapid, there seems to be no epicenter. It acted more like a pandemic. My educated guess for an epicenter would be out west somewhere."

"Well." Garrett mulled over Professor Taylor's hypothesis. "What I know is that a flood of walking dead has been coming to our island for over a week now. They're attracted to sound and smell if they get close enough. They attack the living to feed. If they bite or scratch you, you become infected, die of fever and come back. A bullet to the brain puts them down. That's what I know."

"Well said, Sheriff. That sums the situation up."

"Like hell, it does!" Sanchez exploded from his chair.

"Calm down, Rod."

"Bullshit!" Mr. Sanchez shot back. "I have a pregnant wife! How are we going to have the baby, or survive for that matter?"

Petra bowed her head, rubbing the top of her extended belly. One of the other women, a curvy blonde, came over to her and placed an arm around Petra's shoulders.

"Thanks, Sarah," Petra mouthed, pressing her own hand up to clasp Sarah's and resting her cheek against them.

The other woman, Margie, huddled the kids together.

Sheriff Garrett spoke up.

"We have our own physician, Mr. Sanchez. Doctor Rawlings is quite capable of delivering your baby."

"We ain't staying!"

"Well," Garrett replied, "that's your choice."

"We recently made the decision to head to Atlanta, Sheriff," Taylor added. "Even though the road closures pushed us north we are confident that we can make it to the Center for Disease Control for answers."

"If the major cities were unprepared for the speed of the infection's spread," the Sheriff answered, "what makes you think that the CDC will be able to help? And what makes you think you can even get close to the CDC, or even Atlanta?"

"Good points, Sheriff. But we have decided on a plan and aim to follow through. All we ask from you is supplies and fuel, if possible."

"We will discuss what we can do for you."

"That's all that we can ask, Sheriff."

"What about the children, Taylor?"

"What about them?"

"Where did you pick them up? I don't get the feeling that any of you are their parents."

"Mr. and Mrs. Sanchez found them. They were checking out a middle school in Middleton for shelter and supplies. The children were locked in the cafeteria. Whoever was caring for them did not think they would be safe in the open"

"Christ!" Reynolds muttered. "What the hell is wrong with people?"

"One never knows until the excrement hits the blades, Deputy," Taylor replied.

Felix, Pete, Kyle and Gloria wandered in as a group, Gloria gliding in with her mane of curly brown hair interwoven with satin braided strands.

Behind them, Ms. Greenfield, Sam, Erma and Patrick came in. Sam and the other islanders took up at Sam's usual table, the old man spinning his chair around to face the group. Ms. Greenfield walked over to the counter and picked up one of the menus. Her eyes darted at me while she read the two-week-old Specials of the Day.

"Hey, Lucy."

"Hi, Sebastian. What's new?"

"I would guess the new visitors, no?" Sebastian asked. "And did you hear that John took out the FRACs single-handedly on the Stretch, plus managed to get a little hand-to-hand action in, too?"

"What did he do?" Lucy inquired, her voice measured.

"Well," Sebastian said with a tug of his Mack truck cap, "John figured that since he didn't have any ammo left the smartest thing was to take the Pastor's spade shovel and start digging graves."

"There is something seriously wrong with you, Sergeant," Lucy said with a shake of her head.

"Amen to that," Sebastian agreed, "but what a show!"

Sheriff Garrett and Professor Taylor stood from the table in unison, signifying that the meeting was wrapping up.

"You can stay at the Town Hall. We'll bring pillows and blankets for the main chambers, plus we'll move a couch in for Mrs. Sanchez."

"We appreciate the hospitality, Sheriff."

"We'll talk more over breakfast."

Taylor extended his hand.

Garrett shook it.

The other men at the table stood.

Mr. McDougall walked over and shook hands with Garrett.

The twins and Mr. McDougall then went over to the booths where Sarah and Margie had corralled the tired kids. Mr. Sanchez joined his wife. The children were collected and the group left, led by Felix and Kyle as escorts.

Carol started cleaning up.

"Reynolds," Garrett stopped the two of us in the doorway, "make sure that all of the office and exits are locked. Do it quiet. I don't want Taylor offended, but I don't want them wandering around where they shouldn't be."

"On it, Chief," Reynolds replied before jogging out into the night.

"John," Garrett said with a hand on my chest. "I have something else for you."

34

Inspection

+10 Days – 2145 hours

I slipped up to the bell tower for my shift.

Jackson spun around when I flipped up the trapdoor.

He checked his watch as he sucked in on his cigarette.

"Hey, John. You're a bit early, ain't you?" he asked as he exhaled.

I stole a glance at my watch and shrugged.

Grabbing my M4, I moved to the second window, flipped open the scope covers and looked through it. It provided enough ambient light for a crisp view.

Professor Taylor's caravan stood empty and silent.

Jackson stretched his legs.

"John, is it okay if I take off? I really want to see what's going on at Town Hall."

I waved him away.

"Thanks, man!" Jackson lit up. "You sure you're okay?"

I shot him a thumbs-up.

Jackson put his rifle on the shelf.

"Cool. Thanks again," he said as he disappeared down the ladder.

I took a minute to position the rifle.

Jackson jogged across the grass. Others had formed into loose groups under the plaza's street lamps. Jackson weaved his way through, slowing every so often to chat. He made his way to the Town Hall and took one more look up at me before disappearing inside.

Garrett and Reynolds passed Jackson on their way out.

Erma stood on the sidewalk with Diggs and Sebastian. She gave Reynolds a big hug the moment he was within arm's reach.

Garrett spoke to Diggs and Sebastian during the exchange, gesturing to Mall Street. When Erma was done with Reynolds, Garrett pointed for her to leave.

The Sheriff moved to the next cluster, raising his arms to shoo them away. Reynolds peeled off to another group to do the same. Once done, Garrett and Reynolds stood with their arms crossed until the plaza stood empty.

Reynolds turned back to the Town Hall.

Garrett looked up at my position and gave me a flick of his finger from his temple before following his deputy inside.

I tucked my Glock into the back of my waistband before slipping on a black hooded sweatshirt from the shelf. Sticking the detached scope from the rifle into the front pouch, I slid down the ladder to the alcove. Through the vestibule, only the light patter of my boots broke the silence.

Slipping into the nave and up the center aisle to the altar and ambulatory behind it, I stopped for a moment to gaze up at the Son of God suffering on Mount Calvary's Cross. Nodding to the man with a wound from a lance's impalement on his side, a crown of thorns on his head and spikes hammered through his palms and feet, I exited the church via a side door.

We all have our crappy days.

I made my way up to the barricade.

Leaning against a bumper I peered through the car windows, seeing no movement on the bridge - warm or cold blooded. Moving over to the Atlantic side bridge rail, I straddled it and dropped down to a narrow concrete ledge. Water trickled under the roadway, making its way through the gateways into the impatient slapping ocean.

Once even with the flatbed truck I hopped over the railing to the road. I leaned against the passenger door of the truck and poked my head up to the window. Other than empty food cans, wrappers and bags on the bench, nothing peaked my interest.

I tried the handle.

The door opened.

Pulling out my tactical light, and careful to keep its cast downward, I lit up the glove compartment. The only important item was a snub-nosed revolver. I pulled it out and clicked open the cylinder. The chambers were empty. I flicked the cylinder closed and returned it to where I found it.

Hiding the tactical light's cast against my thigh, I closed the passenger door and moved to the 'Woody' station wagon. Bottled water, toys, and more empty food containers filled the back. The stale, bitter smell of sweat and grease filled my nostrils through the barely opened windows.

I moved to the front of the Winnebago.

The driver's side door was locked.

Walking to the rear of the camper, I climbed up on the bumper and looked through the wide rear window. Open cardboard boxes of non-perishable foods were stacked up on the left side of the bedroom, wedged between the bed and the wall. The compound bows and the quivers of arrows lay on the bedspread. The cabin opened to a hallway with a bi-fold door to a bathroom, a dining and kitchen galley, and the shadowed recesses of the front cabin.

Something flitted inside.

Flicking the light toward the movement, I cupped my hands against the window for a better view.

The Plexiglas slid a little.

Sliding the pane open, I lifted myself to the ladder. With one more look around, I entered the vehicle.

I pulled my weapon out, attached the tactical light to the rail, and stepped off the bed toward the front of the camper. Stopping at the kitchen bay I cupped the light, letting the darkness cover the cabin and listened.

A faint scurrying sound came from behind the captain's chair.

I drew the Glock up, the tactical light's beam shining against the back of the driver's seat. One slow footstep at a time I slid to the right toward the side door and centered my weapon at the steering wheel.

Something moved high to my left.

Sharp white teeth and red eyes flitted through the light and lunged at my face.

I grabbed my attacker by the neck.

Its eyes and sharp teeth seemed less threatening when it emitted a squeaking sound.

The ferret wrapped around my arm, its nose and whiskers twitching. I loosened my grip and set my Glock on the dining table, letting the light illuminate the room.

I readjusted my grip of the animal's scruff. It squeaked some more, its tail flitting, and its legs splayed out, its nose sniffing up at me.

Setting the ferret down, I picked up my gun. The raccoon-eyed brown animal scurried away, his squeaks joined by another. An albino ferret sat on the driver's chair with its front paws draped over the armrest and its ears twitching.

The white ferret sat up and scratched under its armpit before leaping after its companion. They pounced at each other, rolling around and bolting away – only to attack and lunge after each other again.

I smiled and turned to the back of the RV.

The light's brightness bounced off the small spotless kitchen counter.

Boxes of cereal, canned food, and bottled water stacked tight in the hall closet.

I swung out onto the roof ladder.

Closing the windowpane I wiped my palm prints off with my sleeve.

A pale tall shape in a dark suit reflected on the Plexiglas, smoothing his thin black tie.

I spun down to the pavement and brought up my Glock.

Only the station wagon and flatbed truck appeared at the end of my sights, quiet and unassuming. No one else was on the bridge.

The Atlantic crashed against the spillways, not willing to give up anything it might have witnessed.

35

First Light

+11 Days – 0630 hours

As the dawn cracked behind me, I took a moment to appreciate the quiet.

Three FRACs wandered around the Winnebago. They could be handled quickly and quietly when the time came.

Something pale flitted across the camper's back window.

Was it my imagination?

The trapdoor hatch opened behind me with a bang.

For the second time, I spun around with my Glock drawn.

"Whoa, John!" Blake said, one hand raised in surrender. "Sorry, man! Just wanted to make sure you were awake."

Blake dragged his stocky frame through the opening, his rifle and a duffle behind him. He tossed the duffle in the corner and brought the rifle to the second window.

"You may want to put that away, man."

The front sight of the Glock was still centered on his chest, the pressure on the trigger a little too heavy for his health.

I eased my finger off the trigger and put the pistol away.

36

Passing Notes

+11 Days – 0645 hours

The sheriff's department lobby was full.

Weaving my way through the throng of people, I picked up snippets of conversation about Professor Taylor and his group.

I entered Garrett's office.

He ran his hands through his hair, scratching his scalp. I handed over a note. He found his eyeglasses and, after a quick scan, crumpled it up and tossed it in the wastebasket.

"So the worst thing they have are ferrets and an empty snub nose," Garrett mused. "Well, maybe now I can face the masses to figure out what's next."

The novice Sheriff stood and, with a sigh, broke the barrier between safety and madness by walking across the lobby to Sam Sistern, Foster Anderson and Monroe Johnston.

37

Disputes

+11 Days – 0730 hours

Walking across the parking lot from the sheriff's department to the Town Hall, I entered through a lower level side door to the building's basement. Old cushioned office rolling chairs leaned against the concrete block walls, missing casters. Rows of filing cabinets and cubbies lined the walls, filled with island history.

The basement was a firetrap.

I climbed an old wrought iron spiral stairs, the metal vibrating. At the top, I pushed through a more modern fire door.

Two hollering kids from Taylor's group ran past me, the high ceiling bouncing the kids' laughter throughout the lobby.

Walking past the Assembly Hall I climbed an open carpeted stairway out to a visitors' gallery. Sebastian sat in the front row with his feet up on the railing.

"Hey, John," he whispered.

I looked down into the chamber.

Ms. Greenfield sat on one of the benches talking with the very pregnant Petra, using her hands to make soft circular motions between Petra's shoulder blades.

Sarah and Margie sat on the other side of Petra.

Sebastian leaned toward me, the seat creaking a little bit.

"All three of them seem very nice."

I patted Sebastian on the shoulder and took one more look at Ms. Greenfield before returning to the lobby and turning right to the executive offices.

This morning the kids ruled the rooms, jumping on the furniture and running between rooms. The Tewilliger brothers disappeared into the last office. Deputy Reynolds leaned against the hallway wall keeping an alert, but relaxed, watch.

A gold etched placard on the oak door denoted this as Foster Anderson's office.

I checked the doorknob.

It was locked.

Inside the last office, Mike and Mark were giving three of the children "pony rides" around the carpeted interior, whinnying to the kids' delight. The older kids looked on, enjoying the show. The twins suddenly and dramatically collapsed to the carpet, letting the kids tumble off with giggles and grins.

"I see you enjoyed the show as much as these guys," Mark said, thumbing to the other kids. "You got a grin on you."

Michael feigned an Oscar-worthy death on the floor, letting the little kids pile on him in an attempt to revive him.

"Don't worry, friend. John, is it? One of the higher ups, maybe the Sheriff, mentioned that you couldn't speak. I certainly won't take offense that you've cast this elaborate ploy in order to have an excuse to not speak to the likes of me!"

"Heck, Markie! I don't even like talking to you! And I'm your brother." Michael huffed from under a pile of little arms, legs and torsos. "Some twins have a secret language. Hell, I wanted to learn Spanish just to keep from having to include you in conversation!"

A kid grabbed Michael by his mouth and nose, pulling Michael's face toward him to get his renewed attention. "Arrgh!" was all that Michael managed as he contorted into a large-mouth bass on a hook.

Giving Mark a salute I stepped back to the hallway. I passed Reynolds and returned to the vaulted lobby space. Taking the stairway two steps at a time back to the mezzanine, I sat down next to Sebastian.

"Welcome back, young man."

Ms. Greenfield and the other women continued to chat below. "Fine girl, she is."

I agreed.

Ms. Greenfield leaned in toward Petra. From the other side Margie rested her head on Sarah's shoulder.

"No way that girl should be on the road," Sebastian commented. "None of them should."

Petra struggled to her feet, her hands bracing the small of her back. She waddled past Ms. Greenfield and headed up the aisle. Sarah and Margie trailed behind.

Before Petra reached out for the door handle, Anderson made a grand entrance into the chamber.

"Everyone outside, please," Anderson ordered.

He abruptly did an about face, brushing past Sheriff Garrett, Monroe and Sam still walking into the room. They stopped short and spun around.

The women looked at each other and shrugged, following them out.

Ms. Greenfield and I stood at the same time, her eyes locking with mine.

She smiled.

I waved.

In the lobby we joined the growing crowd working their way out to the covered porch.

Professor Taylor, Rod Sanchez, and Noel McDougall sat on the steps, smoking.

Anderson went over to Taylor's group.

"Mr. Taylor," Anderson called out, arms open.

Taylor and Sanchez stood while Mr. McDougall watched from the steps.

"Mr. Anderson. I see you and your council have come to a decision."

"Yes, we have, Mr. Taylor."

"Well, Mr. Anderson, we are certainly interested in hearing you out."

Anderson cleared his throat.

Just as he opened his mouth to speak, the Tewilliger Twins and the kids joined the rest of the women.

Sebastian came out and joined me.

"Mr. Taylor," Anderson said, giving us a stern look, "we can offer you a few boxes of canned goods and non-perishables, as well as fifty gallons of gas."

"We appreciate all that you can spare, sir."

"But those supplies are contingent on one thing."

"What's that, sir?"

"Sheriff Garrett wants to ask the children if they would like to stay on the island."

The Twins stretched their arms around the kids. The children were oblivious to the conversation, poking at each other through Mark and Michael's arms.

Mr. Sanchez stormed up the steps, bumping Taylor. Standing toe to toe with Anderson, Sanchez jabbed a finger into the councilman's massive chest. Garrett moved forward but I grabbed his arm.

"How dare you?" Sanchez spat in the councilman's face. "Either give us the supplies or not! Don't give us ultimatums, hanging gas and food in our faces! Fifty gallons of gas? Look at that tanker across the square, Taylor. This is a joke!"

Anderson studied Sanchez with his deep brown, almost black, eyes.

"Mr. Sanchez," he responded without bothering to remove the prodding finger from his chest. "I understand that you rescued these children from certain death. Regardless, these kids are still orphans and should have a say in their future."

Anderson then took a step forward, bending Sanchez's finger back.

"And for the record," Anderson continued, glancing at Taylor, "I said that the Sheriff should be able to speak to the kids. Garrett will ask his question. Whatever decision is reached, all will abide."

"This is bullshit, Taylor!"

Taylor came to Sanchez's side.

Garrett made another move forward.

I let him go.

Taylor gently placed a hand over Sanchez's prodding fingers, guided them away and pushed him back a step.

"Mr. Anderson," the Professor said. "As you can see, Mr. Sanchez is a passionate man, protective of his family and friends. As soon as we found the children, we fell in love with them."

"Professor Taylor," Garrett spoke up. "We understand your position and feel the same way. In an effort to ease our minds as to their welfare we just want to speak to them. Your group is welcome to sit in."

"I accept your terms," Taylor replied, extending his hand.

"Still bullshit, Prof!"

Professor Taylor stood between Sanchez and the councilman.

"Now is not the time for your pride or your tongue, Rodrigo. Put a cap in it and focus your energies on your wife and where to put the supplies that these generous people have offered us."

Sanchez glared back at the Professor.

"Let it go. Now."

Sanchez stormed down the steps. Mr. McDougall reached for him but Sanchez slapped his hand away.

"Rod!" Petra called after her husband.

He did not slow down.

Anderson puffed out his chest.

"Taylor. Deputy Reynolds will bring the supplies to the barricade. In the meanwhile, Sheriff Garrett will meet the kids in my office."

"I am sure we all want to be there," Professor Taylor replied through thin lips.

"Sounds good." Anderson turned back to the doors. "Noon, if you please."

38

Unexpected Answers

+11 Days – 1155 hours

Anderson sat behind his massive oak desk, his fingers intertwined on the pristine desk blotter. The surface of his desk lay barren, save a gold engraved plaque with his name on it in capital letters.

A nickel-plated .44 Magnum revolver stood in profile under a glass case on the credenza behind him.

I moved to my right.

The barrel lined up with the side of Anderson's head.

Ms. Greenfield and Sam sat on a sectional couch.

Sheriff Garrett leaned against one of the visitor chairs.

He glanced at his watch.

I did the same.

1156 hours.

Anderson stared at the open door.

Thirty seconds later a line of youngsters paraded in, followed by Deputy Reynolds and the adults from Professor Taylor's group. The children talked among themselves, pushing and prodding, making faces and giggling.

Ms. Greenfield stood up from the couch and motioned for Petra to sit down. Everyone found a place to sit or stand. Sanchez remained at the doorway, arms folded. Deputy Reynolds positioned himself next to the windows, his work done for the moment.

Anderson cleared his throat.

Taylor faced the kids. He clapped his hands together three times. The kids quieted down, looking at the Professor for instruction.

"Thanks, boys and girls!" Taylor beamed. "Sheriff Garrett here is going to ask you a question. Please give him your attention. Ok?"

The kids answered 'ok' almost in unison.

"Take it away, Sheriff."

"Thanks, Professor." Garrett sat down, his elbows on his knees. "Hey, guys. We know you have been on the road a little bit. We were wondering if you wanted to stay on the island here with us."

The kids exchanged looks. Petra held a hand to her mouth, her eyes shiny. Sarah and Margie smiled back at the kids, the women's eyes also wet. Even Mr. McDougal looked sad. Mr. Sanchez's stare, though, drilled holes through Anderson's forehead.

The oldest looking of the boys raised his hand.

"Yes, Jacob?" Taylor asked.

"Do we have to stay?"

"Of course not," Garrett replied. "You are welcome to stay here or to go with the Professor when they head out tomorrow."

"As I said, Jacob," Taylor offered, "the choice is yours."

"I want to go with you, Professor, but what about my parents?"

"I know you want to find your parents, Jake," Taylor replied with a sigh. "Once we make it to Atlanta, we can decide where to go next."

"Yeah, but my mom and dad's house is back the way we came, not in Atlanta. We could be at my house in a day!"

Another boy of about thirteen years of age, Donovan, spoke up. "Yeah, my mom is probably worried sick!"

"I want my mommy!" one of the little girls cried out. "I want my mommy!"

Sarah slid off the couch and knelt down to hug and rock the little girl.

"It's okay, Jessica."

Jessica continued to whimper.

The rest of the children's moods soured with Jessica's outburst. A little blonde boy began a hitch at the back of his throat, his lower lip pouting as he held his stuffed lamb tight in the crook of his arm. Sarah swept the little boy into her free arm, holding both children tight.

"It's okay, Kevin," Sarah said.

"Listen kids," Sam interjected. "It'll be alright. It'll be okay."

Sam stood with a crack of his knees and a grimace, digging his hands into his front pocket. With a mock surprised smile and wide-eyed expression, he pulled out a Susan B. Anthony dollar and held it up between his gnarled arthritic index and middle fingers.

"Do any of you kids like magic? Huh? Do ya?"

The kids looked at the old man and the coin, mildly interested.

"Looks like you do!"

Sam ran the shiny dollar across his tops of his knuckles from the index finger to the pinky. The coin disappeared into his palm by way of his thumb to reemerge at the index finger again for another pass across the knuckles.

"Whatcha seeing here, now, is not magic." Sam said. "This is just practice, practice, practice."

Jessica and Kevin stared at the coin.

"Now, the real magic doesn't come from the coin. It comes from you. Watch as I throw the coin up and it disappears!"

Sam palmed the coin into his closed fist and thrust his arm upward, opening his fingers as if to let a captured bird fly away. I swore I saw a glint of silver.

Everyone looked to where the coin should have landed, expecting to see the silver dollar in the deep dark carpet.

"As I said," Sam finished, kneeling over to Kevin's lamb to pull the coin out from under its stuffed ear, "the real magic is not in the coin. It's in you!"

The little kids cheered.

Sarah mouthed a 'thank you' to Sam.

"Now kids," Sam said, "the Sheriff has asked if any of you want to stay. Go ahead and talk it over with the Professor and your friends. Whatever decisions you make will be the right one. Jacob, I cannot promise that we will be in a position to find your family. Or any of your families."

The kids looked at Sam without a word.

"Now, why don't you all go and see what supplies the Professor and the others managed to get rustled up for you!"

The twins, Sarah and Margie led the children out the office.

Jacob and Donovan started their discussion.

'What do you think we should do, Jake?"

"Don't know yet."

Kevin talked to Jessica in a hushed tone.

"Did you see, Jess? How do you think the coin got under lamby's ear?"

The Sheriff stood up and faced Professor Taylor.

"I guess we blew that discussion, Professor."

"You did fine. I am glad Jacob voiced his concerns. We will speak with them and see where their heads are. I assure you that if any wish to stay with you, I surely support a stable and safe environment more than a dangerous nomadic life."

They shook hands, after which Taylor turned to leave.

McDougall followed Taylor out.

Sanchez locked eyes with mine for a moment before he disappeared.

39

Send Off

+12 Days – 0600 hours

Sheriff Garrett, Deputy Reynolds and Foster Anderson stood at the Searing Bridge. Taylor's group walked up to the shield of cars, the children in the center of their processional. Five boxes of food sat on top of the Buick. Ten five-gallon gasoline containers stood lined up on the curb.

Sheriff Garrett and Professor Taylor spoke to each other for a minute and shook hands before Garrett waved up at me.

Six FRACs wandered on the crest of the bridge, moving toward the barricade.

I lined up a shot with the closest walker, a stringy haired teenaged boy with a Ramones T-shirt. A bullet to the temple drove it momentarily to its knees before it crashed onto its face.

After the onslaught two days ago, Sheriff Garrett asked Pete for a suppressor for the M4. The can muffled the flash and the report, reducing both to a simple *phiff* sound.

Two more trigger pulls sent more walkers slumping to the pavement next to the RV. Some of the second walker's gore splattered on the side of it.

A tan woman with blonde hair, matted down by mud and rain, stood at the bridge's railing looking out into the Atlantic. When the third walker thudded into the RV, she craned her neck toward the convoy. Mascara ran down her face into a gaping hole in her right cheek. Another *phiff* and the hole widened to include the cheekbone. The cloudy eyes rolled back and she slumped over the rail.

I pivoted the rifle to track the last FRAC.

Surprisingly, the FRAC had limped off onto Route 5. It wandered down the road, disappearing around the bend.

Reaching for the radio on the windowsill, I squawked the Talk button three times. Two squawks came back and Garrett waved at me.

Mr. Sanchez and the twins hopped up on the trunk of one of the cars, crinkling the metal as they walked across. Mr. McDougall and Professor Taylor helped Sarah and Margie up, with Mike and Mark assisting them on the other side.

Four of the kids came next.

McDougall lifted them up one at a time.

Petra approached Sheriff Garrett, spoke a few soft words and gave him a hug. He patted her on her back. She put her fingertips on the sheriff's badge before walking over to the barricade. Mr. McDougall scooped her up and planted her feet on the trunk of the sedan. She steadied herself, moved with care across the car and let her husband and the Twins help her down.

Sarah and Margie led the children to their vehicles.

The twins grabbed what supplies they could carry.

Sanchez put a hand around his wife's waist and led her toward the Winnebago.

Jacob left Donovan and scrambled over the barricade, beating everyone to the RV and disappearing inside. A moment later he popped back out with a tan leather satchel.

He threw his arms around Margie and hugged her tight. She kissed him on the top of the head and rocked him back and forth.

The smaller kids high-fived Jacob as he worked through the crowd. He stepped up to Petra and touched her jutting belly. She placed a hand over his. Jacob smiled, withdrew his hand, and trotted back to the barricade.

Jacob bound over the cars to rejoin Donovan. He put his friend in a lighthearted headlock and dragged him toward Town Hall.

The supplies were loaded and everyone disappeared into their vehicles.

Engines came to life.

The flatbed and station wagon turned toward the Main.

The RV followed last, triple-tapping its brake lights as a final good-bye.

40

Pour Some Sugar

+13 Days − 0915 hours

Sam stirred and stared at his coffee.

He waved his hand at an empty seat in invitation.

"Yeah. Sit. Jorge is under the weather anyway."

Sam inspected me with his dark eyes.

"Working today, John?"

I nodded.

"I like you, John. You know when to keep your mouth shut."

Sam chuckled a little bit at his own joke.

He leaned over his coffee cup and waited until I leaned in before he spoke again.

"Everyone's carrying on about Taylor and his people," He said, looking around at the other patrons. "It's like they got nothing better to talk about. They should worry more about the goings-on here on the island.

"Do you think we're going to be waist deep in coffee beans a week from now?" He raised his coffee mug. "Foster is looking into rationing like it's World War Two. But he's thinking about it all wrong."

"During World War Two, we still had the milk man coming around and a newspaper slapping against our stoops. We may have gotten our summer season supplies before the outbreak, but that's not going to last. That Exxon truck is the best and only thing we have going for us."

Sam sipped his coffee, grimacing at the bitter taste before taking another drink.

"Foster thinks the government, the military or some goddamn agency is going to swoop in to save the day before we need to worry about food and gas… and heat once winter sets in. What a prick!"

I smiled.

"Yeah. I know you know Foster's a prick," Sam continued. "Let's hope Garrett and I can knock some sense into him. You would think that Professor Taylor's group would have made everyone realize the situation we're in."

He took another sip of coffee and wrinkled his nose. He reached for a sugar packet but eventually dropped his empty gnarled hand to his lap.

41

Torrential

+14 Days – 2310 hours

"...demanding foodstuff rationing based on what each resident contributes." Patrick readjusted his sniper position and continued his monologue. "And Monroe just agreeing with him, all the while tapping that damned leg. I have to say, Garrett really has stepped up his game, though. He's been holding his own."

Patrick chuckled, sounding like his grandfather.

Swirls of ashen charcoal clouds raced across the treetops on the Main. Beneath them, the shadows shimmered with the fall of heavy rain. Lightning flicked down, followed by loud crackles and low rumbles. To the northwest, the white glow of lights from a small town winked out, replaced with a slow spread of flickering yellow.

"We're definitely in for it, John."

Eight FRACs wandered the Stretch, stopping with each clap of thunder. With every boom they stood slack jawed, craning their necks and starting up in low guttural moans.

"What are they doing down there?"

The FRACs shuffled closer together. Their moans grew louder and more harmonious, making my skin crawl.

A curtain of rain raced across the bridge. When it hit the FRACs, their sounds intensified before reducing to whimpers as the rain bore down on them.

"I hope someone got the rain barrels ready. Doctor Rawlings can test the water to his heart's content once we get the barrels filled. As long as the Doc proves that there are no new FRAC contagions in the water, I'll drink it.

"John. Looks like the party is breaking up."

The rain slowed.

The FRACs loosened up to wander around again.
To the northwest, the yellow flickers had already died.

42

Four Bits

+15 Days – 0830 hours

I stopped for some coffee.

Carol poured the bitter brew.

The sugar pack container was empty.

"Sorry, hun. We're rationing."

Sam's predictions had been right.

Lifting the cup, I shuttered at the bitter taste but drained the coffee in four gulps. As I dug into my pocket for change Carol came back.

"No need to pay, dear. Money has been suspended, too. Foster said we should pool our money in a central location until all of this blows over."

I shook my head and slapped fifty cents on the countertop.

Carol smiled at my defiance.

Anderson walked in just then, beads of perspiration on his brow. He spotted the two quarters.

"John, I'm sure Carol told you that we need to pool our money."

"I did tell him, Foster."

Sliding the change off the counter, I swept it into my fist. I turned to Carol, pulled up her hand by the wrist, and put the money in it.

Giving her a wink I adjusted my weapon and left.

"Not too bright are y–?" Foster called after me as the door closed.

In these moments, I wish I still had the power of speech.

43

Ooh-Rah

+15 Days – 1732 hours

I lay down in the former sheriff's bed. In the Corp, one learned to grab rack time as often as possible. This time I drifted off to sleep in a few moments…

… where a thin pale man with a black suit stood in the corner, smiling.

Heart monitor beeped, slowing.

Masked forms blurred into olive drab background.

The gaunt man in the suit smiled wider, stepping between the gurneys.

Beep. Beep. Beep.

He reached out.

Beep.

Lips pulled back. Razor sharp teeth.

Beep.

I screamed. But didn't.

Beep.

He bent over me.

Beep.

"Marine, you and your spotter have served your country well."

Beep.

"This will hurt quite a bit."

Beep.

He pulled out a long black needle.

Beep.

And plunged it into my neck…

… shooting me awake and upright, drenched in sweat with a scream paralyzed behind my frozen vocal cords.

A cool late afternoon breeze blew through the window, the light, gauzy curtains swaying. I flopped back to the mattress, the sheet under me cold and wet.

I got up, padded naked through the house and out to the deck, ending up on the rail of the gazebo.

The sun warmed me.

Closing my eyes, I flipped backward off into the beckoning and forgiving Atlantic.

44

Special Delivery

+15 Days – 2330 hours

Night came.

Another tour in the tower began.

The air carried a salty residue; the crashing of waves keeping me company.

At 2354 hours the rhythm of the ebb and flow of the Atlantic was replaced with a far off rumbling. A flood of light washed the tree line as a car came into view.

It roared onto the bridge.

The station wagon jumped the sidewalk curb and bounced off the concrete railing. Shattering a headlight and crumbling a bumper, the vehicle careened across the blacktop. Its wheels skidded. The vehicle corrected and aimed toward the barricade. One remaining headlamp pierced the darkness.

I grabbed the radio and pressed the squelch button three times.

Hopefully, someone in the sheriff's office had his or her ears on.

Slinging the rifle, I clipped the radio and ran to the trapdoor. I slid down the ladder and ran down two steps at a time to the nave. Left of the altar I slammed into the side exit door, hitting the cool air just as I heard the collision of the station wagon into the barricade.

I swung the rifle around to a firing position as I approached the cars.

Leaping up onto the trunk of the Buick, I dropped to one knee and peered through the belching smoke of the broken radiator to the station wagon's interior. I slid across the barricade, keeping the rifle's sights on the driver's seat.

The driver was slumped against the steering wheel.

157

A scream came from the back seat.

I moved to the back door and grabbed the handle.

The damage to the side of the car was substantial.

Another scream. Louder.

I strained against the pinned door before ripping it completely away from the frame.

Petra Sanchez sat curled up behind the driver seat in a pool of her own fluids, her dress torn and drenched. Her hands held her belly as she grit her teeth.

Sirens got louder.

My military training had not prepared me for this.

45

Hard Labor

+16 Days – 0010 hours

Deputy Reynolds gunned the cruiser through the Tunnel, lighting up the trees under the canopy of leaves and arching branches. Its tires splashed around the soft gravel corners.

The sirens were off but Petra's cries filled the silence.

She lay across the back seat between my legs, digging her fingernails into me.

Rod Sanchez was strapped in the front passenger seat, fresh blood trickling from his forehead.

We raced down into the Presidency.

Reynolds braked hard and swerved left onto Madison Street, squealing to a stop in front of Doctor Rawlings' house.

I leaned my shoulder into the back seat divider and braced Petra from smashing forward. Sanchez, in the first seat, surged against his seatbelt, his arms flailing forward and rapping against the dashboard.

Reynolds got out.

Doctor Rawlings and Basia rolled a wheelchair around the car as the deputy opened the passenger door and pulled us out.

The three of them pulled Petra away from me and lifted her into the chair.

"Get her inside!" Rawlings ordered Basia.

Deputy Reynolds wheeled her up the driveway, Basia running ahead.

Rawlings and I hauled Sanchez out of the front seat, half-dragging him up the ramp and into Rawlings' home office.

"Take him to 2," Doctor Rawlings said.

"Going to call it in to Garrett." Deputy Reynolds passed us, running the other way. "Keep an eye on Sanchez!"

Screams continued from behind the other examination room door.

Rawlings ducked under Sanchez's arm and pressed him against me. He rushed into the other room, the cries more clear and sharp as the door opened.

I dragged Sanchez over to a chair where he slumped down, leaning against the examination table and wall.

I sat on a rolling chair.

"Push, Petra," Basia said, muffled but distinct from behind the wall.

"Bear down now." Doctor Rawlings' voice.

"Save my baby," Petra said in a hushed voice.

Another scream.

"Dinna wan to come back 'ere."

The blood had stopped gushing from the gash above Sanchez's hairline. His face had a puffy, bloated look. It did nothing to mask his contempt.

"Where's Petra?" Sanchez said, trying and failing to get up.

I blew out a sharp short whistle. He looked up, still trying to get his body back under control. I pointed to the wall behind him, the strains of childbirth louder.

Sanchez leaned the side of his face against the wall, running a finger against it.

"Never got close to Atlanta," he spoke again, more clearly. "No way to Atlanta. Never get to Atlanta."

I put my rifle against the wall, opting for a hand on my Glock.

"They're all dead, soldier boy. Left on the road to rot."

He stared along the edge of the wall.

"Kids should never have been on the road. That much you fuckers were right about. They were a liability all the way."

He dug his nails into the uneven painted surface.

"Traffic around Boston. Knew clear roads around here too good to be true. Ran into rags of a National Guard unit overrun by plaguers on the Hutch. Once the ammo ran out, the soldiers didn't stand a chance.

"Prof was stupid enough to get that RV jammed up. Backed right into Noel's truck, pinning them. I pulled Petra out and got her back to the station wagon before anyone realized that we needed to get out of there.

"By the time Prof gave up on the RV and had everyone scurrying up the parkway, they were in our rearview."

Sanchez continued to pick away at the paint, making a well-carved notch.

"Petra's water broke an hour this side of Boston. Stress, I guess."

He stared at me with hate, contradicting his monotone speech and the wall groove he was working on.

I crossed my arms, placing my hand closer to my weapon.

"Anarchy out there. Plaguers everywhere. Looting, fighting the dead and each other.

"They'll find you, you know." Sanchez looked at me with a grin. "You may think you have everything under control but eventually even this little island paradise of yours is going to be nothing but ash –"

The door slammed open.

Basia rushed in, her smock and hands covered in blood and sweat.

"John, we need another set of hands!"

I stood. With another look at Sanchez, I cold-cocked him, sending him back into semi-consciousness.

Grabbing the M4 I went to the other room. Screams and the sight of blood overwhelmed my senses.

"John, hold her down! Get behind her head!"

I placed the M4 on the counter and moved behind Petra, putting my arms around her shoulders. She bucked against me and dug her fingers into my forearms. Pressing her against the side of my face, the heat radiated from her skin.

"Petra, push hard!" Doctor Rawlings ordered. "Basia, open the saline!"

Petra clenched her teeth, dug her nails deeper, and let out a scream.

Rawlings and Basia exchanged looks.

The doctor shook his head.

I hugged Petra tighter.

Her skin burned hot against me.

"One more push, Petra! We're almost there! Just need to get the shoulders out! Push!" Doctor Rawlings yelled.

Petra's face turned red as she pushed, her eyes shut tight and her brow furrowed deeply.

"Good! Good! We got it!"

Basia rushed to Doctor Rawlings and took the baby in her arms. Rawlings clamped off the umbilical cord.

"Okay, Petra," Doctor Rawlings announced. "The baby is out."

"It's a girl!" Basia exclaimed.

"Is she okay?" Petra asked in a tired, weak whisper.

"She's fine. Keep pushing for me."

"Is she okay?" Petra asked again.

"She's fine," Doctor Rawlings repeated, moving back down between Petra's legs. "Give me one more push and we'll be done. Just need to clear the placenta."

"She has to be okay... she has to be okay..." She cried as she pushed again.

"There you go, Petra. You're all set. Great job."

Petra's grip weakened while her body blazed hotter.

I moved to her side, squeezing her hand.

She rolled her head toward me and gave me a thin smile.

I cleared stray hairs from her face.

"She's okay?" she asked again, barely audible.

I nodded.

Her smile expanded, but only a little.

Her breath came out ragged and light.

A single heavy tear disappeared into her hair, leaving a glistening trail. When the next tears streamed from her eyes, her grip softened and she gazed over my shoulder.

As the life left Petra's body, her infant girl cried as loud as her little lungs would allow.

46

Switched At Birth

+16 Days – 0130 hours

"She's gone, John," Doctor Rawlings said, giving me a pat. "Let me clean her up."

A sudden crash came from exam room 2.

I pulled my Glock and ran out of the room.

Basia lay on the floor in the hallway with her hands to her face. Blood gushed between her fingers onto her blue scrubs. An overturned supply cart partially pinned her legs.

Dr. Rawlings bumped past me, knelt down beside Basia and propped her up. He pulled her hand away from her face.

"The baby… Mr. Sanchez…," she muttered.

I ran out of the house and down the driveway.

Deputy Reynolds stood outside the cruiser. When he saw me with my gun drawn, he put a hand on his own sidearm.

"What's happening?"

"Sanchez assaulted Basia and took the baby," Dr. Rawlings said from behind me.

"He didn't come this way," the deputy replied. "I saw John as soon as he rounded the corner. He probably cut through the yards."

I ran back up the driveway into the backyard, the Glock's tactical light on.

A trampled path through the overgrown grass led to the side fence on the opposite side of the yard.

I leaped the fence, following the trail to the next yard, and hurdling to the last side yard before the road. The path continued. Jumping the white picket, I landed on the concrete sidewalk of Rainier Road.

Reynolds emerged from Madison Street, his weapon and penlight drawn.

"Nothing, John," he called.

Shit.

Sanchez was gone.

47

Chewing Out

+16 Days – 0738 hours

Sheriff Garrett shifted his glare between his deputy and me. Reynolds and I stood silently at attention.

"What the hell, John? Lincoln?" With a slow shake of his head, Sheriff Garrett threw both hands up in the air. "We let that asshole back on the island because his wife's in labor and he's bleeding all over. Now she's dead. He and the baby are holed up. I do not have the time, inclination, or damn manpower to deal with this shit!"

"We went door to door last night," Reynolds replied. "Everyone was bewildered as to why we were waking them up. Some were pretty pissed off."

Garrett looked at him.

"Did you account for everyone, Linc?"

"Sir?"

"The last thing we need is a hostage situation."

"Everyone seemed pretty surprised."

"Pull in everyone." Garrett said, pacing. "I want a search of every house in the Presidency. Start at Dr. Rawlings house and circle out block-by-block."

"Gotcha, Chief."

Reynolds jogged back to his cruiser. I turned to follow, but Garrett gripped my bicep.

"John, you're probably the most experienced person we have. Agree?"

I shrugged, but nodded.

"Find that baby girl."

48

Closer

+16 Days – 1130 hours

Deputy Reynolds stood by his cruiser with a two-way radio, directing four teams as they checked in.

"Team 3 here," crackled a voice. "Over."

"What do you got, Lucy? Over."

"Got a missing window pane in a back door. Not broken. Just missing. I see a flag on the meter. Sebastian thought he saw movement, but not one hundred percent positive. Over."

"Where are you? Over."

"We're looking at number 12 on Washington Street. Over"

Reynolds glanced over at me.

I gave him a thumbs-up gesture.

"Team 3. Make your way to Jefferson and Rainier. We're coming to you. Over."

"Roger that. Over and out."

After a minute of rechecking our weapons, Reynolds and I joined Team 3 already positioned at the corner next to a huge Hydrangea bush.

Ms. Greenfield squeezed me on the forearm as Reynolds and I took position next to her. She had her hair pulled back with a blue strip of thin fabric, but a few strays still fell across her tan face. She wore an almost too small gray and red Boston College T-shirt. A 15-round Glock 20 'Short Frame' was wedged in the back waistband of her jeans. She had swapped out the Sig.

Good choice.

Kneeling next to Ms. Greenfield, Sebastian tried to catch his breath.

"Sebastian thinks he heard crying. I didn't hear it," she said. "Sorry, Sebastian."

"I heard it. It was very faint, but I heard it," Sebastian said between pants.

"Okay," Reynolds replied. "John and I will check it out."

49

Breach

+16 Days – 1200 hours

I scanned 12 Washington Street from the second story rear bedroom window of 13 Jefferson Street. Deputy Reynolds stood in the doorway, the homeowner next to him in a floral housecoat.

The glass pane to the rear kitchen door at 12 Washington was indeed knocked out.

"Ready to go, John?"

I pulled away from the windowsill, giving the deputy an OK gesture. We moved out of the room, the elderly woman backing up.

"Would you boys like some sun tea?"

"No. Thank you, Mrs. Saunders."

Mrs. Saunders shuffled after us with one hand sliding along the wall for balance.

"It would be no problem, Lincoln. I put some of my Lipton teabags in a jug of water, and it's been sitting in the sun for about four hours now, " Mrs. Sanders confided. "It should be perfect now."

"We appreciate the offer," the deputy responded. "We may be back."

The homeowner beamed and Reynolds helped her down to the first floor.

"Thank you, dear."

"No problem, ma'am."

We moved to the front porch, leaving Mrs. Saunders behind the screen door.

"Thank you, Mrs. Saunders."

"Go get 'em, deputy. Don't forget my invitation."

"Yes, ma'am."

We joined Ms. Greenfield and Sebastian at the sidewalk.

"What's the verdict?" Ms. Greenfield asked.

"John will be going for a closer look. We'll hang back."

"Be careful, John," Ms. Greenfield said.

I patted my weapon and moved through Ms. Saunders' sideyard. Stopping at the back of the garage, I peeked around the corner to check for movement in the yard of 12 Washington Street.

Nothing.

I hopped the shared fence. Staying low, I moved to the concrete stoop leading to the back door. Pressing my back to the siding next to the stoop, I reached out and tried turning the doorknob.

It didn't budge.

I leaned forward to unlock the door through the missing windowpane.

In the distance a seagull screamed.

A warm breeze puffed across my face.

From somewhere in the house came the faint cries of a newborn.

50

Sweep and Clear

+16 Days – 1225 hours

Fifteen minutes later Ms. Greenfield and I stood at the same rear door of 12 Washington with our Glocks drawn.

Deputy Reynolds and Sebastian had planned to take cover position at the front of the house, taking a 'door buster' with them in case they needed to gain forceful entry.

I tapped the squelch button on the radio.

A moment later, a soft squelch came back.

Moving closer to the door, I quickly looked through the missing windowpane.

The kitchen and dining area were empty.

Reaching through I felt for the deadbolt and drew it back with a scrape and a soft click. Turning the inside knob, I pulled open the door. Ms. Greenfield braced her knee against it, keeping it from swinging shut.

I tapped the squelch button on the radio twice.

Reynolds responded with the same.

After flexing my grip on the Glock, I held my hand up and counted down… three…two…one.

Moving through the dining area, I checked the corners of the room and the adjoining kitchen. Ms. Greenfield stepped in behind me, tapping my shoulder. I moved forward and cleared the hallway. Ms. Greenfield went to the front door, unlocking the deadbolt and opening the door.

Deputy Reynolds entered and disappeared up the stairs. Sebastian followed, opening up the landing closet door and shoving his Beretta M9 inside. A few jacket sleeves lashed out at him as he withdrew his handgun, snagging on the front gun sight. Once untangled, he followed Reynolds upstairs.

I snapped my fingers at Ms. Greenfield.

She joined me at the basement door. I tested the doorknob, pointed to Ms. Greenfield then put a hand flat to the door. She wedged her left boot against it and pointed her sidearm down the hall after me.

I moved a few steps and used my boot to swing open the bathroom door. Stepping in, I pulled the shower curtain back with the gun.

The tub was empty.

I backed out and went to the end of the hall. In the smaller bedroom, I entered with the gun leading the way. The bi-fold doors were open, revealing an empty closet. Dropping to one knee, I lifted up the bed skirting with the Glock.

Again nothing.

The second bedroom was empty. A mattress and disassembled closet door leaned against the wall.

With the first floor cleared, I crossed back to the hallway.

Reynolds and Sebastian's footsteps thumped on the stairs.

I returned to Ms. Greenfield as Reynolds and Sebastian came around to the other side of her.

"Clear upstairs," Reynolds whispered.

Sebastian stood behind Reynolds, his Beretta pointed at the carpet. Flexing the fingers of his empty hand, he scanned the living room.

I pointed to the basement door and patted Lincoln on the chest. I then pointed to the others, waving for them to move back into the living room.

Reynolds nodded, and in a low voice, addressed the other two.

"Sebastian, keep an eye on the doors. Lucy, watch for us."

"Yeah," Sebastian said, his head on a swivel.

I flicked on the tactical light, shining the beam into my hand and adjusting my grip on the Glock. Reynolds opened the basement door. I started down the stairs and he followed with a hand on my shoulder.

At the landing, I flipped up the light switch.

The basement remained dark.

My tactical light bounced off the white painted concrete block wall.

Reynolds clicked on his own flashlight.

Moving left I let Reynolds step down to the landing behind me.

I pointed him to the right with the edge of my hand.

He patted me twice on the shoulder, his weapon and penlight coming up in a crossed-wrist Harries Hold.

Turning, I let the light and weapon point the way.

The basement was a repository of clutter. Haphazard aisles lined with papers, and filled cardboard boxes, cabinets, and shelving slowed my advance.

Sanchez!

Raising the light I put pressure on the trigger.

It was only a dressmaker's form.

No Sanchez.

No infant girl.

Reynolds' flashlight intermittently swept through the unfinished wall and original pipe work.

Backtracking, I returned to the stairs.

Sounds of breaking glass.

Reynolds' light doused.

I squeezed through a hanging rack of clothes, making out Rubbermaid containers stuffed under the stairs and a leather bag of old golf clubs. Quilts and clothes lay on top of taped up U-Haul boxes.

As I swung left something whistled, arcing downward from behind the boxes.

My wrist fell numb, my weapon skittering across the floor.

Another whistling sound preceded the weapon connecting with my left bicep. My arm went numb from the elbow to the fingertips.

I ducked in time to feel the next swish over my head.

The head of the golf club sparked off one of the iron support posts with a dull resonating *thuum*.

Something soft tripped me.

Reynolds' body?

Rolling off, I came up on one knee and reached for my holstered second weapon, the M-45. My numb fingers betrayed me, unable to draw the weapon.

A form loomed, a black silhouette surrounded by patches of light from one of the basement windows and the Glock's tactical light.

He held his weapon in one hand and cradled something in his other. His arm pulled back the pitching wedge and swung it forward.

I warded it off.

A series of thumps and clanks.

"Shit!"

Sanchez's weapon caught up between the joists and a run of black pipe. He tried to pull the club out with his free hand.

Before the golf wedge came loose, I barreled into his waist. We crashed into a stack of cardboard boxes, the pitching wedge left hanging from the ceiling.

"No!" he screamed.

Sanchez twisted and drove his fist into my jaw, dazing me.

He squirmed out from under me, grabbing my Glock from the floor. Pointing my weapon in my face, I stopped advancing.

"Keep the hell away from me," Sanchez warned. "Let us go."

I glanced at the still bundle in his arm.

Sanchez backed away.

I stayed on my knees with my palms up.

He backed up to the stairs, raising my weapon with his finger moving to the trigger.

A shot rang out, lighting up the space.

I cringed.

Sanchez twisted and cried out.

"On the ground, Sanchez!" Reynolds said as he stepped up next to me, smoke rising from the barrel of his weapon. "Put that gun down! Now!"

"John? Lincoln?" Ms. Greenfield called down.

"Stay put, Lucy! Both of you!" Reynolds responded as he moved forward.

Sanchez squared back up, a spot of red blossoming through his shirt by his shoulder and my Glock hanging limp in his hand.

He threw the bundle at Reynolds.

The deputy dove after it.

Hard, heavy steps raced up the stairs.

"Stop!" Ms. Greenfield screamed.

Two more gun shots.

Followed by the sound of breaking glass.

Another three shots fired.

"Lucy?" Reynolds called out.

I pulled myself up and went over to Reynolds.

He struggled to his feet, the bundle in his arms. Reynolds started unwrapping the blanket. I went to the stairs and looked up. The doorway was open and the hallway was clear.

"Sebastian is down! I need help!"

I ran up the stairs.

Several gunshot holes had materialized on the opposite wall since I had descended to the basement.

Ms. Greenfield knelt next to Sebastian.

"We need the doctor," she said into her radio. "Now!"

Sebastian was face down on a bloody patch on the living room carpet. I rushed to turn him over, his gun still tight in his grip.

He stared back up at me, taking ragged watery breaths.

Two red patches seeped high on his shoulder. A third bullet hole left a red, grazing line along the edge of his temple.

Sebastian closed a fist around a bit of my shirt to pull me closer. I pressed my free hand into the shoulder wounds.

"Did you get the girl?" he whispered.

I pressed my forehead to his.

Reynolds came up from the basement.

Ms. Greenfield looked over at the bundle in his hands.

"Lincoln has the baby, Sebastian," she said.

"Good." Sebastian responded. "Damn chest hurts."

"How's the girl, Linc?" Ms. Greenfield asked Reynolds.

Reynolds looked at the three of us, a sticky streak of blood flowing from a gash courtesy of the pitching wedge.

He shook his head.

Sebastian's gun hand moved to clutch his chest, leaving his Beretta on the carpet.

"Shit!" He clenched his teeth and moaned.

His body went rigid as he panted, spittle escaping his lips.

"John," Sebastian begged.

One grunt later and Sebastian relaxed.

His hand slid from his chest to the floor.

He breathed out, but didn't breathe in.

We started CPR.

Lucy watched my chest compressions and administered the two breaths.

I don't know how long we continued, but my arms ached and Lucy had started crying. Covering her mouth with one hand, she reached down and gently closed Sebastian's eyes.

I pulled my M-45 with my good hand and waited.

51

Open Wounds

+16 Days – 1723 hours

We regrouped in Doctor Rawlings' waiting room.
Reynolds sat with a bandage on his forehead.
I flexed my fingers under an ice pack.
Sheriff Garrett paced between us.

"According to Jackson, Mr. Sanchez booked across the Searing Bridge after sunset. Jackson said he took a couple shots but missed. Sanchez was bleeding pretty good from Linc's gunshot."

Reynolds opened his eyes and leaned forward.

"I hope a FRAC got him," he hissed.

"Jackson said that Sanchez shot a couple walkers on the way across," Garrett said, "but managed to get to the Main before they could gang up on him. I don't think we're going to see him again, Linc. His wife is dead. His daughter is dead. There's nothing that would bring him back to the island.

"Sorry about Sebastian, John. Can't believe he had a heart attack."

I should have realized the signs that Sebastian showed since arriving on the Island. All I could to is stare at his Beretta M9 in my good hand.

Dr. Rawlings came out from the examination area, Lucy and Basia behind him.

Rawlings stopped in front of Garrett.

Reynolds stood, grabbing the receptionist windowsill for support.

"What about the baby, Doc?" Garrett inquired.

"We found some red flannel fibers around the baby's mouth, leading me to believe that Mr. Sanchez had pressed the baby against his chest and suffocated her."

"Sorry I asked," Garrett responded.

Reynolds stared through the receptionist window, wiping his eye.

Lucy put one hand on my forearm and the other on the chemical ice pack.

My mind was on Sanchez.

If I ever saw him again I would kill him.

52

Congrats

+17 Days – 1015 hours

The search teams sat around the sheriff's office lobby.

I sat with Lucy, her arm wrapped through mine holding a fresh ice pack on my hand.

Deputy Reynolds and Sheriff Garrett stood outside his office, Reynolds waving his hands as he spoke. Garrett listened to him for a few minutes before stopping him.

The sheriff pulled Reynolds close and whispered something.

Reynolds nodded.

Garrett directed him into his office.

Pete was cleaning his rifle again. He dipped into his jacket pocket and pulled out the rifle's magazine. Satisfied that it was full, he clicked it into the rifle's stock.

"Hey, Chief! Don't forget about my reimbursements for the ammunition!"

"You'll get it when I get it, Pete."

"Yeah. Sure. Oh, and when you get a chance, I got something at the shop for you to look at."

"When I get a second."

"It's good stuff, Chief! Guaranteed!"

"I bet."

Garrett headed to some of the younger men.

Simon Russell and Kyle Foster were in the middle of retelling anyone within earshot their involvement in the search for Sanchez. When Garrett reached them, Kyle looked up and grinned.

"Hey, Sheriff!"

"Hey back, Kyle. I really appreciate what you boys did out there yesterday."

"Yeah, we really drove that sumabitch off, didn't we?"

"We sure did, Kyle. We sure did," Garrett said. "You gonna be on time for your shift tomorrow?"

"Only time will tell, Boss!"

Kyle returned to exaggerating his role in the previous day's events.

Garrett walked over to Felix, Diggs and Donny Matthews.

"Where do you think Sanchez will go, Diggs?"

"I don't know, Felix. There are plenty of houses on Route 5. Without a car, he's going to have a hard go. With the bullet hole, he's not got many options. What you think, Donny?"

"I figure Sanchez won't make it more than three miles," Donny said after some consideration. "The FRACs have thinned out a bit, but I can't imagine he's going to make it far if he's bleeding out."

Garrett made his own prediction.

"If we're lucky he'll collapse of blood loss by the time he reaches the gas station and end up face down on the asphalt as FRAC food."

"We can only hope, Chief!"

"Yeah, Donny. We can only hope."

Diggs slapped Donny on the back, nearly knocking him off his feet. Both laughed and started to wrestle. Felix watched them, shook his head, and returned to reading a paperback.

The sheriff walked over to the last search team.

Doug Chang and Rita Atwood cuddled on one of the benches. Joyce and Willard Richards sat next to them, fingers intertwined and Joyce resting her head on her husband's shoulder.

Garrett shook their hands and spoke to them.

When he turned to leave, Doug and Rita got to their feet. Rita whispered in his ear. Doug shook his head with a smile and turned back to grab his forgotten rifle.

The four of them headed to the entrance.

"See you guys later," Lucy called out. "Good job out there."

"Just wish we were able to get to them sooner," Doug said.

"Sorry about Sebastian, John."

"Thanks, Doug." Lucy squeezed my hand as she answered.

"Yeah. Doesn't make it right though," Willard chimed in.

"Nothing is right nowadays," Joyce added.

Joyce turned to push the door open but the handle jerked out of her hand. She recoiled, her hand snapping to the Sig Sauer at her belt. Willard's hand covered Joyce's, keeping her from drawing the weapon. He wrapped his other arm around her waist and pulled her back out of the entryway.

Foster Anderson walked in, Monroe Johnston following.

"Didn't mean for you to be startled, Mrs. Richards." Anderson flashed Joyce a politician's smile, not slowing as he passed her. "Sheriff!"

Anderson and Monroe walked straight toward Garrett and stopped. Monroe shifted from side to side, his fingernails between his teeth.

"What can I do for you, Foster?"

"Nothing, Jared. Just wanted to congratulate you and your teams for ridding the island of the pestilence that was Mr. Sanchez."

Anderson stuck out his hand.

Garrett hesitated then shot out his own.

"Thank you, Foster."

"Wish that deputy of yours had better aim, though."

"I did what I was trained to do, councilman." Reynolds said from Garrett's office.

"I'm sure you did, deputy. Just would have been nice to know for sure that the matter had been put to bed."

"It's not our job to kill people, councilman. Even if the world has gone to shit!"

"The world has gone to shit, Deputy Reynolds," Anderson replied, empathizing the *has*.

"Foster," Garrett said as he stepped closer to the councilman. "I commend Reynolds for how he handled himself. It may be a brave new world, but I'll be damned if I'll let that be an excuse to toss aside the law. I'm not going to change just because the environment has. Have a good day, councilman."

"Come on Reynolds." Garrett went into his office. "Close the door."

Reynolds did as he was told, never taking his eyes off of Anderson until the closing door broke his line of sight.

Anderson continued with his politician's smile, turning to face the rest of us.

"Thanks to everyone who helped to root out Mr. Sanchez." Anderson held out his arms in gratitude, straightened his shirt cuffs then brushed past Monroe who kept his head down and continued to bite on his fingernails.

Anderson approached the doors and stopped.

Willard opened it for him.

"Thank you, Willard," the Councilman said with a smile and walked through.

As the door began to hiss closed, Monroe hurried to slip through. Although the door didn't hit him in the ass, it did clip his hip.

53

Sparks

+17 Days – 1810 hours

The air felt heavy as the temperature dropped in the late afternoon.

In front of Erma's grocery store Donny and Diggs wrestled by Diggs' truck, hooting and hollering. Felix split off and walked toward the Mall. His collar was up and his hands were in his pockets.

Lucy had said something.

I turned toward her.

"I said, 'How's the hand?'"

I flexed and wriggled my fingers. No pain. Lucy received a thumbs-up from the attacked hand, proving it worked satisfactorily.

"Good."

She grabbed the arm with a strong grip and twisted it. It hurt a little, but I didn't let on.

"Good. Shows that you are a fast healer. That'll come in handy these days!"

She let go and glanced at her watch.

"Another couple of hours 'til night shift. I'm going to the diner."

I looked at my Cobra and realized how much of the day had slipped by. With three hours until my own shift I could still get in a couple hours of rack.

"Wanna come?"

I shook my head. I wasn't hungry.

Sebastian's Beretta weighed down my holster and his death weighed heavy in my mind.

Lucy frowned before putting on a strained smile.

"Okay. I'll see you later," she said as she started to walk away.
I grabbed and spun her around, her hands landing on my chest. She blinked once, tears running down her cheeks.

I finally saw the loss and desperation that she had hidden so well since being trapped on the island.

Leaning forward, I kissed her.

And kept kissing her.

54

Declaration

+17 Days – 1915 hours

After eating peanut butter sandwiches on homemade bread at the Oceanside, Lucy and I left together. She reached up on tiptoe to kiss me before breaking away for the sheriff's office. She looked back and waved. I waved back with my 'bad' hand, pointing at it with mock surprise.

Lucy laughed and faced forward in time to keep from stumbling off the curb. She shrugged, laughed again and pointed at the sheriff's office. This time, she waved without looking back.

I walked onto Mall Street, passing Gloria's soaped over bookstore. The islanders had been shocked that she had left without a word. Lucy had mentioned that Gloria had told her and Diggs that she was worried about her son at Boston College.

Across the street the light to Pete's Guns and Ammo Shop burned bright through the plate glass window, even through the stickers and signage.

I tried the door.

Locked.

I went to press the intercom.

Down the block Felix stumbled onto the sidewalk and reached out for the lamppost in front of The Irish Spirit. He bent over, retching with loud convulsive force. Once the spasm passed he leaned with the post nestled against his neck and shoulder.

I went over and put a hand on his back.

Felix looked up with bloodshot eyes. His skin was pale, even in the dim multi-colored glow of the bar's windows.

"Hey." Felix hugged the post tighter as he dropped to his knees. "This could've been avoided. The FRACs. They're my fault."

55

Find The Spirit

+17 Days – 2005 hours

We sat in silence in the last booth of The Irish Spirit.

Felix picked at the edges of the beer bottle's red, white and blue label, making a pile of shavings. We were down to drinking good ole American beer, the dark Guinness pints expiring a week ago.

Felix's eyes had dried up as he stared at the bottle, melancholy settling onto his thinning frame.

The candlelight wavered a warm cast on the oak paneled walls. Frank Long cleaned beer mugs behind the bar, standing in front of a stained glass mural entitled "Ireland Forever".

According to Sam, Foster Anderson had restricted electricity usage. Frank had negotiated to keep his refrigerators running instead of lights and a dishwasher.

Two other patrons were in the pub. Jorge sat in a booth reading Huxley's *Brave New World* and sipping a double shot of bourbon. Vincent Leone sat at the bar hunched over a beer.

Felix stopped scratching at the label and took a swig of beer.

"This is all because of me," he said with sharper, dryer eyes. "I knew when that little girl showed up it was too late. Strange to see it first hand."

Felix's eyes held no humor, wrinkles more apparent on his face.

"I had it all together, John." Felix returned to scratching the label. "It was all figured out. Every time I sat down to eat, I could see it coming together. I just needed a few more pieces. Just a few more pieces."

He trailed off and diverted his attention to the framed pictures on the wall.

"There's nothing to be done now," Felix said, perhaps finding comfort and strength in the pictures of past patrons. "I didn't have the courage to blow the whistle. Now it's too late. Maybe it was always too late."

I thought hard about where Felix worked. He wasn't affiliated with bio-weapons or pharmaceutical development that I knew of. White collar for sure, Felix struck me as more of a paper pusher.

Felix slid out of the booth.

"Thanks for listening, John. And for the helping hand outside." He smiled weakly and put his hand on my arm for a moment. "Have a good night."

56

Control

+18 Days – 1315 hours

I heard the arguing before I entered the sheriff's department.

Sheriff Garrett and Foster Anderson stood in the middle of the empty lobby.

I eased the lobby door closed behind me.

"… entire island is out of control, Jared. You're letting people get away with theft, indecency, and gods knows what else!" Anderson's chest puffed out as he spoke, although it was a losing battle to his massive gut. His thick index finger, complete with a diamond encrusted gold ring, stabbed the air at Garrett.

Garrett, his arms folded, stared at the councilman.

"People are scared. I am not going to arrest people for trying to scavenge food or for running naked into the Atlantic for a midnight swim," Garrett said. "After you come up with a realistic solution to our current situation, I'll start worrying about public nudity."

Anderson took one step closer.

Garrett's arms remained folded as Anderson's finger came dangerously close to poking him in the chest.

"You're here to uphold the law, Jared."

"And you're here to help make sure this island is safe. Do your job and I will make sure I do mine."

Another step by Anderson brought him to within a foot of the sheriff.

"You would do well to remember your place as a civil servant, Mr. Garrett."

"And you would do well to remember that nobody's buying your bullshit. You may want to come up with something else to sell. My suggestion would be for you to go back to your plush office and figure out how we're going to ride this out. You need a plan whether the United States military comes to call with tanks and choppers within a week to save the day, or whether we find ourselves on our own for good."

"Just make sure you have enough manpower to keep things secure, Sheriff." Anderson backed up two steps and cleared his throat. "The last thing we need is another undead invasion."

"I have all the men and women I need, Councilman," Garrett replied. "Thanks."

Anderson scoffed and turned, realizing I stood at the door.

I gave them each a two-finger salute.

Anderson huffed and started toward me.

I backed up and held the door open for the councilman.

He brushed past me and disappeared.

My two-finger salute became a solitary one as Anderson's wide back receded across the parking lot.

I let go of the door.

"Hey, John. Did you enjoy the show?"

I grinned.

"Bastard." He shook his head. "Oh, that goes for him, and you!"

Garrett laughed and walked back to his office.

"Come on in, John. I may have a couple things for you."

I followed him and waited for him to sit down before I plopped down in one of the visitor's chairs. The seat cushion exhaled, the air racing out of its many loosened seams.

"Keep those seats around in case of serious interrogating." Garrett sat back in his slightly better chair. "Glad I am on this side of the desk.

"After the episode with Sanchez, I started to wonder how far the Professor and the others could have gotten. You think that they're still out there?"

I thought a few seconds before shrugging.

Garrett tapped the desk blotter with the eraser end of a pencil.

"I see them on the side of the road, out of gas, out of hope. We should have tried harder to get them to stay. I can't stand to think of those kids out there."

I snatched the pencil out of his hand and grabbed a Post-It pad. I wrote a note and handed both back to Garrett.

He read it and put them on the center of the desk.

The pencil skittered away.

He stopped the pencil, rolled it back and hovered his hand above it until he was sure it wasn't going to roll away again.

"That's a little harsh, isn't it?"

I stared at the sheriff.

"Maybe Foster was right." Garrett leaned back and folded his arms. "Maybe I'm not cut out for this damned job."

He rubbed his shadowed jaw with what I suspected was sorrow and disappointment.

"I'm not Sheriff Wayne, that's for sure."

I took out Sebastian's Beretta M9 and ejected a round. I caught the bullet in the air and slapped the round down on top of the blotter next to the Post-It pad. The pencil started on another arcing path toward the end of the blotter.

Garrett wasn't quick enough to stop the pencil before it fell off the desk.

He stared at the bullet and the note, not speaking for a minute.

"I'm not going out the same way as Frank," Garrett said, a flit of anger racing across his eyes. "I know you're right, but it doesn't make it right."

Glancing down at the note, I grabbed the bullet and put it into the front pocket of my jeans.

Even upside down, the five words read clearly.

You can't control the world.

57

Close Calls

+18 Days – 1830 hours

The treetops burned gold as the sun dropped toward the horizon, drifting away to bear witness to the west.

Three FRACs wandered beyond the barricade.

I put a slim woman into my crosshairs from my perch in the church tower. Dried blood and mud smeared her white suit and her long flaxen blonde hair. She staggered around, her pantyhose dirty and torn, one of her heels broken off.

Deputy Reynolds and Diggs approached the barricade.

The FRACs craned their necks, snapping their teeth. They bumped into the front bumpers and reached across the hoods with raw and twitching fingers.

Besides the FRAC fashionista was an older man with cargo pants and a faded gray Polo shirt. Wisps of hair stuck straight out from his spotted head. His mouth was opened wide, devoid of teeth.

Next to him a tall burly mustached man in mechanics overalls and a hoop earring gurgled as he attempted to climb the barricade.

Diggs walked to the end of the line of cars with a four-foot crowbar in his hand and nodded to Reynolds.

The deputy rapped his gloved knuckles on the closest trunk.

Mechanic FRAC snapped its neck toward him, a sickening warble rising from its rotten throat. It tried to clamber over the hood, failing to get purchase.

Toothless Joe FRACson and the FRACtionista shambled over to the mechanic, bumping into each other and slapping their arms on the car as they tried to get to the deputy.

Diggs hoisted himself up onto the trunk of the car and stalked over its roof.

Reynolds took out his nightstick and started beating the trunk. The FRACs responded by slapping their hands on the hood. They snapped their teeth, except the old man who flapped his blackened gums. The FRACtionista dragged her ragged fingernails against the hood's paint.

Reynolds continued to pound away at the hood.

Diggs raised the crowbar and struck the curved end into the mechanic's crown. Gore sprayed up in a bloody V. The mechanic's features went slack, his arms dropping to his side.

Diggs yanked out the end of the crowbar, a clump of hair and a fragment of skull coming loose with it.

The mechanic dropped into the FRACtionista's knee, making her falter while she grabbed at Diggs' pant leg.

Diggs swung the crowbar across the FRACtionista's face.

Her head rocked sideways to her shoulder and stayed there. With her broken heel, buckling balance, and Diggs' strike, the FRACtionista knocked into the old man and sent them both careening to the pavement.

Diggs dropped onto the FRACtionista's chest and drove the straight end of the crowbar into her face, his right hand shaking from the vibrations from the strike through her skull into the hard asphalt. He pulled out the bar and stepped over to the tangled Toothless Joe struggling under the weight of his companion. Diggs swung the curved end of the crowbar into the old man's forehead, using both hands and all of his weight.

The handyman placed a work boot on the FRAC's cheek. Diggs pulled out the crowbar from the elder's head and tossed the tool on the car hood.

The deputy scrambled over the cars to join Diggs on the 'no man's land' side.

Diggs dragged both the FRACtionista and Toothless Joe to the sidewalk while the deputy used both hands to grab the mechanic's dirty collar.

All three were quickly lined up on the sidewalk.

They talked, Diggs pointing at the FRACs and tossing a thumb back over his shoulder toward the mainland. Reynolds stood with a hand on the butt of his holstered pistol.

You know they're all going to die, don't you?

I spun to the voice.

In the corner was a gaunt pale man wearing a black suit. He ran his long-fingered hand down the front of his shirt to smooth out his skinny black tie.

They aren't like you. And you are not like them.

I pulled the Beretta and put his heart center in the sights.

John.

The too-tall, too-thin man said, his extremely long fingers splayed out in a surrendering gesture.

I am wounded that you would be so callous towards me.

He made a clicking sound with his tongue, his lips pursed.

I save your life, and this is what I receive for my trouble.

He placed his hands behind him and paced across the room. As he walked his pupils widened, eclipsing his entire eye sockets.

Not very appreciative are you, John.

I followed his movement with the barrel of the pistol.

Let me prove how much I am in your corner.

He said as he drifted back and forth, air-quoting 'in your corner'.

Let me fill you in on a little situation.

I stared at the Gaunt Man.

He sighed and shrugged.

Oh well. You should know that your friends on the bridge are going to get company in a few seconds.

I cautioned a look over my shoulder.

There was actually movement on the bridge.

Shit!

Three farmhand FRACs shambled across the bridge.

They were ten meters away.

I glanced around for the walkie-talkie. It was nowhere to be found.

Shit!

The FRACs came closer.

Seven meters away!

I grabbed the M4 and sighted in on the lead FRAC. I exhaled slowly and squeezed the trigger.

The FRAC's head ruptured. The body dropped out of my sights and the second of the group came into view.

I lined up the shot and pressed against the trigger.

A dark blur swept into the sightline.

My trigger finger jumped to the guard.

I looked over the scope.

Diggs' crowbar stuck out of the second FRAC's skull.

I centered the crosshairs on the last FRAC's forehead as it groped for Diggs shoulder, but it dropped down out of the scope's view.

A pistol shot popped.

A wisp of smoke rose from the barrel of Reynolds' sidearm.

Diggs pulled the crowbar from the FRAC's skull.

"How 'bout we don't wait so long next time, John," Reynolds voice came through faintly. The walkie-talkie was sitting on top of the cooler.

The Gaunt Man was gone.

Reynolds looked up at me from the barricade and shrugged.

I rubbed my eyes before dragging a hand down my face.

Exhaling sharply, I looked out at the bridge.

Diggs and Reynolds dragged the additional corpses to the curb, returning to their conversation.

58

Through the Tunnel

+18 Days – 2200 hours

Shadows danced under the flickering street lamps.

As I crossed the plaza to Mall Street the lights brightened then winked out. 10pm sharp, like clockwork.

Now shrouded in darkness, I could just make out the soaped over shop windows of Gloria's store. I passed her shop and the others on the street, making my way to Rainier Road and its surrounding open fields.

The moon hung bright and high, the sounds of crashing waves coming from both sides of this narrower stretch of island. A half-mile later, the fields widened significantly but became choked with low brush and pines. Soon, the road became overgrown with a thick canopy of overlapping pine branches, providing a natural low ceiling that the moonlight could not penetrate.

I entered the Tunnel.

My eyes adjusted but it was still near pitch black under the canopy.

Halfway through, a twig snapped.

A rustling followed.

Something dragged across gravel.

I stopped and drew Sebastian's Beretta from under my windbreaker, a round already in the breach.

Lovely evening, isn't it?

The Gaunt Man stood in the middle of the road with his hands behind his back. He unnaturally illuminated the road. He smiled, revealing jagged teeth, his tongue flicking in and out between them.

He coiled and lunged at me.

I fired twice at his chest.

He was gone.

As if he had been nothing more than wisps of black oily smoke.

New shadowed movement came from the right side of the road, followed by a low mewing sound.

I pointed the Beretta at the middle of the form.

The shape also lunged toward me, letting loose a guttural growl.

I flicked on the weapon's tactical light, shining up the charging FRAC.

Its arms came up and it slowed its pace.

I squeezed the trigger.

The light and the first muzzle flash showed the aftermath of the bullet as it blew out what remained of its left eye, spraying a thin mist of fluid and matter out the back of its skull.

Another muzzle flash sent another bullet racing out, shattering the ridge of the FRAC's nose and expelling more matter out through the moist gaping hole that the first bullet had created.

Falling backwards with its arms flailing, the walker crashed into the gravel.

I stood quiet – waiting, watching and listening for more FRACs.

After several minutes I turned the tach light on and approached the corpse.

It was a middle-aged man. Its clothes were intact and its skin had a gray pallor. He was bruised from a beating but not too badly decomposed.

The defenses must have broken down.

Nothing could be done until daybreak.

I continued to the Shack.

59

A Meeting of the Minds

+19 Days – 0718 hours

The FRAC looked worse in the pale morning light. Two bullets to the face did nothing to help its bruised, emaciated appearance. Dirty, bloody and dead, it still gave off an aura of something dangerous.

Sheriff Garrett and Doc Rawlings stood over it, talking.

Rawlings lowered to one knobby knee and bent over the remains, his long black hair falling across his eyes. He absently pushed the locks behind his ears with a gloved finger as he looked at the body. The doctor sighed and moved a hand down to the FRAC's chest, pressing against its abdomen under the rib cage. Pulling out a coroner's thermometer, the doctor opened up the man's shirt and pierced into the soft slate-colored skin into the liver. A faint putrid odor followed the squishing sound. The doctor waited a minute then checked the thermometer gauge. Once satisfied, he pulled the instrument out.

Diggs and I stood to the side, watching the examination.

Rawlings stood, knees popping. He removed the gloves, put them in a large plastic bag and put it in his jacket pocket.

"Diggs can dispose of it if you do not have any objections, Sheriff," Rawlings stated.

"Is it post-event, Doc?" Garrett asked.

"The abdomen is putrefied. No organ definition. Even though it looks recently turned, I would guess its skin tone is an anomaly."

"Okay, Doc. I'll take that as a yes. Go ahead, Diggs. I don't need the body."

"No worries, Chief. I'll get right on it." Diggs turned to me with a big toothy smile and slapped me on the shoulder. "Great shootin', John."

I smiled back.

Diggs walked down the road to his pickup.

The rest of us walked toward town.

Rawlings mounted a bicycle he had left leaning against a tree. With a quick salute he pedaled away.

"Smart man, that one," Garrett commented, quickening his pace. "I guess we had better run a perimeter sweep. Something has obviously changed."

60

A Three-Hour Tour

+19 Days – 0915 hours

I sat on a fully fueled Suzuki dirt bike in the municipal parking lot.

Pressing the clutch lever, I turned on the ignition, engaged the shifter to first gear, feathered the throttle, and slowly released the clutch. The bike surged forward unexpectedly but I quickly tuned into the bike's rhythm.

I puttered down North Plaza Street and through Mall Street before I opened up the bike's throttle on Rainier Road's Tunnel. I wound my way east to the service access road to the Norte Bridge.

At the crest of the road I turned off the bike and grabbed a sniper scope from my pocket. The chain link fence on the Main looked secure. A trio of undead wandered around Route 5, but I did not see any perimeter breach points.

I headed east past the Presidency.

As the road curved toward the southern shoreline, I stopped again. Two beachfront McMansions stood quiet, the sandy beaches around them empty and undisturbed. On a curl of the shoreline, Sheriff Wayne's shack sat isolated on the eastern most tailings of the beach. A hooking breakwater invaded the ocean for two hundred meters. The waves crashed into it, leaving the waters under the pier and gazebo calmer.

Opening up the throttle again, I rode along the shoreline road.

In this more barren section of the island, two parcels of farmland sprung up. At the entrance of the first farm two large posts guarded the path beyond. An arched sign connected between them with the etched out but faded letters welcoming guests to 'Dickerson Farms'.

Riding past a half-mile of split rail fencing, I came to the entrance to the second farm. Fencing flanked a straight asphalt road. A goat chewed on the high grass growing up along one of the posts. He looked up and bleated before returning to graze.

Three miles later the end of the island and the fierce gray Atlantic loomed. The road curved to the north as the island narrowed and hooked to a point. A couple of tiny islands peppered the coast, barely more than sand bars during high tides. One outcropping of rocks and two seagulls constituted the largest mass apart from the island proper.

On roughly two and a half acres of barren rock, Lighters' Point Island sat thirty meters north from the island's curl. A wood walkway bridge served as its umbilical to the island. One of Garrett's armed men stared down at me from the rail walk of the Casper Lighthouse.

He gave me a tip of his Red Sox ball cap.

I acknowledged with a wave.

Returning to the bike I traveled north on an asphalt road that soon turned into a gravel and dirt road named Eastern Shore Drive. It hugged the empty northern coast for a few miles before reuniting with Rainier Road at the narrowest point of the island – the Neck. Cooler salty air swept across my face.

Soon Western Shore Drive appeared as a slight fork off of Rainier Road. It was a gravel and dirt road like its eastern brother, running better than three miles.

The view of the dull mindless Atlantic gave way to the jagged forested shoreline of the mainland north of the island. Land loomed closer as the road merged back into Rainier Road between the Presidency and the Norte Bridge.

I raced through the Tunnel and back into the center of town, finishing where I started.

Lucy stood at the head of the parking lot space with her hands on her full hips and an impish smile tugging at the corners of her lips.

From the look of things I had traded one three-hour tour for another.

61

Love Shack, Baby!

+19 Days – 1635 hours

I leaned on the deck's rail and let the breezes dry the sweat off me. Lucy padded barefoot behind me and wrapped her arms around my waist, pressing her bare breasts against me. She sighed, her right leg wrapping around mine. Her hug quickly evolved into kisses on my back, her hands running along my stomach. Her hands still around me, I turned and stared into her dark eyes.

I kissed her full on the mouth.

In spite of the last few hours we had spent at the Shack, my mind was occupied elsewhere. Lucy had helped to distract me and I showed her my appreciation – twice. She was intelligent and intuitive enough to not press me on other business.

I gave her a squeeze on the bottom, a peck on the forehead and left her standing naked on the deck.

"I'm going to stay out here for a while, John."

I nodded then went inside.

Holly the fluffy squat-legged dog with floppy ears and a punched up face – self-proclaimed hero of the canine assault at the Searing Bridge – snorted and hopped up to pad along side me.

62

Cleanliness is next to Godliness

+19 Days – 1713 hours

I heard water splashing in the shower.

The solar panels on the roof were a blessing for hot water – even if only for a few minutes at a time.

Her form silhouetted through the shower curtain.

I picked up my T-shirt from the bathroom floor and put it on.

Holly eyeballed me from the bath mat, her tongue hanging out the side of her mouth.

Grabbing the shoulder holster with the Beretta, I shrugged it on and put my windbreaker over it.

I returned to the bedroom and removed the Beretta from the holster. I took one last moment to honor the memory of my fallen friend before putting his weapon in the top drawer of the dresser.

So long, Sebastian.

Next to it on a pile of T-shirts was my remaining weapon, the M-45.

I gripped its comfortable heft and put it back in the holster where it belonged.

Hello, old friend. It wasn't the Glock but it was a trusted companion.

I left the bedroom and made my way to the living room.

The squeak of shower faucets announced that Lucy was finished.

Lucy wouldn't be surprised that I left without saying goodbye, no pun intended.

She understood.

Nor would she be concerned for her safety, especially with a sawed-off shotgun on top of the toilet tank. Plus, she had the ever vigilant Holly standing guard, too.

I walked outside and straddled the bike parked next to Lucy's Pinto, turning over the ignition. With a few revs, I was soon roaring up Rainier Road to the scene of the crime.

63

Scene of the Crime

+19 Days – 1730 hours

The body was gone.

Diggs had disposed of the FRAC as instructed.

I walked over to the bloody gully the walker had occupied. Taking a knee I looked at the red flecks on the trees and the heavy drops in the gravel.

Closing my eyes I replayed last night's encounter in slow motion. I started with the noise it made on the dried and fallen twigs and ended with the bullets through its brain.

How did the FRAC get onto the island?

I didn't find any incursion points during the perimeter check. The Searing Bridge had not been breached. Norte Bridge's barricade and fence line were undisturbed. No one had reported a new death. Doctor Rawlings had already determined the FRAC to be a well-preserved walker from the first days of the outbreak.

I stood and scanned the gravel.

Ten meters into the tree line were several snapped branches. On one of the low branches clung a swatch of blue cotton, matching what the FRAC had been wearing.

I moved between the trees.

A sloppy path of bent branches and stomped down grass trailed through the pines with a relatively straight sightline to the Presidency.

64

Beer and Cigarettes

+19 Days – 1800 hours

I puttered the dirt bike into the Presidency.

Turning down Madison Street I rode to a blue painted house. It was trimmed with white, all under a black-shingled roof. A wraparound screened-in porch set the house apart from others on the block. Only the porch steps and front door were not screened in. An old reel blade mower leaned against the porch rail, a file and a whetstone on the bottom step.

I went to the front door and knocked three times on the glass.

From inside came a fit of coughing.

"Patrick! Get the door!"

More coughing.

"Son of a bitch! Where is that boy?"

The sound of creaking boards followed.

The yellowing lace curtain darted open.

Sam peered out, a home-rolled cigarette dangling from his mouth. When he recognized me, his lips turning into a rubbery grin. The cigarette defied gravity, traveling up to the corner of his mouth.

"Well," he said, "here's another son of a bitch!"

He opened the door.

"Come on in, Johnny boy. Now I can talk to someone other than myself."

With a couple more coughs, he creaked over to his overstuffed La-Z-Boy.

I closed the door with a soft click and looked up the stairs.

Sam stared at me as he sat down in his well-worn chair.

"If you're wondering about Patrick, I guess he's out."

Sam puffed away, the lazy smoky haze circling around him. Four empty beer cans lay crushed at his feet.

Walking over to a high table, I picked up a framed picture of a younger Sam from his time in the Korean War.

"That one there is me at Outpost Harry, Iron Triangle, June 8th, 1953. That stupid soldier thought he had the world by the balls." He inhaled the last of the cigarette. "But there were dark days to come."

Sam's eyes glazed.

"Damn smoke. I'll have to quit these when I die."

He wiped his eyes with his sleeve.

"Yeah," he muttered, "dark days, indeed."

65

Korea – 1953, Outpost Harry
+19 Days – 1827 hours

Sam lit another cigarette from the butt of his previous one and continued to puff away, in spite of the surgeon general's warnings.

He watched the thick smoke drift to the ceiling before he spoke. "Yeah, we were already gettin' heavy mortar and artillery from the Chinese. Whistling and blasts every minute or two for the entire day. When we went out to fortify our positions, we had to worry about the shells... and snipers.

"Two days later the Reds attacked us outright. Outpost Harry was important. If they had gotten their hands on it, we would have had to retreat over six miles.

"We got over the fact that we were invincible quick.

"When night hit, so did the Chinese. We were outnumbered 10 to 1, defending the post with our rifles and napalm. But they kept coming. Once the fucks got into the trenches, we had to let our artillery rain down on them. But we didn't let those shells burrow. Made sure they exploded in the air. Let the concussive force turn them into jelly.

"We stayed in the bunkers.

"On the 18th the Chinese came at us one last time. More soldiers, more shelling. They got into the trenches 'round 0300. By first light the battle was over. The CPV withdrew with their tails between their ball-less sacks. Combat Ineffective is what the stars and bars called it. I call it a yellow strip over a red ass!"

"That's all official, Johnny." Sam peered at me through the smoke. "You can probably look up the history in the library. Don't think Emily would mind. I even got a Distinguished Unit Citation somewhere around here.

"What the history books don't tell you and what the Brass kept under wraps is what we are dealing with now is the same thing we were dealing with then."

Sam leaned in.

Smoke swirled past his bloodshot, yellow tinged eyes.

"That's the real story, my boy."

66

Korea – 1953, The True Iron Triangle

+19 Days – 1845 hours

Sam leaned back in his recliner.

"We found out why the Chinks took only some of their dead during the night. Soldiers two days dead started crawling into the trenches. Torn up and peeled away faces howling at us.

"Where we succeeded against the living, we failed against the dead. We were overrun. McCain, a Private from San Diego, stomped the butt of his M1 into the jaw of one of 'em, but it kept coming. And then bit him in the neck. Never heard screaming like that.

"We retreated to the bunkers, covering our escape with M3s. Their skin melted off. Their charred bodies stunk of burning flesh. The PFC operating the flamethrower didn't see the walker before it lunged on him. He spun around and lit up two soldiers with their own M3s. The tanks blew and incinerated all of them. The rest of us just made it to the bunker before the flames hit.

"Once the flames died out Private Hamilton opened up a .30 cal through the ports and ripped a bunch of them to shreds. But they kept coming and we ran out of ammunition. I shoved a bayonet into one of their chests. It stood there staring at me. Its jaw was hanging by a few shreds of skin and muscle. Then it dropped all by itself.

"By morning, the Brass came in with reinforcements. Mostly they came to debrief us. They bandaged up Private McCain and choppered him off post. I don't know what happened to him.

"We were sworn to secrecy by a four star general and a man in a dark suit. Threatened with loss of benefits, dishonorable discharges and a stay in a psych ward, we agreed. We knew that no one would believe us."

67

Sam Fades

+19 Days – 1840 hours

Sam returned to silence and what remained of his fourth cigarette. He took one last drag before stamping it out in the ashtray stand.

Tears streamed down his rough cheeks. He didn't bother to wipe them away.

The old man closed his reddened, tired eyes and breathed deeper.

I grabbed a quilt from the couch and covered his lap.

Going to the kitchen table, I grabbed a pencil and jotted down a message on a legal pad for Patrick.

Taking one last look at Sam, I went to the front door and opened it.

Doctor Rawlings stood with his fist in midair, a black satchel at his side.

"Hello, Mister Walken! I didn't realize you lived here. I was sure I had the right address. Is Mr. Sistern at home?"

I opened the door wider.

Doctor Rawlings peeked in.

"Well, I guess I will come back later."

He turned on his heels and stepped back out onto the porch. I closed the door behind me, only a click of the latch and a shaking of the glass to mark our departure.

68

A Short Walk

+19 Days – 1850 hours

We headed toward Rainier Road.

"A beautiful day, Mr. Walken," he said as he tapped his bag against his thigh.

He started to hum.

At the corner, I swung a leg over the bike and settled into the seat.

"Well, Mr. Walken. I am off."

Doctor Rawlings gave me a stiff, slight bow.

"Looks like we may get some rain," Dr. Rawlings said, looking at the sky.

I started the ignition.

"Oh, please be sure that Lucy come see me," he added. "She is still on my list."

He headed away from the darkening clouds, humming again.

69

Fly on the Wall

+19 Days – 1900 hours

The sheriff's station lobby was empty but not silent.

"I don't care!" Garrett yelled. "I don't like the idea of even one FRAC running loose."

A pause.

"What if John wasn't there?"

Another pause.

"Bullshit!"

I stopped at the door.

"We can't figure anything else out now. Diggs got rid of the body. Rawlings said it was an outbreak walker, anyway."

Another long pause then a bang of the receiver in the cradle.

I rapped on the doorframe.

"I read your report," Garrett said, looking up. "We have no gaps, no incursions, no missing islanders. If the FRAC didn't come from the Main, we have bigger problems."

He ran his fingers through his hair.

"I wish Frank was here."

70

Another Shift

+19 Days – 1915 hours

The church doors, painted in long thick red strokes and furnished with wrought iron trim, stood out in stark contrast to the white siding. Red signified good luck in some cultures. These doors had held up their end so far. I gave the door a pat before entering the vestibule.

In the alcove on the landing of the stairway I climbed the ladder to the bell tower, banging the hatch open.

Jackson sat at one of the arched openings facing the bridge, his arms folded and a cigarette between his fingers. His long black hair and thick mustache reminded me of a 1970s rocker – someone from the Eagles, maybe.

I pulled the M4 from the shelf and took up position at the other window. Jackson got to his feet and collected his belongings.

"Not much happening, John," he said, heading to the trapdoor. "Pretty quiet today. See ya later."

He closed the trap door quietly.

Now alone I peered out on the bridge.

Small groups of FRACs milled around.

In the plaza a few islanders did the same. Three stood in a small group chatting. Two others staggered into each other, the 'brown bag' law in full effect.

71

Unexpected Guests

+19 Days – 1941 hours

A shadow moved along Route 5 behind the tree line, too large and fast to be a mob of FRACs. An armored truck came into view, outfitted with a .30 caliber machine gun on a makeshift rotating roof turret.

The truck drifted to the shoulder, plowing over a FRAC who had just turned toward the rumbling engine. The body crunched under the double rear wheels.

I made out three passengers. Two silhouetted shapes sat inside the cab. One man stood behind the roof turret. Without taking my eye from the scope, I signaled the sheriff's station with the walkie-talkie.

The truck came to a stop at the crest of the bridge.

It flashed its lights three times then laid on the horn for a loud honk.

A minute elapsed as four FRACs staggered toward the vehicle.

The passenger door opened.

A tall blond male in a black ball cap, aviator glasses, black T-shirt, and fatigued cargo pants exited.

He looked at the advancing walkers, drawing his pistol. Pulling out a silencer from his pants pocket, he screwed it onto the barrel.

Just as the most ambitious FRAC came within biting distance, the man raised the gun between its outstretched arms and pulled the trigger. Dry chunks blew out from the walker's head. It fell backward to the pavement.

Aviator double tapped each of the remaining walkers in the head. While the FRACs fell, he removed the silencer and holstered his sidearm. He spun the silencer in the air before returning it to his pocket.

215

He grabbed the wrist of one of the walkers and dragged it around the front of the truck. He grabbed another one by its shirt collar and deposited them both at the curb. He repeated the process with the other two.

I checked the second man at the roof turret. The gunner was thicker than his counterpart, although he also wore a black T-shirt. A Boston Red Sox cap was pulled down over his eyes, although the sun has dipped behind him.

Garrett pulled up to the barricade, flashers spinning. He stepped out with a bullhorn.

"What can I do for you?" Garrett's voice boomed along with a few crackles.

The tall muscular blonde waved and walked forward.

"If you intend on coming to me, leave your weapons at the truck."

Aviator wiggled out of his holster and hung it from armored truck's reinforced grill. He raised his hands and turned around once before starting toward the barricade.

I double clicked my radio squelch.

Garrett crackled through with his soft response.

"Just keep an eye on 'em, John. If the guy on the turret starts shooting, I'm gonna make sure their emissary is directly between us. Over."

I responded with a single squawk.

The man approached to within twelve meters of the barricade. Without using the bullhorn Garrett called out, "That's close enough, friend!"

The man stopped, hands raised with palms out.

"What can I do for you?" Garrett repeated.

"Ah... my friend," he started, "We are looking for supplies."

"How many are you?"

"Just three."

"How many included in your entire party back in the woods?"

"Only a few more," Aviator admitted. "I didn't want to parade an entire division of armed men into the bridge."

"I'm sorry, friend," Garrett called out, "we have very limited resources. We can't spare anything."

The man smiled and moved closer.

Garrett's unfastened the strap for his sidearm and rested his palm on the grip.

"Surely you can spare something."

"I'm sorry. We can't."

Aviator stepped forward again, still smiling.

"I would advise you to return to your vehicle," Garrett warned.

Aviator did stop.

He looked past Garrett toward the town and up at the church tower before looking back at the sheriff.

"I am sorry, sir. I respect your decision. I see you are the man in charge."

He gave Garrett a curt bow.

"Good luck to you, sir... and your town."

Aviator trotted back to the truck, grabbing the shoulder holster before hopping back into the cab.

The truck revved with a groan and a sputter. Gears creaked as the driver backed off the bridge to Route 5.

The man on the turret took one last look as the truck curved round the bend.

The lights in the plaza turned on.

The turret operator had already turned away.

A sigh of weary relief escaped my lips.

72

Shift Change

+20 Days – 0055 hours

My shift ended at midnight but it was 0100 when Lucy opened the hatch.

"Sorry I'm late, John," Lucy said.

I waved her off.

She pulled the second scoped M4 off the shelf. She checked the weapon before bringing it to the other bridge-facing window.

"Hell of a day, huh? Garrett told me about the mysterious man and his little armored truck. Strange. Said he was pulling Jackson in early for extra cover for the AM shift with me."

I pulled my weapon up and returned it to the shelf before going to the trapdoor.

Lucy settled in to her position, getting into the mindset of the business at hand.

"See you later, gator," she said, not looking back.

73

Scary Noises

+20 Days – 0120 hours

I zipped up my jacket against the cool night air, stuffing my hands in the pockets. The plaza lamppost lights extinguished, a bleached bone sliver of moon providing the only light.

Keeping to the street, I passed the Exxon gas station with Sebastian's tanker rig and walked through Mall Street. Erma's grocery store was quiet, its produce racks empty.

Noises made me stop.

A faint tinkling carried in the breeze.

I pulled my M-45.

The noise came again but was carried away before I could pinpoint its source.

Something grabbed my shoulder.

I spun around, blocking the arm at the wrist, breaking its hold. The M-45 came up and forward, my finger pressed against the trigger.

"John! John! Whoa!" Doctor Rawlings held his hands up in surrender.

I let go and holstered the weapon.

He rubbed his twisted wrist.

"Sorry, John. Something have you spooked?"

He cocked his head for a moment.

"I don't hear anything but the moaning of wind through the trees. Spooky enough, I guess."

He flexed his wrist in a circular motion.

"Anyway. No harm, no foul, young man."

Rawlings headed up the block but turned back.

"I guess I was wrong about that rain."

74

Alone In The Shack
+20 Days – 0800 hours

I opened the front door to the Shack.

Holly launched off the windowsill, slid on the hardwood and bumped into my legs. She bit into my jeans for a few seconds then skittered away to run laps around the living room.

Shaking my head, I headed to the refrigerator. I quenched my thirst from a glass jug of distilled water. The only other contents were a few zip-lock bags of filleted fish on the bottom shelf.

Holly clicked over to me as I looked through the sliding glass out to the Atlantic.

Returning the water to the fridge, I pulled out the cod. I turned on the stove and poured a capful of olive oil into an iron skillet pan. I tossed the cod in with a dash of seasoning and listened to it sizzle.

I reached for the last of the lemons Erma had given us earlier in the week. In her greenhouses she grew a myriad of fruits and vegetables year round. Whoever thought that citrus fruit only grew south of the Mason Dixon Line never met Mrs. Hilger's green thumb. Carol mentioned Erma had pollinated plants to blossom during the winter months.

Holly sat up on her hind legs, waving her front paws and swishing her tail against the linoleum. A low growling wha-wha sound came from the back of her throat.

I stared at her and she looked away, still pawing the air and wagging her tail. Her right brow arched as she snuck a look back my way as if to let me know a little scrap would be our secret.

Promise.

75

Over the Water

+20 Days – 0918 hours

I sat in an Adirondack chair in the gazebo at the end of the weathered dock.

Lucy plopped onto my lap and threw her arms around my neck. Holly padded around the rails, peeking through them at random intervals.

"What's the matter, John? All those sentry shifts making you lazy?"

She kissed me full on the mouth then pulled her legs up to cuddle deeper on my lap. I hugged her tight and inhaled the scent of her hair.

"Duty was so boring, John! Nothing happening seems worse than something."

With one more hug and kiss, she hopped back to her feet.

"Don't fall asleep and be late for your shift," Lucy advised. "Come on, Holly!"

I turned to watch them both wag back to the Shack.

76

Running Errands

+20 Days – 1115 hours

My errand sent me into the last block of the Presidency.

Erma's property was the only house on the eastern side, backed up to a cultivated field and three greenhouses. The front lawn was freshly cut, the beds along the porch filled with blooming flowers.

I went to the door and rapped on the leaded glass window.

Nothing stirred inside.

I knocked again.

Maybe Erma was in one of her greenhouses.

I placed a list under the lid of her mailbox.

Two boys pedaled past me on Rainier Road.

A flash of white caught my attention.

In the high grasses a flit of curly tail wagged along, the tail appearing one moment before darting out of sight. Holly didn't seem to mind that her pack consisted of a maimed ex-Marine and a gun-toting Army brat.

77

Small Talk

+20 Days – 1236 hours

The sidewalk in front of the diner showed signs of life. Vincent Leone from the Irish Spirit and Sam's friend Jorge had holstered pistols. Several rifles leaned against their chairs.

"Can't believe the shit we're in," Vincent said.

"Is what it is," Jorge responded.

"Bad enough we're running short on food."

"Gonna get worse."

On the door someone – I assumed Carol – had taped a handmade sign reading,

Keep Guns Off the Tables

Priceless.

Sunlight cast warmth and brightness in as far as the counter. I sat, Carol strolling over with a coffee pot and cup.

Thanks to Erma, Mother Nature, and an obscure mention in a *Harpers New Monthly Magazine* in 1886, Carol poured me a cup of roasted and ground dandelion taproot coffee.

With the first taste, I raised my cup to Erma in thanks. As good as the new coffee tasted, though, I could always retreat to the three-pound can of Maxwell House I had found in the Shack's garage.

Carol flitted away to check on everyone.

Sam had abandoned his usual seat at the window to sit with Patrick two stools down.

"How you holding up, Marine?" Sam asked. "Run into any Commies?"

Patrick looked at his grandfather.

"Always with the stories, huh, Pops?"

"You know I love my stories, Patty. And I know you love my stories."

Patrick shook his head with a smile, glancing at me.

Monroe Johnston sat next to Patrick, staring at his chicken soup and absently stirring it with a spoon. Pulling a napkin from the holder he patted his clammy skin.

One stool was open between Monroe and Rita Atwood. She had volunteered to keep the library open after Emily Proctor's suicide. She leaned into her boyfriend Doug, her arms wrapped through his.

The piano-hinged counter walk-thru separated Doug's stool from Joyce and Willard's. Willard had started helping out on patrol and Joyce volunteered to monitor the Norte Bridge's floodgates. Both had a knack for their posts.

Strangely, I could make out all of their conversations.

"There is no way that a random FRAC got onto the island without notice, Pops."

"Yeah, Patty. I know," Sam replied with a grim stare into his coffee cup. "The perimeter's been rechecked. Unless FRACs have decided to take up swimming... this shouldn't be happening."

Monroe stared at his coffee, his spoon still stirring slowing and clinking out the cup's ceramic sides.

Rita and Doug said nothing, cozying against each other with their eyes locked.

Joyce and Willard also leaned into each other in comfortable companionship.

"I didn't hear it, Joyce," Willard said.

"Don't know how you couldn't," Joyce responded.

"The FRAC on the island has you rattled. You probably heard the wind through TV antenna wires... or just your imagination running away."

"I love you, Will. But you need to take me seriously."

"Baby, I take you as serious as a FRAC attack."

"You're a shit head."

"That's why you love me."

"Ass!"

"Another feature you love."

Joyce slugged Willard's arm, defusing her furrowed brow.

I took a sip of coffee and looked at my watch.

It was time for work.

78

Happy Feet

+21 Days – 0910 hours

Louis Stanton and Jackson Parson had relieved me from sniper duty at 0300.

Too tired to travel back to the Shack I caught rack in a pew.

Now the sun was up, warming my face as I walked down the church steps.

I had to report to the sheriff's office at 1000 hours for body disposal duty.

To kill time I crossed the street and sat on the gazebo's steps. Three men cut the grass with whirling manual rotary blade mowers.

I took off my boots and socks, picked them up and walked off the pathway into the plush pre-cut grass. Individual blades crept up between my wiggling toes. Making a slow beeline toward the other side of the plaza I reached the sidewalk and looked up at the chrome of the Oceanside.

Sustenance would go well with my renewed serenity.

79

Beat It

+21 Days – 0930 hours

At the Oceanside, the familiar tinkling over the door marked my entry. Carol looked up from serving coffee to David Chang, grabbed a coffee cup and started down toward my usual spot at the end of the counter.

"Morning, John. You look like you had a night," she said as she poured me some dandelion coffee.

"You want breakfast, hun?"

I put up two fingers then took a sip of the new standard for brew.

"Number 2, Larry! Beat it!" Carol yelled toward the kitchen.

"Okay," Kyle's replacement, Larry Phillips, responded.

"...you hear about Erma?" Jorge asked Carol, a coffee pot hanging in the air between them.

"What happened?"

"She was suppose to deliver produce this morning... and never showed up."

"Well... that happens from time to time, Jorge. Maybe she's cutting more taproot for this fine coffee you love so much. You know she could end up at the lighthouse."

"True. But she didn't leave a note."

"Well, Jorge... we'll have to wait and see, won't we?"

"You know, Carol, you're too sedate sometimes for your own good."

"Just drink up and quit taking your turn at the rumor mill."

I thought about my note left for Erma and hoped that a package of goods would be ready for me. I sipped the coffee, staring into the murky brownness surrounded by the cracked white cup.

A slap connected to the back of my head.

"You didn't come home last night, John."

I swiveled around to meet Lucy's eyes. My gaze only lasted a second before she wrapped her arms around my neck and kissed me with her plush lips.

She pulled back and punched me.

"That, and the previous slap, is for not coming home. See ya."

She bounced away and out of the diner.

I turned back to my coffee.

With a grin, Carol placed my breakfast in front of me.

"You're a pretty lucky man, John."

80

A Few Minutes

+21 Days – 0950 hours

After breakfast, I tapped the counter to thank Carol.
Donning my sunglasses, I moved out into the day.
Ten minutes until disposal duty.
A few of the Mall Street shops had closed over the last three weeks. Erma's grocery store was dark. Swift's barbershop was locked up since Leonard's death. Gloria had disappeared in search of answers or of loved ones.
But life still existed.
Kids biked in the streets, Donovan and Jacob with them.
The three mowers worked to finish before the day got too hot.
Armed men and women sat around the plaza.
Lucy walked from the Town Hall to the municipal building.
I glanced at my Cobra. Five minutes had passed.
Sighing, I started across the lawn.

81

Concern Reports

+21 Days – 1010 hours

Garrett spoke to Lucy, Reynolds and Diggs in his office.

"We now have three concern reports about Erma," Garrett said. "No one has seen her for two days."

"She likes to wander out to the end of the island, Boss." Reynolds replied.

"Yeah, I know. But she doesn't usually go out without letting someone know."

"Keep asking around. Find out her last twenty."

"Sure thing, boss," Reynolds replied.

"Okay," Garrett said as he moved from behind his desk. "Let's get you gentleman out for disposal."

"Erma has been missing since yesterday, John. Did you see her when you dropped off the list?" Lucy asked as we left the office.

I shook my head.

"We have lost too many good people," Garrett said. "She needs to show up in good condition."

"I hope so, Sheriff," Lucy replied, "I hope so."

82

Disposal Units

+21 Days – 1025 hours

We met Felix in the parking lot.

The cracking asphalt of the lot provided a few lanes for stray dandelions, proving that post-event weeds were just as voracious as ever.

"Let's go," Lucy said. "Waiting for Kyle is useless."

"Yeah," Felix responded. "Let's get to work."

We walked to the barricade and the waiting Reynolds.

"Still no Kyle, huh?" Reynolds asked, shaking his head.

"No. He's running late again."

"Well, Lucy, I think I'll ask the Sheriff to give him something worse."

"All that means is that he will skip out on that assignment, too." Lucy chuckled.

"True. Very true."

Diggs puttered his truck to a stop next to the stack of FRACs that the man I had dubbed Aviator had put to the curb.

"Let's go, gang," Reynolds said as he climbed the barricade.

He put out a hand to Lucy, but she hopped up by herself.

"Thanks, Deputy," Felix said as he took Reynolds hand.

Lucy grabbed his other hand.

I thought about giving him a push, but decided against it.

Using the guardrail, I joined the rest on the other side of the barricade.

We headed toward the truck.

I looked back at the church tower. Jackson looked back at me with his rifle cradled in his arm and a cigarette between his lips.

Lucy chatted with Reynolds, Felix and I following behind.

Diggs pulled himself up onto the bed and grabbed a hay bale hook from behind the cab. Felix and I grabbed gloves from a milk crate, grabbed a FRAC and swung it up onto the bed. Diggs jammed the hook under its collarbone and dragged it toward the cab.

With Kyle absent, Lucy and Felix took turns helping me haul the bodies over to the truck. When the last body hit the back bumper its head tore clean off. The flesh-stretched skull bounced off the pavement and rolled under the truck.

"Dammit!" Lucy cursed, bending over to see where the head went.

The hay bale hook flew down and into the walker's chest whipping the body out of my hands.

"Go get that head, Lucy!" Diggs laughed. "Go get it, girl!"

Lucy crawled under the old Ford, reaching out to catch a few strands of filthy blond hair. Dragging the head out, she got up and held it up like a trophy.

"Here you go!" Lucy said triumphantly.

Diggs swung the hook out and impaled the head in the open neck.

"You're getting way too good with that thing, Diggs," Reynolds added.

Diggs raised the hook to turn the FRAC's face towards him. He looked into its cloudy eyes and batted his eyelashes at its slack jaw. Diggs blew it a kiss then shook the head off the hook. It bounced off one of the bodies and came to rest near its owner's shoulder.

"You're a little sick, Diggs," Reynolds said. "Let's get these things out of here."

Diggs jumped off the back to the cab. Felix followed to the passenger side. Lucy and I pulled off our gloves and tossed them into the milk crate. I lifted her onto the bed before pulling myself up.

Reynolds hopped up onto the bed, skirted the pile of bodies, and slapped the cab's roof.

Diggs fired up the engine and we started toward the Main.

We traveled west two miles on Route 5, passing a burned out Exxon gas station. Abandoned vehicles littered the sides of the road. Some had become crypts for their drivers and passengers, or worse, prisons for the dead that had come back to slap against the windows. Only the faint buzzing of small insects droned in the air.

Another mile brought us to a gravel turn-off.

Diggs turned the truck onto the rutted, grassy trail.

Reynolds ducked just in time to avoid being slapped across the face by a swinging low hanging pine branch. He squatted behind the cab, the stock of the shotgun braced against the bed.

I gripped the slanted side rail to keep from pitching off the back, Lucy's arms wrapped tight around my waist.

Tree branches pressed in, scratching against the truck.

The road finally evened out and opened up.

Diggs turned the truck around in a dusty arc then backed it up to the edge of a ravine. It was a rocky crevasse split wide like a wound across the center of the clearing.

Reynolds slapped the cab and Diggs stopped.

The scar in the earth ran twenty-five meters deep and ten meters across at its widest, with craggy outcroppings of granite on the steep slopes. The bottom was littered with what seemed like a hundred withered, picked-over bodies.

I stabbed a body with the bale hook and dragged it to the back of the truck. Prying the hook from its rib cage, I pushed the body over the edge with the bottom of my boot. It fell into the ravine, flopping and bouncing off the outcroppings until it hit bottom.

Lucy and Reynolds each pulled a body to the bumper and pitched them off the end. I hooked and dragged the last corpse to the edge, flicking my wrist and watching it roll into the pit.

"Heads up, John!"

I ducked as Reynolds punted the wispy blonde shriveled walker skull. The head sailed into the middle of the ravine. It bounced off a pile of bodies before rolling under the armpit of a young woman with her cheek ripped open, staring at her own outstretched arm with wide-open cataract eyes.

Reynolds and Lucy joined me. We stared at the gaping opening. Felix and Diggs stood on the step-ups of the cab, looking over the wood side rail slats.

"Does anyone want to say anything?" Lucy asked.

"Fuck 'em all!" Felix called back to us. "Can't say eulogies every time we come out here."

"Felix!"

"Man's entitled to an opinion, Lucy," Reynolds said in defense. "Diggs, anything?"

"Nah, Linc. I'm with Felix. I've been out here too many times for last words."

"Everyone deserves last words, Diggs."

"I'm sure they do, Lucy. I'm just not the man for the job."

"Well, then let me just say a little prayer?"

"Sure, Linc," Lucy said.

Reynolds gazed into the gash's shadowed interior, looking at the same sores and rot as the rest of us. Then he looked up to the cloudless sky.

"God, we commit these people to your care in the hopes that their souls will be accepted into your welcome embrace. Have mercy on the actions their bodies committed after death and forgive them their trespasses. In Jesus' name we pray. Amen."

"Amen," Lucy whispered in acknowledgement.

Felix and Diggs got back into the truck.

WHERE am I? ... What are you DOING to me? The Gaunt Man's voice mocked.

"Where are you, John?"

I turned to Lucy, giving her a hug.

"Let's get back to the island." Reynolds slapped the roof of the cab, letting Diggs know we were ready to leave the smell of death behind us.

83

Missing Persons

+21 Days – 1324 hours

Felix walked across the plaza. The rest of us headed to the sheriff's department.

"I'm really worried about him, Linc," Lucy said.

"Me too. He really hasn't been the same since the girl."

"Yeah. I thought he would bounce back by now."

"Maybe he should see Dr. Rawlings."

"Rawlings isn't a psychologist."

"Yeah, but he *is* the closest thing we have."

Reynolds pushed open the doors and headed into Garrett's office. Lucy and I sat down in adjoining chairs in the lobby.

Through the smoked glass window, Reynolds' silhouette stood in front of Garrett's desk, his arms waving as he spoke.

"I can't hear anything they're saying." Lucy said, leaning in.

They continued to talk in low murmurs.

I felt the comfortable weight of the holstered M-45 and Lucy's grip.

Deputy Reynolds and Sheriff Garrett came out, both with grim looks.

"John, go with Linc," Garrett directed. "Someone found Erma."

84

Bulrushes

+21 Days – 1405 hours

Reynolds and I rode in silence.

A lanky teenager stood at the dam's service road, waving frantically as we approached. A dark-skinned muscular young man looked at his friend and shook his head.

"Wait in the car," Reynolds ordered. "I'll see what's up with Stan and Donell."

Reynolds pulled to a stop, got out and approached the pair.

After a minute with the young men, Reynolds gestured to me.

As I opened the door, Reynolds came back and leaned over the window frame.

"Erma's out there past the utility fence line," Reynolds said, blocking my view to the teenagers. "Stanley says he saw her wandering around with a backpack."

We walked to the back of the cruiser. Popping the truck, he pulled out a pump-action shotgun and a body armor vest. I took them as he leaned in for the same gear for himself.

Slipping the armor over our heads, we adjusted the Velcro. Reynolds slammed the trunk lid and we walked to the barricade.

"I'm sure she's fine, Linc," Stanley said, following close behind.

"I'm sure she is, Stan."

Reynolds stopped and Stan, in his excitement, collided into him.

"Any chance you going to move your ass back over there with Donell?"

Stanley raised his hands in surrender and stepped away, grinning.

We walked past the barricade, the gravel loose under our boots.

"Not sure why she would go through so much trouble on the Main." Reynolds looked at me. "Dandelion root isn't that important."

He led the way across the spillway service road.

We stepped onto the mainland and headed to the gate. Reynolds pulled out a key and unlocked the padlock, loosening the chain enough for us to slip through before hooking the lock back through the chain.

We walked in silence for a quarter mile, the buzz of insects and the swish of the ocean disrupting the quiet.

The combination of heat and the Kevlar vests, plus the stress of the situation did nothing to keep us cool. Reynolds wiped his hands on his pants, switching the shotgun from one hand to the other.

Reynolds stopped short, putting up a fist.

I turned and watched our six.

Reynolds sounded out a quick, short whistle. He gestured me over and pointed into an open area off the right side of the road.

The clearing was surrounded by a sparse tree line, ending in a berm with peatland bulrushes beyond it. Seasonally flooded, but dry now, the peatlands thrived with the tall wheat-like reeds.

Erma worked furiously on her knees in the high grass at the base of a knot of pines.

"Erma!" Reynolds called out.

She didn't respond, continuing to work.

Reynolds approached her, motioning for me to stay put.

I scanned the road.

A slight breeze swayed the pines.

Reynolds circled wide to the right.

"Erma," he called out again.

Erma continued to dig, partially hidden by tall grass.

Reynolds moved closer, waving me over.

Sinatra's 'Luck Be A Lady' blared from Erma's earbuds.

"I don't want to scare her into a heart attack," Lincoln muttered. "Erma!"

She stopped working and looked up.

"Erma!"

She struggled to her feet.

Even standing she was partially hidden from view. She wore her big floppy hat. Erma cut a new path through the tall grass toward us.

I looked around the berm.

The grass and reeds split open.

Erma lunged at Reynolds.

Blood covered her mouth, dripping off her chin.

Reynolds wedged his shotgun against her, the barrel pressed against Erma's cheek and neck. Blood and saliva sprayed onto Reynolds' face.

I rammed the butt of my shotgun over his shoulder into the center of Erma's face. The hardened composite stock crushed her nose and cheekbone.

She staggered backwards, disappearing back into the thicket.

Reynolds fell against me.

I leaned into his body and steadied him by the vest's grab handle.

"I'm alright," Reynolds said between breaths. "I'm alright."

We followed the trail that Erma's bloody face had left for us. Reynolds took point and treaded into the trampled reeds.

Whistling, I made a flanking gesture with the edge of my hand.

He nodded and moved forward.

I walked on the crest of the berm parallel to Reynolds, only catching sight of the top of his head. The bulrushes shook five meters ahead of him.

I whistled twice to get Reynolds' attention.

He continued stalking the rustling reeds. When he was three meters from the spot the reeds stopped moving.

Reynolds stopped, too.

I dropped the shotgun and drew the M-45.

Erma plunged toward him.

I fired but she kept moving toward Reynolds.

Just as the separating reeds narrowed to Reynolds' position, a bang filled the air.

A second later came another shotgun blast.

Silence followed.

I scooped up the shotgun and scanned the bulrushes.

The reeds at the berm's edge separated.

I raised the pistol and the shotgun.

Reynolds, his face muddy and streaked with sweat, put a hand up in defense. He held out his smoking shotgun. I holstered the M-45, took his weapon and slung both shotguns on my shoulder.

Reynolds reached out for my hand.

I clasped it and leaned back. Heavier than expected, I strained to pull him out of the soft earth.

Reynolds dragged out Erma's bloody body behind him, both of us pulling her dead weight out of the stubborn but eventually relenting muck.

Laying Erma on the grass, Reynolds dropped to his knees and brushed a lock of gray hair away on her now hatless and ruined face.

He slumped his shoulders and cried for her.

85

Precious Cargo

+21 Days – 1613 hours

Deputy Reynolds and I returned to Rainier Island.

"Stanley!" Reynolds yelled.

The teenager raced into view.

"What can I do for ya, Deputy?"

"Go to the trunk and get me the blue tarp."

Reynolds raised his keyring, pointed it at the police cruiser and pressed the trunk release button.

Without another word, Stanley ran to the sedan and lifted the trunk lid.

"Don't fucking touch anything else in there!"

Stanley slammed the lid closed and brought us the tarp.

"Give it."

Stanley did as he was told. Reynolds caught the tarp.

"Now get back over with Donell."

"Yes, sir."

Stanley walked off without another word.

Reynolds brushed past me and headed back across the service road to the mainland.

We walked down the center stripe and made our way to the clearing. The deputy hitched the tarp and walked over to Erma. I checked the road for FRACs as we moved to the body.

"Don't know how she got like this out here," Reynolds muttered as he unrolled the tarp. "Makes no sense."

We squatted down.

Reynolds grabbed Erma under her arms.

I lifted her by the ankles.

We swung her gently onto the tarp.

Reynolds reached down for a corner of the canvas.

I pulled my M-45.

Reynolds looked at me in surprise and ducked.

I fired an echoing shot.

The FRAC took the shot in the collarbone, twisting back but still moving forward.

I pulled the trigger again.

The walker's head snapped back as it slipped off into the bulrushes with a splash of mud. Its jeans and boots were the only things still visible.

"Christ!" Reynolds exclaimed. "What the hell today?"

He walked over to the FRAC and kicked its calf with his steel-toed boot, stomping on it well after the snap of its femur.

With spittle coming out his mouth and his eyes red, Reynolds returned to Erma and me. Silent tears and sweat rode down his face.

"Let's get her back," he said softly.

86

On the Table

+21 Days – 1823 hours

Dr. Rawlings rolled Erma's body onto the autopsy table.

Garrett stood in the corner of the room, rubbing his mouth.

Walking down the corridor to the locker room, I stripped out of the body armor and my T-shirt. I went to the sink and turned on the hot water. The fluorescent bar above the mirror left my stubbled face gaunt, blood-splattered and haunted.

Another face shared the mirror.

The Gaunt Man reached for me.

I spun around with my fists up.

The changing room was empty.

Damn it!

I leaned against the sink, the water running behind me. Turning, I ran my arms under the scalding water to rinse off the death. The dirty water swirled around the drain. When the water cleared, I turned off the faucet, dried off and grabbed a gray Rainier PD sweatshirt from a shelf.

Dumping the towel and my soiled T-shirt into a hamper, I grabbed the vest and went back through the receiving area. Picking up Reynolds' discarded vest and weapon, I hauled everything back to his cruiser.

When I returned to the basement, Sheriff Garrett and Doctor Rawlings' voices carried throughout the receiving area.

"What happened to her, Doc?"

"Hard to say, Sheriff. Her liver temp is 90 degrees, leading me to believe that she just turned. It's possible that she had a coronary event out there, died and reanimated."

"Yeah, but why did she turn? I thought that the reanimation process for natural death had stopped. When Lenny Swift passed a week ago, he didn't come back. Shit! We stood around his body with rifles, waiting in shifts for twenty-four hours."

"We had to be sure."

"What are you sure of now, Doc?"

"I can't be sure, Sheriff," Rawlings responded. "I know Erma complained last week of a slight fever, but it certainly wasn't the raging temp spike I've seen from a FRAC bite."

"Maybe it was from transfer. She was always digging through the brush and bushes. Is it possible that she scratched herself on a branch that had FRAC blood on it?"

"Interesting concept, but unless the hematological makeup has changed or mutated, the lethality of FRAC blood and saliva is only contagious upon immediate and direct contact with our blood."

"I'm at my wits end, Bill. We've had a FRAC roaming around, materializing out of thin air. Now Erma's reanimated without any good reason!"

"Easy, Jared. Let me do my autopsy. I'll have answers for you."

"You treat her with respect, Bill." Garrett pointed a finger at the doctor.

"I know, Jared." Doctor Rawlings raised his hands up, the blade of a scalpel glinting in the weak flickering fluorescent lights. "She was important to me, too."

87

Night Surf

+21 Days – 2141 hours

The house was dark and empty.

Lucy was on sentry duty.

Holly was out looking for adventure.

I went out to the deck.

The waves reflected their white foamy caps against the rising three quarter moon.

Striping off my holstered weapon and clothes, I left them in a pile on the deck bench and walked down the steps to the still warm sand. My feet sank in the deep grains. Running headlong into the oncoming surf, I dove into the surf between cresting waves.

I paddled up and over the incoming surges. When they evened out, I floated and felt the tug of an unsure current as it struggled with whether to take me back to shore or carry me farther out. Eventually the ocean relented and I inched back toward the beach.

Still floating on my back, I could hear the waves slapping into the beach, bubbling, and receding. I submerged my head, drowning my senses in thick watery silence.

As I neared the shoreline, the waves increased in strength. I rolled over on my belly. A wave crested through me as it grew bigger and crashed me into the beach. The water pulled at me as it rushed back to form the next wave.

The ocean left me dripping and alone.

Spitting out salty water, I found myself a hundred meters west of the Shack. I stood dripping, sandy and naked.

I started the walk back, staying in the semi-wet sands.

A rustling in the grasses caught my attention.

I stopped and peered into the dune.

A breeze kept whatever it was camouflaged and hidden from the cold moonlight.

My nudity came with its own problems, namely the fact that the M-45 sat on a pile of clothes on the deck.

I veered a couple meters toward the roiling surf and kept walking.

The rustling continued.

Walking backwards, I scanned the tall grasses.

When I closed within touching distance of the Shack's deck, I lost sight of the dunes. Moving back to the steps, I caught my heel on the riser's front edge. I slammed my bare ass on the deck.

Scrambling to the clothes, I heard a slapping noise.

I pulled the pistol from the holster and rolled over toward the noise, pressure on the trigger.

Holly barked at me.

With her head sticking out of a makeshift doggy door, Holly laid her muzzle with her front paws on the bottom of the doggy doorframe, the rubber flap sitting on her head.

She barked once more before rolling onto her back. Holly growled playfully, pumping her front paws at me. With a *rawowha, rawowha* sound, she rolled her eyes with her tongue hanging out.

I stood on the top deck step. Slapping away the sand, I retrieved my clothes and went to the weathered bench to dress.

Still hanging halfway out of the doggy door, Holly watched me.

Holstering the M-45, I lay it on the bench. I hopped into my boxers and pulled on the sweatpants. The sweatshirt I had borrowed was draped on my shoulder.

Holly barked again, a low deep growl crept from the back of her throat.

A second more guttural sound came from the edge of the deck. I grabbed for the M-45 and pivoted it into the darkness.

Nothing stared back.

I stepped to the deck's edge.

With a clear sightline around the corner of the house, I saw nothing. The grasses swayed and the dune continued its run under the Cape's pilings.

Not taking my eyes from where the dune ran under the house, I dropped to the sand.

A searing pain!

A hiss escaped my clenched teeth.

Pitching away from the deck, I rolled onto my back with a jagged piece of driftwood impaled in my foot.

A groan drifted out from under the deck.

Two gray hands with broken fingernails lunged out of the darkness.

Prone on my back in the sand, I fired twice.

The muzzle flash lit the underside of the deck as the bullets ruptured the walker's skull, spraying the wood's underside with matter, gore and bullet fragments.

The FRAC fell forward between my spread legs.

The gaping wound oozed with dark, pus-like substance, thicker and slower than blood. Larva from inside the skull slinked out of the new orifice.

I turned my head and threw up.

After the retching slowed to dry-heaves saliva returned enough for me to spit out the residue. I swept a hand across the sand to cover what my stomach had unleashed. I crawled away from the body.

The driftwood still stuck out of my foot, blood dripping off my heel. I dropped the handgun on my belly and pulled my leg up to look at the injury.

I yanked out the spike, sucking air in through my teeth. The bleeding from the wound flowed more freely. I tossed the driftwood away. The 'Property of…' sweatshirt still clung to my shoulder. I grabbed it and tied it tight around the wound. Putting my weapon in my waistband, I inched back to the deck.

Pulling myself up on my good foot, I used the deck supports for bracing. When I was shoulder level with the deck, I found myself face to face with another menace.

Holly, now completely extricated from the doggy door, stood on her haunches. She barked in my face before lunging to nip me on the nose.

88

Dotted Lines

+22 Days – 0655 hours

Sitting in a gazebo chair, I stared out at the sun as it crept up from the horizon.

A pile of cotton rags lay next to the chair, joined by a bottle of hydrogen peroxide, heavy gauge sewing thread, a pincushion with needles, scissors and a pair of latex gloves.

Holly tucked herself into a ball under the chair, her snores tempting me to sleep.

The sewing thread was holding together the puncture. The clean wound was clotting well.

Dotting the length of the pier to the Shack, the blood trail from my wound had quickly soaked into the deck. Beyond, the FRAC lay in the brightening sands.

I calculated how much weight I could put on my foot without tearing the stitches open. Adding a couple pieces of gauze to the sole of my foot I wrapped it tight with athletic tape. Collecting the supplies and bloody rags in a plastic bag, I hobbled onto the pier and followed the dots of bloody footprints.

I whistled.

The clicking of claws followed. Holly caught up to my slower pace, sniffing at the bag of bloody rags and gruffing her displeasure at being awoken. At the sliding door, she trotted in front of me. Putting the plastic bag on the counter, I walked to the wall phone. I picked up the receiver and realized that my call would be nothing better than a prank.

I hung up.

Going back outside I looked at the FRAC. It lay face down, desecrating the beach as ooze from its open skull stained the sand.

"What the hell is that?"

Lucy stood at the top of the dune with her hands on her Sig. Her shift in the church tower had left her with bags under her eyes and a slump in her shoulders. She stepped down toward the body.

"Looks like you were busier than I was last night."

She approached the FRAC and kicked it with her boot.

No movement.

She dug the same boot under its shoulder and pushed it over onto its back.

"Nice grouping on the shots."

Lucy knelt with her weapon still pointed at it.

"Something familiar with this one?" She frowned.

I looked closer.

A female with wide hips, small frame, and longish hair, it wore the remnants of a long gypsy skirt and peasant blouse. An orange-and yellow-knotted satin ribbon hung limply in what remained of her hair.

"It's Gloria," Lucy said in horror.

Gloria Steiner had not closed up her second-hand bookstore.

She had not soaped over the windows.

And she had not left the island in search of her son.

89

More Bodies, More Problems

+22 Days – 0919 hours

Reynolds and Diggs stood on the edge of the deck, staring down at the rotting corpse. Sheriff Garrett and Doctor Rawlings walked over to Gloria. The doctor donned latex gloves and looked over the body before touching it.

"You moved the body, John?"

"I did, Sheriff," Lucy responded, emphasizing the *I*. "I thought there was something familiar about the clothes and kicked the body over to satisfy my curiosity."

"You're lucky the procedures for walkers differs from that of murder," Reynolds chimed in with a grin.

"Keep a lid on it, Linc," Garrett replied, not looking up.

"Sorry, Chief."

"I'm sorry, Sheriff," replied Lucy. "I think I've been on the disposal unit too long. All we do is lug the damned things around."

"Yeah, I reckon."

The sheriff looked at what was left of Gloria's face. The cheekbones and jaw line on the rotting stretched skin had degraded some but was still recognizable.

"Yeah. It's her."

Gloria Steiner could now be taken off the list of island MIAs. The sheriff struggled to his feet and stepped back.

"Do what you need to, Bill."

"Thanks, Sheriff."

Garrett walked toward the water and stared out at the Atlantic.

Doctor Rawlings bent over the body, poking at the entry wounds. After a few moments, he shifted his attention to the torso. He pulled at the blouse to reveal her pale chest. Touching the sallow skin, Rawlings pressed against the sternum.

"Well?" Sheriff Garrett called out.

"I'd say we're in the clear."

"Hurray for us," Garrett mumbled.

"Linc, get Gloria back to the station," the sheriff said in a louder voice.

Diggs grabbed Reynolds by the shoulders and pushed him toward the deck steps.

Lucy and I stayed put in the sand. She leaned into me.

"We haven't seen Gloria since the second week. How is it that she disappeared and came back as a FRAC?"

I shook my head.

Doctor Rawlings walked over to the sheriff. They talked with their shoulders close together, the Doctor moving his arms about.

"… no way that Gloria managed to keep a low profile this long," Lucy continued.

Gently breaking the hold she had on my arm, I wrapped my arms around her waist. I looked into her eyes, kissed her on the forehead and guided her back to the Shack.

I had seen and heard enough.

90

Bilco

+22 Days – 2310 hours

The streetlights around the empty plaza had been turned off for an hour. I headed to the gazebo under the moonlight and took a seat on the bench that faced Mall Street.

Why were Gloria's shop windows soaped over, John?

The Gaunt Man leaned against the alley wall between the Oceanside Diner the Mall shops, glowing with a luminescent quality. He pulled off the wall and bowed at the waist with his feet together and arms extended – a ghoulish circus ringmaster without the top hat.

I stood and drew the M-45.

No need for theatrics, John. That's my job.

I left the gazebo, keeping my gun trained on the thin pale man. A screaming gull circled overhead.

I looked back at the alley.

The Gaunt Man was gone.

On the whitewashed concrete block wall, someone had spray painted a rotted walker caricature with FRAC spelled out in pillowy letters.

Where the moon's light could not quite reach, a second alley joined in from the left, serving the back of the diner. The smacking of pots and pans could be heard.

I kicked a raised concrete footing. Bilco cellar doors angled out from the wall. I felt around for the handles. A length of chain wrapped through the handles, joined by a padlock.

Mumbles of Carol and Larry's conversation drifted to my ears.

I pulled out the tactical light and wished a painful death on the man who stole its gun. Cupping the light towards the chains, I lifted the padlock. I knew that it could be picked with the right tools.

I would have to come back.

91

Eco-Friendly

+23 Days – 0839 hours

I stared at the gore spotted sand, leaning on a spade shovel. Though Gloria's body was gone, the wind had yet to smooth over her impression. Scooping up Gloria's dried blood, I flung the sand up into the brush. The sand sifted through the blades of tall grass.

Returning to the deck, I sat on the steps.

The cries of the same lone circling gull sounded too much like Petra's birthing screams.

Rattled, I went inside the garage and hung up the shovel.

A vehicle sat covered under a large white paint splattered drop cloth. I grabbed the cover and pulled it off, letting it pool at my feet.

The Suzuki Amigo had oversized knobby tires, a removable black hard top, a roll bar and a bank of roof mounted and custom steel tube grille mounted lights. The left front wheel well was missing its tire, the rotor disc sitting on a concrete block topped with a cut down 4x4 wood block. An electric generator motor cut into the upper right corner of the well's plastic cover, bolted to the frame.

The cab interior was spotless, with bucket seats and a second row bench. Hybrid battery packs had been mounted at the base of the small trunk area.

I ran my hands across the vehicle's top and gave it a pat.

Grabbing the car cover, I swung it back over the Amigo. It billowed up and drifted down across the car's shape, coming to rest – if slightly askew.

92

Special Skills

+23 Days – 1951 hours

As the day's light bled out, I glided to a stop at the mouth of the diner's alley. Walking the ticking bike into the corridor, I propped the Schwinn I commandeered from the former sheriff's garage against the wall next to the Bilco entrance.

The alley had been undisturbed since my last visit.

Muffled banging, clanking and conversation crept over from the Oceanside like it had the night before.

I pulled out a small pouch, unzipped it and selected two small tools.

I knelt down and slipped the picks into the key slot of the padlock. Closing my eyes I felt the tools running across the tumblers. Within a few moments the lock slipped open and the chains went slack. I slipped the chain through the handle quietly, placing it and the lock to the side.

After another glance around the alley, I opened one of the steel double doors. The hinges faint squeaks answered me, both beckoning me in and warding me away.

I took a step down and pulled my tactical light. The light pierced the storage space, shining on old metal bookshelves, cardboard boxes stacked on pallets, wooden chairs and file cabinets. The basement was an open rectangle ten by twenty meters. In the far corner an iron staircase spiraled up to the store.

An unfinished sheetrock wall with two framed-in doors stood next to me. I inched to the first door and checked the handle. The door opened easily with a fainter squeak than the cellar doors. A silent boiler, a spider web of copper piping and a sink sat inside.

I closed the door and went to the next one.

It was an empty three-quarter bathroom.

No cot, bedding or supplies.

I didn't see anything to support that Gloria had holed up here.

Maybe she had stayed up in the store.

A thump and shadowed movement flicked to my right.

I pulled the M-45 and held it over the light.

Boxes crashed to the floor, a dark blot in the center of it.

I cast the light down and pressed against the trigger.

A book flew up at me.

Ducking as the shape ran across the overturned shelf, I dropped the tach light and dove to grab his ankle.

The leg tried to twist away.

A glint of blade came at me.

I blocked the serrated blade with the slide of the gun.

My assailant stabbed out of the darkness again, the point spearing at my belly.

I leaned back out of its reach.

I dragged my assailant into the tach light's beam.

He recoiled and covered his eyes. Small of frame with long hair and a hoodie, the face was still obscured.

I pulled the ankle farther out of the debris.

"Let go!" came a high voice, still kicking and trying to twist away.

Another book sailed it at me, spinning off my shoulder.

I pulled the ankle up higher.

"Let go, shit head!"

Putting my gun in my waistband, I reached for the tach light and cast the light into my assailant's face.

The hoodie had fallen back. Dark almond eyes glared at me.

I let go of the ankle and backed away, shining the light off the white ceiling tiles.

"Damn it, John!" Lucy cursed as she got to her feet. "You really did a number on my ankle... and my wrist!"

She tested the ankle, dusted off and retrieved her knife.

"Help me."

We pulled the short bookcase upright and gathered up the stray books. Once done our skirmish had been erased enough to pass casual inspection.

I put my hand to the small of Lucy's back and nudged her toward the stairs.

"You know, John. You may not be able to talk, but you still need to communicate. I saw a bike and the open Bilco doors. Things could have gone all sorts of wrong down here!"

I gave her a slap on the ass to get her moving up the stairs into the night air.

93

One-Armed Bandits

+24 Days – 0628 hours

The sun warmed my back.

Scraping noises came from the belfry ladder and the trapdoor creaked open.

"Hey, John," he called out. "It's Steve."

After hearing about my tendency to draw on people entering the belfry, Steve was a little wary of coming up unannounced.

Steve grabbed his scoped rifle and leaned it against the windowsill. He bit the top of his sweat jacket and unzipped it with his remaining hand. Shrugging it off, Steve grabbed the jacket as it fell down his good arm. He caught it by the hood and put it on one of the pegs.

The doctor had done an excellent job salvaging Steve's upper left arm. Unable to save any of the meat or bone in the forearm, Dr. Rawlings amputated cleanly below the crook of the elbow. Steve wore a compression sleeve cap on what remained.

He seemed to have physically bounced back pretty well.

Sheriff Garrett was still suspect about his condition.

Steve seemed okay to me. I wouldn't allow a nut job in the tower with a rifle.

"Saw your bike downstairs, John," Steve commented as he settled into position with his rifle on a sandbag. "Foot still slowing you down?

"It's really fucked up what happened at your place. I can't believe it was Gloria. Where was she? Makes you wonder if security is all its cracked up to be.

"Present company excluded, of course," he added. "Don't want you to think…"

I drowned out the rest of Steve's monologue.

DAY ZERO

Yeah... where had Gloria been all this time, John?

The Gaunt Man asked from the other side of the barricade.

Gloria's shop had been untouched and locked up. Only the scuffle between Lucy and I proved anything had changed since the windows were soaped over.

Whether she went to the Main and returned unseen with the infection or not, how was it that no one had seen her? And if she never left the island, where and why had she been hiding? And why were the windows soaped over?

Who did that, John?

I closed the flaps on the scope, and folded the M4's tripod. I put the weapon on the shelf and gave Steven's foot a tap.

"Hey...," he stuttered. "Have a good day, man."

94

No Matter How Unlikely

+24 Days – 0715 hours

Reynolds and two security teams stood in the sheriff's office lobby, theorizing about Gloria's death.

On my way across the lobby, a few acknowledged me with quick looks. Others just stared at me outright.

I rapped on Garrett's doorframe.

"Come on in, John. Take a seat."

Lucy sat in the other chair.

"John," Garrett said. "Lucy told me that you are guilty of B&E. That's a serious offense."

I glanced at Lucy.

She shrugged.

I looked back at the sheriff and shrugged too.

"John. I'm trying to keep some semblance of law and order here. I thought you understood that." Garrett leaned forward. "The question is, what did you find?"

I shook my head.

"Figures. I've been in that alley dozens of times. The Bilcos were always chained, even before the shop closed up. Walkers are certainly not adept enough for breaking and entering."

Garrett slapped the desk

"Damn! I spoke to every one of them out there. They're not always on the ball, but when it comes to letting Gloria slip through, I believe they didn't see her."

"What about by water?"

"What do you mean, Lucy?"

"Maybe Gloria came in by water."

"Gloria could have swam the length of the Bridge, but why bother?"

"Maybe there were FRACs."

"Maybe, but why swim? Our spotters would have seen her."

"Maybe she wasn't sure there would be spotters. What about by boat?"

"There is not a boat launch within 5 miles of the island. The shoreline to the north is marshy. No private residences for at least 7 miles. John?"

I thought about my trip down the coast with Sebastian and nodded.

"And to the west, the coastline is sheer cliff face for ten miles," the sheriff continued.

I raised two fingers.

"20 miles. She would have been smart to keep to the water. But any craft large enough to be practical to get here – something with a motor, a canopy – would have been seen eventually."

I held up a hand like a shark fin and rotated it in the air.

"What are you, John?" Garrett raised an eyebrow. "The Queen of England?"

"I think he means a sailboat, Sheriff. I had a little beat-up curved mast two-man fiberglass sailboat when I was a kid. Inherited it from a neighbor who got it out of a Sears Roebucks catalog, if you believe it. Would have been light enough to get back here, and quick and small enough for one person to pilot if she stayed close to the shoreline."

"But we still have same problem. Where is the sailboat? I don't think she'd haul it so far inland that no one would see it."

"True."

"Then there is the other thing."

"What's that, Sheriff?"

"Let's say she made it back to the island. By boat, on foot, parachute, teleporter… take your pick. She's set foot on the island. If she was alive, why didn't she reach out to anyone? If she died, how did she go unnoticed?

"And how is it that two FRACs managed to wander onto the island within a week of each other?"

Lucy clucked her tongue.

"No patrols have seen any evidence that Gloria returned to the island, yeah?"

"Correct"

"Well, then the answer is obvious."

Garrett glanced at me.

I shrugged.

"Enlighten me."

"If it's impossible that she returned to the island unnoticed, then she must have never left."

"If that's true, where has she been all this time?"

"I bet whoever soaped over her windows knows."

95

New Recruit

+24 Days – 1041 hours

Lucy and I leaned against the brick façade of the sheriff's office.

Jackson Parson came over, a tall muscular blond man behind him. In jeans and a gray UnderArmor compression shirt, the new man's steel gray eyes darted around before settling on me. A ragged scar ran from the corner of his left eye to his jaw line.

"Hey, Lucy." Jackson shook my hand. "Glad you didn't get eaten, John. The last thing we need is for you to take your training to the other side. Knowing you, you would be the only FRAC that could handle a weapon. Then we would really be outclassed!"

He gave out a hearty laugh.

"Oh, by the way, this is Dexter Holloway. Dexter... Lucy and John. Lucy and John... Dexter."

Dexter Holloway held out his large hand. I shook it with three pumps.

"Good to meet ya," he said in a deep voice.

He turned to Lucy, shaking her hand with more restraint.

"Dexter came across the Norte yesterday. He was ex-military with law enforcement up north before the infection. Garrett gave me the green light to show him the ropes."

"Welcome, Mr. Holloway."

"Thanks. Lucy, right?"

"Yep."

"And John," she added, pointing to me.

"Sorry. I'm really bad with names and faces. Please don't take offense."

"No problem, Mr. Holloway," Lucy replied.

"Thanks," Mr. Holloway said. "You can call me Dexter."

"Don't worry, Mr. Hollo...er, Dexter. You'll get the hang of it soon enough."

"Alright. Enough chitchat, Dexter," Jackson announced. "Time to run you through the wringer."

Jackson slapped him on the back and started walking him toward the parking lot.

"Nice meeting you," Dexter said. "I'll see you soon."

"You, too, Dexter." Lucy waved.

Jackson escorted Dexter away and we found ourselves alone again.

"Well, babe. I'm going." Lucy growled and shook me in what she considered a bear hug. "I'll see you at the Shack later. Dr. Rawlings has been bugging me to get a flu shot. Apparently, he told you to remind me but you never mentioned it. Can't imagine that happening."

She rolled her eyes.

I kissed her on her forehead.

"Anyway. I'm going to swing by his office. I'll see you at home later. I may even take Holly out to the beach for a while, if she's home."

Lucy released her grip, made a pouty face and stomped her foot.

"I hate needles!"

She turned, her black hair bouncing as she walked away.

96

Visiting Old Friends
+24 Days – 1200 hours

I hopped off the Schwinn in front of Sam's house.

Walking up to Sam's front door, I rapped on the glass a couple times. When there was no answer I went to the window and peered in. Sam sat in his oversized La-Z-Boy chair with a book. I rapped on the bay window.

He looked up, smiled, and waved me in. "Hey, Johnny Boy!"

I took his gnarled clammy hand in mine.

Sam patted my wrist.

"Good to see yo–" Sam coughed, grabbing a cotton handkerchief to cover his mouth. "Sorry about that, Johnny. I thought getting a flu shot was supposed to keep you from getting sick. Oh, well. Give me a few days."

I sat down next to him.

He returned to patting my wrist.

"Anderson giving you trouble?"

I shook my head.

"Well, be on the lookou–" followed by a phlegm-filled cough. "Foster will eventually try to pull the rug out from under the entire town. If Foster had his way, every penny of this town would be hidden away in that office safe of his."

He coughed into the handkerchief, checked it, and put it back in his pocket. Grabbing the neck of a Goebel's beer bottle, Sam took a swig and cleared his throat. He took another swig before wedging the bottle between the seat cushion and the armrest.

"Feeling a little under the weather, Johnny. Don't be offended if I take a little nap on ya." He rubbed his eyes. "You're a good kid, Johnny. Rainier would have been in trouble without you. Especially without that trigger finger of yours!"

He cackled until another bout of coughing staved off his amusement. Another tip of the beer bottle followed.

"Jesus wept."

Sam stuffed the bottle in the cushion and wagged a finger at me.

"I hear that you and Ms. Greenfield have been getting cozy at Frank's love shack on the beach." He smiled, but shook his head. "All kidding aside, we may need to send out scavengers off-island soon. The seasons are going to change and I'm running low on supplies."

He held up his Goebel's bottle, tilting it to see how much beer remained. Then he emptied it in one swig.

"Seriously. We'll need to get some supplies stockpiled. Foster says he is worried that we'll lose people or, worse, lead people and FRACs back. But without food we'll eventually lose everyone. I think he's worried that once the bubble pops, he's going to lose whatever control he thinks he's got."

Sam made a few groans and mouth smacks along with a quick scratch under the left armpit. A few beads of sweat had formed on his brow and upper lip.

"Feeling a little worse, Johnny. Not to be rude, but I need to lie down. Help me?" He grabbed my hands and pulled himself out of the chair with my help. "Yeah. Feeling a little warm, too."

I walked Sam to the smaller of the two bedrooms and dropped him gently on the bed.

"Thanks, my boy."

He patted me on the arm.

"Now, get back to that chickadee of yours!"

He laughed as I closed the door behind me. The door muffled the cackle, but not before the laughter turned into more coughing.

97

Roadkill

+24 Days – 1430 hours

I biked toward Jacob and Donovan as they grinded skateboards on the curb. Three other skater boys had integrated them into their group.

Jacob waved.

"Don't worry, Mr. Walken! Jax and Daisy are fine. Mr. Dickerson built a bitchin' coop for them at Mrs. Fendry's. You should see it. Chicken wire, ramps, and all sorts of cubbies, tubes, and stuff. It's very cool."

Giving him a thumbs-up, I continued pedaling.

My foot still itched a little.

I gained momentum down the hill and closed my eyes on the straightaway. Fingers of wind ran through my hair. Its disembodied voice whispered something unintelligible, but comforting, in my ears. I smirked, trying to recapture what the kids at the top of the hill hadn't lost yet.

Knowing that the bottom of the hill curled to the right, I opened my eyes.

Something lay in the road.

I slammed on the brakes, skidding the back tire around to a stop inches from it.

Holly opened her eyes. She yawned and stretched out so far that her back legs quivered. Turning her head she sniffed the bike's tire, sneezed and rolled onto her belly. She wagged her tail and greeted me with a hearty woof.

Getting off the bike, I knelt down next to the white fuzzy canine. She licked my hand before gnawing on the edge of my palm, wrapping her front paws around my wrist.

I scratched her belly, her tail swishing away the dust on the asphalt. For the hand she was chewing on, I wrapped my fingers around her snout and shook her muzzle.

Hearing the teens, Holly broke her grip and rolled over onto her short legs. She gave me a last look before sprinting up the hill.

Traitor.

98

Helo

+24 Days – 1710 hours

I sat on the rail of the Shack's weathered gazebo.

My boots and socks on the worn deck, I unwrapped my foot and inspected the wound. The wound had almost healed over. The stitching could be taken out now, but a day or two more wouldn't hurt.

Going to the edge of the pier I put my feet in the water.

The waves – unaware that the end of the world had already started – continued to pound against the pilings on their way to dry land.

Thump. Thump. Thwap...

... Thwap. Thwap. Thwap.

The rotors lifted the helicopter into the air.

The lights of the base camp grew smaller as the craft gained altitude. The Black Bird pitched forward and rolled to the right, sliding the gurney with me on it head first toward the fuselage's closed side door.

"Keep your eyes open, Sergeant!" I heard above the din of the cabin.

I opened my eyes wider, although I thought I had them open. A fatigued shadow leaned in over my face.

"We're going to the base command hospital, Sergeant! Don't speak! You have a needle in your throat! Don't speak! Don't try to take it out!"

The voice receded, still dark in front of the dim red cabin lights. The medic moved back, disappearing into the cargo-netted back panel.

Only the high pressure slapping of the helo's blades remained.

It hurt to swallow, my windpipe swollen and raw. An itch ran across my throat.

Looking over to the bench, I still couldn't make out the medic. I tried to reach out, but the straps stopped me.

"What do you need, Marine?"

The medic loomed above me. Darkness covered his eyes, turning his dim face into a bloody skull. The lips peeled back to reveal pointed teeth. Bits of flesh and skin caught between the yellowed enamel.

I fought against my straps.

"Don't worry, son," the specter cooed.

Its lips curled into a wide grin.

A hypodermic needle hovered over my face, held by gray decaying fingers. With a slight press of the plunger, dark fluid dribbled out the needle's tip. The scent of copper and sulfur filled the cabin. I choked back the bile that attempted to escape my brutalized throat.

Wrapped in ragged and ripped fatigues hiding a dark suit, the thing held the needle above me with both of its skeletal hands. Before the hypodermic could fade into the blackness of the cabin, the rotted medic swung it down into my chest.

The apparition cackled.

The needle and his hands sunk into my chest. My lungs and the ragged edges of my ribcage lay exposed, blood spurting into my face.

"Wait. I need that!"

The Gaunt Man dug around my chest cavity, rummaging through my vital organs. With a triumphant laugh, it pulled out my still-beating heart, snapping it away from the muscle, arteries and sinew that had held it in place.

I started to pass out.

"Now that's good..."

" –thing to eat?"

Lucy stood above me, the sun shimmering off her hair.

"Are you in pain? It looks like you were crying."

I wiped away the unfelt wetness from my cheeks, shrugging.

"Well. Come inside. I brought food from Carol."

She walked back to the house, her steps thumping on the deck top.

"I'm making fried cod. Them's good eats!"

99

Straight to Dessert

+24 Days – 1730 hours

Lucy stood at the stove, bits of oil crackling and sputtering as the wet breaded cod hit it. She covered the skillet and moved to a cutting board and a wedge of lemon.

I tried to shake her 'good eats' remark, not quite remembering why it bothered me. The more I thought about it, the less important it seemed. I finally dismissed the comment, focusing on the way Lucy's tight gray yoga pants accentuated her body.

Lucy stood on tiptoes, reaching for a tin of paprika. When she moved to a balancing act on one foot, I got up from the table and moved in behind her, lifting her by the waist off the cracked linoleum.

"Ohh!"

She grabbed the spice and set it on the counter.

"Thanks, muscles!"

As I set her down she spun around in my loosened grip. Her hands landed on my chest and she angled up to kiss me. I lifted her onto the counter, knocking over the paprika.

"That's better."

Lucy wrapped her legs around my waist and her arms around my neck. Her fingers found their way into the back of my hair. She pulled me in and our lips met for a moment.

"That's much better." Lucy smiled.

She plunged in for another kiss, longer this time. Our hold on each other tightened. I picked her up with my hands on her firm bottom, her lips still pressed to mine.

I detoured to the stove, shutting it off and moving the skillet to a back burner.

"Always thinking ahead, Marine. Let's see if I can break you of that."

Slapping her on the ass with my free hand, she cried out then kissed me with force. Her tongue found its way into my mouth and a soft moan hummed from her throat.

I carried her to the bedroom and leaned her crossways over the bed.

She unbuckled the belt on my tightening jeans and made quick work of the zipper. Lucy released her leg lock and I dropped my pants and boxers, kicking them off my legs. I peeled her yoga pants and panties off her firm legs and tossed them on the floor.

Lucy spread her legs, guiding me inside. She dug her fingers into me, straining to take all I could give. Closing her eyes, she bit her lower lip. I pulled her up enough to kiss her, joining us together by lips of both reason and life.

She tensed up, her back arching and her fingers laced behind my neck. I lifted her off the bed. Lucy's body tightened and she screamed out. I released, and released her a moment later.

Lucy let go, flopping onto the comforter. She rolled over toward the head of the bed and I fell in behind her, pulling her to my chest to smell her raven hair. She wrapped her arms around mine and kissed my bicep. The sweat cooling on our skin mingled.

Spent and breathless, Lucy still managed to get in the last word.

"Not bad. I think I'll keep ya."

I pinched her soft belly.

"Ouch! You're such an ass!"

She slapped my forearm then bit it.

I kissed her on the neck behind the ear.

She hugged my arms and scooted her hips into mine. We lay there for a while, feeling our subsiding heat. We fell into a light drowsiness.

Before I drifted off completely, Lucy whispered to me.

"I love you, John."

100

Game of Catch

+24 Days – 1845 hours

The fried cod tasted good, even after cooling in oil.

I cleaned up the pan and our plates.

Lucy came up behind me and hugged me, her fingers lingering along my abdomen before she retreated to the table. With a dry cough, she sat down.

"One really needs to remain hydrated," she said, clearing her throat, "when exercising."

She had on one of my black compression T-shirts like a dress. Her breasts stretched out the front, while the rest of her curves hid underneath.

"Like what you see, big boy?"

Lucy struck a pose with an inverted wrist on a flared out hip, pouting her lips and running her fingers through her hair. I crossed the kitchen and wrapped her in my arms. After exploring each other with lingering lips and flicking tongues, we finally pulled away from each other.

"I like ya. You get the job done."

I tickled her sides.

Lucy shrieked, trying to twist away.

As I ran my fingers under her arms, Lucy yelped, slapping at me in self-defense.

I finally let her go.

Her face had reddened and tears had escaped to the highlands of her cheeks. She doubled over to catch her breath, panting and coughing. After a minute, she straightened up and put her hands back on her hips.

She cleared her throat.

"I will have my revenge, Mr. Walken," she warned. "Mark my words."

I backed up to the counter with my hands up in mock surrender.

"Yeah. You better run," she said with a smile.

I grinned.

"Just watch yourself, mister."

Lucy waggled a finger in my direction, letting me know she was keeping an eye on me. I continued to keep my hands up. She backed out of the kitchen – eyes still on me – and flitted out of sight to the bedroom with a flick of hair.

A minute later, she reappeared with a pair of well-worn tight stretch blue jeans and her cowboy boots. She clipped her sidearm holster to the back of her belt.

"Well, champ, I gotta run back to town."

She headed off to the front door, opening it while looking at me.

A blur raced past her legs.

"Shit!" Lucy exclaimed, reaching for her Sig.

Holly ran through the living room and leaped onto the top of the recliner. As it rocked, Holly plopped down with her tail swishing.

Lucy gripped her chest.

"Damn it! That dog is going to be the death of me! Way before any FRAC."

Holly rolled her neck to Lucy and woofed. The tail wagged faster.

Lucy gave Holly the same gesture she had given me, putting the canine on notice. Holly acknowledged her with another playful bark.

Lucy moved her finger to me.

"Deal with your mutt. I'm out of here."

My mutt?

She gave me a quick wink before closing the door.

I looked at Holly.

She looked at me. The wagging slowed. I patted her on the head and scratched her behind the ear.

Lucy's Pinto sputtered to life, the whine of the transmission following as she backed out of the gravel drive.

I headed out to the deck.

Holly launched off the furniture and bounded out the door in front of me. She bounced up and down, ruffing at me. Grabbing a worn scuffed tennis ball, I threw it down the beach.

Holly dashed after it, her little legs kicking up sand. She scooped up the ball and skidded to a stop. Running back, her floppy ears flowed back in her slipstream. Coming to a stop, she let the ball go and watched it bounce several times before it came to a rest between my feet. Holly's ass shot up with her tail waving like a white flag of surrender, her face nestled down on top of her paws.

I picked up the ball and flung it down the beach.

Holly bolted off the deck again in pursuit of the green fuzzy orb. As Holly caught up to the ball, the wall phone rang. I went inside to answer it.

Pressing the 3 key, I waited.

"John?" Reynolds voiced crackled through the earpiece.

Pressing the 1 key, I followed with the 4 and the 0 keys then waited.

"Okay. This is Reynolds. Forget Norte Bridge. Steve will cover your shift. We have another body. Meet me at Rainier and Van Buren in ten minutes."

I pressed the 1 key.

"Okay, See you there."

I hung up.

Holly sat up on her back legs, the tennis ball in her mouth and sand in her hair. She dropped the ball and watched it peter out under the kitchen cabinets. I picked it up and put it in a saucer on top of the refrigerator. It tried to roll away but only had the edges of the saucer to escape to.

I slipped into my holster with my M-45.

Damn. I missed my Glock.

I double-checked the window and door locks before heading to the front door.

In the center of the kitchen floor, Holly sat and stared at the top of the refrigerator, willing the ball to roll off.

101

Dish Served Cold

+24 Days – 1905 hours

Deputy Reynolds pulled up in his cruiser just as I rode up on my bike.

"Thanks for coming, John. Sheriff wants your impression on this. With all of the shit going on, he's tired of missed opportunities."

We walked up the block to a gray house sitting behind a row of hedges and a towering oak tree. Reynolds lumbered up the steps to the portico. He opened the door and motioned me inside.

The living room was spotless.

"What you need to see is this way."

Reynolds closed the front door, revealing an archway to a room behind him. The walls were a burnt umber color, finished off with white trim. Windows occupied the centers of the front and sidewall. A simple modern lacquered three-leaf dining table occupied the middle of the room. Five chairs were pushed in around it.

Felix leaned back against the sixth and last chair.

His mouth hung open and his eyes stared at the ceiling.

A bead of blood dried from the corner of his mouth.

A silver dollar-sized exit wound opened up the back of his head, matting his hair with more thickening fluid.

Blood had splattered on the wall behind him.

To the left of his bare foot sat a .38 Special revolver.

"Here, John," Reynolds said, handing me a latex glove.

I wrapped the revolver with the glove and picked it up. The smell of expended gunpowder grew stronger as I brought the barrel up to eye level.

"I'll take that."

Reynolds, with his own gloves, took the weapon by the barrel and placed it in a brown paper bag. He folded it and wrapped it with a rubber band.

"Looks like a suicide."

The visible gun powder residue on the right hand, the angle of the shot through the mouth and out the upper back of the skull, the lack of defensive wounds, and the general slight upturn of the mouth led me to the same conclusion.

I circled the table.

The black lacquered surfaces gleamed. In front of Felix sat a white plate and an empty glass filmy with the last bastions of powdered milk, both on a placemat. Breadcrumbs and a light smear of peanut butter caught the edge of the plate.

I made one more circuit of the room.

Deputy Reynolds glanced up from his notepad.

"Anything?"

I shook my head.

"I guess it's no surprise that it would come to this, with all the drinking."

Deputy Reynolds took a last look at the room, jotting down a few more notes before flipping his notebook closed and putting it away.

"Okay, John. Thanks for your eyes on this."

The deputy headed to the front door and hesitated at the threshold.

"I wish Felix hadn't called me," Reynolds said with a cracking voice. "I didn't need to come over to this."

The Deputy patted the heavy door and stepped outside.

"Sheriff," Reynolds spoke into his radio.

"Yeah, Linc?"

"John's done here. You can let Rawlings know he's clear. Over."

"Okay. Over."

I stood alone with the man who claimed responsibility for everything, culminating with the staggering girl in the white nightgown in the middle of the plaza.

Glancing from the look of peace that death had given Felix to the pieces of Felix that had escaped with some velocity to the wall behind him, I walked up to the mural that Felix and his Smith and Wesson had created. A closer look at the still sticky and drying medium revealed fragments of bone that had become embedded in the pocked plaster.

At the center of the picture I dubbed the "Grand Exit", a larger round hole outlined the entry point of the bullet that had served as the brush for Felix's last masterpiece.

102

Homework

+25 Days – 0615 hours

Felix's body had been removed.

His blood and matter still hung on the wall, now dry.

Standing in the dining room, I was unable to shake the feeling that I had missed something. Felix's dead finger scratched away at the corners of my mind like they had that beer bottle label in the Irish Spirit. He had tried to communicate something important to Reynolds – but what?

I pulled out the chair opposite where Felix had died. My chair had well-worn scars of use, more than any of the other chairs. I sat on it and tapped my fingers on the table.

The saucer and glass sat on the placemat. Only the 'mural' on the wall seemed to want to reveal something. It screamed at me. My eyes dropped back to the dishes, the crusty film inside the glass.

I continued to tap.

The room was clean, aside from the blood cast and the dishes. Felix had prepared the entire house before his departure. Yet the plate and glass sat dirty on the placemat.

Why would Felix leave the dishes from his last meal without clearing them?

Every time I sat down to eat, I could see the pieces coming together.

Felix's words from the pub echoed through my head. I looked at Felix's empty chair. The chair was not worn like the one I sat in.

I had it all together, John...Every time I sat down to eat...

The dried flaky powder gnawed at me. The plate sat silent, indifferent to the crumbs that scattered across its cracked surface. The glass, though, demanded my attention.

Standing and circling the table, I grabbed the dishes and the placemat.

I looked at the wall, examining the bullet hole with my nose almost touching the plaster. The smell of copper still clung on the surface. The swirling plaster was muted from years of repainting, and now blood. Around the entry hole, behind the brain matter, a fleck of masking tape poked through. What I had thought were natural pockmarks in the plaster surface were actually small puncture holes.

I went to the kitchen and placed the plate and glass in the old porcelain sink. I shook out the placemat, folded it and put it on an open shelf with the others. The sponge was on the counter but the dish soap was not. I opened the cabinet under the sink. The dish soap sat at the cabinet's front edge.

I grabbed the bottle. A paper box sat behind it. Pulling its handle, I slid the box from around the cast iron P-trap to the linoleum floor and popped the lid.

On the top sat an official document with the letterhead embossed with the name Roanoke & Raleigh. A cobalt blue eagle soared with its wings outstretched and its beak opened in a shriek. Its talons carried a three-pronged trident piercing a lotus flower. At the bottom, also printed in raised embossed blue, read five cities with tiny lotus flowers between them - New York, North Carolina, Atlanta, Las Vegas, and Los Angeles.

Between the header and footer scrawled with a thick black Sharpie marker simply read.

It really didn't matter.

103

Put A Pin In It

+25 Days – 2023 hours

The evening sun bruised and darkened as I carried the box to the garage.

The Amigo still sat silent and almost finished, the tarp covering most of it.

I turned on the lights.

On the rear wall hung new sheetrock, a plywood and lumber counter lining its length.

Perfect.

Popping off the lid of the box and letting it fall to the concrete floor, I pulled out a container of pushpins and grabbed a few.

The message Felix had left on the Roanoke & Raleigh letterhead went onto the virgin sheetrock, directly in the center of the wall. I dug back into the box and pulled out an internal memo from the head of the Scientific Research and Development business unit to an executive at the Roanoke & Raleigh Defense Contracting arm, another business unit of R&R.

I read an excerpt of the memo again.

Concerning lab rat group #129F, test subjects #1 through #7 of 21... after exposure to serum #USDoD-2AZ049-237A and immediate euthanasia, showed immediate physical muscular reanimation.

Test subject #1 of group #129F was separated and euthanized at 0730 hours on June 11th. At 0732 hours, test subject revived and showed aggressive tendencies to the other living test subjects, even with cage separation.

Test subject #2 of group #129F was separated and euthanized at 0730 hours on June 12th, At 0735 hours, it showed similar tendencies as test subject #1.

Put into separated, but close proximity between subject #1 and the rest of the non-euthanized subjects, subject #2 showed no aggression to subject #1. Both #1 and #2 still show violence toward non-euthanized subjects.

Test subject #3 of group #129F was...

It was tacked to the right of Felix's note.

I found a copy of the lab photo I had looked at earlier. It showed the results of the test subjects of group #129F. In the picture, three wire cages sat on a white counter behind Plexiglas. In the leftmost cage, seven white lab rats lay at the bottom of the cage on their sides. In the center cage, seven white lab rats stood at the right side of their cage. Some had their teeth on the wires, others had their front paws pushed through the separations. One of the middle cage mice had stuffed its entire head through one of the openings, stuck at the shoulders. In the rightmost cage, seven rats huddled together at the far back right corner of the cage.

A Sharpie note from Felix on the edge of the photocopy read

Sums it all up

I tacked it up.

Finding more spiral-bound reports, I put them in a pile on the floor. Most of the reports were very clinical. They dealt with theoretical or practical development of extended soldiering in the battle theater.

Felix had added small yellow Post-Its to several pages.

On one of the reports, Felix used a pink Post-It. On the visible edge, I could see a large exclamation mark in red Sharpie marker. I opened it to the page that Felix marked. In the middle, marked in the same thick red marker, Felix had circled and drawn arrows to two specific paragraphs.

Developed by the scientific division of the military of the Red Communist Chinese government during the Korean Conflict, 'supplementary soldiering' was specifically and practically implemented at Outpost Harry, Iron Triangle, starting June 8th, 1953 against American and Allied forces.

The United States Department of Defense, after debriefing and compartmentalizing the surviving American soldiers from the battle, had collected samples (designated USDoD-2AZ049) from the battlefield for analysis state side.

I put the document down to find a hammer and a few nails. Picking it up again, I opened it to the page just read and hammered it into the wall.

Dragging out a few legal pads from the box, I lost control of one of them and it slapped to the floor. I plucked it up, revealing a page Felix had written on. I read his commentary on the conspiracy he thought the United States government had perpetrated against the American public.

In the middle of the page was a map of the United States. A red arrow swept in a small arc from the American southwest to the Atlantic Ocean. Five dots accompanied the arrow. The dots represented spots in New York, North Carolina, Atlanta, Las Vegas, and Los Angeles – the same as were on the Roanoke & Raleigh letterhead. The Las Vegas dot served as the starting point of the arrow across the map, with two expanded circles creating a bull's eye around it. To the west of Las Vegas, Felix had drawn a series of diagonal but parallel hash marks, running from Baja, California up through the Rocky Mountains into Washington state. What happened in Vegas apparently did not stay in Vegas.

I tore out the page and added it to the wall.

Looks like my tax dollars had been very hard at work, indeed.

104

Fits

+26 Days – 0510 hours

I woke to the sounds of muffled coughing.
The bedroom still clung to the predawn dimness behind the linen curtains.
Lucy's side of the bed was cool to the touch.
More coughs from down the hallway.
I slipped on my sweats and followed the sounds.
Lucy sat in the bathroom on the closed lid of the toilet seat, her elbows propping her head over the edge of the vanity. A mix of mucus and blood clung to the porcelain.
I put a hand on her back.
Heat and sweat radiated through her sweatshirt. She stirred after a few moments, puffy bloodshot eyes looking up at me through her wet hair. Wiping her mouth with her sleeve, Lucy moved her hair out of her face.
"Hey," she whispered.
The damp hair dropped back down in front of her eyes.
"Sorry." Lucy licked her lips and swallowed. "I didn't mean to wake you."
I squeezed her neck and knelt beside her.
"I feel like shit." She glanced at the basin. "Been coughing up blood and snot all morning. Can't shake this fever, either."
She barely managed a weak smile.
"So much for getting a flu shot."
I rubbed her back while she coughed again. Her body shuttered as she spit out a mix of milky and scarlet phlegm.
She sunk back down to the toilet lid.
"I need the doc, John."
Agreed.

105

Walk-In

+26 Days – 0545 hours

Lucy's weight seemed insignificant in my arms.

Her feverish temperature radiated through her clothes.

I quickened my jog up the hill on Rainier Road. I hadn't found the keys to Lucy's Pinto, and hadn't wanted to waste time searching for them.

Holly ran after me.

"Feel FRAC'd up...," Lucy muttered.

I would have thought the same thing if I thought she had come in contact with a walker, let alone bitten by one.

On Madison Street, I broke into a run to Doctor Rawlings' driveway. I raced up the ramp and kicked on the office storm door, leaning my elbow into the doorbell.

Holly helped by adding a series of loud barks.

The door opened.

Basia looked at Lucy and opened the screen door.

"Get her to Exam 2." She led the way. "Put her on the table."

I lay Lucy down on the examination table where Petra had died not too long ago.

Basia pushed past me and felt Lucy's forehead.

"You're burning up, lady."

She pulled out her stethoscope and listened to Lucy's respiration and heartbeat. She pressed in a few spots on Lucy's chest and sides of her abdomen then leaned over Lucy with a penlight.

"How many days has this been going on?"

I touched my forefinger and thumb into a zero.

"Just started? Any symptoms before today?"

288

I pantomimed coughing with a closed fist then opened it into a peace sign.

"Coughing for two days. Bad?"

I shook my head.

"Any bites or cuts?"

I shook my head.

"I'm going to have to perform a physical exam to rule out the infection. She has all of the signs. Geez, she was just here."

Basia left the room, the echoes of her footfalls receding down to the basement.

I moved to Lucy's side and held her lax clammy hand.

Holly whimpered from the foot of the table.

Basia's steps grew louder as she returned with a saline bag.

Holly padded over to sit beneath the visitor's chair.

Basia hung the saline bag then tied a rubber tourniquet around Lucy's bicep. She inserted an IV needle and secured it with white tape, adjusting the thumbwheel for the drip chamber until she was satisfied with its flow.

Lucy hissed, arching her back as the cool saline hit her blood stream. Before we could react, she returned to a prone position. Basia pressed her hand against Lucy's abdomen until she was confident there wouldn't be more convulsions.

"Dr. Rawlings is at Town Hall. He'll be back in ten minutes."

I looked at my watch.

My shift in the tower had started thirty-five minutes ago.

Lucy seemed to be more relaxed with the saline.

Basia clipped a restraint across her waist.

"Just in case," Basia commented. "There isn't much to do but wait."

I checked my watch again.

"I'll take good care of her, John. I'll call the sheriff if anything changes."

I kissed Lucy's cooling cheek.

I whistled for Holly to follow.

Holly whimpered but did not move.

At least one family member would keep an eye on Lucy.

106

Campaigns

+26 Days – 0640 hours

I double-timed it from Doctor Rawlings' office to the church. Barely out of breath I climbed the ladder leading to the belfry, knocking three times before swinging the trap door up.

Jackson sat in the window with a rolled up cigarette between his lips, a scoped deer rifle cradled in his arm.

"Hey, John! I didn't think you were goin' make it!"

He smiled as he took a long draw on the short cigarette. The end smoldered a bright red before turning to ash, the wind taking it out the window.

I closed the trapdoor and retrieved my M4 rifle. I positioned at the window and flipped open the scope covers.

Five FRACs wandered around the road at the far end of the bridge, one bumping off the guardrail. Two of them staggered up the ramp approach, but walked back down again.

"What's new, John? Nothing? Good. Anderson is still fucking with everyone. Lincoln was talking with the sheriff. Says Foster has no clue what to do next. That guy would steal your baby if he thought he could sell it for a profit. Not a sympathetic bone in that sonofabitch."

I smiled at Jackson's last comment.

"Did you hear? Sam's under the weather. Got a cough or something. Been bed-ridden for a day or two now, according to Patrick. Sam better get back to work or Anderson will take over everything in a coup."

Sam did have the cough. I had seen it firsthand.

Maybe Lucy had just a garden variety cold or flu. Dr. Rawlings could manage regular illnesses just fine. He still had plenty of antibiotics in his cabinets. If need be, I would hike the six miles to the pharmacy in Hampton.

"John? What's that?"

At the farthest part of Route 5 visible from our position idled a familiar armored truck. Oily exhaust rose from its muffler stacks.

The truck revved toward the bridge.

The FRACs turned their heads just as the armored truck smashed its reinforced grill into three of them. They bounced off to the pavement in front of the truck, run over by the truck's double rear wheels. Their heads exploded under the tires' weight. The remaining FRACs shambled after the truck as it passed, chasing as quick as their rotting muscles could carry them.

One of them suddenly stopped as its milky left eye ruptured in an explosion of black ooze. It fell face forward.

I scanned the treeline but didn't see a sniper nest. The shooter had to be in a camouflaged position with a silenced rifle. Unless he shot again, I wouldn't be able to zero in on him.

The truck roared across the bridge. It skidded to a stop about ten meters from the barricade. The window tint and the glare from the sun rising behind our position obscured any view into the interior.

On the truck's modified reinforced grille were two pikes, each with the decapitated head of a FRAC adorning it. One of them had its eyes rolled up and its swollen tongue lolling out between blistered, fat lips. The other head was smaller with long golden hair and a huge gash across its face.

The passenger side door squeaked open and a booted man stepped down.

I zeroed in on the figure.

Coming around to stand in full view was the Aviator.

107

Take Me To Your Leader

+26 Days – 0650 hours

"I want to speak to the man in charge!" Aviator hollered, pointing a gloved finger at our position.

"What now, John?"

I picked up the radio and tossed it to Jackson. I motioned with a 'Hang Loose' gesture.

"Sheriff." He paused. "Sheriff. We got what looks like military down at the bridge asking for the person in charge. Over."

A steady stream of static came back.

"Sheriff's talking to Anderson," Lincoln finally responded. "Hang tight. Over."

I glanced over at the Town Hall in time to see the curtains of one of Foster Anderson's office windows fall shut.

"Copy, Lincoln," Jackson responded. "Over and out."

Jackson drew his hand down over his chin stubble.

"What the hell, John?"

I responded by pointing out the window. He gripped the stock of his rifle tight and positioned himself against the windowsill.

Movement drew my attention from the barricade back to the steps of Town Hall. Anderson strolled out. Sheriff Garrett followed him. Anderson paid him no mind as he trotted his sizable girth down the steps with his chin high and chest out. Strapped in a holster on his belt was the nickel-plated ivory inlaid handled .44 Magnum from his office display.

Garrett grabbed at Anderson's shoulder, but the councilman shrugged it off and kept walking. The Sheriff looked up at the tower – at me directly, I was sure – and pointed at his eyes with his index finger.

They hurried across the grass to the bridge, the large councilman moving surprisingly quickly. Anderson stopped, the barricade between him and the Aviator. Garrett took up position at one of the bumpers, his service pistol out.

"My name is Councilman Foster Anderson." His words rang sharp and crisp.

The Aviator stepped forward.

"Mister Councilman, my name is Lieutenant Colonel Randall Wallace in the service of the United States Army. I am requesting food and fuel."

Anderson and Garrett looked at each other.

"I do not see any men, sir," Anderson stated.

"I figured you wouldn't care for a battalion of men parading across your bridge, sir. A show of force would be a little unnerving, agreed?"

"Agreed," Anderson responded. "Is that armored truck military issue?"

The Lt. Colonel stepped over to one of the heads mounted on the pikes, wrinkling up his nose at the smell.

"You have to be able to adapt if you want to survive these days. That is why you see the armored truck like it is. As for the heads, they may not be air fresheners but they do keep the Zekes from zeroing in on us when we stop for the night."

Anderson mulled over the officer's answer. Garrett kept his eyes on the shoreline.

"How many do you have in this battalion of yours?"

"137 at last count. We were at 500, but even rifles and grenades can't keep the Zekes out past a perimeter forever. Looks like you have yourself fortified well enough."

"We do alright," Sheriff Garrett chimed in. "You were here looking for supplies a week ago."

The Lt. Colonel flashed the sheriff a smile, too.

"Yes, sir. You are correct. We were rebuffed then, as you may remember."

"Yeah, I remember. I was the one who rebuffed you."

"Yes you were, Sheriff... That's why, this time, I asked for the man in charge."

Wallace pointed a finger at Anderson.

"And here he is. I figured I may get a more favorable answer this time." The officer walked to the barricade. "What do you say, councilman? Can you help a fellow American down on his luck?"

"I'm afraid I can't help you or your men." Anderson cleared his throat, his hands on his love handles. "I have enough problems dealing with the residents."

The Lt. Colonel's grin faltered, but only a little.

"Well, I am sorry to hear that, Councilman." He put his hands on his own slim hips, mirroring Anderson. "You are the man in charge, the man who makes the final decisions in these matters?"

"Yes. I am."

"Okay, then."

The Lt. Colonel walked back to the FRAC adorned truck. He slapped the panel of the still open passenger side door.

The remaining FRAC who had pursued the vehicle across the bridge's span finally arrived. I flipped off the rifle's safety. The Lt. Colonel punched it square in the nose, driving it off its feet. He straddled the FRAC and drove his boot heel through its face repeatedly. It stopped squirming.

The Lt. Colonel turned to face the sheriff and councilman.

"Sorry about that. They're like cockroaches. Except they don't scatter when the lights come on."

He laughed good-naturedly, raising his hand in a wave and shouted.

"You are the man, Councilman!"

Anderson waved back.

The Lt. Colonel dropped his hand.

The back of councilman Foster Anderson's head splattered open. He fell backward with his hand still raised and fingers still splayed.

"Shit!" Jackson shouted.

Sheriff Garrett ducked, but not quickly enough to avoid a bullet to the shoulder. He screamed in pain.

The Lt. Colonel ran to the barricade and jumped across it. He pulled his gun and pointed it at the Sheriff.

"Are you the man in charge?" Wallace shouted.

Sheriff Garrett shook his head.

I zeroed the Lt. Colonel in my sights.

My finger pressed against the trigger as I exhaled.

A whistling sound pierced the still air.

Rocket propelled grenade?

The tower exploded.

The world went bright, followed by heat and pain.

Then darkness.

108

Incursion

+26 Days – Afternoon

Ringing in my ears.

A heavy weight on my chest.

Difficulty taking in a breath.

Hot rippling air burned my throat and lungs.

I covered my mouth with my sleeve and opened my eyes to blurry slits.

Jackson lay on top of me.

His burned face and eyes stared back at me, tufts of hair smoldering. I pushed two fingers under his jaw line to his carotid.

Nothing pulsed under the flaking blackened skin.

Dead weight.

I rolled him off, getting onto my elbows and knees.

Sore and bleeding from several open cuts, I had still escaped worse injury.

The wall opposite the bridge had taken much of the blast.

The ringing in my ears was replaced by the sound of licking flames and crumbling supports.

Shouted orders came from below.

Boots thudded on the ladder rungs.

Weapons scraped against the brick walls.

Lt. Colonel Randall Wallace had landed forces on the island and had launched a successful incursion.

I slid behind the trapdoor, feeling for the M-45 in my shoulder holster.

The smoking trapdoor lifted in front of me. A flash bang grenade bounced off the far wall. I grabbed for the door handle before it could drop shut, ducking behind it.

The grenade exploded.

"Fucking door stuck open!" from below.

"Get up there and clear the space!" from another voice.

A man in green digital fatigues, helmet and goggles came up through the opening. As he got his footing on the belfry floor, I closed the trapdoor. As he spun around I pulled the barrel of his M16A2 and drove a closed fist through his mouth and nose. He slumped before he could get off a shot.

Pulling the weapon out of his hand, I swung it around by the barrel into the side of his helmet. He struck the floor with a thud, landing on top of a pile of burning wood and brick.

I got my finger on the M16's trigger and dropped to one knee.

"Is it clear?" the second voice called up.

I raised the rifle and lined the sights to the square target of the closed trap door.

"Damn it!" The door creaked open. "Private?"

The hand and head of another soldier came into view.

I fired a three-round burst into his face. He dropped out of view and crashed on the deck below, the trap door slamming shut.

"Fire!"

I rolled onto the back of the Private.

Bullets cut through the floor, splintering wood.

Several rounds pumped into the body beneath me, moving him from critically injured to actually deceased.

The firing stopped.

Barely audible voices hummed below.

I turned the soldier's bleeding body over and removed his Personal Load Carrying Equipment mesh harness, filled with magazines. I slung the PLCE over my shoulder.

The hum of discussion continued.

I stood up and edged around the room until I reached the gaping hole that the RPG had left behind. Keeping the rifle facing the trapdoor, I peeked out.

Soldiers ran toward the church's main entrance.

Rifles chattered in the distance, coupled by a series of explosions.

Dark smoke rose into the air.

Loud orders and screams filled the lulls of manufactured carnage.

The trapdoor creaked and flipped open, a hand swinging forward.

I shot it along its wrist and forearm.

A scream followed another crash to the landing.

A second flash bang grenade exploded below, the alcove lighting up like a strobe.

Moving over the opening, I emptied the rifle's magazine. I counted seven soldiers – disoriented after the blast and gunfire – dead or injured.

Dropping through the opening, I landed squarely on the armored vest of one of the dead soldiers. His ribcage cracked.

Two groaning soldiers received a close range single shot to the head as a cure-all. I moved from soldier to soldier, collecting ammo and two more PLCEs. I shouldered three more rifles and clipped two radios.

I piled the rest of the weapons under the ladder.

Going down to the first floor landing, I pulled two of the scavenged fragment grenades, pulled the pins and tossed them into the alcove. I ducked behind the wall as the grenades exploded. Their blasts thundered in the enclosed space.

Anything salvageable would be of little use.

As I listened to the increased chatter on the radios – most of it about the explosion moments ago – I slipped out the side exit and disappeared.

109

Working My Way Back To You, Babe

+26 Days – 0833 hours

From my vantage point, in the pines beside the road through the Tunnel, several columns of black oily smoke rose up between the trees and large diesel motors reverberated from the Norte Bridge.

I edged closer.

Wallace's pre-dawn assault had surprised the sentries. Stanley, Donell and Donny Matthews were propped up against a small concrete building next to the barricade, riddled with bullets.

They never stood a chance.

Men and equipment now rumbled across the dam.

If I hadn't been late for duty or if Lucy had not needed Rawlings, I may have realized what was happening. So wrapped up in safeguarding against the dead we forgot that living, thinking threats also existed on the Main.

One of the radios I confiscated squawked into life.

"Colonel! We have nine soldiers dead at the church. Over."

The voice was young and unsure.

The responding voice was clear, confident, and commanding.

"What about the sniper? Over."

"We have one dead non-military with a modified M4 weapons system. Over."

"Good news, soldier. That man fought hard. We will honor our dead later. Carry on. Over and out."

In death Jackson had become an inadvertent decoy.

The Private in Wallace's command had shit for brains when it came to tactical and battlefield forensics. The cache of destroyed weapons – and the fact that Jackson had suffered only post-mortem bullet wounds – was a dead giveaway of my escape.

300

I hunkered down in the thickest part of the woods just as a truck drove past. I trained one of the M16A rifles on the vehicle, following its path toward town. The heavy-duty flatbed truck was loaded with eleven armed men in fatigues and an assortment of wooden crates.

My finger moved from the guard to the trigger before I realized it.

The truck disappeared.

I turned into the thicket and started toward the Presidency. The dense brush hindered my progress until I found myself on the same overgrown trail I had used when reverse tracking the FRAC I had shot.

Making my way to Rainier Road, I crouched behind a grove of trees across from Jefferson Street. Four soldiers in a muddy and rusting JEEP Wrangler headed east past my position. The sputter of their engine faded.

I moved low across the pavement and along a picket fence holding back hedges until the white washed wood became a low chain link fence at the west corner of Madison Street. Easing over the fence, I stopped next to the front stoop of Madison #1.

Rawlings' house was across the street three houses down.

Something brushed against my arm, climbing to the top of the rifle stock.

Daisy the ferret stared at me, her nose wrinkled up and sniffing. She twitched her ears as her black paws clung around the barrel stock. She wore a pink body harness. A connected leash ran to a tiny doggy-door, disappearing under the rubber flap.

Daisy chattered at me.

I scratched under her chin. She chuckled. I picked her up by her scruff, put her on the porch and patted her on the rump to get her back inside. Instead, she sat up on her back legs and rotated her ears.

A moment later I heard what she heard.

The 6-cylinder engine of the JEEP Wrangler roared back up the hill.

I had left myself in the open.

The ferret squeaked and ran back to the doggy door. She slapped at it with her front paws and slithered inside.

Traitor!

The door opened.

"John!" Donovan said. "What's with all the hardware, dude?"

Instead of an attempt at a pantomimed answer, I leaped onto the porch and unapologetically jammed my way past the boy, slamming the door behind us.

I looked out the peephole.

The JEEP drove out of sight toward Jefferson Street. I breathed a sigh of relief until I heard the shriek of worn brakes, voices, and the slamming of doors.

"Who is that, John?" Donovan let go of the curtain, the fabric falling back into place.

I sunk to the floor with my back to the door, the rifle butts clanking on the hardwood floor.

All I could do is shake my head.

110

House Guests

+26 Days – 1101 hours

Two soldiers peered through open curtained windows on the other side of the street. At the third house one of the soldiers even peeked through the front door's mail slot.

When the soldiers worked their way to Dr. Rawlings' house, I gripped the rifle tight with one hand and the doorknob with the other. The heavier of the two walked onto the porch. He looked through the windows and tried the doorknob. The other soldier with a pimply face walked along the side of the house and out of my sightline.

I turned the doorknob after ten seconds.

"Don't do it, John," Donovan warned, peeking through a narrow slit between the curtains. "I mean it! The other two are smoking at the Jeep, but they're looking this way. You'll never make it."

Daisy stood up and leaned her front paws on my leg, as if to say 'Don't go'.

The younger soldier returned. He thumbed over his shoulder and said something to his partner. Hefty soldier acknowledged him with a wave of his rifle.

I backed away from the peephole, plopped onto the third step and let out a long ragged breath. Daisy and Jax the albino ferret scampered up to curl up between my legs.

"Should we go upstairs?"

The soldiers would continue their sweep and work their way back down our side of the street. Dr. Rawlings was the only remaining resident on this block. The rest had moved onto Washington and Jefferson after the outbreak.

"John?"

The rifles and mesh ammo pouches ended up on the couch. Jax and Daisy stayed on the stairs.

Donovan stood by the curtain.

I whistled and pointed upstairs. Donovan untied the ferrets' leashes from a table leg, scooped up their limp bodies and retreated up the steps. When he turned around at the top landing I pointed to the bedroom to the left. He drew the ferrets close and disappeared.

Peeking through the curtain, I spotted Hefty and Bootcamp one house away. I checked that the door was unlocked and moved to the foyer closet. Sliding it halfway open, I stepped inside between two long wool coats. Pulling the M-45, I chambered a round.

I closed my eyes and waited.

Three minutes later, Bootcamp chattered away as he stomped up to the porch.

I opened my eyes to a slapping sound

The young soldier's head poked through the doggy door. He looked toward the living room.

"Shit!" the young recruit exclaimed. "Hey! Ackers! I found weapons!"

The head disappeared.

The door swung open and Bootcamp stepped inside, heading toward the couch.

I pocketed my weapon and stepped out, tapping the front door and closing the distance to the soldier.

I cupped one hand over his mouth, nose and jaw line. Barring my other forearm across the back of his neck, I twisted his neck with a sick crack.

As I eased him to the floor the door creaked.

I rushed over, grabbing the rifle barrel that appeared through the widening crack. Forcing the weapon against the doorframe I yanked Ackers into the house.

Keeping him off-balance, I drove an elbow into his Adam's apple. He wheezed and clucked, attempting to draw breath. I jammed the heel of my hand into the bridge of his nose. As bone fragments impaled his brain and blood dribbled from his nose, the soldier made one last glugging sound as his eyes rolled back.

Now dead weight, I dragged Ackers next to Bootcamp.

Patting them down, I scavenged their ammo vests, rifles, sidearms, and an oversized Bowie knife that certainly wasn't military issue. I tossed the equipment on the sofa.

Both their radios came to life.

"What's taking you so long, Ackers? Find something good? Over."

I stared at Ackers' radio a moment before turning it off.

"Garrish? What the hell are you two doing? The Lieutenant Colonel wants us to clear this subdivision ASAP! Respond. Over!"

I turned off Garrish's radio, too.

"John," Donovan whispered from upstairs. 'They're coming."

Grabbing the Bowie knife, I went to the foot of the stairs and jabbed the air in the direction of the bedroom.

Donovan went back inside.

Running through the kitchen, I snuck out to the back yard. I stayed low behind a row of bushes to the side yard.

The third soldier, a PFC, ran across the front lawn.

A voice rang out.

"Sarge! They're dead!"

The Sergeant sprinted onto the lawn, a cigarette between his lips and an M16 in his hands.

He passed the corner of the house and I followed.

"Behind you, Sarge!" the PFC shouted.

PFC, on the stoop, pointed his rifle at me.

Sarge turned, tripping over something in the overgrown lawn.

PFC squeezed the trigger.

I grabbed the harness of the twisting Sarge. The PFC's rifle erupted in semi-controlled bursts. The Sergeant took the brunt of the weapons fire, his body reverberating with the impact of at least half a dozen rounds. A few stray rounds spun past me into the grass.

The PFC's mouth gaped as his rifle clicked empty.

He looked down at his weapon with shock.

I pushed Sarge forward and, using our momentum, hurled his body into the PFC. He put his hands out and tried to catch Sarge with his free hand. I plunged the Bowie knife between the PFC's ribs to his heart. His helmet slammed against the concrete stoop, the Sarge partially across his thighs. I was straddled on top with both hands on the knife's hilt.

A gurgle from the PFC turned into a dribble of blood. He stared at me with a furrowed brow and wide eyes until one last wet bubbling exhale smoothed out his face.

Donovan clicked at the window, the curtain draped behind him. Daisy pressed her nose and front paws against the pane. I pulled the knife from the PFC's chest after some effort and cleaned both sides of the blade on the Private's shirt before sticking it through my belt.

I patted down the bodies.

Donovan opened the front door and I handed him the equipment. The PFC had a wallet filled with one hundred dollar bills and a portrait of a young blond girl with a gold embossed 'Class of 2019' on the corner.

The Sarge carried two folded New England gas station maps with towns circled with red marker. All the towns north of Rainier Island had Xs through them, recent dates and arrows running between the towns down the Atlantic coastline. He also carried a military-issued compass and loose bills.

I dragged the soldiers inside and dropped them next to their teammates. Donovan closed the door behind me.

Their weapons and supplies sat on the couch with the equipment I had scavenged.

Good kid.

I unfolded the map again. The dates started two days after the outbreak. The earliest date was next to a crossed out circle in Portland, Maine. Five other crossed-out circles peppered the coastline, the dates three or four days apart. Rainier Island and other towns to the south were circled without any dates next to them.

I tapped Donovan on the shoulder and pointed to the stairs.

He pouted but grabbed the ferrets and mounted the steps again.

The bedroom door clicked closed.

I needed to get to Lucy.

Taking a last look around the living room I crossed to the front door.

Opening the door, pain exploded across my jaw.

Slamming into the stairs, my spine jammed on the steps.

A dark shape straddled me in a watery blur.

A rifle butt came down again before I could get my hands up.

The world went painfully black.

Again.

111

Crosses to Bear

+26 Days – Afternoon

Vibration and dust coated my vision.

Sharp pain shot through my body with every bump.

My eyes were no more than blurry slits through my swollen face.

Asphalt ran like a conveyor under me.

My arms stretched out behind me, my lower legs disappearing under a rust pitted chrome bar.

Gravel sprayed across my face.

A white pick-up truck with patches of green rolled down the road in front of me.

The air went dark and cool with the smell of pine.

The Tunnel's canopy flickered sunlight.

We rounded a corner.

More vehicles in the convoy rumbled into town.

I flexed, my arms firmly and painfully restrained.

The vehicle hit a pothole.

Sharp aches like stabbing knives radiated out from the center of my shoulder blades.

The day brightened again.

A breeze mixed with smoky blue exhaust splashed across my face.

The asphalt gave way to cobblestones as we passed over Mall Street. The shops blurred past me, their windows dark.

Cobblestones turned into asphalt again.

With a squeak of brakes, the convoy came to a halt in front of the Oceanside Diner.

Doors eased opened and slammed shut.

A silhouette blocked out the sunlight, accompanied by smaller wavering forms.

"So this is the man who has become the hemorrhoid in my ass?" the largest shape asked.

The owner of the voice dropped to one knee.

I squinted up at the man with the name Wallace embroidered on a patch on his breast pocket.

The Lt. Colonel gazed at me.

A faint scar ran from his clean-shaven chin to the corner of his right eye. Without that scar, Wallace could have made a living as a model.

He ran his smooth manicured hand across my face, turning my head side to side.

"I calculated you would be the only real problem here. That one scope reflection in the church tower on my first visit told me everything I needed to know. I thought one well-placed RPG would rid me of you, but luck is a fickle bitch, isn't she?"

His arms perched across his knee and he leaned in.

"You must realize that you're going to be made an example."

I glared back, my vision clearing.

Ropes whined and tightened as I struggled forward.

"Always the warrior. Let's see how you enjoy being a tribute."

Wallace brushed off his fatigues and walked away. I dropped my head, the pain and exhaustion in my neck suddenly overwhelming.

Two sets of boots came into my line of vision. One set was military issue, the other a new pair of tan work boots. One military boot scratched the back calf of the other.

"This the one you told me about?"

Tan Boots rocked back on his heels.

"Yeah. That's him."

A hand grabbed my hair and yanked my head up.

Dropping to eye level, Tan Boots stared at me. His foul breath exhaled through crooked yellowing teeth.

"I have a bullet in my shoulder courtesy of you, Walken."

Rodrigo Sanchez pressed the barrel of my Glock to my temple. My vision blurred.

"The Lt. Colonel says that I can't fuck you up. Says you're to be put on display." Sanchez pulled away my Glock and displayed it. "At least I have a souvenir."

His fingers tightened on my hair, pulling my face closer.

"Just to let you know, you will pay for what you did to my family."

He cocked my weapon back and crashed the bottom of the grip into my temple.

My neck snapped to the side and the world faded for a time.

112

A Little Ribbing

+26 Days – Evening

Wake up, John.

As I came out from under the warm blanket of unconsciousness, the pain in my arms and shoulders returned with the feel of hot serrated blades.

A hiss escaped through my teeth.

"Walken. Wake up."

I tried to turn my head. My arms were still bound, now at a more severe upward angle. Although in the same forward pitched position, the hot front grill and rolled steel had been replaced with some sort of post running up my back. Duct tape wrapped around my forehead, waist and ankles. Salt and a tinge of cut grass hung in the heavy dusky air.

"John!"

The cobwebs cleared from all but the darkest corners.

"Can you hear me?" Sheriff Garrett called out.

I answered with a quick whistle.

"Damn, John! You okay? One whistle, yes. Two whistles, no."

I hesitated then whistled once in response.

"Good. Listen, John. That Lt. Colonel Wallace is one crazy fuck," Garrett responded between tired breaths. "If you haven't figured it out yet, they strung us up in the plaza like we're shit-pole scarecrows. Had the audacity to clean and dress my gunshot wound before stringing me up. Guess they want us to last awhile.

"Wallace's men were clearing the Presidency until you took down some of his men. What's your body count? Thirteen?"

I whistled once.

Garrett exhaled then fell into a fit of coughs. When it subsided he spit out whatever had come up.

"You haven't made many friends, John," he said, clearing his throat and spitting again. "You and me are warnings. After Anderson's shot to the head and you and me on display, most have surrendered and are corralled in the diner. I heard Wallace's men. Once he's finished, I know we will end up dead on these poles."

I whistled twice.

"Always the optimist." He chuckled until another fit of coughing stopped him. "Don't know how we came to this. I thought the end of the world would be enough. When the rules break, I guess people do too. Wallace comes across as a diplomat, until his charm becomes a bullet to the head. Foster was a shit heel, but even he didn't deserve what he got."

Light flickered. My left eye worked better than expected, the swelling already going down. The fluorescents from inside the diner spilled light onto the sidewalk. Shadows crossed through the glow, both inside and on the curb.

Garrett's quiet sobbing carried on faint puffs of breeze. The slightest of whistling through the gazebo's lattice joined in.

The crack of a slap.

The Sheriff exhaled.

"What's the matter, Sheriff? The beautiful summer night breaking your romantic heart?"

Shuffling of boots on the pavers and a round of laughter followed.

"Screw you," Garrett hissed.

"Yeah Sheriff, I don't think that is going to happen. In case you haven't noticed, you're a little tied up at the moment. Unless you happen to be into that, I guess. Are you a little freak, Sheriff? Use those handcuffs for a little more than upholding the law?"

"He must, Roscoe! Not like there was much to do around here before the shit hit."

The comment elicited a couple snickers.

Another slap and hiss, followed by a spitting sound.

"Sonofabitch!" from a new voice. "You're going to pay for that, Sheriff."

"Hey, Roscoe, I hope he wasn't infected," from the second voice. "I wouldn't want you to get Necromonia!"

More laughter. Sounded like four or five men.

"Fuck you, Wright," Roscoe said. "You infected, Sheriff? You trying to give me Necromonia?"

The clicks of buckles as someone unslung a rifle. That was followed by a *humpf* as the rifle butt drove into Garrett. There may have been a snap of a rib. Garrett wretched and started another coughing fit.

The men laughed again.

Someone struck a match.

Another gut shot from a rifle butt made Garrett cry out before falling into ragged breathing.

More laughter.

This time joined by hooting and high fives.

I whistled.

When the noise did not die down, I whistled louder.

"Sounds like someone's finally awake," Roscoe said.

A twenty-something PFC came up to me, his stenciled nametag indeed spelling out Roscoe. I spit in his face, between his eyes.

"Fuck!"

"Oh shit, Roscoe! You're definitely going to need a vaccination now!"

The PFC wiped his face, a fierce look in his eyes.

"Shut the fuck up, Wright!"

Wright, standing off to the right with two men, doubled over in laughter. I smiled.

"Think you're funny?"

I looked from Wright to Roscoe, not breaking my grin or gaze. Spittle still clung to his cheek. His arm tensed up, ready to swing.

"Be careful, PFC. He did take out thirteen men."

Roscoe turned to a smoking soldier in the shade of an oak tree, unseen except for his boots.

"All the more reason to beat him to the last inch, Bowers."

"Sergeant, if you please, PFC." Bowers responded softly. "Problem is, you don't want to get to that last inch and let the Lt. Colonel find out you couldn't manage to reel it back in. Am I clear enough for you, soldier?"

He looked back at me.

My gaze and smile hadn't changed.

PFC Roscoe, either unnerved by me or by the rational suggestion by Sergeant Bowers, loosened up the tension in his shoulders and moved to within a few inches of me.

"Lucky you're on display for Wallace, fucker. Otherwise..."

I stared back and broadened my smile.

He backed up and walked away. The other soldiers followed, giving me dirty looks. Bowers finished his cigarette and flicked it away, leaving Garrett and me alone in the darkness with only the crashing of the ocean for company.

113

Young and Restless

+27 Days – Pre-Dawn

The pain had dulled to a numbed ache. My vision had cleared. Had I not been crucified in the center of the plaza, I would have thought I was recovering nicely.

Soldiers patrolled the perimeter, walking repeating circuits but not venturing close to us like Bowers, Roscoe and their squad had during the night.

I tried to stay alert, but unconsciousness did not mean the same as sleep. With no other soldiers coming around to torture us, I let myself relax.

Soon I drifted off…

… and due to the nature of the injection and the position of the entry track, both your left and right vocal cords have suffered vocal paresis or what we call vocal cord paralysis. Neither of the folds can move. It's still uncertain whether the paralysis is due to damage to the nerves going to the vocal cords or if the muscles themselves are suffering full paralysis."

I tried to ask a question but my throat wouldn't cooperate.

"We will be shipping you stateside in a few days," the military doctor continued. "Bethesda will continue research and aid in your recovery."

He leafed through my chart, his eyes scanning through the sheets. He got up from the metal stool, its legs screeching on the hospital tiles.

I grit my teeth.

"Sorry about that. If you have any questions, you can write them down." He pointed at the end table to the right of the hospital

*bed. A clear glass vase with water and an assortment of flowers sat
in the center of the tabletop, a legal pad and a pen next to them.*

*I shook my head. I wasn't in the mood to facilitate any more
bad news.*

"Okay. Get some rest."

The doctor hung the clipboard at the end of the bed and left.

*As the door started its hissing swing close, a gaunt pale man in
a 'government issued' black suit and mirrored sunglasses slipped
in. Without a word, he picked up the medical chart and leafed
through the paperwork.*

"Sergeant John Walken. We hope you are recuperating well."

*He put the clipboard back and walked to the right corner of
the bed. The man smiled, revealing perfect white teeth.*

He tapped the top of the footboard.

*"You were on death's door, Sergeant. Lucky for you, one of
our support team medics was onsite at your base camp when you
and what was left of your team were brought in. One injection
later and here you are on the road to recovery."*

He shot me another smile.

*And materialized at the side of the bed, stroking the bed
covers.*

"I can imagine you are very appreciative."

*He took off his sunglasses and looked through the lenses,
blowing a speck of dust off and putting them away inside his
jacket.*

His pupils seemed too dilated for this bright, white tiled room.

*"We apologize for the injury you have sustained. We are
confident you will have a full recovery. Of course, I am no
doctor." He continued to grin, standing motionless.*

*I glanced at his fingers, still making swirling motions on the
bedspread.*

"We wouldn't want you to become disgruntled, Sergeant."

*He suddenly stood directly beside me, his face leaning in. His
teeth revealed semi sharp edges. He held up a syringe, squeezing*

the plunger with his thumb and producing a bead of yellow fluid at the needle's tip. The bead grew until it dangled from the thin-gauged needle. It lost its grip of the metal shaft and fell onto the bedspread. The drop fizzed and smoked as it ate through the fabric.

I looked back up at the Gaunt Man.

He was watching the fluid with interest.

The fluid burned through the top cover then the bed sheet beneath, finally losing its caustic properties enough for me to keep my hospital gown intact.

"Good thing I didn't push out any more." His grin opened wide, the corners of his mouth seeming to reach his earlobes. "I wouldn't want to put you through more pain. Definitely would not want you to suffer more than you have. Agreed?"

He pressed the syringe against my face, stroking my cheek and jaw with the tip. I stared back at those black oily eyes with as much defiance as I could muster. When I did not flinch, the Gaunt Man raised the syringe. He flipped it around and plunged it deep into my chest...

... and forced out a ragged noiseless gasp to bring me fully awake.

The duct tape restraints kept me from moving but my body still managed to shake uncontrollably. I sucked in a series of haggard breaths. The shuddering slowed just a bit.

The corners of the still vivid dream started to wither, but I continued to feel its effects. Some of it was cast from actual memory, some from pain and subconscious reconstruction. The problem was I couldn't remember the line where reality broke down.

The sun started to rise, casting a feeble light across the waves.

Hearing Garrett's own ragged breathing, I wondered how many more sunrises we had left.

114

Full House

+27 Days – Late Morning

Sweat beaded down my neck into my collar. I had the overhang and the bulk of the gazebo to shelter me but Garrett had an unobstructed view of the sun as it beat down on him.

I watched the soldiers.

Teams stood at each corner of the plaza. Trucks came and went. Twelve to fifteen men worked in shifts inside the Oceanside Diner. Before the sun made the windows of the diner a blinding reflection, islanders huddled in groups supervised by one or two guards. The security details would swap out every thirty to forty-five minutes.

Three teams of soldiers with M14s surrounded the Exxon station – more importantly, Sebastian's tanker truck.

A panel truck roared in from Mall Street, coughing out exhaust. The truck pulled up to the curb opposite the diner to block my view of the restaurant.

Two soldiers outside the diner stepped over to the back of the truck, hovering five meters back from the rollup door with their rifles up.

The driver jumped down from the cab and moved to the rear. He slammed the butt of his pistol along the side panel as he walked.

The other guards laughed.

The driver put his gun away, unlatched the roll-up door and let it chatter open. He barked orders to people in the back, pointing toward the diner.

First came Donovan with his satchel. His face was swollen and discolored. After him Steve hopped down from the rear bumper. Once his boots hit the pavement, the guards yelled at him to get his hands up. Steve exchanged a shrug with Donovan, and put his one arm up. Both of them disappeared into the diner.

Pete, looking naked without his weapons, got out. He lunged at the closest soldier, receiving a rifle butt to the temple long before he got a hand on the guard. The old gun shop owner slumped to the curb, half in the dry gutter.

A blur jumped down from the truck and rushed to Pete's side. Dr. Rawlings knelt down to check his condition. The doctor pointed a finger and yelled at the soldier who had assaulted Pete. The soldier shrugged, responding with a mock swing of the rifle butt.

Basia jumped from the truck and stormed over to the soldier. She slapped him across the face. The other soldiers roared with laughter as the young gun's cheek, then whole face, reddened.

He raised his weapon.

She stood there with her hands on her slender hips.

"You're a dead woman!" the guard yelled.

After a few tense moments between healer and death dealer, the driver tapered off his laughter enough to step between them.

"Go help your doctor," he pointed at Basia. He turned to the soldier. "Take a walk, Wright."

The soldier glared at his superior before slinging his rifle and walking away.

More people were unloaded from the truck and ordered into the diner. A couple of the young guys, Kyle and Simon helped Dr. Rawlings carry Pete from the curb. Basia followed behind them, keeping a wary eye on the remaining soldiers.

The driver shouldered his rifle and extended his hand to the open panel. The remaining guard came up and extended his hand as well. They helped the eighty-three-year-old Mrs. Saunders down.

It wasn't Lucy.

I closed my eyes and said an unfamiliar prayer.

115

In God We Trust

+27 Days – Afternoon

The sun continued to beat down.

I twisted my wrists, the sweat on my skin working through the gluey bindings.

"John?" Garrett called out, his voice weaker.

I whistled backed.

"My body is numb and my face is tingling." His voice broke and hitched as he talked. "If Wayne was still here, he would have shot that bastard straight away."

Garrett cleared his throat.

"Whatever he went through on the Main that day must have been brutal."

Another pause, longer and more ominous.

"...we're not going to last another night," his voice almost a whisper. "We're going to rot on these crosses. God help us."

I could only hope that someone could help us, because I knew from experience God didn't seem to be listening.

116

Languish

+27 Days – Evening

The sun drifted lower into the western sky. The gazebo's shadow stretched out across the grass. An unseasonal drop in temperature and the shade should have been a relief, but the cooler air bit at my damp skin.

Sweat and blood rolled down from my bound wrists, soaking through the cotton cuffs of my T-shirt. I could twist my arms a full forty-five degrees, making the work to loosen the restraints more productive.

Sheriff Garrett had fallen silent since his terse prayer. He had come a long way from that uncertain deputy on the day of the outbreak, but he wasn't seasoned enough to endure a crucifixion.

Someone slapped me.

"Sorry to disturb you gentlemen," Lt. Colonel Wallace said.

He stuck a finger between my lips to check out my teeth before heading toward the Sheriff.

"Corporal Ames, did you feed these men?"

A gangly freckled-faced redhead bolted over to the Lt. Colonel.

"You said you wanted them to suffer, Sir."

"The world may have gone sideways, Corporal, but there is still a thing as mercy. I want them as living examples. Christ."

The last word came across the breeze softer than the rest.

"Private Douglas!"

"Sir!"

Private Douglas, a muscular Asian man, ran across my vision.

"Get some food from the diner for these men."

"Yes, Sir!"

The corporal and private double-timed across the plaza.

Lt. Colonel Wallace stood ruler straight with his thumbs tucked behind an oversized belt buckle that was not Army issue. Behind him the rest of his detail stood at ease.

"You're holding up well, Marine. I believe you'll outlast the Sheriff by a day or two, maybe three." His breath smelled of mint. "You do realize that you will die here, don't you?"

I glared back without changing expression. Our staring contest ended when he busted out in genuine laughter. His face lit up in an almost humanizing way.

"Good for you, Marine." His laughter tapered down to chuckles. "Good for you. I could use more like you."

Wallace patted me on the chest, reverberating shards of pain through my body.

"You will die here," Wallace spoke softly, leaning in as if to kiss my check, "and suffer until you beg me to end it for you. My men you killed will be satisfied knowing your death will be slow and languishing."

Wallace stepped back, smacking me softly on the cheek before turning towards the diner. The other soldiers in his detail fell into step behind him. Ames and Douglas saluted their commander as the Lt. Colonel stepped off the curb.

Ames and Douglas double-timed past me. The bag Ames had been carrying crinkled as he rummaged through it. A quiet snap and a plastic grating followed.

"Here. Take a drink."

"Ames! You're spilling it all over him. He can't tilt his head back, idiot. Use the straw. The lady at the diner put it in the bag."

"Oh, yeah! Here, Sheriff. Drink."

A few more seconds of silence was followed by a fit of coughing and gurgling.

"Slowly, Sheriff! Shit!"

"Easy, Ames. Give the man a break. Use the napkins."

I tuned out the soldiers and went back to observing the patterns of Wallace's men.

117

Rude Awakenings

+27 Days – Night

Sudden pain shot through my belly.

" – and shine, muthafucka!"

I opened my eyes to a darkened world.

A fist connected against the side of my jaw, lighting up my vision. I tried to shake my head to clear the stars but the duct tape restricted me.

With sweaty skin, dirty clothes and a left arm wrapped in a dingy sling with a pint of whiskey poking out, Sanchez looked at me with a twitch that pulled at the corner of his mouth.

"I always knew that I would get another shot at you," he spat at me as he talked. "You ain't so tough now, are you?"

Spittle sprayed from his mouth, dribbling down his unshaved chin. His pupils nearly eclipsed the faint dark ring of iris, the whites bloodshot.

He paced, his slung fist clenching in unison with his free hand. "Look at me!"

He danced from one foot to the other, reaching back and swinging his fist.

I felt a crunch then numbness under my left eye. A wet sting seeped from my cheek. One side of vision blurred and wavered into darkness.

Whiskey from the open bottle splashed onto his shirt.

"Muthafucka!"

Sanchez dropped the bottle to the walkway where it shattered.

"Leave him alone!" Sheriff Garrett yelled out.

Sanchez's grin faltered for a moment. When it reappeared, the grin was wider than before. He reached into his windbreaker.

"Remember this, Johnny?"

He held up my Glock.

Grit and dirt caked along its slide. The front sight was scratched.

Sanchez ran the side of it down my cheek, blood staining the end of the barrel. He waggled the gun at me and snickered.

"Leave him alone," Garrett said in a more even tone.

"I guess you'll have to wait." Sanchez sighed. He started walking away but turned back. "Don't go away."

That set him into a fit of laughs that continued as he disappeared from my dim view.

Sanchez slapped Garrett once, then again.

"As a sheriff, you ain't so tough either, are you? Got a hick police commandant and a self-proclaimed war hero on the same island, and you're both strung up."

"Why don't you go sleep it off?"

"Let me respond in the form of a question. Why don't you kiss my culo?"

"No one's to blame for the death of your wife."

"Says who? You? There's plenty of blame to go 'round. That stupid Professor… McDougall.. and you two! If Captain America had just let me go instead of hunting me down like a dog I would still have a daughter!"

"No one killed your little girl but you."

The breeze died down and silence followed.

Minutes seemed to go by.

I could only make out pieces of Rod's quiet whispers, none of it making sense.

Sheriff Garrett did not temper his response.

"Listen, shithead! You killed your wife as soon as you decided to leave this island. You killed your little girl when you smothered her to death trying to hide. Don't fucking project your stupidity and blame on us! Why don't you take your drunk ass somewhere before you do something you can't recover from?"

"You're small town! Small sheriff, small island, small fuckin' existence. I'm not the one strung up like butcher meat, am I?"

The familiar sound of a slide pulled back and let go, a bullet now chambered.

"Say it's your fault."

I strained against the duct tape, trying to get a glimpse of Garrett and Sanchez. My muscles stood out but I only managed to turn my head enough to make out blurry shapes.

"I won't do it."

"Say it!" Sanchez hissed.

"No."

A shot rang out.

Wood splintered.

I raged against the restraints. Some of the tape tore, but not enough to break free.

"Say it!"

"No! Get that through your head!" Garrett shot back.

Shadowy movement invaded the darkened left side of my vision. Two soldiers ran toward us. They flanked, moving with quiet precision with their M14s drawn.

"I lost everything 'cause of you people!" Sanchez shouted.

He moved back into my sightline, waving the pistol at Garrett.

"This fucking island was the worst place we could have wasted time on. I knew it from the start! That professor wasn't as smart as he thought he was!"

Garrett responded in slow, soft words.

"We asked you and your wife to stay."

Sanchez reverted to pacing and using the pistol to scratch at his scabbed hairline.

"Sanchez!" one of the soldier's voices boomed.

They arrived, their weapons at full draw. The one who shouted at Sanchez stood five meters to my two o'clock. The other soldier came up and positioned himself inside the gazebo. He flipped off his weapon's safety.

These two were young, but experienced.

The soldier in front of me spoke in an authoritative Kentucky accent.

"Let's lay down that weapon, Mister Sanchez. Nice and easy now!"

Sanchez approached Kentucky, waving my Glock.

Kentucky raised his rifle barrel slightly.

"They killed my wife!"

"That may be the case, sir, but this is not the place to air those grievances."

Sanchez spun and aimed the weapon at Garrett.

"Sir!" Kentucky asserted, moving in a step.

The gazebo soldier thudded into a better position.

Sanchez looked at Kentucky, his neck straining with the gun pointed behind him. He brought the gun back around and pointed it at me.

"You don't understand what I've been through!"

"We've all suffered, sir. Now put the weapon down or I will put you down."

"You don't have the balls."

"I do, sir. And I have standing orders from Lt. Colonel Wallace to back those balls up at my discretion."

Kentucky flipped off his safety and placed a finger on the trigger.

"Last chance, sir."

Sanchez looked from Kentucky to me. He licked his lips and glanced at the soldier in the gazebo before looking back at Kentucky.

He raised his good arm over his head, letting the Glock go limp in his finger. The gazebo soldier approached Sanchez with his weapon trained on him. Circling around Sanchez and lifting the Glock off his finger, the soldier tucked the weapon into the front of his gear. He patted Sanchez down for any other weapons, stepped back and gave Kentucky a thumbs-up.

"Roger that, Corporal." Kentucky nodded. "Okay, sir. We'll hold on to your weapon for now. You can see the Lt. Colonel about retrieving it tomorrow. Let's move along."

Kentucky waved his rifle barrel from Sanchez to the diner in three quick motions. Sanchez walked away, Kentucky and the Corporal stepping in behind him in a tight processional.

Kentucky gave me a passing glance as he went by.

I hung in the center of the plaza with blood dribbling down my face, my lip split open and my cheek swelling up again. I wondered if Sanchez would come back for more justice or if we would even last long enough for him to get a second chance.

118

Early to Bed, Early to Rise

+28 Days – Morning

The sun warmed my cheek, comforting me as it baked away the chills from my tired, aching muscles. I opened my eyes to the glint of the rising sun over the Atlantic, its rays splashing across the tips of the waves.

Wallace had his soldiers fully deployed, walking the plaza's perimeter and standing post in front of the Oceanside. Two more soldiers paced the diner's roof.

I licked my split lip, the coppery metallic scabbed remnants not stinging as much as expected. The swelling had subsided and my vision had returned.

Lucy was right. I *was* a quick healer.

In spite of that, all feeling had left my arms. The numbness drifted down to what felt like a central rusty railroad spike driven between my shoulders.

Coughing interrupted my assessment.

Garrett was waking up.

"John? You still there?"

I whistled once.

"Good," he said weakly. "Hell of a night, huh?"

He chuckled to himself, the light sarcastic laugh turning into a fit of phlegm-filled coughing. He spat out what he had brought up and settled into more even breathing.

"Think Sanchez shot me. Or maybe just reopened the gunshot from Wallace."

A pang of fear knotted my stomach.

I whistled once.

"Yeah. Maybe nicked me. I don't know. Stings. Figured it would hurt more. Maybe it's splinters. I don't know."

Garrett went silent as the sun pulled itself out of the Atlantic. Once it fully escaped the ocean, Garrett spoke up again.

"Hope we get more food soon. I really could use a drink, you know?"

I doubled whistled.

I pulled at the duct tape binding my wrists. The tape had stretched and the glue had started failing, but the twisting of the tape made my intended progress counterproductive. I couldn't pull my palms past the handyman's shackles.

Activity stirred at the corner of the plaza.

The soldiers on duty finished their circuit and headed to the diner, idling about and waiting – more on edge.

A tired looking Kentucky stood in the group. A fresher looking Douglas and Ames seemed no worse for wear after Ames' lapse of judgment. Kentucky's partner, the Corporal, stood off smoking at the edge of the lawn. Bowers and his men, including Roscoe, stood in front of the diner. The spy Dexter Holloway was there – outfitted with an M4 and a red bandanna. Some of the others I recognized from their patrols, only knowing them by rank and visual description. In total, I counted the current contingency of Wallace's men at sixty-seven.

Others may never have set foot in the plaza or Wallace may have exaggerated the strength of his troops from the onset. Maybe the others were spread throughout the island or still on the Main.

Most of them seemed young and rag-tag, fresh out of boot – maybe even the academy or reservists – but some, like Kentucky and his partner, had more tactical experience. It was easy to spot the 'boots' from the vets, although it usually had little or nothing to do with how fresh of face they were.

Radios were raised, orders were shouted and fingers were pointed. Several of the patrolling soldiers stood at ease on the sidewalk. Other soldiers stood in front of the diner. Only the soldiers in rotation at the Exxon station and on the diner's roof stood to post.

Wallace's armored truck turned onto North Plaza Drive, stopping in front of the diner. Wallace's driver got down from the cab, hurried around the piked FRAC heads to open the passenger door.

Lt. Colonel Wallace stepped down and marched around the vehicle with the Sergeant behind. Wallace crossed the street and spoke with one of his men.

I followed the Sergeant's movement as he drove the truck down the block and stopped in front of Town Hall. He hopped down and stood at ease next to the door.

Wallace had disappeared.

After a minute he came out from the Oceanside.

Ames followed but slammed into the closing door. Ames gave Wallace a dirty look but held the door open.

All of the soldiers who had been at ease stepped away from the diner in a widening ring, their weapons at full draw. The men positioned on the roof aimed their weapons into the circle.

Wallace faced the diner, his hands clasped behind his back.

People were ushered out of the restaurant, their clothes dirty and wrinkled. They lined up inside the circle of Wallace's men. The crowd grew as the diner emptied. Carol, Doctor Rawlings, Basia, and Donovan stood at the front of the group, each with grim faces and darting eyes.

Over two hundred residents stood crowded together. A last soldier walked out from the Oceanside and gestured to Wallace. The Lt. Colonel cleared his throat.

"As you know, we are moving you to Town Hall. Once there, my men will escort you into the main chambers."

He nodded to another sergeant.

"Alright people, let's move!" The subordinate ordered.

Wallace turned about at the head of the column and walked toward us. With nudging and a few shouts, the remaining residents started their reluctant march.

Wallace stopped in front of me.

"We are not oppressors," he addressed the crowd with arms out. "We are your protectors from the villainy, torment and brutality that exists past your borders!"

Wallace pointed out to the direction of the Searing Bridge.

"Some of you may wonder why you have not encountered more survivors. The truth is the road is too treacherous for all but the most experienced and most well armed to move from city to city, and town to town. The Zekes, the ones you call FRACs, roam free. Entire cities have been laid to ruin with fires and dissent. Gangs of thugs and marauders take everything they want. We have the ability to move freely and protect our own and those who stand with us.

"Some chose to blindly fight with a misplaced sense of duty or honor." He flipped a thumb over his shoulder to the sheriff and me. "Do not end up like them. I beg you."

Wallace suddenly spun around and resumed his march toward Town Hall. A few more barked orders got the crowd moving again.

Carol looked up at me as she passed, covering her mouth. I smiled and threw her a wink. I couldn't tell if she smiled back.

Doctor Rawlings and Basia came next. He took one look at me and gritted his teeth. Basia gasped and tried to come to my side. A soldier, anticipating that, responded with a raised rifle barrel and orders to keep moving. Rawlings grabbed her around the waist and escorted her past us, shielding her from the spectacle of our crucifixion.

Donovan, Steve and Pete shuffled by. Donovan mouthed the word 'Sorry', a tear falling down his cheek.

I nodded at him.

From under the cover of the satchel a furry domino masked muzzle poked out. Steve held his stump with his good arm, hugging himself. Pete, still hobbling from his post-truck ride rifle whipping, took one look at me with bright eyes and spat on the boots of the nearest soldier. He received a hard shove for his trouble but smiled at me in solidarity before he disappeared out of sight.

Other residents walked by.

Most took a quick look.

Some kept their heads bowed.

A few stared with shared defiance.

Tricia Reynolds was in the processional, but not Lincoln. Foster's pet councilman Monroe was MIA. The Sistern men were not in attendance. A couple of Donovan's new skateboarder friends and Jacob were missing. No David and Rita.

And Lucy was gone.

As the throng of people thinned out and the last of the armed soldiers filled in behind them, I realized just how few of us had survived. The processional had added more burdens to my already heavy heart.

The last soldier, Bowers, walked by with a quick glance before following on with the rest of the crowd. The air grew quiet and the streets took on the appearance of a ghost town.

"John."

I whistled back.

"I don't think we have much longer, friend."

As much as I didn't want to believe it, the sheriff's words had started to ring with more truth.

119

Stragglers

+28 Days – Early Afternoon

The activity throughout the rest of the day remained the same as the breeze - still and quiet, with brief flits of movement. The roving patrols had pulled back to Town Hall. The snipers stationed on the diner's roof had disappeared, though men still guarded the Exxon station and Sebastian's truck.

Occasionally, a patrol walked by.

For a late lunch, Ames and Douglas came back with peanut butter sandwiches and water. This time, they didn't speak to us or to each other. When done, they retreated to the street in time to meet a flat bed truck pulling up in front of Town Hall.

Wallace's men had picked up over a dozen more islanders. Among them was a bruised and bloody Lincoln Reynolds. Three of the skateboarder crew – Paul, Dillon, and Frankie – sat in the back of the truck, looking incomplete without their boards. An older couple huddled against the back of the cab holding hands.

The rest of the people I couldn't identify.

I just knew Lucy was not with them.

120

Tale of the Tape

+28 Days – Night

The lampposts didn't go on, leaving the plaza dim and gray. The Lt. Colonel either hadn't figured out how to turn on the lights, figured they didn't work, or hadn't beaten the information out of anyone yet.

Sheriff Garrett hadn't spoken since eating. I had whistled a couple times but received only rattled breathing in response.

The roaming patrols had disappeared. Even the Exxon station sentries were gone.

I pulled at the duct tape around my wrists. Three days of blood and sweat had loosened the glue but had rolled the tape into rope-like cords.

The muscles in my arms and shoulders didn't ache anymore. In fact, I couldn't feel them at all.

The temperature dropped and a mist rose from the ground, swirling lazily across the grass and walks. The lawn's perimeter was lost in the fog in spite of the rising moon's light.

Something danced in and out of the farthest edge of my vision. *Miss me, John?* The Gaunt Man asked.

The blotchy shadow darted at me.

I balled up my fists, but could do little else.

The slight black form came at me with a glint of pointed silver. The thing rushed between the Sheriff and me, light footfalls on the steps.

Long fingers wrapped themselves across my mouth.

Heavy breathing warmed my ear.

"Don't worry, Mr. Walken. I'm here to get you out."

Was I confused? Or just dreaming?

The fingers disappeared and cold metal slid against my wrist under the duct tape. After several sawing motions my arm dropped to my side. Agonizing shards of pain replaced the numbness I had been enjoying.

My rescuer hacked against the duct tape wrapping my legs to the pole. When the tape broke free, my legs were left dangling. He moved to cut through the other wrist restraint.

A noise drifted through the night.

The blade stopped.

Three blotted forms glided along the curb behind the veil of fog, stopping at the corner of the plaza. A matchstick flared to life and danced in the air before snuffing out. Three cigarette tips brightened and faded.

The barely bodied voices carried across the lawn, faint but understandable.

"This duty is starting to get a little screwed up," A young voice, cracking and high pitched, spoke up.

"Starting? That's an understatement," replied a deeper voice.

"Stow that shit, gentlemen. Unless you want to be strung up as fast as the sheriff and the Marine over there."

"Come on, LT. Aren't we just stealing what we want and weeding out new recruits? Isn't this how the militias build armies in South Africa? Going after ten-year-old boys and forcing them through boot camp with a rifle in their hands?"

"I would advise you stop talking and finish that smoke, soldier," the lieutenant said with a tired edge.

"Yes, sir."

The floating glow of cigarettes brightened in unison. One of the red embers sailed through the air and hit the ground with a spark of embers. The other two red tips dropped to the ground without fanfare and were extinguished.

The dark shapes drifted toward Mall Street, their voices receding.

My rescuer returned to slashing through my other wrist restraint. My arm dropped like a stone, buzzing needles working through it. The duct tape around my forehead was cut through, pitching my sore head and neck forward. My waist and chest loosened from the post, my weight stretching the bindings.

I suddenly fell, landing in a heap on the grass between two small shrubs.

"Shit! Sorry, Mr. Walken," he whispered.

Spitting out a few blades of grass, I tried to get up.

Quick hollow thuds from the gazebo.

The black clad man grabbed me under the armpits. As he pulled at me, the sensation of pulverized glass between my muscles roared back to life, making me wince and inhale sharply.

"Come on," he whispered, "we don't have time."

I got on my hands and knees then onto my shaky legs. He leaned me against the gazebo's entry post, my shoulder hitting it with another painful jar.

The slender shadow put a hand on my chest.

"Stay here. I have to cut down the Sheriff. We still need to get to better cover. So be ready."

He disappeared back into the darkness. He whispered something to Garrett and the sheriff mumbled something back.

I stretched. My muscles were more accommodating than expected, the pain and numbness already fading. I pulled the remnants of bloody duct tape from my body.

Both of the Sheriff's arms, his legs, and head were hanging loose, leaving his chest and waist held tight with tape.

Grasping out to the post I pulled myself along until I stood under the sheriff.

In the moonlight he looked pale and swollen with blood caked down his face. An image of Emily Proctor hanging from the library staircase flashed through my mind.

Garrett exhaled a puff of breath in the cold night air.

"Just another minute, Mr. Walken."

As each strip of tape around the sheriff's chest snapped loose Garrett leaned more forward. I cradled his head on my shoulder. After a snapping sound Garrett's full weight fell against me. I leaned back, controlling his momentum to the ground.

The cutter rushed over and knelt beside us.

"Okay… okay," he muttered.

He rolled the sheriff off me and helped me to my knees.

"We need to get off the plaza."

I looked at the masked and camouflaged face, unable to place his eyes.

He grabbed the sheriff under the arm.

"Come on. Help me."

As much weight as Garrett had shed, he was still dead weight. We finally got him up and moved to the pathway.

The fog blanketed the ground in a thin gauzy haze, slow wispy tendrils wrapping around the extinguished lampposts.

"Okay. Let's go," the masked man ordered.

We dragged the sheriff across the lawn to the sidewalk. His legs helped with a random step or two.

"We need to get to Pete's."

We staggered into the street, like a trio of drunkards - or the undead.

121

Dark Alleys

+28 Days – Night

The rear entrance to Pete's shop was three doors away.

The fog settled thicker in this sunken channel, veiling discarded pallets, dumpsters, garbage cans and other debris that had piled up over the weeks.

We pulled the sheriff along, keeping close to the store wall, unable to see farther than a meter in any direction.

Sudden clashing.

An aluminum trashcan tipped over at the far end of the alley. We stopped.

My heart pounded as laughter drifted over to us.

"Knock it off, dickhead!" a voice said.

"Sorry, man!" was the response between cackles.

"Come on, man! I can't see where the fuck I'm goin' in this soup! I just want to take a piss, for Santa's sake!"

"Dude, that saying is never going to catch on! Hurry up, man. We need to get back to Town Hall!"

"Quit rushing me," Santa said. "You're giving me performance anxiety!"

Laughter came from Funnybone.

"Quit it!" Santa whined.

More laughter from Funnybone, wrapping up with a snort.

I motioned to the Shadow.

We guided Garrett onto the closest stoop. The Shadow sat down with Garrett's arm around his shoulder. The Sherriff slumped against the handrail.

I put a finger to my lips.

The Shadow held up his knife.

I took it.

With Garrett's weight off my shoulders, my muscles felt better.

I moved toward the two voices.

When I looked back, Garrett and the Shadow had already faded into dull cut out forms.

These two voice were the same as two of the three soldiers from the cigarette break in the plaza. While the fog worked to conceal me, it worked just as well for the soldiers. If they were spread out across the alley, I would not be able to keep the element of surprise for long.

Creeping next to a decaying smell rising from a steel dumpster, I passed two rear store entrances before I caught movement.

Standing by a dumpster across from the rear entrance of Pete's store Santa tried to relieve himself.

I hunkered down.

Neither of the other two soldiers was visible.

The weak-bladder, but piss-shy, soldier shifted his weight.

"Come on," he mumbled. "Damn it."

I crept up behind him.

With a quickness that startled me, I covered his mouth, nose and jaw with my right hand. With one quick forceful twist of the knife, I severed his spinal cord.

He went limp.

I laid him out slowly on the wet pavement next to the dumpster, his urine finally starting to flow.

I felt around his waist and found a Bowie knife and a Beretta M9. I sprung and checked the magazine before sliding it back into the grip with a faint click that seemed too loud. After a count of ten, I put the pistol in my waistband and slid up next to the corner of the dumpster

"Come on, Stokes! Aren't you done with that piss?"

"Go get him, Wilkes," came from a third voice.

"Yeah, okay, LT."

I gripped the Bowie knife in a hammer grip.

Wilkes appeared at the corner of the dumpster. I thrust the knife upward between his ribs.

Directly into his lung and heart.

My other hand swung behind Wilkes' neck.

I drove his body onto the blade, burying his mouth into my shoulder.

He fell forward.

I stepped back and controlled his descent, pulling the knife out at the same time.

With two men dead, I had better odds against the Lieutenant. I was cornered, but the alternative would be running into the Lieutenant as I moved to a better position.

"Wilkes! Stokes!" The Lieutenant's voice boomed, echoing off the walls. "You better be ready for an ass-kicking!"

The safety on his M14 flicked off.

"Wilkes! Stokes! Sound off!"

I scooted past Wilkes and peered around the corner of the dumpster. A flicker of a dark form wavered in the fog, but did not solidify. If I shot at it I was not guaranteed to hit anything, and I would give away my position.

A shrill laugh came from behind me.

It scared the shit out of me.

It trailed off into giggles.

I backed away from the corner, grabbing Wilkes' collar and inching his body along with me.

"Wilkes! Why are you two always screwing with me?"

The cackles continued.

"I should leave you two here for Wallace to fuck up!" The lieutenant's voice boomed closer. "That would teach you to screw with the chain of command!"

I pulled out the M9 and grabbed the tied top of a small garbage bag.

After several seconds the Lieutenant's appeared.

His rifle was raised, but not at a full draw.

He saw the bodies on the ground and pivoted his gun around.

I raised the garbage bag.

His smile turned into an "O" of shock.

I shot through the makeshift silencer, sending a bullet through his forehead.

The muffled retort still bounced off the hollow metal of the dumpster, ringing long after the lieutenant's body thudded to the ground.

122

Shopping Spree

+29 Days – 0445 hours

After I whistled the all clear, the Small Shadow brought the semi-conscious Sheriff Garrett to my position, opposite the rear entrance to Pete's store.

I pulled the lieutenant's body over to Wilkes and Stokes.

His patch said his name was Lenard.

I scavenged their weapons and gear and put them in a wooden crate.

"Like my laugh?"

I gave the Shadow the thumbs up and pointed to the steel dead bolted rear entrance door.

"No problem."

He jangled a set of keys in the air. He sat Garrett down on the steps and unlocked the two deadbolts. Using the key as a grip he pulled open the smooth-faced door.

The Small Shadow pulled Garrett up and guided him into the dark shop. Following with the crate as the door hissed closed behind me, I locked the deadbolts.

The Shadow flicked on a flashlight and helped Garrett down the hall into an office, plopping the sheriff down onto a ratty orange cushioned futon. Garrett made a grunting sound and laid his head back, eyes closed.

The small man shone his light in my face. I set the crate on the paper-strewn desk and raised Stokes' pistol back at him, thumbing back the hammer.

"Whoa!" He raised his hands with the light from the flashlight reflecting off the ceiling.

He lifted his ski mask and tossed it at the crate. Even with his long stringy hair covering his smeared face, I recognized him. He was the missing Monroe Johnston.

I dropped the M9's hammer back and tucked it into my waistband.

"Listen, Mr. Walken. Before the soldiers got to up the majority of islanders, Pete handed out spare keys to four of us. Doc Rawlings got caught on the second day and Deputy Reynolds got rounded up yesterday. Diggs and me still managed to keep off their radar. He's at the farm."

I grabbed a nubbed-down pencil and wrote on the back of an ammunition delivery slip. I showed it to Monroe. His mouth moved as he read the words.

Where's Lucy? Still alive?

Monroe looked from the paper to me, expressionless. Before he answered, he leaned against the wall and ran his fingers through his hair.

"She was in pretty bad shape, Mr. Walken. When the soldiers came around, she was running a fever over 104. The Doc tried to bring her temp down, but the soldiers broke in before he could."

My hopes dropped. I started pacing.

"Diggs said that when Wallace's men came in, Rawlings and Basia rushed upstairs so that he would have time to get Lucy out through the cellar doors."

She was alive.

"Diggs said to get you guys, get supplies then get back to the farm. When I left, Lucy still had a fever but it was breaking."

I had to get to Diggs' place.

"We gotta get ammo and guns, and get back to the farm. He says he's got a plan, but he needs you."

That sounded like a good start.

Dried blood covered half of Garrett's face and the front of his shirt. He looked like he could sleep for a month. He wouldn't make it to Diggs' place on foot.

I swiped the flashlight from Monroe and walked out of the office. Keeping the torchlight focused I found a large canvas duffle bag behind the counter. Unzipping the bag I slid open the doors to the storage cabinets under the display racks. With a quick flash of light, I pinpointed the ammo cases I wanted, slid the bag below and dumped the boxes in.

As I lifted the bag onto the counter Monroe rapped the glass top.

"Diggs said he wants handguns and a sniper rifle."

I pointed to the end counter case and slid the duffle across the countertop. Monroe grabbed an assortment of 9mm handguns and added them to the bag.

Dust lingered in the moonlight seeping through the barred front windows. The outlines of Winchester 30/30s, pump-action shotguns, and other weapons lined the wall, but there were no sniper rifles. The sheriff's department had 'borrowed' all of the larger, more powerful rifles. Diggs would have to be content with the pistols.

"Okay, Mr. Walken. I think I have everything we can carry."

After filling the duffle to capacity, he had stuffed pistols into his waistband.

I had to smile at his new bravado.

Monroe grabbed the duffle's handles and pulled it off the counter top. Gravity and Monroe's slight physique let the bag drop to the floor with a bang.

"Shit! Sorry, Mr. Walken."

I shrugged, shook my head and glanced out between the bars of the front window. The fog had thickened to a point where the plaza's curb was behind a white blanket.

Crossing the store, I shouldered the duffle, the contents shifting.

Nodding to Monroe, I headed back to the office. Light danced off the walls as he picked up the flashlight and followed me. Garrett snored softly.

"We're not going to be able to move him, are we?"

No.

I calculated the sheriff's and the duffle's weight, plus the three miles distance from the shop to Digg's farm. Even with optimal fog cover, I don't think the three of us would get far enough.

"I'll stay here with Garrett. Get to Diggs and let him know what's happening. If the sheriff has enough strength to move before dawn, we'll try to make it to the farm."

Garrett slept.

I grabbed a Glock 17 and three 15-round magazines from the crate then went to the rear door with Monroe, the duffle on my shoulder.

He turned the deadbolt latches as quietly and slowly as he could. The click of the bolts seemed too loud as each of them opened.

On a white dry erase board next to the door I wrote:

Check the sheriff's wounds

Monroe shone his flashlight on the message.

"Ok."

I leaned against the delivery door, letting the Glock match its slow swing open. When fog started to sift inside, I stepped down to the alley.

The fog hid everything.

Monroe closed the door.

The deadbolts clicked into place.

After a moment, I move forward into the white-washed unknown.

123

Mist

+29 Days – 0525 hours

Even with the dense fog and the weight of the duffle, I made good time across open ground. The only sounds were the slap of my boots on the asphalt and my breathing.

Ten minutes later, I found myself socked in with zero visibility. The canopy of the north shore's tunnel compressed the mist to such a point that I veered onto the road's soft shoulder before realizing to course correct.

Muffled popping sounds punctuated the still air.

Picking up my pace, I navigated the middle of the road by feel more than by sight. My visibility expanded back out to three meters as I got to the end of the canopy.

More gunshots peppered the air, from the north. Wallace's men must be busy stemming back a FRAC pack on the Norte Bridge crossing. With all the activity over the past few days, more walkers must have been attracted to the island.

I jogged down Rainier Road as it curved toward the Presidency.

The fog thinned a bit.

The street sign for Washington Street loomed to my left.

The fog vibrated with the rumble of a truck in low gear coming from the east.

I crouched next to a picket fence and drew the Glock up.

The vehicle's large dark shape shimmered, becoming more distinct. The edges of the flat bed truck pierced the fog's veil, its headlights burning through as it lumbered up the hill.

I pivoted on my back foot as the truck passed, twisting for a good sightline.

Two soldiers occupied the flatbed. One stood behind the cab and the other sat on the back edge looking out into the fog as it kicked up in the truck's wake.

The truck drifted back into the fog.

A few seconds later, three metallic slaps rang out.

The brake lights glowed bright.

After some mumbling, the red taillights disappeared after a brief flicker of white.

A door creaked open and a pair of boots thudded to the asphalt.

I retreated to a vantage point farther down the fence line.

More boots on the asphalt, three pairs in all. The truck stood idling and empty as the soldiers advanced toward me.

I stepped into the front yard of Jefferson Street #2, drifting toward the house behind the cover of the bushes.

"Something was right here, Deacon." One of the soldiers pointed out.

"There's nothing here now, is there?"

"Come on, Jack, this fog's effed up, but I know I saw someone in front of the fence."

'What do you think, Jeffers? Do we reconnoiter?"

"In this fog? Nah. Let's get back to Town Hall. Wallace wants to start the eliminations before the end of tomorrow."

Jeffers sounded as weary as the fog was thick, but he also sounded committed to Wallace. Jack and Deacon just sounded weary.

"Come on. Let's get back."

"Yeah, I'm hungry," Deacon said.

"Agreed," Jack said.

The boots padded away.

I stepped away from the overgrown bushes. With a clear outline of the retreating soldiers, I let out a piercing whistle. The three turned in unison, their weapons coming up.

I fired three times.

Three soldiers went down.

The echoes of the Glock's discharges faded quickly.

What was left was the truck's idling motor and a faint groan.

One of the soldiers writhed in pain.

I stood above him, the soldier with the patch Deacon on his camo jacket putting a hand up to ward me off.

I shot through the hand into his forehead.

The other two didn't require additional medical attention.

I dragged them to the truck and dumped them onto the flatbed. After collecting their weapons, I went to the driver's side and tossed them and the duffle up on the bench. I hopped in and backed the truck onto Jefferson Street and turned to the east.

124

Diggs' Digs

+29 Days – 0545 hours

The truck bounced as it rumbled over a hundred meters of gravel to the main house of Dickerson Farm. I parked in the turnaround. Taking the keys, I grabbed the duffle bag and hopped down to the stone driveway.

I went to the front door and knocked.

No answer.

I rapped on the screen door, the metallic rattle echoing on the frame.

After a minute I squeaked opened the screen door and turned the doorknob. I pushed the door open an inch and whistled.

No answer.

I push the door open a bit more.

A handgun hammer clicked behind me as its barrel pressed against the base of my neck.

"Don't move."

I stopped. My hand clenched the doorknob.

"Step back. Close the door."

I complied.

"Turn around slow. Hands up."

I put up my hands and inched around.

The owner of the gun stepped back far enough to stay out of reach.

Once I completed my 'about face', he spoke again.

"Fuck, John! You almost gave me a heart attack."

Diggs lowered the gun and gave me a big bear hug. He released me just before my ribs thought to give way. He pulled back, his meaty hands still on my arms.

His grin turned to a frown.

"Where's Monroe? Where's the sheriff?"

After a thumbs-up I made a writing gesture in the air.

"Okay. Okay," he replied with a slap to the side of his head. "Yeah. Yeah. Let's get inside."

I turned toward the front door.

"Not that way! You open that door and you'll get a gut full of buckshot! Come around to the side."

He patted me hard on the back and hurried to the end of the porch, dropping off and disappearing around the corner.

I hitched up the duffle's strap and followed.

At the corner, Diggs' silhouette stood at the side steps with a hand through the barely open door.

"Come on in, John. I disengaged this door."

We went inside.

Heavy curtains covered the windows in the kitchen and living room, making the space dim and oppressive.

Duct taped to two chairs was a double-barreled shotgun pointed at the door. Fish line filament connected from the trigger through a series of eyehooks from the back of the chair, to the ceiling and to the outside kitchen wall above the door. Running down the wall to the backside of the door, the fish line ended in a snare over the doorknob, easily removed by someone who knew what he or she was doing.

Diggs put his gun on a coffee table, picked up a flashlight and headed toward the hallway.

"Come on, John," Diggs said, looking back at me. "I'm sure you're wondering how Lucy's doing."

She's still alive. Thank god.

"She's fine, by the way."

Diggs went to the larger bedroom. The bed was empty.

I frowned.

Diggs opened a bedside table drawer and rummaged through it.

"There you are!"

350

He swirled a pen on a note pad then handed them to me.

"What happened to Monroe?"

I scribbled on the pad then showed it to him.

Sheriff too weak. Both at Pete's.

"And the truck?"

I wrote another message.

Killed 3 men to get it.

"Well done, Johnny. We'll thin these bastards out yet!"

I wrote on the pad, flipping it around.

"What's the plan? We're going to raise some hell, boy! Slap that Lieutenant Colonel with the Hand of God!"

Diggs smile cracked wider.

"The Hand of God, Johnny!"

He slapped me on the shoulder as he slipped into the hallway.

"Now let's go see how your girlfriend is doing!"

I took the pad and pen and followed Diggs back through the house.

Diggs picked up his gun and went back out to the side yard.

I slipped through the screen door before it slapped closed behind me. Diggs walked over to the front of a shed extension built off the farm's original red barn.

"Come on, Johnny." Diggs waved me over. "Hurry up."

The fog had thinned considerably, its weakening swirls clinging around Digg's legs. The barn's silhouette stood in dark bloody relief, looming above him while a single hooded bulb provided a large pool of light.

The shed extension ran the length of the original barn's sidewall, jutting out with a sloping metal roof. Washed in barn red with white trim, the structure glimmered in the moist early morning light. On closer inspection I realized that the red on the walls had started peeling in spots and the window was full of spidery cracks.

Diggs pushed open the steel door.

I stepped in as Diggs closed the door, the darkness of the room overwhelming. A mixture of industrial cleaners and rot hung in the air.

"Hold on, let me get the generator going."

He shuffled around in the darkness. The sound of a pull-cord preceded the sputtering and accelerating chug of a gas-powered generator. Bare fluorescent bars clinked and flickered into cold life.

The room was a combination workroom and storage shed. Gardening tools hung neatly on corkboards on the far interior wall. An old tabletop electric stove with a saucepan sat on a wooden bench. Diggs hunched over a generator, adjusting its throttle. A flexible aluminum exhaust pipe ran from the generator to a hole at the top of the wall.

"There we go."

Using a hand on his knee, Diggs got to his feet with a grunt.

"Let's go see your girlfriend."

Unlocking the deadbolt to a second door, Diggs swung it open and gestured me forward.

The room was pitch black, blackened further as Diggs blocked most of the available light in the doorway.

"Let me get these lights. Hold on."

The heavy smells assaulted me. The cleaners could not cover up the underlying stench of decay. Exhaust fans whirred above me.

"Hold on. It's always a bitch finding the switches. Should have moved them closer to the door when I realized the contractor was an idiot!"

A series of clicks lead to more cold light.

"Sorry for the smell. When the horses died, they did so in violent fashion. I tried to clean it up as best I could."

Diggs' shadow moved to the right. As the light from the overhead fluorescent bars stabilized, I could make out a row of several wooden stalls along the space's length.

Diggs continued to the far end.

"I figured if Lucy was in here, any of Wallace's men coming around would check the house and maybe the main barn, but would be put off by the smell in here," Diggs called back. "I don't think Lucy minds, though."

Diggs leaned a shoulder against the far rail of the last stall.

"You can put the duffle down anywhere."

I shrugged off the cache of guns and bullets.

Diggs waved a hand into the last stall.

I scrawled two words on the pad then handed them back to him.

"You're welcome, John."

I slipped past him with a smile and a pat on the arm.

Lucy sat in the corner on a bed of straw.

She was covered with a horse blanket. Her hair hung in her eyes, her head drooped down to her chest. Her skin was sallow, accentuated by the cold light.

I rushed to her side.

Her skin was damp and cold.

The smell of excrement, musky sweat and urine permeated the stall.

Lucy raised her head.

I brushed the loose hair from her face.

Dark gray circles were painted under her eyes, her sockets hollow. Her eyes had changed from a dark brown to a flecked red and gold, laced with spider webs of ruptured blood vessels.

Lucy smiled with dark teeth.

She let loose a guttural scream and lunged at me. Lucy snapped her jaws, nearly sinking her teeth into my arm. I fell back, scurrying away on my hands and feet. Her forward motion came to a sudden halt. Lucy swayed at the end of a length of chain linked to a leather collar around her neck - previously hidden by her hair.

I backed up until I slammed against the corner of the stall.

Getting to my feet, I reached for the Glock and spun toward Diggs.

He smashed me in the face with the flat of a coal shovel.

The Glock skittered away as I fell against the wall.

Diggs' blurry shape hovered over me.

Lucy grunted and snapped against her restraints behind him.

My vision darkened.

Diggs' shadow moved closer, blotting out more light.

"You like Ms. Greenfield's makeover?"

125

Before the Devil Knows You're Dead

+29 Days – Morning

My eyes focused on the intricate swirls in the wood grain.

An ant walked between flecks of straw with a bit of grain in its jaws.

Each exhale through my bloody nose and mouth blew dust away.

I squashed my hands and toes under me as I twisted onto my back, the pain evident but distant.

I was hog-tied in the same stall as Lucy.

She sat on her knees, leaning towards me with her hands outstretched, the chain and collar holding her at an obscene angle. Her jaws snapped slowly, her raw fingers with ragged and cracked fingernails reaching out.

A stray tear streaked into my hairline.

"Don't cry, John."

I spun my head around.

A jolt of pain stabbed through my neck.

Diggs sat on a milking stool. A flashlight shined on his face. Supported by the handle of the coal shovel, Diggs looked ghoulish in the light.

"Sorry about all the misdirection, Johnny." Diggs grinned. "I didn't want you to give up hope before you saw your girl."

I stared at him with impotent rage.

He stared back.

"I mean, the look on your face. Priceless! Remember those old credit card commercials?"

Diggs looked at Lucy.

"People are fun. Just look at her. I gotta tell ya, spiking farm animals with FRAC blood just ended up messy, with a big hole to be dug. People, though, they dance around and provide all sorts of entertainment."

I raged against my bindings.

"Relax, Johnny. I'll untie you soon enough. I got big plans for you and your girl. You may hate me, but that Wallace is screwing up my playtime. And you, sir, will play a big part in taking care of that problem for me."

Diggs sat back, bringing all of the peg legs back to rest on the plank floor. He looked up at the rafters and rubbed his unshaven face.

"I tell ya. It was divine intervention when I finally took those overdue books to the library. I felt so bad for Ms. Proctor after that first attack. She was such a wreck. I figured returning some books would cheer her up, you know. But there she was, seconds away from climbing into a noose at the top of the stairs. What a shame!"

He leaned down at me, his breath a warm, acrid expulsion. His eyes were dark, the pupils dilated. The whites had suffered some.

"I didn't stop her. She was so wrapped up in killing herself that she didn't even realize I was there. I have to admit that curiosity got the best of me. She was just as timid trying to take her life as she was trying to save it at the bridge. And when she jumped off that top landing, boy did she skitter!"

Diggs smiled wide, enjoying his storytelling.

Then the grin quickly faded.

"But she didn't turn into a FRAC, John."

He mocked shock and shrugged.

"Yeah, right? I know! Here I am, enjoying the view at the bottom of the stairwell, watching her legs twitch. Then nothing!

"I'm not a perv, John. I can see that you think I was looking up Ms. Proctor's dress while she was lurching about up there under the rafters. That's a disgusting thought and I don't appreciate it!"

He shouted the last bit with spittle flying out of his mouth at me. His cheeks flushed, he stepped over me and started pacing.

I rolled over to face him.

"Son of a bitch, John! I'm not the bad guy here! Wallace and his men are! They just come here and think they deserve anything they want. My food, my water, my fuel, my cattle! But they ain't gonna get away with it. Once I'm done with things, those military assholes will have their hands too full to be my problem."

He stood with his hands in his pockets.

Lucy lunged at him but was choked back a solid meter from him.

"They just don't understand what's at stake here. But you and me are going to make them understand!"

Diggs dove at me, dropping to his knees and bringing his hands out of his pockets. He gripped a syringe filled with dark fluid, pulling off the cap with an expert flick of the thumb. Pushing my head away with his other palm pressed into my chin, Diggs stuck the needle into my carotid.

He pushed the plunger, a cool numbing in my neck running out to my shoulders. Diggs pulled out the syringe and tossed it into the corner.

He got up, favoring his left knee.

"Getting too old for this kind of work, John.

"Oh. I forgot to ask you. Did you enjoy Gloria's homecoming? She was one of my early works. Her, Emily and the FRAC in the tunnel. You have definitely been more than a match for the surprises I have left you."

Diggs stepped over me and left the stall.

"Kudos to your success, my friend. It looks like I can finally announce checkmate against such a worthy, if not victorious, adversary!"

He swung the gate closed and latched it.

"I'll be back for you later. We got important work to do, you and me. Too bad the sheriff and Monroe couldn't have attended too."

The fluorescent lights turned off a section at a time, fading the stalls into darkness. What took almost a minute to come to life died in seconds.

I struggled against the ropes.

A cool numbing tingle traveled out into the rest of my body. When the icy tendrils reached my chest, the coolness changed to a fiery burning coal in my heart.

Razor sharp blood pumped out to the ends of my body. It felt like my arteries were tearing to shreds. I grit my teeth, contorting against the pain. Sweat poured off my skin.

The pounding of my heart doubled.

Then tripled.

The tainted blood reached my brain, setting it on fire.

My vision filled with burst blood vessels and red tinged spots.

My limbs convulsed, snapping the ropes.

Foamy spittle slid from my mouth, pooling and congealing with the dust.

Lucy stopped lunging at me, slumping back onto the horse blanket.

I spasmed.

A railroad spike of pain slipped into the back of my skull.

A blinding whiteness darkened to a pinprick of deep crimson.

My breathing labored.

My heart slowed.

Sweat bled off my skin.

My breathing slowed.

The Gaunt Man appeared, his long fingers stroking Lucy's hair.

The red in my vision deepened to a dark gray dusk.

The pain was gone.

My heart fluttered.

My breathing hitched.

The thunder of an ant clicked across a plank.

My body relaxed.

Breathing thinned, then stopped.
Heart skipped a beat. Then two.
Then stopped.
The Gaunt Man stopped petting Lucy.
Welcome to the jungle, Johnny.

126

Brilliance

+29 Days – Time Unknown

You'll be the first of many. The point of the spear.
I felt cold.

The room was sterile and white, the tiles gleaming under harsh cold fluorescent lights.

The Gaunt Man stared at me from the corner of the room, although the two walls somehow did not meet at a proper angle.

I was strapped in a hospital gurney, immobilized by leather and buckles. The gurney tilted at a 45-degree angle, giving me the perfect perspective to view the too pale, too thin man.

You were such a waste, you know.

His thin red chapped lips moved, but the voice seemed to come from my own head. Scratchy, with the hint of buzzing bees, the voice sunk its bony fingers into the creases of my brain's soft tissue. I tried to shake my head against the deepening sound, but the straps held me firmly in place.

You never accepted it.

The Gaunt Man looked at his long fingernails and picked at something underneath one of them, absently flicking it away. When done he smiled at me with his sharp shark teeth.

Just accept it. You will feel so much better. I promise.

I tried to pull out of the wrist restraints.

He sighed and shrugged.

It's up to you, but you need to make a decision soon. Everything hangs in the balance. Tick tock.

He brushed off his sleeve and walked toward me, halving the ten meters to the gurney in only a few steps. With one more step he stood next to me.

He bowed at the waist and whispered in my ear. His voice rattled inside my skull.

You could have been a contender. You could have been somebody. Instead of a bum, which is what you are, let's face it.

The Gaunt Man's thin lips parted, revealing more glistening rows of pointed teeth. He blinked and the white around his eyes disappeared into a solid onyx. He brought his bony hand up and patted me on my chest.

Use the force, John.

He cackled.

A tear slid from the corner of my eye.

Wake up!

The Gaunt Man clapped his hands.

The room shook.

Wake up!

Another clap boomed like thunder, setting tremors through the room. The gurney started to slide but the Gaunt Man grabbed the side rail to stop it.

Wake up!

His voice sent the room into a quake. The vibrations split some of the porcelain tiles and popped others off the wall. They crashed to the floor, shattering without a sound.

The gurney hovered for a moment before slamming to the floor. Another bump held the gurney in midair before crashing it down again. The frame's piping snapped from their weld points. The gurney collapsed, the mattress landing on a pile of metal, padding and rubber.

I ripped one of my wrist straps entirely from the side rail. The other rail came away with the strap. I tore off the leather around my leg, not bothering to unbuckle them. I ripped off the wrist restraint still connected to the rail as I climbed off the debris.

The Gaunt Man stood in his non-corner again. I walked toward him, but couldn't reach him – no matter how many steps I took.

The fluorescent ballasts pitched above me, sparking and flickering. They swayed before breaking from their mounts.

The entire room jumped.

More tiles fell.

Light filtered through the cracks, each tremor expanding the fissures. As the fluorescents died, light streamed into the room through the broken walls with a blinding brilliance.

The Gaunt Man turned into a translucent shimmer before disappearing altogether.

More tiles fell and wider cracks formed.

I went to the wall and pounded my fist through the biggest fissure. Grabbing the corners of the crack I pulled it in. A large section of wall crashed back into the room.

Through the gash in the wall were the fields west of the Tunnel. The endless waves of the Atlantic crashed into the beaches and bubbled back out. The scent of high grasses and salt filled my nostrils.

A hand pressed my shoulder, sending a strange sense of calm through me.

Petra stood awash in a soft brilliance, a cooing blanketed bundle in her arms.

You have much to do, John. Go back, she said as she pointed toward the wall.

I looked through the cracks to the blue and green landscape.

When I looked back, Petra and her daughter were gone.

I grabbed both sides of the opening.

Taking one last look for the Gaunt Man, I pulled myself through the tiled fracture to the other side.

127

Cattle

+29 Days – 0949 hours

I slammed against an aluminum wall lined with horizontal slats. Fresh air puffed in, but not enough to disperse the rotting stench in the enclosed metal space.

My rope restraints were gone.

I turned around.

Walkers in various stages of decomposition pressed together in the metal confines of the livestock truck. The FRACs swayed with every bump and curve from the moving vehicle.

Lucy stood against the opposite side staring out one of the slats. Another bump knocked me off balance, sending me into a reanimated Sam Sistern. He gurgled and slowly yawned back at me but made no move to attack.

Poor Sam.

With the sun streaming in, I could make out others. Doug Chang leaned against two unknown FRACs next to me while Rita Atwood pressed against four of Wallace's soldiers in the middle of the trailer. At least a dozen others crowded in the rest of the space.

One of the unknown FRACs, neither island resident nor soldier, bumped me.

I expected the stringy blonde female to snap at me, but she bounced off without incident. Her gray face was marred by a deep slash through her nose and left cheekbone, clotted maroon blood covering blackened muscle tissue. One eye was milked over while the other had a deceptive amber clarity.

We passed through the Tunnel, its cool, dark canopy doing little to alleviate the smell and heat inside the metal box. Just when the coolness started to drift in, we drove into the sunlight again.

I shuffled past Doug for a better vantage point at the front of the metal box. I bumped the swinging remnants of a trio of dripping chicken carcasses hung from fishing wire.

Clever.

Through the slats, I could make out Diggs as he sat behind the steering wheel. He didn't look back or check his rearview mirror.

The dirt road entrance to the Norte Bridge came up on our right. Wallace's men turned around just as Diggs whooped like a cowboy and floored the accelerator.

The soldiers got off a few errant rounds before Diggs plowed them broadside into their own truck. We slammed to a stop from the impact, the other 'passengers' in the truck piling up against me.

Diggs threw the truck into reverse and sputtered ten meters from its impact point. Diggs got out, leaving the engine idling.

The FRACs shuffled back to the rest of the box.

With a shotgun in hand, Diggs went over to the closest soldier and blasted him in the chest. He went over to the next sentry, pumped the weapon and fired again. Pumping the shotgun a last time, he strolled over to the last soldier.

The young man said something to Diggs, his hands coming up in a feeble fending off gesture. Diggs lowered his weapon to waist level, still pointed in the young man's direction. The soldier smiled a sigh of relief and dropped his hands heavily to his lap. Diggs said something and the soldier responded with a nod.

Diggs nodded back.

Then he shot the soldier in the face.

Matter and blood spattered against the side of the truck, dripping sluggishly down the side door.

What was the last thing to go through the fly's mind before it died? Give up? The windshield! The bodiless Gaunt Man whispered.

Diggs turned back to the truck, but stopped.

He returned to the soldiers' truck and rummaged through a lock box behind the cab, coming out with a pair of bolt cutters.

Walking past the dead soldiers with the bolt cutters on his shoulder, he disappeared around the curve of the dam's service road.

I pushed my way to the doors. Although Diggs had not padlocked the latches, there was no way I could reach through the openings with my fingers to reach the latch, let alone flip it open for my freedom.

Pushing against the metal doors, I could feel the corner of the door starting to bend. I worked on the corner of the door for a few minutes, but the latches still kept me from getting out.

I returned to the front of the truck.

Diggs was back.

He stuffed rags into the gas tank of the truck he had been rummaging through. With the flick of a lighter, he lit the end and watched flames burn up its length into the gas tank opening. After admiring his work, he put the bolt cutters under his arm, grabbed his shotgun, and walked back to the livestock truck.

When he was in the cab with the door closed, the barricade truck exploded into flames and oily black smoke.

Diggs let out a whoop, his grin visible in the large side mirror.

128

Public Service Announcement

+29 Days – 1030 hours

Diggs parked on the grassy shoulder of Rainier Road. He fiddled with a knife as he cleaned his fingernails. When done, he spiked the knife into the bench cushion.

He pulled a cassette tape out of the breast pocket of his flannel shirt. After flipping it around in his fingers a couple times, he pushed it into the tape deck. Turning up the volume, he tapped his fingers on the steering wheel to the intro of AC/DC's "Hell's Bells".

I looked out the sidewall slats.

The black smoke from Diggs handiwork on the Norte Bridge billowed up a straight column of smoke.

The island's air raid siren whirred to life, roaring for two minutes before winding down again. Feedback from a bullhorn pierced the air. I moved past Doug and two other FRACs.

"Attention! Attention!" The Lt. Colonel's voice boomed.

Diggs turned off the radio.

"Sergeant John Walken. I see smoke coming up from the east. Bodies of three of my men were found in the alley behind the shops. Be on the plaza lawn in the next five minutes. If not, I will execute one of your precious islanders. Every five minutes will bring another execution."

The bullhorn emitted a series of mechanized clicks, followed by murmuring.

"I know you can hear me," Wallace continued. "I will give you free entry into the plaza. Let my men take you into custody and the executions will be stopped.

"The choice is yours… over and out."

Diggs started to laugh.

366

"Hey, John! Should I let you out now?"

After several seconds, Diggs' laughter tapered off. He wiped the tears from his eyes. He turned the radio's volume up and hummed along to a live version of "Thunder Struck".

I banged against the aluminum enclosure separating me from Diggs, denting the metal into the shapes of my fists.

"Hey! Keep it down back there," Diggs hollered.

I returned to looking for a way out of the box. The aluminum sidewalls and roof were reinforced. The back swing doors were latched shut. All the slats and vents were too small to slip through.

The FRACs crowded against each other, their noses sniffing the air and their teeth clicking together.

They looked at me. Even Lucy's vacant stare bore into me. None of them attacked, but their close proximity and milky eyes unnerved me. A faint humming came from nowhere and everywhere, giving me a headache.

Just then, a shot rang out.

My first five minutes were up.

129

The Next Five Minutes

+29 Days – 1035 hours

"Now we're talking!" Diggs hollered after the echo from the first gunshot crack faded away. "John, ole buddy, you're the center of attention! Funny Wallace doesn't realize how close you are."

The bullhorn clicked back to life.

"John. One of your fellow islanders is dead. I am sure you can see me, but if you are not down range, the name of your friend was…"

There was a pause and a click.

"Carol. I remember her serving me a bitter cup of coffee when I arrived. Nice woman."

Several seconds passed.

"Your next five minutes start now."

I slammed my fists against the front of the enclosure. The other FRACs started a low rumbling moan. They stared where I had slammed against the metal. A few seconds later they averted their milky gazes around the enclosure again.

Whatever Diggs had injected me with hadn't infected me. Or killed me. Whatever he did to me, the walkers didn't seem interested in me.

Looking at the dents in the enclosure from my fists, I realized I was stronger.

Murmurs filled my ears. The saltiness from the Atlantic and pine resin filled my nostrils, comforting scents under the rot of the FRACs.

I slid through the crowd and stood next to Lucy, looking at her bloody and muddy face. I moved away an errant wet strand of her hair. She reacted with a slow snapping of her jaw at my wrist. The reaction held no malice.

She slowly looked down at my hands as I squeezed her arms. Her dark eyes had not milked over completely, still gleaming with flecks of red and gold and a slight glimmer of dull animated life.

I placed my hands to her cheeks.

Was there a glimmer of life? Was there a spark of memory or a sliver of soul?

Lucy gazed at me and emitted a low mewing sound.

My heart broke as I ran my fingers across her bloody and waxen skin.

Lucy's hands pressed against my wrists, responding to my touch. Too soon, she pressed harder to break my grip.

I released her.

She dropped her arms and turned away, leaning against the aluminum, pressing her face through the narrow opening and sniffing the air.

"Three minutes, John!" Wallace alerted me through the bullhorn.

Diggs turned down the radio, currently playing the original "Mad World" from Tears for Fears. He fiddled with a black Casio watch, pressing the side buttons. Removing the watch he buckled it around the top of the steering wheel. The readout displayed 2:21… 2:20… 2:19.

Diggs turned the key, letting the engine sputter to life. He dropped the transmission into first gear and revved forward, the walkers and me lurching against each other. Tapping the accelerator, Diggs coasted down the brick-lined street until the corner of Town Hall came into view.

In the plaza the gazebo stood in stark relief against lush wet green, the fog leaving a glistening landscape. On the Town Hall porch, Wallace and his men had tightly corralled the islanders. Some hugged, others sobbed or glared at their captors with disdain. I could see them as if I were standing in front of them.

Below them, Carol lay with her arms spread out and her eyes open. Lines of dripping red traveled down the stone steps. A large crimson crater lined the left side of her temple, partnered with a smaller circular dot on her right.

Diggs revved the engine with his foot still on the clutch.

The soldiers raised their weapons. Wallace waved them off with a grin.

Popping the clutch, Diggs' fully loaded truck squealed forward, its back tires sliding and spinning for a moment on the still wet asphalt. The truck accelerated then screeched to a halt halfway down North Plaza Drive.

Behind me a sea of FRAC arms, legs and torsos twisted together.

Diggs fiddled with a loop of rope next to him. 1:07 displayed on the mounted watch. Disappearing through the cab's roof to the top of the enclosure, the rope produced a metallic slap each time it was pulled.

"We are at one minute, John," Wallace's voice shot through the bullhorn. "Again."

Diggs pulled over the weapons duffle and grabbed a Beretta. He holstered another in an underarm rig, squeezing two more between his thigh and the flaking bench upholstery.

"Forty-five seconds. Here's your new candidate."

Wallace dragged Donovan over.

Steve broke free from the soldiers. He received a rifle stock to the face and fell back into the crowd.

Jacob rushed after his friend.

A gunshot rang out.

Jacob fell forward, skidding to a stop next to Donovan.

"Jacob!" Donovan screamed.

Wallace put his still smoking nickel-plated Mark VII .44 Desert Eagle against Donovan's head. Wallace's driver, the Sergeant, held the bullhorn in front of him.

"Twenty seconds, Marine. I guess saving women is not a priority. She was a cow, anyway. Not worth the effort on your part or the bullet on mine. But not coming to the aid of a child, John?

370

Surely a child would elicit an honorable response from such a patriot. I mean, even this young man dead at my feet tried to save his friend!"

I slammed my fists into the container's front walls, turning the dents into craters.

The Sergeant mouthed something to Wallace.

"Ten seconds," Wallace updated. "Your choice."

Diggs rigged up more rope between the steering wheel and handmade mounts on the dash. He positioned a 2x4 next to his leg then stomped the accelerator and popped the clutch.

The truck jumped over the curb. We streaked across the lawn on a collision course with Wallace. Tying the ropes to eyebolts on the dash, Diggs ducked down just as rifle fire chattered. Bullets ricocheted off the cab's hood, grille and enclosure. The windshield cracked, then exploded, with the hail of ammunition. The truck hurled onto West Plaza Drive, roaring onto the sidewalk and up the Town Hall steps.

Wallace continued to grin as the truck bore down on him.

Donovan tried to twist away.

The soldiers continued to fire.

The truck crushed over Carol's body. Wallace dove out of the way at the last moment, pushing Donovan into its path. The truck missed them both. It thumped over Jacob and accelerated toward the lobby doors.

The massive double doors and sandstone walls were no match for the speeding panel truck. The grille and hood smashed through the entry, slamming to a wedged halt in the doorframe.

We hurled forward, my shoulder banging into the front wall. A sound like a tuning fork resonated in my ears. I stumbled to my feet, using the sidewalls for balance.

I couldn't see Diggs in the cab through the dust, but heard the same slapping metallic sound at the back of the trailer. After a couple hard slaps, the back double doors flew open.

Hard light washed the interior of the trailer.

Intermittent gunfire filled the air, followed by the islanders' screams and soldier's yelled orders.

The FRACs, attracted to the open doors and the noise outside, staggered to the back of the trailer and fell off the edge.

They slowly regained their feet and sniffed the air.

The FRACs, including Lucy, went off in pursuit of fresh meat.

130

The Last Minutes
+29 Days − 1058 hours

Islanders fled down the steps and away from Town Hall, soldiers shooting some of them in the back. Steve went down on the grass. Basia and Dr. Rawlings, in spite of the gunfire, went to his side.

Three soldiers had their throats torn out by Doug, Patrick and Sam before they realized the FRACs had dropped off the back of the truck. As the men went down, other soldiers turned to face the new threat flanking them. The soldiers fired their M14s in a panic, riddling the walkers with bullets.

Doug went down with a lucky shot to the head. Rita shambled past her fallen lover with a growl and outstretched arms toward the soldiers. She was put down. Sam took a shot to the neck before being dropped with a fatal bullet to the forehead.

A trio of soldier FRACs shambled past me in pursuit of a lone soldier trying to fire on the retreating crowd. As their shadows reached his feet, he spun with his rifle raised and barrel flashing.

One FRAC received a strafe of bullets from his ribcage to his head before he dropped to the ground. The soldier fired on the second FRAC, but didn't land the kill shot before the rifle clicked empty. The FRAC, and his remaining flesh-eating partner, tackled the serviceman. The soldier's screams quickly drowned out into wet gurgles.

While the fallen serviceman was feasted on by two of the FRAC soldiers and Patrick, I reached between them for the rifle, two magazines and his sidearm. The walkers didn't flinch as I scavenged off the soldier's body.

Maybe they realized I'm trying to survive, just like them.

I shot the soldier in the forehead. Then I shot the two FRACs execution style before they realized their food was getting cold.

I paused for a moment.

Then shot Patrick in the back of the head.

I stepped back to the crashed truck.

Wallace had disappeared.

His soldiers fought against the walking dead. They seemed to be winning. Most of Diggs' FRACs and a couple islanders were strewn out on the steps and the street.

Several FRACs with mouths and arms red with fresh blood lumbered after the soldiers. The men formed a protective circle, the front line on one knee. Gunfire erupted and a line of walking dead dropped in their tracks on the lawn.

A FRAC crossed in front of me. I shot him in the back of the head.

A series of low moans came from behind me. The soldiers just killed under the porch's awning struggled to get to their feet. I shot them dead - this time for good.

The islanders ran toward Mall Street or the church. The soldiers who weren't trying to round up the islanders continued to fire at the walkers.

Pete ran across the grass. He scooped up an M14. As he brought the weapon up, he was shot. He tumbled to the grass and remained still. I spun and placed a round in PFC Roscoe's temple. He fell with the still smoking barrel clutched in his hands.

Two reanimated soldiers moaned and stumbled by, oblivious to my presence.

I shot them both in quick succession.

Lucy stood in front of the gazebo.

She cocked her head to the right, sensing for something to chase.

Her lips gleamed red.

Fresh blood dripped from her chin.

I carefully took aim.

Lucy's left eye disintegrated in a mist of red and gray. Her jaw slacked as she pitched unceremoniously forward to the ground, her arms spread out.

What the fuck?

Rod Sanchez stood at the top step of the gazebo with my Glock in his hands. A wisp of smoke rose from its barrel.

I kept the gun sight trained on Sanchez's forehead and walked toward him.

Rod stood his ground and fired.

A bullet buzzed past my ear.

I kept walking.

My vision turned red with flashes of light, my temples filled with sharp pain.

Sanchez adjusted his grip, squinted and pulled the trigger.

The muzzle flashed in slow motion.

I sidestepped as a clump of grass split open beside me.

Blinking the pain away, I exhaled and squeezed the trigger as I walked. Sanchez cried out as I put another bullet in his wounded shoulder.

He let go of my Glock.

It slid across the planks and hit a post.

Sanchez lay on the steps with his blood pooling under him.

I pressed a boot to his throat. He grabbed my heel with both hands.

"Maricon," he sputtered.

I leaned on his neck.

He grimaced and gurgled against the pain.

Then I shot him in the fucking skull.

Stepping over Sanchez's body, I retrieved my Glock 18. First checking the breach, then ejecting the magazine to see the remaining rounds, I hammered it back home with a comfortable and familiar click. I tossed the borrowed gun into the grass.

Returning the Glock to its rightful holster, I stepped over Sanchez' cooling body. Once my boots touched the stone walkway, my vision cleared of the painful rose tinted flashes.

Wallace was nowhere to be seen.

Seventeen soldiers remained in the plaza. Residents continued running towards the church.

Two men with sniper rifles had repositioned to the diner's rooftop. Sergeant Bowers shouted orders from the sidewalk. Three four-man teams ran out from the curb, stripping their fallen comrades of their gear. A few of the fallen soldiers received a bullet to the head as a preventive measure.

I headed to Town Hall and hoisted myself into the trailer. With the dust cleared, I could see through the front slats to the cab. The driver's side door stood wide open inside the splintered and powdery mess beyond the lobby's doorframe.

No Diggs.

I retreated to the rear doors and stepped down to the porch.

A rifle stock snapped across my face.

My thoughts went hazy.

I crashed to the porch.

My head bounced off the stone patio.

I shook my head and propped up on my hand.

It was kicked out.

Lieutenant Colonel Randall Wallace stood above me, the rifle barrel pressed against my ear.

"Sorry, Sergeant. As the cliché goes, 'This town ain't big enough for the both of us'. Once you're gone, I will go find your delivery man."

I closed my eyes and waited for the bullet.

131

Crossfire

+29 Days – 1136 hours

Motionless on my hands and knees, I focused on my breathing. The sudden thought of death seemed welcoming.

"Good bye, Sergeant," Wallace said.

I exhaled slowly and waited.

"Wallace!" screamed someone, followed by a cracking sound.

Splinters fell around me as Wallace's shadow disappeared.

Donovan held a section of the Town Hall's doorframe. The end was split and dangling.

Using the truck's bumper I struggled to my feet.

Donovan tossed away the wood.

"Come on, John," he said as he propped me up.

Lt. Colonel Wallace was sprawled out cold.

I pulled my Glock to finish him off.

"John! Look out!" Donovan warned, shoving me into the truck trailer.

Bullets sparked and pinged off of the aluminum.

Wallace's men fired on our position, both from the middle of the lawn and from overwatch on the diner's roof.

I returned fire.

The last brass shell ejected and the slide locked open.

I had lost count.

Whistling, I handed Donovan the Glock and a spare magazine from my rig. I swung the rifle around and brought it up into a firing position.

Men had taken up behind the gazebo where Sheriff Garrett and I had been less than twelve hours ago. Duct tape still hung in tattered bloody strips.

The roof snipers were out of view. I would have to expose my position for a better sightline. Or shoot through the side ports.

Instead, I focused on the soldiers on the plaza.

I flipped off the M14's safety.

Without needing the scope, I squeezed the trigger.

The muzzle flashed and the air cracked.

A millisecond later a spray of crimson mist clouded behind one of the soldier's head. He sunk from view.

I shot a three-round burst of cover fire.

Sounds like heavy rocks off metal pinged the left side of the trailer.

"John! The guys on the roof are shooting at us!"

I took my eyes off my targets and slid back a few feet. Grabbing Donovan by the collar, I pulled him to the rear of the enclosure just as a bullet buried itself into the deck beside him. The safest spot was behind the swung open rear doors. The snipers would not have a clear sightline. They could get lucky with a blind shot, but for now their distance and angle served as a disadvantage.

I slid to the opening.

Two of the gazebo soldiers were breaking right toward the church.

I fired at the trailing soldier. The bullet tore into his side under the arm. He fell forward, his momentum crashing him into his teammate. They both went down in a heap.

The larger young man in fatigues pushed out from under his downed companion and clawed to his feet. I shot him in the base of the skull.

The last soldier at the gazebo had stopped firing at the truck, taking cover behind a post. I peeked through one of the side slats. Another rain of bullets pinged the truck.

Rolling back to the rear of the deck, I grabbed Donovan by the waist and jumped out. Bullets whizzed by as we took cover behind the double rear wheel.

Wallace was gone.

Damn it!

Donovan thumped against the massive rubber profile of the tire. I pointed to the gap under the truck leading into the building.

He shook his head, not understanding.

I pointed again. He looked again, nodded and scurried through the rubble to the wall, sliding past a massive column that the truck had barely missed on its collision course.

I reloaded the rifle.

Donovan tossed over the Glock. "It's reloaded!"

Pulling the slide, I holstered the weapon.

Damn! I didn't have a good sightline to the diner's roof.

We needed better cover.

I inched to the rear of the truck. The last soldier had abandoned the gazebo, flanking for better cover behind the curbed trucks in front of the diner. With the two soldiers nested in high cover on the roof, I was at a decided tactical disadvantage. Having only the livestock truck and the unsure Town Hall as cover – and with Donovan – I was running out of viable options.

Two soldiers pulled out a military hard case from one of the commandeered pickups. I brought up the rifle but had to duck as bullets spattered around me.

When they stopped, I chanced another look.

One of them had brought up a rocket propelled grenade launcher.

Snapping up the rifle, I pressed the trigger.

A disappointing click responded.

I had lost count of the rounds. Again!

I pulled out the Glock.

A whooshing sound came as the RPG raced from its launcher with a smoking white trail.

I dove to cover Donovan.

The grenade impacted the rear of the truck.

And exploded.

133

Re-Up

+29 Days – Noon

Donovan was trapped under me.

Flaming sections of the livestock truck lay on top of us.

I kicked away the twisted paneling then patted down my jeans where the gasoline fueled flames still licked the denim.

The truck was a wreck, both from the grenade and the resulting gasoline tank explosion. Oily smoke and intense flames swirled from what remained. The explosion had tossed sticky flames against the stone and concrete walls.

We had been protected from the brunt of the explosive by the column.

Donovan stirred.

As the fire pried its way into Town Hall, I knew we were in an untenable defensive position. I looked to the open ground between the Town Hall steps and the church, calculating our chances to make it across without being shot. Looking under the truck chassis, I saw the shimmering shapes of soldiers making their way toward us using the parked cars as cover.

We had to move now.

I got up and reached for Donovan.

He was gone.

Shit!

I tossed the rifle and checked the Glock.

Dust was scraped away in a straight line to an opening next to the truck's cab. The explosion had widened the hole, dislodging the truck and breaking away more of the wall.

Donovan must have escaped inside.

I squeezed through to the darkened interior.

Smoke was thickening under the lobby's thirty-foot ceiling.

I let out a piercing whistle and waited ten seconds.

No response.

Heading to the gallery staircase with my weapon up, I flanked left to the opposite wall at the landing. My hip crashed hard into the brass handrail. The rest of the stairway was dim, but empty.

Taking the second set of stairs two at a time, I cleared both sides of the mezzanine before exposing my position on the balcony.

I went to the railing and looked down into the main chamber.

The benches and council table were empty. The only evidence of use was discarded gear and food containers from Wallace and his men.

A clunking sound got my attention.

Donovan's legs poked from under one of the benches, his Keds clearly visible.

I whistled again.

Another pronounced thunk was followed by a curse. Donovan looked up from between the wooden benches with his hand rubbing the back of his head.

I whistled again and waved.

He spotted me and waved back.

"I'm trying to get Jax back in the satchel," he called up. "He thinks its playtime."

Just as he finished his sentence, the albino ferret clicked his way onto the bench and padded above Donovan. He jumped on Donovan's chest and nipped him on the nose. Donovan grabbed the animal by the scruff and got to his feet, the ferret curling up.

Donovan hurried back to the main table, unbuckled the satchel and dropped Jax in. Sniffing each other, he and Daisy disappeared to the bottom of the bag. Donovan dropped and buckled the flap.

"All set," Donovan said with a thumb's up, throwing the bag's strap across his shoulder. "I don't think anyone else is here."

Gesturing for him to stay put, I backed up to the stairway.

The corridor lit up.

Searing heat tore through my right shoulder, throwing me against the metal handrail.

I hissed in pain and reacted by firing down the stairwell.

My bullets missed a flitting shape.

A shape leaped up on the landing.

It connected a fist downward to my jaw before I could get off another shot.

I dropped to my knees.

Wallace kicked away my Glock. My gun twirled down the stairs and skated across the marbled floor.

Wallace punched me in the fresh wound.

Pain flared through my chest and arm.

He cupped the back of my neck and drove his knee into my face.

I blocked it with my left forearm, but the knee and my forearm connected with my nose anyway.

He drove the knee up again.

I shot him a glancing fist between the thigh and groin.

With him off-balanced, I swiped his ankle.

He tumbled hard to the carpet, kicking my grip away. He rolled back to a kneeling position against the wall. His gun came up.

I kicked off the railing, driving my left shoulder into his ribs.

His weapon went off with a sharp reverberation.

I head-butted his jaw.

He slammed his pistol's grip into the back of my neck before twisting me away.

I tumbled down the stairs and sprawled hard to the floor. Skidding to a stop with my palms squeaking against the marble, I rolled away as a bullet sparked off the stone next to me.

Three more shots rang out as I rolled out of Wallace's line of sight.

I came up onto my feet.

My gun was too far away and in Wallace's sightline.

Calculating his descent, I rushed the stairwell.

As he reached the bottom of the stairs, I connected with a running right-hand punch to the side of his head. Pain spread out to my shoulder, chest and neck. Wallace staggered to the corner of the stairwell, still on his feet.

He swung his gun around. I stepped into his body, blocking his arm with my left forearm and twisting around with a straight-fingered right hand to his wrist. His gun skittered away and banged off the far wall.

Wallace caught me with a swinging left elbow to the right temple, stunning me. I didn't see the hook-kick to my chest coming, either.

I fell backward.

Using that momentum, I reversed rolled into a crouching position.

The smoke had thickened and the flames had now begun to eat away at the lobby. It peeled up and down the walls, engulfing the lobby doors.

"Son, you've been such a pain in my ass that I'm starting to rethink coming to this shit hole island in the first place. That fuel truck was so damn inviting, though."

Wallace stepped to the right then stopped in the middle of the lobby. Both of our guns were at least three meters in opposite directions. Wallace didn't seem interested in retrieving either of them.

"A simple yokel in the church tower. What could be simpler to dispatch, huh?"

Wallace unbuckled his mesh rig and dropped it to the floor with a hollow thud. He took off his shirt and dropped it on top of the pile.

"Well, Marine, let's get this over with."

He curled his hands into fists and started moving around on his toes.

I stood up and wheeled my right arm. There was a surprising lack of pain. The blood had stopped seeping from the wound. Cracking my neck and shrugging my shoulders, I stepped forward.

We circled just out of reach.

I quickly tired of the dance and lunged at Wallace with a flying kick. He sidestepped with a forearm block, spinning and punching me in the back of the neck. I hurled backward with a spinning elbow that landed on his cheekbone.

I felt bone crunch.

Continuing my pivot, I landed a haymaker on the same spot. Wallace dropped to one knee. He quickly retaliated with an uppercut to my jaw. My head snapped back. I stepped away with both hands up. Wallace landed a hook kick between them.

My vision blurred and went red.

Wallace spun around and kicked my swelling face.

I tumbled to the floor.

Wallace punted my downturned face.

I rolled onto my back.

Wallace stomped on my chest.

I saw stars.

More blood, more pain.

I couldn't breathe. My lungs burned.

I tried to roll away.

Wallace stopped me with a boot to my wounded shoulder. He lifted his foot and drove it down again.

I grabbed it with both hands, twisting it.

Snap!

Wallace howled in pain.

He collapsed to the floor, grabbing his ankle.

I rolled onto my side. Taking an agonizing deep breath, I got my hands under me. Blood flowed from my mouth, nose and cheek. I stood on shaky legs.

Wallace had crawled more than five meters away, obscured by the smoke.

I stalked after him.

Just then, a small voice called out. "John! Where are you?"
Donovan was in the direction of the main chamber doors.

I looked back for Wallace. He was lost in the haze.

A shot rang out.

Donovan screamed.

No!

I ran in the direction of the muzzle flash.

Wallace appeared as a dark shape in the smoke. He was leaning against an antique table. I tackled Wallace at full speed, crashing him into the wall. Plaster and lathing crumbled. The mirror above the bureau shook.

We dropped to the floor, me on top.

Wall fragments rained down.

I grabbed Wallace around his windpipe, stood him up and lifted him off the floor.

All I could see was red as the piercing buzzing headache hammered at my temples.

Wallace tried to break my grip.

I barely felt his efforts.

He looked into my eyes, his own widening.

With a strained effort through my tightening grip, he spoke in a gurgled whisper.

"You're one... one of... them."

I tightened my grip further.

"You're dead. They're all... dead..."

Wallace smiled, still struggling against me. But it faded as I crushed his windpipe. Blood stained his teeth in a pale film, bubbling out between his lips with his last breath. His grip slackened and his arms fell to his side. His eyelids fluttered and his pupils dilated.

I felt his pulse stop in my hand.

I released him and let his body crash to the floor.

My vision still ran red. The white painful flashes flanked the edges. In the flame flickered lobby mirror, my hazel eyes were now flecked with gold, red and black streaks. I closed them and pushed my fingers to the bridge of my nose. Surprisingly not broken, the cartilage still hurt like a motherfucker. White flashes exploded behind my eyelids.

A series of coughs caught my attention.

I headed toward the sound, stepping on something. I knelt down and retrieved my Glock, putting it back home in its holster.

More coughs.

Lying against the double doors, Donovan continued his fit.

I lifted his head.

"Hey, John," Donovan said, looking up at me. "Did you win? What's up with your eyes?"

He inhaled too deeply and ended up hacking, eyes closed tight. When it subsided, he looked at me again.

"Must be my imagination. Thought your eyes were weird."

I looked him over. No bullet holes. No blood.

The canvas satchel, though, did have a dark spot on its side.

I unbuckled the straps and opened the flap.

Daisy popped out her head but did not leap out. A bit of crimson laced her nose, tongue and whiskers. Jax lay on his side with a gaping bullet wound. Blood covered his fur and the bottom of the bag. Daisy dropped back down and curled herself around her companion, mewing softly.

Daisy bared her teeth as I reached in. When I starting petting Jax on the head, she licked my hand instead.

I closed the satchel and patted the side.

Lifting Donovan off the floor, I carried him over to Wallace.

Shielding Donovan, I pulled my pistol. Putting the weapon to Wallace's forehead I pulled the trigger. The echoes diminished, quickly eaten up by the flames.

I holstered the Glock and grabbed Wallace by the collar with my free hand. Dragging him through the smoke and flames, the three of us made our way to the north end of the lobby.

133

Out of the Frying Pan

+29 Days – 1225 hours

The emergency door slapped open.

I stepped out to the municipal parking lot.

Cradling Donovan, I headed toward the sheriff's station. I dropped Wallace in the middle of the asphalt. At the municipal building, I opened the lobby door and gently placed Donovan on a bench inside.

He looked up and coughed a little.

"Thanks," he smiled. "I think I'll hang out here a while. I'm a little tired."

I placed my hand on his cheek. He leaned into it.

"You've been shot."

I patted him on the head and put the Glock in his lap. He gripped the weapon like a teddy bear, curled up on the bench and closed his eyes.

When he started breathing more deeply, I left the lobby and returned to the middle of the lot. I picked Wallace up and slung him over my shoulder.

I passed the library before one the roof sentries caught sight of me.

"Heads up! Heads up! Sidewalk!" Kentucky shouted as he trained his Barrett on me.

The second roof sniper followed suit, He was the same soldier who had accompanied Kentucky during the Rod Sanchez Gazebo incident. The eight soldiers in front of the diner took cover, their weapons pointed at me. Two 4-man squads returning from recon circled behind me, boxing me in.

I tossed Wallace to the sidewalk.

Hammers cocked and breaches filled.

"Hold fast," Sergeant Bowers ordered. "Hold fast."

I had hoped he was the ranking officer, even if he was a NCO. He seemed like he was a good man.

Sergeant Bowers walked past his men. He kneeled to check Wallace for a pulse, in spite of the gaping head wound. Bowers glared at me with a cold stare.

"You kill him?"

Bowers leaned close and whispered in my ear. "I'm sorry."

He walked behind his men at the diner. A few glanced back at the sergeant. Fingers slid to triggers.

"Men, you ca–" Bowers began.

Screams!

A throng of islanders ran into the plaza from Mall Street.

Sergeant Bowers and all but Kentucky looked back at the commotion racing toward them. I continued to stand at parade rest, careful not to give Bowers' men an excuse to shoot me.

Before Bowers could figure out the resident's erratic behavior, several FRACs shambled down the Mall Street cobblestones after them. A couple walkers sniffed out the soldiers and bee-lined toward us.

Bowers pulled his sidearm and fired on the advancing hoard. One, then another, collapsed to the sidewalk. The gunshots alerted more walkers on the grass who veered toward us.

The sergeant shifted to the new threat and fired.

A skinny FRAC with a scraggy white and red beard caught a bullet in his cheek, tipping backward to the grass.

"Get your guns on that corridor!" Bowers barked, pointing toward Mall Street.

He hopped on a car hood and whistled at the two snipers.

"Daley! Wick! Get your eyes on that chokepoint!"

Wick continued to work his mouth noiselessly.

"What, Wick?" Bowers asked.

Wick came closer to the roof's edge.

"Sarge, we got a sea of walkers coming in!"

"How many?"

Wick looked over his shoulder.

"Wick!"

"A least a couple... couple hundred, Sarge."

Bowers looked down at me.

"Marine, we need all hands."

I went to the truck, grabbing an M14 and an empty duffle. I slung the rifle and filled the bag with full magazines.

"Hey!" Ames protested.

I answered by firing a three-round burst into a FRAC face trying to get between two trucks in front of him.

"Get your heads out of your ass. Any of those things get through and you won't have to worry about ammo!"

I finished filling the duffle. When done I retreated back to the sheriff's station. Pops of intermittent rifle fire started, mostly from Daley and Wick.

Islanders were heading to the church.

Inside the sheriff's office lobby, Donovan still sat on the bench. He leaned against the wall and pointed the Glock at me.

Good boy.

He dropped the weapon to his lap when he recognized me.

I ruffed his hair then pointed across the plaza to the church.

Donovan would be safer there with the others.

He nodded and got to his feet.

"I know Jax saved my life." He patted his satchel. "I'll give him a proper burial later."

I squeezed his shoulder and pointed to the church again.

"You coming?"

I nodded.

We moved through the parking lot, across the street and to the nearest patch of lawn.

The walkers chased down a group of islanders on the plaza.

One screamed as a FRAC snagged the strap of his backpack.

I flipped the rifle to single fire and squeezed the trigger.

The FRAC dropped to the ground with a ragged hole in his head. The walker's death grip on the pack's strap dragged the elderly man, Mr. Tyson, to the ground with him. Two other walkers slowed and dropped beside Mr. Tyson as he struggled to twist out of the pack.

I cleared two more shots from the rifle. The FRACs interested in Mr. Tyson slumped to the grass. We moved across the lawn. I stepped on the first FRAC's wrist. The fingers opened enough for me to pull the strap loose.

On my six, Donovan helped Mr. Tyson up. While the others in his group had continued without him, the boy put his arm around Mr. Tyson and helped him toward the house of an absent god.

I covered our retreat.

A FRAC came at us at a ragged trot.

I dropped him with a single shot.

As I stepped onto the plaza's sidewalk, a young male and female FRAC charged at me with eager speed. I double-tapped them in the head. They crashed into each other before they dropped to the ground at my feet.

We crossed the street to the church sidewalk.

Mr. Tyson's 'friends' helped him up the steps, taking over for Donovan.

I whistled at the boy and gave him a thumbs-up. He smiled, hiked the strap of the satchel, patted his shirt over the Glock and went inside. The door slammed shut, leaving me alone.

The lawn was scattered with FRACs, with more pouring in from Mall Street.

Some shambled toward the church while others focused on Bowers and his men. Daley and Wick stood on the east end of the diner's roof, slowly picking their shots into the mass of walkers. The rest of Bowers' men focused on the closest to their position.

It was a smart tactical move on Bowers part, although his position was exposed on open ground. Rationing their ammo, they were making every shot count. Their disadvantage was that the FRACs were attacking in force. Soon, they would be overrun.

They should all get to the diner's roof.

I walked across the lawn, dropping several FRACs until my rifle was empty. I reloaded.

Time slowed with every squeeze of the trigger.

A waxy-skinned woman with an unraveling bun in her hair took a shot to the eye. A Massachusetts State Police officer with his shoulder 2-way radio knocking against his thigh dropped after a bullet entered his septum. Two teenage boys with Boston Celtic basketball shorts and jerseys, and a woman with a bloody apron still tied around her waist, all had their un-lives ended by a whizzing bullet.

Firing from the open lawn, I managed to divide the attentions of the oncoming walkers. Some of them staggered toward the sound of my gunfire while some wandered around in front of the church behind me.

I swung the M14 in a 120-degree cone of fire in quick sharp pivots. As each magazine emptied and left one round in the chamber, I reloaded.

Bowers and his men were holding their own, but barely. FRACs shuffled up the sidewalk, getting as far as the alleyway between the diner and the back of the bookstore before the soldiers sprayed FRAC brains into the faces of the walkers behind them. The resulting piles of bodies served as growing barricades that the FRACs needed to navigate over or around.

The mass of undead streaming through Mall Street continued.

I grabbed the now much lighter duffle, and double-timed it toward Bowers' position.

I flipped the rifle's switch to semi-automatic.

Halfway to the diner, I opened up with three-round bursts on the advancing FRACs. They fell into each other as bullets shredded through their skulls. Gray matter splashed onto the sidewall of the bookstore.

By the time I reached North Plaza Drive, the FRACs were within two meters of me and even closer to Bowers and his men. The walkers had moved along the barricade of bodies, inadvertently flanking Bowers' perimeter. The vehicles at the curb helped as cover, but the FRACs were still overwhelming the position with sheer numbers.

The soldiers fired into the crowd. I sidestepped to the west to make sure I didn't catch a stray bullet.

The sea of walkers raged against the nest.

Daley and Wick fired into the crowd, slowing down the FRACs' advance.

Bowers and his men continued to fire.

Ames ran out of ammo and, in a panic, broke the line. He climbed onto one of the curbside vehicle's hoods. He slipped and fell headlong into the walkers. He screamed as the FRACs clawed into him, dragging him down and ripping chunks of flesh out of his body.

Bowers slid across the hood, brought up his pistol and shot Ames in the head. The private's screams squelched for good. The sergeant emptied the rest of his magazine into the throng of undead with a yell.

When his weapon's slide locked open, Bowers slid back into the midst of his men.

Pointy exposed-bone fingers clawed at the soldiers, scratching at their fatigues. The FRACs grabbed at their rifle barrels; even as bullets tore through their hands into their brains.

I strafed across the line of FRACs, heads exploding in quick succession. As they fell, I emptied the magazine on the next advancing row of undead. Reaching into the duffle I reloaded one of the last two magazines and pocketed the other. I flipped to single-fire.

A dozen FRACs milled behind me. They were more attracted to the billowing inferno of Town Hall than us. A FRAC did bump into me. He staggered off to one side, mewed and continued his course to the fire.

I focused on the main group of walkers.

The herd crowding through the cobblestones of Mall Street was thinning out.

Bowers and his men were exhausted.

After a few shots into the open mouth of a FRAC with an already unhinged jaw, the slide on Bowers' Glock locked open. He withdrew it from the falling ghoul's mouth and drove its grip into the brittle shell of the next FRAC's skull.

Sighting the closest group of FRACs, I pressed the rifle's trigger in a smooth rhythm, dropping the undead with every shot. Reloading with the last magazine, I fired until pressing the trigger resulted in an unsatisfying click.

I gripped the rifle by the hot barrel stock, advanced on the closest dark-skinned FRAC and swung the rifle into the side of its head with a crack. His neck snapped and he staggered to his knees. Another walker, a plump raven-haired woman, fell over him.

Like a wave against the shore, the advancing line of FRACs crashed against the pile of bodies. They spilled over into the soldiers' nest.

The FRACs stretched open their rotted and bloody mouths, emitting a haunting moan.

My head buzzed.

They grabbed at the soldiers, tearing at their fatigues and pulling themselves closer to their prey. One of the soldiers, with the name patch Epps, screamed as he reloaded his rifle. He shot one of them in the chest as he struggled to bring up his rifle barrel.

Wright finished off the job with a shot to the FRAC's temple. Two other FRACs dragged Epps over the line of bodies, the soldier kicking, punching and screaming. Wright shot the second and third FRAC in the face with an assault shotgun. As each crumpled to the ground in an oozing bloody mess, more FRACs pulled Epps further into the crowd.

Sliding across a car hood, I hurled headlong into the middle of the nest of panicking soldiers. The closest FRACs clawed at their sleeves.

"Hold the line!" Bowers screamed, taking deliberate single shots from his rifle.

I swung the butt of my rifle around, crushing the side of one fat FRAC's face. The stock sunk into its brittle skull with a thunk and a faint crack. The momentum of the blow crashed the FRAC into a waifish girl, sending them both into the brick wall.

More walkers advanced.

I hook kicked a young pale redheaded woman with a pivoting shot. Her face caved in, sending her backward into the outstretched arms of a balding middle aged FRAC in an expensive, but now tattered and bloody suit. They fell to the ground, Banker FRAC wiggling around like a turtle on its back.

The FRACs ignored me. I used that as a tactical advantage. As each pushed into the nest, I delivered a killing blow.

"We need higher ground," Bowers yelled. "Get ammo. Fall back to the alley to the diner's roof. Two at a time!"

Sweat poured down the soldiers' faces. None of them spoke, only responding with gunfire and yells. Some shots found their marks, but more missed the crucial headshot on the first try – even in closed quarters.

"Tanner! Sheridan! Move!"

Bowers' orders were barely heard over the deafening weapons fire. Two soldiers pulled from the line. They slung their rifles, rushed to get ammo cases from the back of a truck and headed toward the alleyway.

"Greer! Williams!"

Two more soldiers pulled themselves from the perimeter.

The firepower in the nest dwindled.

The perimeter was collapsing.

Bowers killed a FRAC squeezed between two cars. He fired at another walker trying to climb over the first, effectively using them both to choke the chromed corridor.

Bowers pulled out a tactical knife and tossed it to me. He followed up with a Glock 17 and a spare magazine. I clenched the knife in my teeth. Pocketing the extra magazine, I checked the weapon.

I nodded to Bowers.

He nodded with a grim look.

"Everyone fall back now! Full retreat!"

The soldiers pulled off the line in quick succession. Rifle fire suddenly stopped as they rushed to the truck, grabbed an ammo box and ran to the alley.

The FRACs rushed the nest. Sixteen shots later, I let the magazine drop from the grip, reloaded, and started firing again. Sensing the weapon as a threat, the undead moaned and reach out for the gun.

I continued to fire.

Too quickly, the slide ejected the last round. I holstered the Glock and grabbed the knife still between my teeth.

A shirtless FRAC with a huge gaping shotgun blast wound to the right side of his chest lunged at me with his long spindly arms. His teeth clicked together in anticipation. I drove the knife into his brain through his over-sized left ear. His cataract covered eyes rolled back.

Where is my cover fire?

I pulled the knife out before the FRAC collapsed. Spinning right, as groping hands pulled at my shoulder and snagged at my shirt, I slammed the knife into the temple of a long-haired, acne-faced kid. The blade pierced out the top of his skull. I drew back the knife, spinning around and arcing the blade upward into the soft tissue under the boy's chin. I let him fall forward, twisting his head sideways off the blade.

Where were Bowers and his men?

Another walker received a hook kick into the jaw. The bone detached and impaled into the base of his brain. A female FRAC grabbed at my outstretched trailing arm, bringing my momentum to a halt. I replanted my foot and head butted her. Her face erupted in dark, thick streams of blood as she slumped to the pavement with a grip still on my elbow.

I ripped my arm away.

A FRAC in denim overalls and flannel growled at me. I landed the knife into Farmer FRAC's cheek. He chomped down. I couldn't pull out the blade. The harder I pulled the harder he bit down. Letting go of the knife, I grabbed the FRAC by his lapel. I threw Farmer FRAC over me, sailing him headlong into the outstretched arms of a blonde walker in bloody nurses' whites.

I grabbed the now loose knife and tried kicking both of them away, but I couldn't extend my leg as the other FRACs pressed in. Running out of maneuvering room I resorted to using my fists.

Farmer FRAC regained his legs. I swung an uppercut to his chin. Something audibly cracked as his head snapped back. He stumbled before tumbling to the ground for good.

The bloody nurse snarled at me, her fingers whittled down to the second knuckle. I rushed forward, interlocking my hands behind her neck and driving up my knee. Her cheekbones and the bridge of her nose crunched. I drove the knee once more, ensuring the nurse became dead weight. As gravity grabbed at her, I swung her into the advancing undead.

The FRACs still pressed against me.

Losing balance and leverage, I could only flail at the closest set of peeled back rotten lips and snapping filmy teeth. One nipped me on the arm. After he did he lost interest, but still was as stuck in the crowd as I was. My feet slid out from under me.

Bowers had left me to die after all.

The whistling whine cut through the air.

A firecracker popped in the sky with a blast of white.

Seconds later there was an eruption of gunfire. It was the continuous bratta-bratta of a single high-caliber weapon.

Pressure loosened on one side as the FRACs started herding toward the new sights and sounds. I regained my feet but was almost knocked to the ground as the FRACs behind me tried to shamble past.

More bottle rockets whistled into the air.

Reaching the supply truck, I hopped onto the bed. I found a stash of magazines loaded with high capacity 9mm rounds. I reloaded the Glock. A couple FRACs looked over the sidewall. I reloaded my holster with four magazines, stuffing three more in each of my back pockets.

One of the FRACs, a pixie-cut bottled blonde with androgynous features, pulled herself up the sidewall.

I slammed the grip of the Glock into her skull. Twice.

More piercing whistles were followed by a barrage of gunfire.

Sheriff Garrett knelt at the roof's edge of Pete's Guns, Ammo and Bait Shop with a strangely configured Gatling gun. Mounted on a heavy-duty tripod, the gun looked brand new with a nickel-plated body and black barrels. Instead of a side mounted ammo box feeder, the cartridges fed from underneath.

Monroe Johnston was on the roof too. He stood under a PVC cup attached to a long thick dowel in the process of lighting up another bottle rocket. The firecracker fuse fizzed before the rocket took off into the air with an angry shriek.

The FRACs were pushing back into Mall Street in front of the store. Over eighty walkers remained in the corridor reaching up at the pair on the roof. Then sixty-five. Then forty. Every trigger pull mowed down a clump of walkers. The remaining FRACs filled in the gaps, stumbling over the fallen bodies.

The doors to the church banged opened.

Basia, two of Wallace's men, Simon Russell, Kyle Foster and Deputy Reynolds ran out. Simon and Kyle scooped up discarded weapons. Lincoln and the soldiers were already carrying their weapons. They crossed the street and raced across the lawn toward us.

Monroe disappeared from the roof's edge, reappearing a moment later hefting a set of tanks on his shoulders. He tightened a canvas strap before picking up something that looked like the cross between a rifle barrel and a nozzle. Garrett stopped firing long enough to help Monroe double check the tank and open two valves. Monroe pressed a button on the side of the handheld unit and lit a flame at the end of the nozzle, stepped to the edge, leaned over and pressed the trigger.

A stream of sticky fire spat from the flamethrower into the crowd of FRACs below. Dried flesh, soiled clothes, and stringy hair ignited. The FRACs continued to pool beneath the whirring Gatling gun, ignoring the flames that ate at them.

Only the walkers under the awning, pressing and clawing against the security bars, were safe from the hail of bullets and fire streaming from above.

One of the flaming FRACs staggered into the back of the group pressing against the gun shop doors. The fire jumped from him to the clothes of some of the others. Their clothes popped into flames, spreading without hesitation.

Deputy Reynolds and the soldiers opened fire on the deserters.

"Come on, suckers!" Kyle yelled as he fired wildly at the walkers.

"Take this!" Simon hollered in agreement.

Basia went to the gazebo and scavenged a rifle from one of Wallace's dead soldiers. She brought up the too big weapon as she jumped to the walkway. She pulled the trigger. Nothing happened.

"Shit!" she exclaimed.

Basia looked at the side of the M14. She found the safety and flipped the lever. She brought up the rifle in time to fire through the torso and neck of a FRAC.

The walker still grabbed at her.

I fired and nicked it high on the arm.

The walker bit into Basia's shoulder and drove her to the grass.

She screamed and tried to pull away as she fell, spinning and firing a strafe of bullets.

Sparks bounced off the lower side of Sebastian's tanker.

Reynolds shot the FRAC and rushed over to Basia.

Kyle and Simon went to her, shooting wildly at any FRACs closing in.

I shot two walkers and they crashed to the ground.

Startled, Simon reacted by shooting one of them in the head.

The two soldiers retreated back to the church in a full sprint.

"She's losing too much blood," Reynolds shouted. "We're losing her. Shit!"

More walkers peeled away from the main group in front of the gun shop, realizing easier food was available on the plaza. Maybe it was smell of fresh blood.

Kyle and Simon fired on them. Too quickly, they ran out of ammo.

I shot several FRACs as I flanked toward Reynolds' position.

In front of the store, walkers fell like dominoes under the barrage of bullets from Garrett's Gatling gun. More FRACs fell on top of the growing pyres for the dead. Some snuffed out the spreading fire while others simply added more fuel for the flames. The flames ate through the FRACs' muscle tissue. Their ability to move grew worse. Some wandered away while others bumped off the storefronts.

Reynolds, Kyle and Simon made the decision to abandon the now dead Basia and retreated back to the church. Reynolds pushed the other two ahead of him, tears flowing freely.

I holstered my Glock and picked up a fire ax left in the grass. FRACs milled about in no particular direction, only a few shambling after Reynolds' group. Most had stopped to feed indiscriminately on the entrails of the scattered, still warm corpses of soldiers and islanders on the lawn.

Swinging the ax down, the blade sliced cleanly through the neck of a FRAC chewing on a section of large intestines. The head fell cleanly away, its teeth clamped down on the string of guts.

I moved to the next kneeling walker and drove the ax head square into the back of its skull. Lifting the handle up, the FRAC came with it. I stepped on its neck and wriggled the ax free. I spun the ax around, the blood and gray matter rolling off the steel.

Stepping over the two bodies I marched toward a walker who sensed my presence a moment before I plunged the spiked end of the fire ax into its forehead.

A one-armed FRAC approached me.

Steve had died from his bullet wounds and from an unlucky bloody nip in the shoulder from a FRAC. I looked at the fire ax, slowly spinning the handle around. As Steve wandered past me, I swung the axe through the back of his neck.

As Steve's head and body dropped in different directions, I threw the fire axe to the ground. Its head sparked off the cobblestone.

I looked at the inferno at Town Hall. Fire and smoke billowed to the sky, leaving a skeletal framework of steel and stone behind. The fire had not jumped over to the municipal building.

I turned back to Mall Street.

The rest of the undead fell under the rain of bullets and fire that Monroe and Garrett continued to unleash from the roof. The flames had started to eat away at the fronts of some of the other stores.

One of the FRACs, shirt licking with flames, limped away from the gun shop barrage. Shuffling down the center of East Plaza Drive, he wandered slowly toward the other side of the island. The fire on his shirt expanded to his sweat pants, eating away at the muddy cotton.

Basia slowly got to her feet, the wound on her shoulder seeping through her scrubs. Her skin was waxen, her eyes scarlet and gold. She bared her teeth and sniffed the air.

Rivers of gasoline poured from the underbelly of the gas tanker truck into the street. The flaming FRAC was only a meter from the spill. I pulled my weapon and fired.

The FRAC dropped into the pool of gasoline. The gas absorbed into the walker's clothes. The flames engulfing the body whooshed back toward the gas station under the truck. A moment later, the flames jumped up into the tanker.

Basia was three meters away, snarling and reaching for my gun.

The hot explosion blew me off my feet.

My skin singed and burned.

I landed in the grass, my lungs burning.

Christ!

I rolled to my side and struggled to my feet.

The gas station was ablaze, flames sweeping across the street and grass.

A high-pitched moan surfaced through the blast.

Basia stood at an awkward stance, her hair and clothes completely burned off and her skin blackened with veins of still burning flesh. Her lidless white eyes stared at me, her movements like a choppy slow-motion marionette. The surrounding flames cast her in a surreal silhouette.

She snapped at the air, not sensing me as I approached. I wrapped her up in my arm from behind, pinning her against me. She squirmed against the restraint as her skin still sizzled.

"Shusssh," I breathed as I sunk the blade of Bowers' tactical knife into the soft tissue under her jaw.

She relaxed in my arm as I lowered her to the ground.

The breeze from the ocean had picked up, swirling the oily smoke into a lazy column trailing off to the northeast. Through the fires, the FRACs around the base of Pete's store had thinned out. The stream of the undead from Diggs' opened gate at the Norte Bridge had stopped altogether.

The Gatling gun fell silent, but the air was still filled with the sound of licking flames. Monroe slipped out of the tank harness and leaned against it.

A few stragglers struggled to navigate around the deep smoking and flaming piles of bodies. A female FRAC drifted past me. I picked up the discarded axe and jammed the pick into the side of her head. I pulled the axe out as she fell, blackened goo trailing off the edge of the blade into the waiting grass.

Human and FRAC fluids stained the wooden handle, my skin and clothes.

I twirled the handle of the ax and headed off to Mall Street to deal with what was left.

134

Aftermath

+29 Days – 1505 hours

After I dispatched another dozen FRACs on Mall Street, Monroe opened the shop's steel door. He and Garrett came out with fire extinguishers. They put out the flames that had crawled onto the storefronts, leaving the FRAC bonfires to burn.

The smell closed up my throat. My lungs were desperate to expel the oily smoke and stench of burning human flesh.

Monroe wrapped a bandanna around his nose and mouth.

"You okay, John? Looks like you got popped in the eye."

I buried the ax into a FRAC's head that was probably already dead.

Where did Bowers go?

Leaning the axe against the brick wall of Gloria's bookstore, I walked past the empty and dark Oceanside to the far alleyway where Bowers and his men had retreated.

At the dark mouth I stopped short.

Soldiers were strewn across the alley floor, their throats ripped out or stomachs opened up. A pool of blood streamed to a storm drain in the center of the corridor. Most of their weapons were still slung or holstered. Four walkers lay scattered across the opening with headshots – a fifth with a knife in its eye socket.

A few walkers must have detoured through the alley between the bookstore and the Oceanside, coming up behind Bowers' nest position in an accidental strategic flanking maneuver. Bowers and his men had rushed right out of one hot zone and into another. With their hands full of ammo boxes and their focus on retreat, they had been ambushed.

Why didn't Daley and Wick defend them?

I walked into the dim corridor, careful not to step in the seeping bloody river. A Barrett sniper rifle lay at my feet. I pulled at the weapon. The soldier had a dead man's grip on the strap. I turned him over. It was Wick.

Looking up at the roof ladder, I figured that Wick and Daley had come down to hoist up their mates and ammunition, only to be pulled down by the walkers who had converged in the closed quarters.

I went around to each soldier. From their pallor and physical condition, they were not getting up again. Two of them were shot in the back of the head, most likely from friendly fire. One soldier had managed to get his firearm drawn and trigger a suicide round.

Bowers was not among them.

Pulling the Glock, I went to the far end of the alley. At the turn a corridor ran the length of the restaurant to join with the Bilco alley behind Gloria's bookstore.

I swung far to the left, giving a wide berth to anything that might be lurking around the corner. I cleared two Waste Management dumpsters against the diner's rear wall.

Beyond the dumpsters a stack of wooden pallets had been pulled down, creating a tangle of wooden splintery planks. A slender walker with black hair and sporting a gaping hole through his sternum and skull lay across the top of the pile, his arms reaching through gaps in the slats. Fresh splatters of blood sprayed across two of the pallets.

I pulled the walker off by the collar. The front of his graphic Tee was adorned with a smiling feline inside a heart with the words 'Don't Worry! Be Happy!'.

The end of a shotgun barrel was pushed through the pallet slats.

I holstered the Glock and pulled the top pallet, flinging it across the alley to shatter against the opposite concrete block wall. I tossed two more pallets behind me. One of them landed on the

Bobby McFerrin fan, breaking in half. I hurled the last three pallets against the closest dumpster.

The shotgun barrel fell to the ground, slapping against Sergeant Bowers' leg. His hand still clutched the trigger. Bowers had been shot twice, once in the shoulder and another in the hip. His right leg twisted. He held his Glock close to his chest. Blood ran down from a huge gash above his hairline, just starting to clot.

I didn't see any other scratches, tears or bites, but I pushed the pistol's barrel against his temple.

Bowers mumbled and tried to raise the shotgun.

I put away my weapon and disarmed him of the Remington 870 shotgun. Prying his pistol away was more difficult.

Bowers moaned in incoherent protests as I lifted him out of the remaining pile of wooden pallets and into a fireman's carry. I scanned the alley for any other sign of life or un-life but I was met with silence.

I carried Bowers up the bookstore's alley, not interested in backtracking through the carnage and blood of Bowers' men.

My senses were assaulted as I stepped back out onto the sidewalk. The oily exhaust from the burning pyres burned heavy in the air.

Garrett leaned against the wall next to my fire ax.

He smelled of blood, sweat, gunpowder and napalm.

Garrett looked at Bowers slung across my shoulders.

With an air of disgust, he pointed across the plaza.

"If the man is worth it, Doc Rawlings is triaging in the church."

I hefted my load and stepped off the curb.

135

Triage

+29 Days – 1418 hours

The church doors clicked closed behind me.

People lay on the marble floor, muddy and bloody. Some were crying or rocking back and forth. Others stared at nothing. The rest huddled and hugged each other.

I carried Bowers past them into the house of the Lord.

Three pews away, Dr. Rawlings was administering a visual exam on Mrs. Saunders. He looked for scratches or bite marks. She didn't look good; sweat beading up on her skin and brow.

Joyce Richards rushed in from the side aisle with a handful of folded table clothes and a gallon glass jug of water.

"Doc! There is more water in the basement. I figured you wanted what I found for bandages."

"Thanks, Joyce."

I walked a few steps, blocking Dr. Rawlings' light.

"Sorry, John. Put him over there." He pointed across the aisle.

I rolled Bowers onto the wooden bench.

He moaned for a moment.

I leaned his Remington against the bench. As I pressed the Glock to his chest he put his hand over it.

I looked around at the scattered groups of survivors. The two soldiers who had come out with Reynolds earlier sat separate from the others, no one bothering them.

In the front row, Donovan's scruffy hair and dirty ears could be seen above the back of the bench. He sat next to a larger figure covered with an army blanket.

Safe.

I left Bowers and headed up the center aisle.

When I reached the second pew the person next to Donovan stood. He threw off the blanket and grabbed Donovan up by the arm. As he twisted around, I could see the clean vertical lines down Donovan's cheeks.

I reached for my weapon.

"Stop!" Donovan's captor hissed.

Harlan "Diggs" Dickerson held Donovan against him with a large syringe filled with his special opaque fluid pointed at his neck.

"You reach for that gun and this sidekick of yours will get a nice vitamin B12 shot of his own," he whispered.

Diggs cocked his head and squinted with one twitchy eye, his smile not faltering.

"Curious how you're still... you. That dose should have FRAC-ified the shit outta ya. Curious, and curiouser. No matter. Toss that gun of yours away so I know you understand my intent. I already took a pistol off your boy here. Just a couple fingers of the off-hand, if you please."

Reaching up to the holster with my left hand, I pinched the borrowed Glock's grip and slowly pulled it out. With a smiling tilt of the head from Diggs, I flung it away. It landed with a hard click and spun across the floor.

"So now what, Johnny?"

I shrugged, not taking my eyes off Donovan.

The vestibule's doors squeaked open and thudded closed again. Diggs looked to the back of the church but didn't seem worried about whoever had entered or left.

"Quite a day, huh?"

He backed up toward the altar, dragging Donovan with him.

I stood helpless.

The Gaunt Man appeared at the pulpit with his hands on either side of the wood. His long fingernails clicked on the corners of the lacquered wood in a low, continuous rhythm.

He disappeared, but the clicking sound remained.

Diggs didn't hear the clicking sound or didn't care, his grin plastered on his face.

I put my hands up and sat on the pew.

Diggs pulled Donovan back a step toward the empty pulpit.

The ripping of sheets suddenly filled the chamber as Joyce tore up a tablecloth for bandages.

The Gaunt Man reappeared at the pulpit, clicking his talons against the wood.

"Tell you what, Johnny," Diggs pondered, "I think I'll stick this kid anyway. He seems to be a favorite of yours. You've been a pain in my ass, so it seems fair."

He pulled Donovan close, letting go long enough to swing his arm around his chest and pull his jaw to one side. Diggs adjusted his grip on the syringe. He raised his arm back and swung the needle down.

With a growl, Holly leaped forward from under the front pew.

Diggs swung out the hand with the syringe to ward her off.

Holly promptly bit into his wrist.

He howled in pain.

Donovan drove his elbow into Diggs' crotch. Diggs doubled over, allowing Donovan to twist away. Diggs grabbed at his attacked testicles with both hands, Holly still shaking away at his right wrist with a vise-like grip.

I charged at Diggs.

Holly let go and dropped neatly to the floor.

I heard an audible snap as I slammed Diggs' ribs into the front edges of the marble altar steps. With my knees on either side, I drove my right fist into Diggs nose. Cartilage broke and blood spurted from the center of his face.

Pulling back my fist, I realized my other hand was clamped around his throat. Even with the broken ribs, broken nose, and fractured check bones, Diggs smiled.

"Guh on, Juhn," Diggs breathed through blood bubbles, "eh dare yeh."

He slapped at me with his bloody, punctured arm.

I pushed his hand away.

He laughed, blood gurgling out of his mouth.

"Trah egan."

I pulled back for another punch.

Diggs swung the syringe up.

I blocked it with a forearm to his injured arm.

Grabbing his wrist, I slid my other forearm down to the crook of his elbow. Twisting his fist back, I leaned my weight on his forearm. The syringe tilted back at him.

Diggs foamed up blood, spitting it up on my shirt as he struggled to keep the tip of the needle away from his face.

Slamming all of my weight downward, the syringe pierced through his eyeball, sinking halfway into the soft matter of his skull.

I pressed the plunger.

The rose-colored bloody foam from Diggs mouth turned a rabid white as he wretched and convulsed.

Holly growled and backed away to the cover of the pew.

Donovan stared at Diggs, his head partially hidden in his arms. His foot tapped.

Wallace's men stood behind me, their guns angled at the floor. Joyce and Doc Rawlings stared from the center aisle, Joyce with a stack of bandages and Rawlings with a bloody pair of blue gloves.

Joyce's husband Willard looked in from the vestibule. Bowers sat up with a bandage wrapped around his head, barely conscious.

Everyone was paralyzed.

Diggs let out a blood-curdling howl.

Holly barked.

With the syringe sticking out of his eye socket and a red and gold working eye, he lunged at me.

I kicked Diggs in the face, sending the syringe deeper into his skull. He staggered back but did not fall.

He surged forward again with a howl.

A deafening shot rang out, echoing through the chamber. The left side of Diggs' head exploded in a stream of brain and blood. The force of the blast pushed him sideways for a moment before he skidded to the floor.

Donovan stood in the corner holding my discharged smoking Glock. I placed a hand on the weapon's slide and pulled it out of his shaking grip.

He wrapped his arms around my waist.

I hugged him back as tight as I dared.

EPILOGUE

1

Assessment

+29 Days – 1630 hours

I stared at my reflection in the church's lavatory mirror, my hands curled around the sides of the porcelain sink.

My irises had taken on the tiny gold flecks again. A tinge of red dashed across them as my eyes dilated in the cold fluorescent glow.

I took slow deep breaths.

Thump… thump.

My heart rate slowed.

The red and gold receded.

I splashed away the blood, dirt and sweat from my face.

When I looked at my face again my eyes had returned to their normal dark brown color.

I turned off the water, reducing it to a single drip that would not be staved off no matter how hard I would have turned the squeaky faucets.

Grabbing a paper towel from the dispenser, I wiped my face and the sink top. Spidery cracks had formed where I had grabbed the edges of the porcelain.

2

Follow up

+29 Days – 1645 hours

The bathroom door bumped into the back of my leg.

I instinctively drew my Glock.

Donovan, who had been waiting outside, rushed in and grabbed my shirt. I squeezed his shivering arm and led him back out to the vestibule.

The boy was still in shock.

He needed food and rest.

Joyce looked up from folding linens between the pews and gasped.

Sheriff Garrett and some of his men had returned, their clothes bloodied and their hands scraped.

"Don't worry." Garrett raised his hands in surrender. "We ran into a few FRACs at the Norte Bridge, but we're good. These scratches are from fixing a massive tear in the chain link fence. We added some barbed wire, but it bites hard when you're rushing and don't have the right gloves."

"Well, come get checked out," Dr. Rawlings said from the side aisle, ushering the sheriff's men to a pew. "We don't need any unnecessary infections."

Garrett waited for his men to be seated before walking toward Donovan and me.

"What happened, John?" Garrett asked, looking at the pool of drying blood under Diggs' body at the altar.

I gestured for Garrett's pad.

He handed it and a pen to me.

I wrote down seven words and handed both back.

" 'Diggs was a FRAC. Donovan shot him'," Garrett read the note aloud then appraised the boy. "That the way it happened, son?"

Donovan nodded, his eyes wide.

"Diggs was family." Garrett sighed and nodded back. "And I can't believe the shit he did. But it was the least he deserved after what he did to Gloria. And Lucy. If he was a FRAC, it was for the best."

Garrett winked at Donovan, eliciting a small smile from the boy.

"Take care of him, John," he commented to me.

I nodded and put a hand on Donovan's shoulder.

Garrett departed to Dr. Rawlings triage station, putting his notebook back into his breast pocket.

Donovan showed his resolve and led the way up the aisle. Daisy the ferret clucked inside his satchel. Holly padded along behind us, slowing to drop her white snout to the carpet every so often.

The sun warmed our faces as we stepped outside.

Town Hall still burned.

Plumes of gray and black smoke rose from the remains of the structure. Islanders were busy carrying FRAC bodies across the grass and through a gaping hole in a partially collapsed wall that the fire in the Town Hall had created.

On Mall Street, Monroe was pointing and shouting out orders. He still wore his bandanna like an outlaw. His crew hustled pails of water and fire extinguishers to douse the remaining licks of flames trying to survive on the storefronts.

I bumped into Donovan.

"Shit," the boy muttered, staring at the Searing Bridge. "Shit. Shit."

At the top of the ramp, behind the barricade of cars, pushed a clawing and moaning mob of FRACs. They swayed and bobbed at least twenty rows deep. Their familiar guttural groans rose up in unison.

I put a hand on Donovan's trembling shoulder.

The spectral Gaunt Man shook his head as he came up beside me.

My fingers gripped my Glock.

I hadn't realized I had drawn it.

You're going to need more bullets than that, Johnny, the Gaunt Man murmured softly, his voice laced with an underlying tsk-tsk sound.

"Yeah," I gravelly whispered in agreement, my voice finally returning.

About the Author

Charles Ingersoll is a Detroit area native who transplanted to New York City for the Great American experience of contributing to the local economy.

A lover of comics, comic cons and cosplay, movies and television, the supernatural and all things undead; writing happened to be a lifelong passion that has become his next personal adventure.

He currently lives on Long Island, New York.

Other Books by the Author

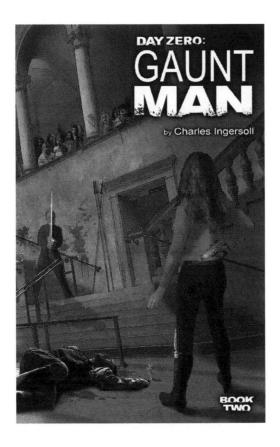

Find out what's next for John in book two of the series.

Day Zero: Gaunt Man

Now available in paperback and eBook!

43273085R00241

Made in the USA
Middletown, DE
05 May 2017